EMILY & JEN

Emily & Jen Dance for Deeron is the debut work in a series of fantasy adventures, each of which will follow two ordinary girls with an extraordinay gift to conjure magic through dance.

In each book, the courage, fortitude and friendship of Emily and Jen will be tested to the extreme, as they battle at every turn many evil and dark dangerous forces, in other worlds as well as our own.

Praise for *Emily & Jen Dance for Deeron*:

'An original and engaging tale.'
Bloomsbury Publishing

Coming soon

EMILY & JEN AND THE CURSE OF AGARA

www.novuvisus.com
www.emilyandjen.com
www.dancefordeeron.com

Jayn E Winslade

EMILY & JEN
Dance for Deeron

EDITED

BY

SIMON M WINSLADE

Grosvenor House
Publishing Limited

Book cover illustrations and artwork,
copyright © Simon M Winslade 2008.

This book is published by
Grosvenor House Publishing Ltd
28-30 High Street, Guildford, Surrey, GU1 3HY.
www.grosvenorhousepublishing.co.uk

A CIP record for this book
is available from the British Library

ISBN 978-1-907211-48-5

ABOUT THE AUTHOR

Jayn E Winslade was born in Birmingham, and has been involved with dance since childhood. An early career in ice skating led her to study at the London Contemporary Dance School and, more recently, the Laban Centre London.

Latterly, as a dance practitioner Jayn has instructed Further and Higher Education students, and directed many performances. She lives amongst a magical herd of deer in the vast ancient Needwood Forest.

ACKNOWLEDGEMENTS

To my husband Simon M Winslade, this book and I owe a great debt. In the dark times of writing he cast a light upon the imagery and plot, and gave a skilled editorial hand to the work's narrative flow. Ultimately, through words and music he helped make this project an enriching and creative collaboration.

THANKS

Many thanks go to Erena and Bexs for their dancing, and to Marilyn for her invaluable proofreading.

This book is dedicated to Simon for his brilliance and the music to which they dance, and to Elle for her steadfast belief.

EMILY & JEN
Dance for Deeron
by JAYN E WINSLADE

The Start of the Holiday

Emily King stared out of the coach window, absently gazing at the countryside drifting by. It was the first week of the summer holiday, and to be honest, she wasn't sure what was about to happen. Her break from school had not got off to a good start, as her mum and dad were constantly arguing and there was no money to go on holiday. Just when she thought things couldn't possibly get any worse, Emily's mum had come up with the bright idea of sending her to stay with the daughter of an old school friend whom she hadn't even spoken to in years! In a flash it seemed, Emily found herself aboard a coach heading off into the Staffordshire countryside; bound for Needwood, wherever that was! She didn't know much about the trip at all, except that the daughter's name was Jen, they were the same age, and she was alone for the holiday as well. Those were two things they had in common, anyway. Emily repeatedly ruffled her boyishly cut short black hair as she contemplated spending the entire summer with a total stranger.

The truth about Emily was that when she wasn't fed up she was actually a very positive girl, with a knack for smoothing over difficult situations. Fortunately - or unfortunately depending upon how you look at it - her mum and dad had given her lots of practice. There had been many arguments at home recently, and Emily had become expert at calming things down.

The dark rolling hills and stormy sky outside seemed to match Emily's mood on that coach, although she did have to admit to herself that the passing scenery was quite spectacular. Actually, it had been a long time since she had seen countryside like this - dry-stone walls separating rugged fields in front of a blanket of pine trees - as city life was really all she knew. Looking out, her attention was grabbed by a piercing ray of sunlight suddenly shooting down through the clouds, lighting the landscape beneath dramatically. With her gloom distracted, Emily suddenly felt quite optimistic again, and decided to abandon her despair of feeling like a parcel shunted off in the post. Besides, it wasn't going to change anything. Instead, she decided to think of herself as a strong tall tree, bathed in a warm golden light.

In reality, it was probably a good thing that Emily was getting away this summer. Her mum was about to have a baby, and there were going to be lots of visitors, including Aunt Ivy and cousin Steven with the runny-nose. Emily couldn't stand those two at the best of times, and the thought of them cooing over an infant was more than she could take right now. The only thing she was really going to miss were her holiday dance classes, because dancing was the one thing she loved to do. When Emily danced, it felt like she was floating above the ground, leaving the real world behind her and entering some strange magical land.

Her mother had told her that it was all in her imagination - of which Emily, without doubt, had plenty - and that she should be thinking more about her future career prospects. Emily didn't know whether she wanted to be a professional dancer, or even pursue anything remotely connected with dance. All she wanted, right now, was to be able to make up her own mind about what was best for her. Besides, at this moment in time, she didn't really think that either of her parents was especially well equipped to offer any useful advice. She gazed out at all the trees, standing tall and proud in the distance. 'They must have been here for many years,' she thought. 'I'll bet they're wise.'

Finally, the coach pulled into the curb. As the doors swung open, a strong country smell wafted in.

"Oak Dale Farm!" the driver called. Emily fumbled about in her pocket and produced a piece of paper, upon which was written the address of her stay. After a quick glance, she called out,

"Yes, that's me!" Her father had stowed her case well back in the overhead locker, denying poor Emily any chance of retrieving it herself. Fortunately, the driver came to her rescue.

"All right now, love?" he smiled, kindly.

"Thank you. Bye," she called as the doors closed, and the coach drove away.

Emily stared at the white gate in front of her, with the name *Oak Dale Farm* engraved upon a brass plaque. A gravel path swept up to the house, while ploughed fields and a forest of pine trees spread out far behind. The farmhouse itself possessed an enormous thatched roof that appeared far larger than it needed to be, making the house look like a small face peeking out from underneath an enormous straw hat. Emily gazed at the forest, curving tall and dark around the edges of the fields. As she stared, the wind began to rustle through the trees, while a strange sound like whispering rose into the air. Emily suddenly felt an overwhelming urge to dance. As the sound grew louder, she thought she could hear a voice calling her.

"Come to us, Emily," it seemed to say. *"Come to us."*

Emily felt dizzy, and quickly caught hold of the gate. The house somehow didn't look real anymore. It was like a dream! She took a deep breath, steadied herself and closed her eyes. The calling soon after then began to fade, to be replaced by birdsong once more. She opened her eyes to find everything back to normal, just as it was.

Suddenly, an excited golden retriever came bounding towards her along the path, barking loudly and announcing her arrival. A girl ran out of the house after the dog, followed by a man.

"Sit Bill, sit!" the girl called after the dog, who obediently stopped and sat down. Emily cautiously opened the gate.

"Hello, Emily. I'm Jen."

"Hello, Jen. Pleased to meet you," replied Emily, nervously. She tried to drag her heavy suitcase through the gate.

"Give it 'ere," the man alongside Jen said, lifting the case with ease before striding off with it towards the house.

Emily looked at Jen, who smiled welcomingly. She was about the same height as her, with long blond pigtails hanging over her shoulders. Her healthy face glowed with freckles, while her teeth shone pearly-white. Emily immediately warmed to her new friend.

"Mum told me a little bit about you, but I s'pose she doesn't know very much."

"Just as well," teased Emily.

"Well, I don't like goody-goodies," laughed Jen, sliding her arm through Emily's as she led her towards the house. Bill raced past, nearly knocking them both over. "Welcome to Oak Dale Farm!" They entered a cosy pine kitchen where a homely fire glowed in the grate, and the smell of newly baked bread suddenly made Emily feel rather hungry. "Come on, I'll show you your room."

Emily had never before been in a house like this, except once when she stayed in a hotel with Aunt Ivy and runny-nose Steven. As she followed Jen up the creaky old staircase, she noticed a strong smell of polish and lavender. At the top, there was a lovely arched window looking out across the farm towards the forest beyond.

"Wow, this house must be really old!"

"S'pose…" Jen gave a disinterested shrug. "Your room's nice, it's just been decorated." She led Emily along the hallway and into a bedroom at the end, where everything in the room was coloured yellow. It had yellow walls, yellow ceiling, yellow curtains and a yellow bedspread, with even yellow flowers inside a yellow vase! About the only thing that wasn't yellow was a dark wooden beam across the ceiling. Emily stared in amazement.

"Oh it's lovely! How kind of your mum to go to so much trouble!" Emily was thrilled with her new accommodation.

"It wasn't her, actually," scoffed Jen, "and anyway, it was less trouble than taking me with them." Emily eyed her new friend cautiously in this sudden change of mood, as she asked,

"Why, where have they gone?"

"To France to find themselves, or something like that," she shrugged, slumping down onto the bed. "Anyway, never mind me. What's your story?"

"What do you mean?" asked Emily, guardedly.

"Well, we're both on our own this summer, and our mums who haven't seen each other in years, have thrown us together to get on with it. So, how come?"

Emily wasn't sure that Jen would understand her own situation at home, as it was very different from her life.

"Well, it's difficult really, 'cause my mum's pregnant, and there's also…"

"All right," interrupted Jen, suddenly and loudly. "I'll tell you why I'm here on my own! I'm here because my parents might get divorced!" With that, she jumped up from the bed, burst into tears and ran out of the room, leaving poor Emily to feel completely bewildered.

"Oh great," she sighed. "More trouble!"

Jen soon returned, clutching a wad of tissues. She wiped her eyes, kicked the door to, and sat down despondently beside Emily.

"Tell me," said Emily, kindly. "I'm a good listener." Jen blew her nose.

"You can't imagine what it's like. All they do is argue." Emily was, of course, able to completely imagine what it was like.

"My parents row a lot as well," she confessed. "Dad lost his job, and now there's no money to pay the bills."

Jen squeezed Emily's arm, and began to feel guilty for being so self-absorbed. Obviously, Emily's lot wasn't so great either.

"I'll bet you didn't want a complete stranger coming to stay, did you?" asked Emily.

"I didn't want anyone from school coming, 'cause I knew they would all talk about it when we got back. I'm sorry I blurted out like that. You must think I'm mad already."

"It's fine Jen, don't worry," she replied. "We'll have a great time together. It'll be fun, you'll see"

Actually, it really was okay, as these things are often better out in the open anyway. Emily knew just how desperate her mum had been to sort something out for the summer, and so felt that she would just have to make it work. Jen, on the other hand, considered herself more used to bad luck than good, and lately had rarely looked on the bright side of anything. All in all, though, Emily's presence was making Jen feel a bit brighter, to the extent that having a new friend around this summer was definitely preferable to having no one. Suddenly, the bedroom door swung open, and a large round lady in a blue-check dress and red apron came bustling into the room.

"We were talking," muttered Jen, resenting the intrusion. The woman took no notice, and set about closing the windows.

"Supper's ready," she said, matter-of-factly, "and there's a big jug of fresh orange juice." The intruder left as swiftly as she had entered.

"That's Martha, the boss," Jen gave a wry smile. "Come on, she's impossible if you're late."

Supper was laid in the kitchen, on a big oak table placed by the fire. Emily thought this was a bit odd for a summer's evening, but it was nice all the same. Bill lay dozing by the fire, stretched out like a big golden hearthrug.

"This is Emily, by the way," said Jen sarcastically, as they entered the room. Martha simply smiled as she set down huge dishes of food on the table. There was enough there to feed an army!

"Dig in. You must be starving," she urged. Emily watched Martha move busily around the kitchen. She had a neat bun on the back of her head just like a ballet dancer and her cheeks were rosy, while her sharp blue eyes occasionally met Emily's with an inquisitive stare.

When they had finished eating, Emily made a quick telephone call home to let her parents know that she had arrived safely. Afterwards, she followed Jen out into the farmyard. The summer's day was drawing to a close, and the red sky promised a good day tomorrow. As usual, Jen had to go and help Martha in the kitchen, and so Emily followed the path around the edge of the field to where the man she had seen earlier was digging.

"Hello," she said, politely. "Still working hard?"

"Mmm," he muttered.

"It's lovely here," she persisted.

"Mmm." He carried on digging. Emily watched as he turned over the great clods of earth with his fork, and decided to dig a bit further herself.

"Does the forest have a name?" she enquired. The man flashed a hard look at Emily, and immediately stopped digging. He slowly stood upright, and glared into her eyes.

"Now why would you be askin' that?" he very suspiciously demanded. Emily suddenly felt afraid, and also quite insulted at his response. She suddenly wished she hadn't spoken to him at all, let alone asked anything.

"I just thought it might have a name," she replied, sheepishly. "I didn't mean to…"

"Oh, er," the man, perhaps realizing his harshness, dropped his glare and looked back down at his fork. He fumbled about for a few moments, as though composing an embarrassed apology, but instead muttered, "Well, er, let's see now… this part 'ere round the farm is Needwood," he pointed a long bony finger in the direction of the forest. "Further on is 'untswood, and beyond it lies Bagot." He quickly returned to his digging.

Emily was fascinated by the unusual names, and was dying to know more about it. She decided to try once more, and so asked, as pleasantly as she could,

"Are there lots of nice walks?"

The man's mood instantly hardened again. He stood upright, letting his fork drop to the ground, and glared at her. Then he leant forward, pushing his leathery face right up to hers, almost touching her. "There are no walks in there, do you 'ear? That forest is dangerous, dangerous!"

His dark eyes continued to glare, as Emily turned and ran back to the farmhouse as fast as she could. A gust of cold air blew from across the field, seeming to follow Emily as she fled. Bill came bounding towards her barking happily, frantically looking for a stick to play fetch with. Emily stopped running when she reached Bill, and turned back to see the man digging again as though nothing had happened. She shuddered at what had just occurred, but also felt chilled from the blast of cold air that had seemed to wrap itself around her, and then disappear suddenly.

'It's all very weird here,' she thought. Emily had never experienced such hostility before, and certainly hadn't expected it at a place where she was a guest. Jen appeared from the kitchen and waved.

"Sorry I've been so long," she called. "Are you ok?" Emily chose her words carefully to describe what had just happened. After all, she was a stranger here, and perhaps that was normal behaviour in the country. Jen listened, and then laughed.

"That's Nick, and I know what you're thinking, and yes he's a bit odd, but he's all right really. He acts as if he owns the farm, but I think he does the least work. He is the boss, though." Emily picked up Bill's slimy chewed stick and threw it for him.

"Where does he live?" she asked.

"Here," replied Jen, "has done for years, since before I was born. So does Martha." Emily half-laughed in an attempt to show Jen an easy-going side to herself.

"He probably thinks I'm a nosy townie," she said, glancing back at him. "I'll try again another day."

As she climbed the old staircase for bed, Emily felt as though she would drop with tiredness. She lay down on the crisp yellow sheets, closed her eyes and thought about her day. She pictured her mum's tearful face as the coach had pulled out of the station. She saw Jen at the gate, happy and smiling, and then on the bed, unhappy and crying. In her usual positive way, Emily decided that her and Jen were going to be good for each other this holiday, and maybe help one another through their rocky patches. She pictured Martha in the kitchen, and then Nick digging away in the field.

'What a strange man,' she thought. His voice echoed in her head… 'Beyond it lies Bagot… That forest is dangerous, dangerous!' Whoever heard of a forest being dangerous! Her head was beginning to spin, and her eyes felt as heavy as marbles. Then, the voice in the breeze began to ring in her ears once more.

"Come to us, Emily. Come to us."

She covered her head with the quilt and closed her eyes tight. In her mind, Emily was gliding over the trees looking down at the forest and the fields far below. It was an incredible experience, and she felt warm and safe. Within minutes, she had fallen into a deep sleep.

Late into the night, she was disturbed by the sound of rain hammering against the window, and thunder drumming across the sky. A flash of lightening dramatically lit the room, causing her to dart under the quilt once more; but before long, she was back fast asleep.

Deer in the Sky

Emily opened her eyes and stared at the dark wooden beam above her head. She heard a clock ticking, and men's voices calling to each other somewhere outside. She tried to remember where she was. Then, she heard a dog barking. Of course! It was Bill! She excitedly leapt out of bed, ran to the window and swept back the curtains. There it was, the wonderful view of the farm and the forest, all freshly washed and drying in the sunlight. She gazed at the scene, trying to imagine all the animals that lived there. There must be squirrels, badgers, foxes and rabbits, all going about their everyday lives under a big umbrella of pine trees.

The door creaked open, and Jen came into the room rattling a huge breakfast tray.

"Wow! What a treat!" gasped Emily, helping Jen to set the tray down on the window seat. She only ever got breakfast in bed at home if she was really ill. They tucked into the eggs, hot-buttered toast and marmalade. "Let's go for a walk today," she suggested, as Jen busily dabbed up crumbs with her finger.

"There aren't really any walks around here," she mumbled. "Only the road." Emily stared at her in astonishment.

"What about the forest?" she exclaimed. "We've got to explore that!"

"Nick says," Jen adopted a sarcastic imitation of Nick's voice, "you can't walk through the forest 'cause you'll get lost!" Jen had never really thought through this rather brash and dismissive explanation before, and she had to admit to herself that it did actually sound pretty pathetic.

"Well then, we'll mark our way with this!" Emily rooted in her bag and pulled out a large ball of blue string. Jen shrieked, and burst out laughing.

"What on earth did you bring that for?" she teased.

"Macramé," replied Emily, rather defensively. "But we can use it to mark our way as well."

Emily was determined to see her plan through, and so after breakfast hurried to dress and meet Jen, as agreed, downstairs. As Jen couldn't think of a single good reason not to go, she soon found herself wandering along the woodland footpath, with Emily striding off ahead. The sun was shining brightly, while a gentle breeze sent sprays of raindrops down from the trees. There was nothing scary about this forest at all! That was of course until the path began to disappear, and they found themselves walking along a muddy track, snaking off into the trees.

"Come on, hurry up," demanded Emily, impatiently. Jen was beginning to despair of her new friend's bravery.

"Emily, no! I don't think we should go down there!" But Emily had already gone, and so once again, Jen had no choice but to follow her. When they finally stopped to rest, Jen realized that they had climbed quite high, and could now see the forest sloping down to meet a grassy bank below. A lake glistened in the sunlight at the bottom.

"Let's go down there," shouted Emily, from up ahead. Jen, however, finally cracked.

"No Emily, we can't go any further, Martha'll go mad! And Nick, well I dread to think what he'll say!" Emily was beginning to lose her patience.

"Look, we've come all this way. We won't get lost going that little bit further, will we?" Jen suddenly felt pretty feeble. After all, she was the country girl who, it just so happens, had never had the courage to explore the forest before. Now this townie was dragging her off into the depths of it, apparently fearless. Reluctantly, she gave in to Emily.

"Alright, but if we get lost I'll kill you." They marked the way carefully, tying blue string to the trees as they went. It was hard work in the heat, causing beads of sweat to soon glisten upon their faces. "I hate these flies!" yelled Jen, manically swatting at them. It was a waste of time though, as they came straight back again regardless.

"I wonder what caused this?" Emily poked a burnt hole in a fallen tree. Lightning was a possibility, but as Jen explained, you can't rule out tourists who start forest fires every year with their barbecues.

Time was abandoned in the forest. Neither of them was wearing a watch anyway, and today was one of those summer days when you didn't even think about it. As they reached the treeline, the grassy slope spread before them like a welcoming rug. Excitedly, both girls ran down to the water in triumph, spreading their arms like wings and yelling for all they were worth. The lake was as clear and blue as the sky above.

"It's fantastic!" exclaimed Jen, thrilled after all that she'd stuck with the plan.

"I wonder if this lake has a name," pondered Emily.

"You what?" Jen began skimming pebbles across the water.

"Well, Nick said something about the forest having names for different parts, so this must be called something."

Emily lay down on the grass to rest, and stared up at the sky. Bright white wisps of cloud were moving across quite swiftly, which struck Emily as a bit odd given that there was hardly any breeze. She continued to watch as more fragments appeared, all quite suddenly and together. Then, the most amazing thing happened. A picture began to assemble itself from the delicate threads of cloud, set against the blue-sky backdrop. It looked like some sort of animal.

"Jen," she whispered. "Look at this!" Jen lay down beside Emily and gazed up at the cloud formation.

"What is it?" she gasped, in equal wonderment. A set of enormous antlers slowly appeared, and then an animal's head. "It's a deer! A stag!"

Suddenly, the image above them sprang to life. The head nodded, and then peered at them inquisitively. It looked so real and came so close that Emily wondered if she might be able to stroke him, but decided against trying.

"Hello. Who are you?" Jen asked instead, not expecting an answer, which was just as well because she didn't receive one. The stag image did, however, continue to smile and nod as its big eyes gazed down upon them both.

"I wonder where the rest of him is?" asked Emily quietly, but found Jen to be as lacking in answers as the ghostly stag.

Emily and Jen lay on the grassy bank watching the cloud-formed apparition for what must have been ages. Nothing happened, there was no noise, and the day was as still as could be. After a while they began to feel drowsy, as their eyes turned heavy from all the staring. Emily tried to keep them both awake by repeatedly prodding Jen, for she didn't want either of them to fall asleep and miss anything that might happen.

As it was, nothing else did happen except for the slow fade of the stag image, becoming thin wispy cloud once more and floating apart across the deep blue sky before disappearing completely. The stag at last was gone. Both girls sat up, as though having suddenly awoken from a dream.

"That was freaky!" exclaimed Jen.

"Freaky? It was amazing!" gasped Emily. They sat for a while longer continuing to gaze up at the sky, both disbelieving of what they had just witnessed. Then, brushing grass off each other, thoughts returned to the task of getting home.

"We'd best get back, Em, otherwise Martha'll go nuts if we're late." Jen was worried about putting Martha in a bad mood, so they followed the bright blue markings back to the fallen tree, and then retraced their route back onto the road. Jen slid her arm into Emily's as they walked. She was eager to hear a solution to the picture in the sky.

"What do you think it was, Em?"

"Who knows? Some sort of freak cloud, I suppose, would be the sensible explanation."

"Oh yeah! In the shape of a deer?" challenged Jen, sarcastically.

"Well I don't know!" Emily's reply was loaded with defensiveness, as though the very idea that she should even possess a suggestion was ludicrous in itself. "Ask a UFO expert or something." Whatever it was, the image had certainly been an amazing sight, but there just didn't seem to be an adequate explanation for it right now. They carried on walking in silence, lost in their own thoughts.

Unfortunately, their bewilderment vanished the second they arrived back at the farmhouse and saw Martha's face. She stood in the kitchen, arms folded, wearing her '*where on earth have you been?*' look. She complained, as only Martha could, that she had been given no prior warning as to them being out all day, and to make matters even worse, they were both late for supper!

"Look at the state of you both!" she scolded. "You've got grass everywhere! What on earth have you been doing?"

"Sorry," Jen always grovelled slightly when Martha was like this. "We weren't dressed for the forest." They ran upstairs to quickly change for supper. When they returned to the kitchen, Martha was at the sink, muttering to herself.

"Storm, storm in the forest! Yes, that's right. It was a storm in the forest!"

"Martha," interrupted Jen calmly, as she hated it when adults started talking to themselves. "Are you okay?"

"Your supper is ruined!" she shouted crossly, as she then proceeded to bang around the pots and pans, loudly. Jen knew Martha well enough to know that engaging her in conversation was often the best way to improve her mood and encourage her to forget something, at least temporarily. With this in mind, Jen proceeded to tell her all about their day in the forest, although she thought it best not to mention the deer head they had seen in the sky. Emily was ravenous, and far more concerned with satisfying her groaning stomach than placating Martha. She tucked in with her usual gusto.

As Jen began describing the day's woodland adventure, however, her Martha-calming tactics were starting to backfire, badly. Martha had put the tea towel down on the table, and was leaning forward to fix Jen with a cold stony stare.

"You will lose yourself in that forest! You mark my words!" Martha hissed through clenched teeth, and with her entire body pressed up hard against the table, just like a cat about to pounce. Jen stared at Martha open-mouthed, in part amazement and part fear. She wondered if at any second Martha was going to grab and shake her, she was so irate. Instead, Martha sighed and then slumped, as if having exhaled all the oxygen out of her body. She veered back from Jen, took a deep breath, and promptly left the room.

"What was that?" gasped Jen to Emily, who was also staring in complete bewilderment. Jen had never known Martha to behave quite so oddly, let alone be so angry as to come across as vicious or threatening. For the first time in her life, Jen was wary of her old friend and guardian, who baked delicious bread and was always in the kitchen.

Deer on the Ground

The days and weeks that followed were long, hot and exciting.

Emily and Jen had kitted themselves out with caps and rucksacks found amongst the garage jumble, so as to not be so bothered by the forest flies anymore. Also, they now had something in which to carry Martha's scrumptious picnics. The strange deer head had not made a second appearance thus far, but Emily was hopeful that it would. Jen secretly hoped so as well, but didn't want to encourage Emily too much at the moment, so thought it best to avoid the subject. What was obvious to them both, however, was that for some reason Martha did not approve of their days out, and kept muttering on about a storm in the forest. Her piercing eyes could be seen from the kitchen window every day as they set off along the road. It made Jen feel nervous about their trips, as she really didn't want anything to go wrong.

Today, however, Martha was being exceptionally grumpy, tutting and clattering the crockery about as she prepared their picnic. Jen decided to try and convince her that the forest was safe, by telling her all about their carefully marked path to the lake. She also emphasized that there really wasn't much danger of them falling down a hole or getting lost; and as for a storm, they'd never had such good weather!

Martha, though, wasn't having any of it. She tossed the picnic box onto the table, and grabbed Jen by the shoulder as

DEER ON THE GROUND

she moved to pick it up. Her pursed lips quivered as though she were about to say something, while her eyes probed so deeply Jen felt her knees go weak. But instead of saying anything, Martha simply let go and rushed out of the room, leaving Jen yet again feeling totally confused. After all, she knew full well that Martha was a countrywoman born and bred, and was the sort of person who liked plain talking and always spoke her mind. This was really strange behaviour for someone like her.

However, Jen remained determined that throughout Emily's stay, Martha would not spoil their days out. She had never had so much fun, and Martha's bizarre antics were not going to put a stop to it. Even Bill was having a great time on the walks, bounding off ahead to investigate every sound and smell. He was annoyed by all the flies, of course, and continually snapped at them until he ended up chasing his tail.

"We need a hat for Bill," was Emily's suggestion during one such incident. The image of Bill wearing a sunhat had Jen in stitches of laughter for ages. Watching Emily then stride off ahead with the rucksack while her short black hair bounced about purposefully, caused Jen to marvel at her confidence and wish that she could possess just a tiny part of it. Most recently, Jen hadn't felt secure or assured in anything.

"You're not bad for a townie!" she quipped, jokingly.

"Oh, I know about the countryside," replied Emily, slightly missing the joke. "I went walking once with the school in the Lake District. It was great except for this boy, Woody, who spoilt it because he stole a walking stick from a gift shop, pushing it down the leg of his trousers and limping out with it. After that we weren't allowed in any of the shops, so we couldn't buy presents."

"That's the trouble with school. One person does something, and everyone suffers!" Jen had her own memories of this kind of injustice.

"The boys got their own back on him though," continued Emily, "because someone sewed the walking stick inside his pyjama trousers. They said it was hilarious, watching him limp around the dorm." They both laughed at the image. "One thing that was really good was when we swam in the lake. If the weather stays this good, I'd like to swim here before the end of the holiday." Memories of Martha's stern face earlier that morning flooded back into Jen's mind, causing her to think it best to ignore that idea for the time being.

They sat down at the fallen tree and threw sticks for Bill. This place had become so familiar now that it was hard for Jen to believe she had lived so close to the forest all her life, and yet had not wandered here before. Also striking was just how close she had grown to Emily these last weeks, as though they had been friends for years. It was an easy friendship, where you trusted the other person with secrets, and were not afraid of being belittled or laughed at. Jen thought that they could probably talk about anything.

"When are your parents coming back, Jen?" asked Emily, secretly hoping that they weren't returning for at least another week, when she would have to return home herself.

"They didn't give a date, though to be honest it's a good sign that they're still there. I thought they would argue and come straight back. I guess it just proves it's me that's the problem."

"What are you on about?" demanded Emily, rather crossly.

"Well, I just think it must be my fault, though I don't know how."

"Don't be so daft! It's not your fault, how could it be? They are grown ups, after all."

"Yeah, well, we'll see. Come on, Bill." Jen pulled her rucksack onto her back and resumed walking, so Emily did likewise. When they'd first met, Emily considered Jen to be the luckiest girl in the world, as she seemed at first sight to have everything. She was pretty, and her family was obviously rich, but in many ways, Jen's problems were worse than her own; and she was unhappy, that was a fact. Even so, Emily still wished that she could have a friend like Jen back home; someone who could be trusted, and who wouldn't stir things up behind her back.

Emily's thoughts were suddenly interrupted as Bill raced past, leapt into the air, and then landed flat down onto his stomach behind some shrubbery. They both stared dumbfounded as he then crawled into the undergrowth. All they could hear was his golden tail, slowly thumping on the ground.

"What is it, Bill?" whispered Jen, tiptoeing cautiously over to him. She then quickly turned, grabbed Emily, and pulled her behind a huge old oak tree. "Look!" she whispered.

Peering out from behind the tree, Emily and Jen witnessed an incredible sight. Standing in a clearing and congregated within a large circle stood a gathering of twelve stags, all moving in a strange and quite beautiful way. Slowly, they dipped their heads from side to side, causing their huge antlers to rise and fall as they did so. Each stag moved perfectly in time with the others, all combining to create a display of majesty and great poise. As they swayed back and forth, a single stag moved into the centre of the circle and bowed his head to the ground. After bowing, he raised his antlers and then spiralled away from the middle, peering up towards the sky as he did so. Another stag then did the same - moved into the circle, bowed, and then spiralled away - coming to a stop opposite the first stag.

Gradually, two straight lines facing each other were being formed inside the original circle. This sequence continued until the last stag had spiralled, after which each then bowed low to his opposite number, walked towards, and then past the other, in order to change sides. This was a dance! These stags were actually dancing, with such perfect rhythm and timing as to make Emily wonder whether they were moving to music that only they could hear. Through the sound of their hooves beating the ground as they moved, Jen and Emily could both make out a quite distinct, flowing rhythm. Jen decided it was in $^3/_4$, or waltz time, a time signature she loved to play. Emily just wanted to join in and dance alongside the stags - the very idea being so incredible - but she was petrified of moving and scaring them off. Instead, they both stood absolutely still, agog at the wonderful sight ahead of them. Bill lay silent and flat in the bracken.

After more passes, bows, and a two-stag circular movement that reminded Jen of when Bill chases his tail, the dance seemed to come to an end. Emily assumed at this point that they would start behaving like stags again by grazing or some-thing, but they simply stopped, separated, and then disappeared through the trees. The clearing was soon silent once more, except for birdsong and a light-rustling breeze.

They waited for a while, still transfixed and utterly speechless at what they had just seen. Emily then slowly crept into the clearing to see if she could spot any of the stags through the trees, but they had disappeared completely. Jen ran further in to look, but they were definitely gone, with not even a hoof mark remaining upon the ground. Just like the stag in the sky, the whole thing was as though it had simply been a dream. Bill joined them quietly in the clearing, appearing quite stunned himself, and Jen patted him for his excellent behaviour.

"There are deer in the sky AND on the ground in this forest!" she finally exclaimed, completely flummoxed.

They carried on walking, keeping their eyes peeled for any other stags along the way. They eventually arrived at their picnic spot by the lake, and hungrily spread out the food. Emily's eyes widened at the sight of it. Whatever Martha's objections to their days out, she was not letting them go hungry. Emily had never tasted such wonderful picnics in her life.

"I don't know anything about deer," mumbled Jen, pushing a cheese and pickle sandwich into her mouth.

"Nor me, but they seemed to be dancing, and even talking to each other." Emily rose to her feet. "It was so lovely and graceful! Like swans on a river." She spun around on the spot and then skipped in a circle, making a figure of eight with her arms as she went. Her pathway weaved circles within circles. Jen watched with interest, and it looked very impressive.

"Hey, where did you learn to do that?" she asked.

"I go to dance classes every week." Emily was beginning to enjoy herself now, and began to show off a little. Whirling around, she jumped pulling one leg underneath her, helped no doubt by her light and agile body. Repeating the phrase, she scaled higher and higher each time, eventually placing her hands above her head to look like pretend antlers.

"You look like the deer!" yelled Jen, jumping up to join in. They then danced together, with Emily leading and Jen copying. Round and around, jumping through the air, just like the stags.

Suddenly and at once, both girls crashed to the ground, their legs having gone straight from under them. Emily, quite shocked after having had the wind knocked out of her, took a deep breath and tried to compose herself. Had something hit her? She couldn't be sure. She looked about quickly to see what was happening.

Bizarrely, everything around them now appeared faint and blurry, as though they were peering out from the inside of a gigantic goldfish bowl. Also, every bird, insect, falling leaf and anything else that moved, now travelled in slow motion before fading from view completely. Not only that, but the very colours of the forest seemed to be changing as well; everything, from the blue sky above to the grass on the ground, began to swirl and merge together, like the mixing up of many colours on a paint palette. Both girls started to feel nauseous very quickly.

They soon then became aware of noise above, causing them both to look up. Threads of brilliant-white and golden light were spinning just above their heads, and creating this very loud, almost deafening *zuzzing* noise - like a cross between the crackling of an electricity pylon and the whooshing sound of a long whip.

"What's happening?" cried Jen, barely audible above the din.

"I don't know!" was all Emily could yell back in return.

21

Holding tightly onto each other, they managed to stagger to their feet. Jen and Emily stood dazed as the light and noise swirled around them. The white light-threads then suddenly separated from the gold, descended, and spun directly in front of them. The noise changed as well - the crackling sound was obviously coming from the white light-threads, whilst the whooshing sound came from the gold. As the golden threads continued to spin above, the white began to wrap itself around their arms and legs. At first they just both stared quite calmly, as the piercing-bright white threads danced around and encircled them. Except for a light tingling sensation, it felt harmless enough, and the light display was fantastic! Showers of light, like stardust, fell all around them. It was spellbinding! Even the noise died down.

But then, playfulness rapidly gave way to pain and fear. The white light-threads suddenly tightened their grip around them, first along the arms and then the legs, locking up each limb completely. In moments, they were unable to move, while all the time the threads continued to spin, now around their bodies. The noise also increased again, just as powerful and deafening as before. As the threads wrapped themselves evermore around them, they began to cling to both girls like frost in a freezer. Emily and Jen then felt deep and penetrating cold, coming up from their legs and through their torsos to their arms. Both were petrified at what was going on. It was so cold!

"Emily! Help!"

"Help…me!" The frost was now at the top of Emily's neck, and beginning to freeze her face! She peered upwards - her eyes now being the only part of her body she could still move - and saw the golden light-threads still swirling above both their heads. She didn't know what to do or think, but wished that something would come and help them, fast!

As if answering Emily's call, the golden light-threads instantly dived down onto both her and Jen, wrapping around their icy shoulders. Then, like an image appearing on a computer screen line by line, the golden light-threads began scanning all over their bodies, starting at the neck and along the arms, to their legs and finally feet. Moving side-to-side at tremendous speed, the golden threads thawed the frost as they went, hurling the white light-threads off them like some mad knitting machine gone haywire. The deafening noise then reduced to a soft hum, and for a moment it was so warm and cosy, Emily thought they were at last safe again.

But safe they were not. Right above their heads, the frosty white threads had reshaped into a gigantic hand, dwarfing in size the golden thread by many times, and big enough to grab both Jen and Emily effortlessly! Jen felt her stomach knot up again at the prospect of another assault.

The golden light-threads surrounding Jen and Emily suddenly sped up, spinning around them much faster. The *zuzzing* noise also became louder, reaching its near-deafening level in barely a few seconds. Then, just as Jen was about to scream out in pain due to the noise, the golden threads spun upwards and off of both girls' bodies.

Emily shuddered, then looked at Jen. They both appeared to be okay, which was the main thing, and Jen was mightily glad that nothing was touching her any more. The noise, thankfully less ear splitting but still loud, now floated above them. Very slowly, Emily glanced upwards to see what fresh nightmare lay ahead.

Above their heads and suspended in mid-air now appeared the huge white hand, while directly facing it spun a ferocious golden tornado! Every piece of thread combining to make either shape, spun around its own area at incredible speed. Not only that, but each shape was increasing in size all the time. The sense of power and energy was awesome.

"What are they doing, Em?"

"Wish I knew…sizing eachother up, maybe."

Once the golden whirlwind had reached the same height as the hand, it suddenly spun outwards, increasing its size massively. Then, like some vast shoal of fish, the threads pulsated and expanded outwards in all directions, almost reaching the white hand before diving back together again, reshaping themselves in furious activity. Now however, the golden threads no longer resembled a tempest. Now, they had reformed as another hand - a hand much bigger and more powerful than the one in opposition!

Two giant fists now faced each other, directly in combat. Instantly, they lunged together and began to wrestle, each trying to force the other downwards. Then they separated, retreated back slightly, and charged at each other again. The golden hand reached the white hand first, and with incredible strength grabbed and shook it ferociously from side to side. Then it squeezed, hard. The white hand quickly resembled a rubber glove filled with air, and soon looked fit to burst! The golden hand threw it down with relentless force onto the ground, right in front of Jen and Emily.

Not content with this, the golden hand then dived after it, grabbing and squeezing again. The white hand now appeared so damaged that it simply crumpled up, just like a snowball. The white threads were barely spinning, and its energy had been all but crushed. With almost contempt, the golden hand threw the white one far off into the distance. Silence and safety appeared to have been restored, with only a soft hum audible once more.

"Well, I'm glad it's on our side," said Jen quietly, relieved beyond words to see the back of the white threads, and the noise.

"Me too," agreed Emily, still shivering from her deep-freeze experience. The golden hand lowered itself gently to ground level, and opened out from a fist to a cupped position. The index finger then extended outwards, like a walkway.

"I think it wants us to get on, Jen," said Emily. "What do you think?" The fact that they had absolutely no idea where they were right now, sort of answered that question for them. Nothing was the same as before, and this hand, or whatever it was, seemed to be protecting them, so...

The walkway finger closed after Emily stepped on board, and the hand gently glided up into the air. Moments later, they were flying through what could only be described as thick white fog. Sitting in the palm of the golden hand, both girls cautiously peered through the gaps between fingers for any clue that might indicate where they were, or better still, were going. Nothing, however, could be seen above, below or even to the sides of them.

On and on they travelled, until gradually, thinner patches of fog revealed glimpses of something far off and in the distance. Catching Jen's eye first, she grabbed Emily's arm and pointed. Staring hard, they could both soon make out passing flashes of a vast mountain plateau, scarred by deep crevasses and wide-open ravines. Before long the fog reduced further, revealing a much clearer view of many dark mountain ridges capped with ice, both ahead and to the left of them. It looked freezing cold, but thankfully both girls were snug inside the palm of the flying hand.

Still they journeyed further on, across more mountains and over more forest, until finally the hand floated down and descended gently into a clearing by a lake, coming to rest on a crisp bed of dry leaves. The index finger walkway extended outwards and so Emily, closely followed by Jen, disembarked from their transport. As soon as Jen was clear the hand pulled away, uncurling its long golden fingers as it did so. Then, in front of their eyes, the golden hand simply dissolved into millions of spinning light-threads! Like tiny golden tadpoles scattering themselves amongst a vast lake, both the light-threads and the hand they had combined to be disintegrated into thin air.

"No wait!" cried Jen, "Don't go! How will we get back?" That sinking-stomach feeling returned to them both, as they could do nothing but despairingly watch the golden hand disappear. What immediately captured both girls' attention, however, was that coming into view now from behind the hand was a large stag, standing still with apparently gleaming steel antlers! He was tall and golden, with eyes that appeared different somehow, although both were clearly looking straight at them.

"Wow!" gasped Emily. "Where'd he come from?"

"Dunno," replied Jen, cautiously. "I guess he must have been standing behind the hand. What should we do?" For a few moments, they stared at the stag while he stared back at them. No one moved or said anything. Emily took a quick glance at their surroundings. The area looked very much like the clearing by the lake where they had supposedly just come from, except that the leaves on the trees were now dark brown and golden while the grass was parched and lifeless, and the lake itself appeared to be frozen over. The flawless summer that, up until now, had supplied perfect weather seemed to have dramatically given way to a cold and dead autumn.

The crisp sound of leafy footsteps behind him caused the stag to turn his head and peer back towards the treeline. Two lines of stags in single file then stepped out into the clearing and walked forward, coming to a halt once they had formed two closely spaced parallel and facing lines. With every set of antlers poised upright and almost touching its opposite number, Emily wondered if they might be about to dance again, but instead they stood regimented and still. Then, in sequence from the treeline coming towards them, the stags all took one step backwards to create a passageway, and reveal the emergence of an even stranger creature. He was tall and both looked and walked like a man, but had enormous antlers growing out of the top of his head! He wore a cloak of glittering golden leaves, with a wide leather belt hanging around his middle. Even more extraordinary than his appearance, however, was the fact that his feet made no sound on the forest floor, as he slowly walked towards them.

Emily gasped again. A voice inside her head was screaming, 'RUN!' but her legs just wouldn't move. As he approached, she saw that he had a kind face, brown and wrinkled now by a broad smile. He stopped, held out his hands, and with a deep booming voice announced,

"I am Deeron. Welcome to our magical world."

Emily and Jen simply stared in utter disbelief as they limply shook his hand. A dark-brown beard enhanced his rugged and handsome features, while his eyes sparkled as he spoke.

"Please, follow me," he said, then strode off with the steel-antlered golden stag by his side. The rest of the deer followed, except for two stags that presumably were waiting for Emily and Jen, although they appeared to be not in the least bit frightened or concerned. As for the girls themselves, they were not feeling anything like as brave, given the decidedly worried expression Jen gave Emily. However, all Emily could offer Jen in return was a simple shrug, as there weren't exactly many alternatives to choose from. So they followed, escorted by the two deer.

The strange party moved quickly and in silence along a path, venturing deep into the forest. Before long, Emily and Jen caught sight of what appeared to be spires, rising above the canopy up ahead of them. Drawing closer, Jen wondered if they might belong to some long-forgotten cathedral or stately home. As it turned out, their path led them straight to the door, whereupon Emily and Jen simply stared in amazement at the sight of a gigantic woodland castle, towering majestically before them. It was as beautiful and grand as any cathedral either of them had ever seen, with its entire structure built from wood. Large ornamental carvings of deer adorned the arches and doorways, while smaller gargoyle-type figures jutted out just beneath the roofline. In fact, every feature of the building - every finial, tracery and buttress - was decorated to represent deer in some way. To that end, a gigantic set of antlers jutted out just above the main arched entrance.

"Come," beckoned Deeron, "and enter Deeron's Hall. Please, join our company."

They stepped through the enormous doorway and into the warm candlelit glow of a large hall, in which many tall tree trunk pillars towered seemingly ever upwards to support high lofty rafters. Iron candelabras hung down from the beams, each burning huge candles dripping heavily with wax. Carved deer heads stared down from the walls, while upon the floor lay a carpet of soft golden leaves. In the centre of the hall stood a magnificent wooden throne, decorated by a set of ornate wooden antlers forming its back.

Deeron stood at the throne and gestured Emily and Jen to a small wooden table, on which sat three goblets. The party of deer stood before him with their graceful heads held high as if waiting for him to speak, but it was Emily who broke the silence.

"Who are you and where are we?" she managed to blurt out, all in one breath. Jen grabbed her arm as an offer of support.

"My friends," replied Deeron softly, "you have nothing to fear from us." He handed a goblet to each of them. "Take our welcoming drink, and then I will tell you all there is to know." Nervously, they put the goblet to their lips. The drink was delicious, warm and sweet, tasting of honey and herbs. Deeron threw back his head, draining his goblet in one go. "Please, be at home here. You were brought to us for a very special reason."

"Brought here?" Emily tried to sound tough-minded. "Who brought us here?"

"It will take some time for me to explain. Please understand, the deer are my family, and now they are your friends." Emily glanced at the stag standing next to her, whose gentle face gazed sadly upon her. There was certainly nothing to fear from him.

"What do you want from us?" she asked, as Deeron sat down on the throne.

"We need your help," he replied, earnestly.

Jen was amazed at Emily's courage and, although not possessing much herself, made a bold effort to stand stoically by her side. Deeron raised his head and breathed deeply, as his mighty antlers glowed in the candlelight. The deer crouched down before him, and so Jen and Emily took their cue and settled down onto the leafy floor as well.

The tale of Smolder Bagot

In the lofty Great Hall, Deeron's voice echoed like a storm across the sky as he carefully told his tale.

"Years ago," he began, "our home was on the other side of the forest, in the land of Hawkwood. We were a larger herd then, living at peace with our world. We had magic powers but they were never used for evil, only ever for good. Then one day, Smolder Bagot came and destroyed our happiness. Smolder is our enemy. He is the son of Lord and Lady Bagot of Bagot Hall, who were a kind, happy and peaceful folk. They cared for the forest, and loved the deer very much."

"During one especially long and hard winter, Lord Bagot made us a gift of six stags. He told us that they possessed magic in their antlers, and to keep them safe for they would help ensure our herd prospered in the years ahead. As you can imagine, we were very grateful for this offering, and our lives improved for a while. Then sometime later, after Lady Bagot had passed away, Lord Bagot came to see me once more. Forlorn and nearing the end himself, he said he could no longer entrust his son with the welfare of the forest after he died. He also said that his son must never be allowed to retake the magic stags, for their power would be corrupted and the White Light of Evil would take hold in our forest."

"Whilst we had all heard of the White Light," explained Deeron, "I did wonder whether Lord Bagot might have been exaggerating, but he was most anxious concerning the dangers that lay before us. The very last thing he said to me, clasping only my hands in his, were the words *"Prevent at all costs my son from retaking those stags or their antlers, for only then when the time comes will you possess the means to face the White Light. With the golden shield, banish from o'er these lands all that is evil. Peace must prevail here. This is my will. Remember I told you so."* I realized then that those words were important to Lord Bagot and so I did remember them, but even now I'm not sure what they mean." Deeron sat back in his throne as he briefly paused to recall that moment long ago, before resuming the story.

"Soon after, when Smolder learned that his father had given away the stags, he became consumed with jealousy, vowing that when his father died he would create an army to come and steal the antlers back for himself. Lord Bagot found out about his son's plot, and so burned down Bagot Hall to stop him from inheriting anything. Smolder was so angry he struck his father, killing him instantly. He then hid in tunnels beneath the forest floor, all the time strengthening his own powers. Later, he destroyed many trees and built a fortress of wood surrounding the ruins of Bagot Hall. Finally, he shrouded the territory in a veil of invisible fog, concealing his castle from view completely." Jen stared at Emily with a combined look of horror and bewilderment, as she squeezed her arm tightly.

"Very soon," continued Deeron, "Smolder had gathered together an army of powerful fighters. They came from the boglands beyond Marching Cliff, and were well used to war and battle. One night, when we were least able to defend ourselves, he came with his army and axed the magic antlers from the stags' heads. Then he made off, howling his tormenting laugh into the depths of the forest. In the years since, he has used and corrupted the antlers' power to unleash devastation upon us, and imprisoned many of the forest's animals."

Deeron paused to look at his herd. He never ceased to be overwhelmed at their loyalty and innocence. Now, there were two young visitors from the human world waiting to hear the facts. There was no easy way to explain all this, and he knew deep in his heart that he had to tell them the whole, true, horrible story.

"One summer's night, we attempted to get back the antlers. Smolder's magic was already stronger than ours, and he drove us back with torrential ice storms that beat us to the ground. Then he sent dark clouds from the sky that surrounded and engulfed us in dense fog. We sank in mud, we boiled in heat, and we shivered in freezing cold rain. Every trick that Smolder had, he used against us. Many of my army were killed. Brave does and stags were lost in battle, and all for nothing."

Deeron took a deep breath. His eyes stared straight ahead as though he could still see the battle going on.

"I led those who were able to follow, through the forest into Huntswood and then Needwood, which is where we have lived ever since. A storm raged for months here, and the forest was flooded and torn apart. Many animals died, either from lack of food or from the terrible force of the rain that crashed relentlessly from the sky. Night after night, we lay anguished by Smolder's laughter at our suffering. The forest will not recover until we have the antlers back, and he is destroyed."

"But," spoke a nervous and timid Jen, "I live in Needwood, and we weren't flooded. Besides," she stammered, anxiously eyeing Emily for some support, "this summer's been the best…"

"Our world is very different to yours, Jen," he calmly interrupted her, leaning forward. "Although we do share many things…" Deeron paused, as he thought carefully for a moment. "Perhaps," he continued, "I should also explain to you our distant past as well." He stroked his beard softly, as he began to recall the long since spoken of details surrounding the earliest-known history of the herd.

"Almost eight hundred years ago," he began, "all that existed right here beneath our feet, was frozen and barren rock. There were no trees, no lakes, and the temperature remained perishingly cold throughout the year. That was until one day, when suddenly something changed, and trees began to sprout and grow. It was slow at first, but growth increased as the arctic winds eased, and heat from the sun soared. Before long, a vast area of pristine forest had been created. Soon after, the Bagot's earliest ancestors arrived, and they became guardians of this forest. Our herd was then born, and for centuries - right up until Smolder appeared, in fact - the family carried on the role of caring for the forest through each generation." Both girls' heads were spinning with questions.

"So," asked Emily, struggling for a moment to find the right words, "there are two identical forests, one in your world and one in our world, right?"

"Well," replied Deeron cautiously, "not identical, no, as our forest is considerably larger than yours, but it is similar. We have a Needwood, a Huntswood and a Bagot Wood, just as you do, while our lakes, such as Deerbrook, are also much the same as yours."

"How come?" Jen asked.

"Because of something called the Horn Dance," he replied. "You see, every year since these trees first began to grow here eight centuries ago, mortals in your world have danced with imitation antlers, pretending to be deer. It is a ritual that still takes place today, and is the reason why we exist."

"I think I've seen this," said Jen, excitedly. "It happens every year near where I live."

"That's right," replied Deeron, with a soft smile. "When it was first performed, a special magic was conjured that created a duplicate of your forest, here in our world. What you see here now is how your forest would have appeared in autumn, eight hundred years ago."

"Wow," both girls whispered as they gazed at each other, their eyes suddenly ablaze with wonder. In both their minds, the chance to essentially time travel and see how England looked in mediaeval times was an opportunity way too good to miss.

"I should stress," emphasized Deeron, not wanting to be misunderstood, "that beyond this forest, our two worlds are very different. In your world, you have many towns, cities and people, competing with nature for scarce land and resources. Here, much of the land beyond lies unexplored - by us at least - and being rugged and mountainous, is of no interest to us. Our only desire is to live here in peace and harmony, upon the land our forefathers grazed and cared for."

"Oh." Emily tried hard not to show her disappointment as she quickly glanced at Jen, hoping she'd do the same. Jen simply shrugged despondently with her eyebrows.

"Anyway," resumed Deeron as he sat upright, resting his elbows upon the arms of the throne and linking both hands. "Until recently, the magic created from every Horn Dance would go directly to the forest. However, having seen how his son could so easily corrupt it, Lord Bagot instead directed the magic to the antlers of six young stags, the very same stags he presented to us as a gift and that are with us now. His intention was that all the goodness generated from the Horn Dance would still remain in the forest. So you see, now that Smolder has the antlers, that magic goes to him, and he is using it to do terrible things."

"But how can he use good magic to do terrible things?" asked Jen, now feeling a bit braver.

"Ah well," sighed Deeron, his voice suddenly becoming strained and wearisome. "Smolder has Deity, the Goddess of the forest. He shrouded himself in a golden glow and then roamed through the forest, crying for her help. Deity only saw the golden light and so followed, thinking it was a wounded animal needing her. Smolder led her to his castle and, when it was too late to escape, captured her. He has held her ever since, although we do not know where. Deity should never be imprisoned, for she brings beauty to the forest, and guides and protects every soul as it moves from one existence to another. Without her, plants cannot sprout to life and grow in the summer sun. So you see, the forest is forever locked in autumn, and I'm afraid that all life around us is slowly dying. As the trees and plants disappear, so too will what's left of the animals and birds, and so eventually shall we."

Emily and Jen looked up as Deeron lifted his strong body off the throne, and paced thoughtfully across the room.

"But what can *we* do?" asked Emily, getting up off the floor, and suddenly feeling very small and insignificant in comparison to the problem.

"We need you to take the antlers back from Smolder," he replied, turning towards her.

"But if you can't do it," she asked, almost pleading, "how on earth can we?" Deeron walked towards her, and placing his hand on Emily's shoulder, gazed into her eyes with a sudden look of hope, as he replied,

"Because you can enter his castle. Having tried and failed, we are blocked from entering it, but you have the power, for you are both Wandiacates."

"We're what?" asked Emily, with a look of disbelief.

"Wandiacates," explained Deeron, "are mortals who possess Chiron, a very special combination of honesty, fortitude and unity. When they dance, they collect goodness and destroy evil."

"I don't understand," she stammered.

"Your dance is magical," he continued calmly, "and is the key to entering Smolder's kingdom. We felt it when you danced by the lake, and realized then that you are not ordinary mortals, but Wandiacates. When you dance, you step out of the mortal world and enter Wandiacatum."

"Wandia what?" blurted out Jen, now just as perplexed as Emily. She also stood up and gripped Emily's arm more tightly than before, as though suddenly realizing her outburst of bravery.

"Wandiacatum is the space between your mortal world and our magical world, and where time does not exist. It is where the Golden Light of Goodness and the White Light of Evil spin constantly around each other, waiting for something good or evil to happen in either world that will make one stronger than the other. When you both danced by the lake you entered this space, and the golden hand brought you here into our world of magic." Both girls' heads were really beginning to go numb now.

"Many faces are frozen solid in the mountains of Wandiacatum," he continued. "Their souls remain imprisoned far away by the White Light of Evil, where they wander endlessly in search of golden light and a way out. As everything that is wicked makes the white light stronger, their captivity helps make all the evil in both your world and our world more powerful. It is love, kindness, and goodness that makes the golden light stronger, and Wandiacates have more of that than any other mortals on earth. They have the power to collect the golden light, and carry its magic with them to where it is most needed."

"So, what were you saying about this Horn Dance thing?" butted in Emily, trying to keep hold of as many details as she could.

"The Horn Dance is to be performed again in six days," replied Deeron. "When this happens, it will enhance the magic of the antlers, making Smolder more powerful than he has ever been. Then…" his eyes fell to the ground.

"Then what?" asked Jen, softly.

"Then he will come for us all, for his power will be strong enough and we shall be too weak. We will lose the battle and Smolder will kill us, for he hates us all." A deep knowing sigh passed around the deer, as they stared lovingly at Deeron. "Come," he beckoned, moving towards the main arched entrance, "I want to show you something."

Emily and Jen, with the stags filing along behind them, followed Deeron outside and along a tree-lined passageway, to a smaller hall where does and their fawns were grazing and lazing about. Some scampered around playfully, while others chewed grass from huge pottery bowls. Jen held out her hand to beckon them, and a fawn trotted happily up to her and nuzzled her palm with his soft wet nose.

"Oh, aren't they sweet!" she exclaimed, thrilled to bits.

"These are our next generation," he said. "We must try to preserve our herd, or else we will become extinct. Smolder hates the deer simply because his father loved them, while his jealousy and desire for power have warped him in every way imaginable."

"What a hideous and wicked person he is!" cried Emily. "To kill his father and then want to kill the deer!"

"We want to help, really we do," added Jen, still overcome by the sight of the fawns. "But what exactly can we do?" Deeron smiled and led them back outside to a clearing where the stags were waiting.

"The day after tomorrow," he began, "we must head for the edge of Bagot Wood, where lies Smolder's Castle. Our journey will be long and hard, taking several days due to the route we shall have to take because of the many forces that protect Smolder and surround his kingdom. Once we reach his territory, you two must perform your deer dance, as the magic created will lure him out into a valley nearby. We will keep him and his army busy there while you two enter the castle and retrieve the six pairs of magic antlers. We know roughly whereabouts they are hidden, but taking them will be the most dangerous task of all. Once we have those antlers, we shall reunite them with our six magic stags. Only then will we have any chance of defeating Smolder, freeing Deity, and returning triumphant to our home. We will do our best not to put you in any danger, but you must understand that this is a perilous task, and Smolder is a frightening and powerful force. Above all, you must be brave. You are special because you are Wandiacates, but many things that you will see on this journey are not meant for your eyes. It will take great courage and fortitude from you both to step into the unknown." Suddenly, all eyes focused upon Emily and Jen.

"Will you help us?" he asked, in a suddenly stern and warrior-like voice, standing now so tall that he peered down at both Emily and Jen from what, to them, seemed like an astonishing height.

Emily desperately wanted to say yes, but she was terrified that her voice was going to come out as a tiny little squeak, so she nodded her head hard. Jen, momentarily confused at Emily's unusual loss of speech, nevertheless quickly joined in with the nodding. Deeron clapped his hands, and exclaimed joyfully,

"Make ready, for we shall begin our fight against evil!" The deer quickly dispersed, leaving Emily, Jen and Deeron standing alone.

"Thank you for giving us this hope," he said, sincerely. "Do not enter the forest tomorrow, as you may be being watched by someone in your world. Smolder must not know about the dance, in case he finds some means for weakening your power. However, on the day after tomorrow, you must dance again at the same place by the lake, where you will be met by one of my herd. We shall rest, plan and then begin our journey."

"We will do as you ask, Deeron," said Emily, not quite knowing what she was saying or letting herself in for, but meaning it nonetheless.

Deeron, bowing his head graciously, then knelt down and placed his hands upon the floor. Before their very eyes his shape began to change, as first his head and shoulders, followed by his body, arms and legs, all stretched and widened. In a few moments, a large golden stag stood before them.

"Wow!" exclaimed Jen. "That's incredible!"

"I'll say," concurred Emily quietly, more out of shock than anything else.

"Now, climb onto my back and I will return you. Hold on tightly, as there is much evil white light in Wandiacatum right now. Your passage will feel very cold."

Jen, followed by Emily, climbed onto Deeron's back. He then slowly began to turn on the spot, first going one way, and then the other. Jen held tightly onto Deeron's antlers, while Emily held onto Jen. The forest around them then began spinning faster and faster, causing both girls to close their eyes as the air around them turned bitterly cold. They were moving, that was for sure, but it had become so cold so quickly, neither of them could tell whether they were flying, rotating, or still on the ground. Icicles began to form on their eyebrows and noses while their hair stiffened like cardboard. Emily felt a wave of sickness rise from her stomach and stick in her throat. Jen was trying desperately to bury her head into her arms and chest for some cover from the searing blasts of freezing air, coming at them from all directions. Both tried to breath slowly.

A strange sensation came over Emily, as if long bony fingers were poking at her. At first, the pokes were soft enough, but they soon became jabs, and finally stabs, causing her immense pain as she struggled to hold on. They increased not just in their ferocity, but also in their frequency. It felt as though there were many fingers now, all stabbing at her harder and harder, more and more. They came from everywhere, prodding at her body, arms, legs and head. Emily buried her face hard into Jen's back, sensing that the stabbers were trying to get at her eyes. She daren't risk trying to beat them off, as that would mean losing an arm around Jen's waist. She was finding it difficult to breathe now as well, having her face pressed so hard up against Jen's spine, but she had to keep going! Worse still, she couldn't *see* anything, as the wind was just too fierce. Even her lips were beginning to freeze together now. Her situation was becoming desperate.

Just as she was about to scream out to Deeron while she still could, a finger suddenly lunged hard into Emily's ribs. This time, the force and resulting pain was just too much. Her grip around Jen's waist collapsed, and in one almighty jolt, she was hauled off Deeron's back and lifted up high into the air. Up, up into the sky she rose, as if suddenly catapulted by some invisible high-speed elevator. In seconds, Emily had reached a height normally the preserve of large birds and small aircraft, seldom schoolgirls with nothing between themselves and the ground. She closed her eyes and tried to will herself to blackout, as everything now was way beyond comprehension or courage anyway. The view may have been magnificent from that height, but Emily was far too petrified to care.

Still conscious, she felt a sudden jolt, and quickly realized that she was no longer rising. No movement at all, in fact, just complete stillness. Had this all been a hideous nightmare, she wondered? Perhaps if she opened her eyes, she would find herself back in her cosy bed at the farmhouse, with warm sunlight blazing in through the window, and Martha's wonderful cooking smells wafting in from downstairs. Now that would definitely be worth opening your eyes for!

Emily prized open one eye nervously, but the vision that greeted her was seriously *not* what she had hoped for. Her eye registered jagged ridges of snow-capped mountains, and frozen streams far below her. Valleys, forests and lakes could all be seen from where she now was. There was no denying it; Emily was suspended in mid-air! She stared, horrified.

From the corner of her eye she spotted movement, way down on a mountain path. It was Deeron! Jen as well, clinging onto his antlers and waving madly up at her. Emily tried to call to them but she was way too high, and her voice was weak anyway. Even her hands were too cold to wave back. How *could* she be so high? Then she spotted something else, to the side of her - white light-threads!

"Noooo!" The sound that passed from Emily's lips barely registered as anything, she was so cold. White light-threads had surrounded her again. Emily resolved to herself that this really was the end. Her eyes closed, and she promptly lost consciousness.

Unbeknownst to her, the white light-threads had begun to wrap around her head, plunging Emily into a dense and freezing fog. The hideous, deafening, crackling noise that had accompanied her previous encounter with them returned, as before, with a vengeance. It was so loud it brought her round, at least partially. She half-opened her eyes to see nothing but a pea soup of whitish grey ice crystals, as if stuck within some vast, freezing rain cloud. She tried, one last time, to cry out for someone, something, to help her. As her mouth finally opened, it stuck, and Emily realized that she was frozen solid!

All she could do now was wait, motionless, for whatever fate befell her.

Out of the fog came strange white faces towards her, with sunken black eyes and gaping mouths. Emily guessed, in as much as she could think or do anything right now, that these were the frozen souls of which Deeron had spoken. Faces aimlessly wandering the mountains, held for all eternity by the White Light of Evil. Soon, Emily thought, she would be one of them. Also, jabbing through the fog like the rods of maybe a hundred medieaval jousters, Emily could finally see the pointing, bony, skeletal fingers that had caused all this horror. They were everywhere she could see, surrounding her in a spiked, spherical cage. She could do nothing but wait to be consumed, as though she were a tiny fly enmeshed within a giant web.

Down on the ground, Deeron and Jen were beginning to dance. Jen was facing Deeron with her arms held above her head as antlers. Slowly and calmly, they walked around each other ceremoniously, then stopped and bowed. Deeron crouched down low, so that Jen could wrap her arms around his antlers. Then he lifted her, turned her around and like two ballet dancers, they gracefully glided along the mountain path. Threads of golden light then appeared, as though from nowhere, and began swirling around their feet. The light grew stronger and warmer, until eventually, they were surrounded by it completely, and encased within a large golden ball. This was just as well, for Jen was finding it increasingly tough just seeing Deeron through all the golden light, what with him now being a golden stag!

"Climb up, Jen. Quickly!" instructed Deeron loudly, trying to be heard amongst all the whooshing noise from the light-threads. "We're off to get Emily!" Jen jumped up onto Deeron's back, just as the globe began to rise into the air. It then shot upwards like a rocket, forcing Jen to grab hard onto Deeron's antlers once more.

"Hang on, Emily!" shouted Jen as they neared, hoping to be heard. Jen's only concern right now was with Emily's condition, even though both the energy and power of the light surrounding them was immense. As they approached her, the strong golden glow emitted began to thaw Emily, and melt away almost instantly the icy-white threads that held her. The jousting skeletal fingers caging her made no attempt to confront such supremacy. They simply scattered in all directions.

In moments, and with a thud, Emily fell through the light and straight onto Deeron's back behind Jen, precisely from where she had been taken. Then all three, still protected by the golden sphere, flew off at tremendous speed through the air, with Jen holding onto Emily and Deeron for all she was worth. Over frozen lakes they soared, across mountain ridges and above forest trees. On and on, at terrific speed, outrunning easily the long, skeletal bony fingers chasing after them.

Emily's senses began to return, rendering her able to grab onto an antler with one hand and Jen with the other. Even with all the warmth given off from the golden light, she'd truly never felt this bad before. The view around them was becoming distorted and increasingly foggy, just like when they'd danced by the lake only a few hours before. Within a short space of time, they could see nothing. Emily decided to fix her gaze upon the antler she was holding, and wait for the dreadful journey to end.

At last, they began to slow down. Breaking through the rapidly diminishing fog up ahead, a green grassy bank rolled out to greet them. They descended and then landed softly by a lake, back once again in the mortal world. Emily slid off Deeron's back and collapsed onto the grass. Jen ran over to her, grabbing her hand, and sat in silence as tears welled up in her eyes. For a while no one spoke, as words were simply not appropriate. Deeron, having shapeshifted back to his manlike figure, finally broke the silence.

"My most precious Wandiacates, you have experienced the evil that exists in Wandiacatum, and I am so sorry this has happened. I now realize that Smolder is as determined to destroy you as he is us, and it was never our intention to subject you to such danger. I will leave you now, and never return. Go home, and forget all you have heard, especially the name Smolder Bagot." Deeron slowly walked away.

"Stop," whispered Emily, but Deeron carried on walking. Realizing the weakness of her voice, Emily tried to get up but could manage only as far as her knees. Knelt on the grass, she screamed with all the force her aching body could muster. "Stop! Don't go!" Deeron stopped, but did not turn around.

"I saw faces," she called, weakly. "Dead faces, frozen in the light! That's what will happen to you, isn't it?"

"Yes, but I can't let it happen to you," he replied, choking back emotion.

"But it will happen to us in the end, won't it?"

"Yes," he admitted, almost whispering. "Smolder can already enter your world, for his power is now so strong." Emily, now on her feet thanks largely to Jen, looked at him in earnest. A tall powerful leader, Deeron stooped under the weight of despair and destiny.

"We can't let this happen," she gasped, leaning heavily on Jen for balance and support. "Not to you or anyone. Our gift was given for a reason, and we have to use it to destroy evil. That's why we are here." Deeron turned and gazed at the small frail figures of two young girls, somehow strengthened by the power of their wonderful magical gift. "We can't walk away now," she added firmly. Emily had seen the awful truth, and it was never going to leave her mind. The only way forward was to ensure that Smolder Bagot could never hurt another innocent soul. Jen stood firmly by her side.

"She's right, Deeron. We have to do this." Deeron walked back to them and stared lovingly into their eyes.

"I am in awe of you both," he said, bowing his head. "Wandiacates are special indeed. Never before have I seen such courage and such tenderness, in mortals so young. I thank you for all that you are, from the bottom of my heart."

"We shall come to the forest the day after tomorrow, and join your herd in the fight against Smolder." Emily spoke like a general making battle plans for an army. Something outside of herself was filling her with the most amazing courage. Jen felt it too.

"Thank you," said Deeron once more, and then simply turned and disappeared into the trees. They watched him go.

Jen and Emily stood for a moment, staring into the forest. A summer's day stillness hung in the air like a soft mist. Birdsong gently broke the silence. Water lilies bobbed playfully on the lake, and their picnic was right where they had left it. At that moment, the world seemed so calm, so normal and so at peace, that all they had seen and experienced felt utterly unreal to them both, like awakening from just another weird dream.

"Did all that actually just happen?" whispered Jen.

"Yes, it did." Emily turned away, immediately cringing with agony. She keeled over, grabbing the right side of her chest, as the sudden movement caused tremendous pain. It felt as though the fingers were still there, jabbing remorselessly into her ribs. 'It had happened all right,' Emily thought, as she had the bruises to prove it.

"Are you alright, Em?" Immediately concerned once more, Jen tried to comfort Emily by placing an arm around her, as her face revealed almost total panic.

"I'm fine… really, it's okay. It'll go." Emily cautiously waited for the pain to subside, which it did quite quickly. She was actually very relieved at this, for it meant her injuries weren't really that bad. She did ache though, and felt incredibly tired. She longed to sleep, but they both had yet to undertake the long walk back to the farmhouse. That, she dreaded. Suddenly, a cold wet nose touched Emily's hand.

"Bill!" cried Jen, excitedly. "Good boy, Bill! Very good dog!" They both fussed him for a while and then stood quietly once more, just gazing into the forest, trying to take it all in.

Bill had seen Deeron, and was clever enough to understand that something very important was taking place. He stood alongside Emily, gently nuzzling her hand.

This world seemed strange now, compared to where they had just been. How long would it be before the White Light of Evil had a hold over the mortal world? According to Deeron, just one week, when the Horn Dance was due to be performed again, and Smolder would finally complete his power. Then, what would happen to mankind? Emily was certain of one thing - this battle against Smolder had to be won, for everyone's sake.

They gathered up the picnic, and wearily pulled their rucksacks onto their backs. The walk back seemed endless, and it was such a relief to finally reach the farm gates and be home again. Jen looked up at the old farmhouse. She had never grown tired of Oak Dale, even in the darkest moments when she was really lonely, as had often been the case. She smiled to herself as they passed through the rickety green kitchen door that she'd helped her dad paint the previous summer. Events were now about to follow seriously uncharted waters, and she wondered how on earth it would all turn out.

Deer in the Picture

They were home in time for supper, which thankfully meant that they didn't have Martha's bad mood to contend with. Instead she was actually quite jolly, scurrying them out of the kitchen to go and change, and then proceeding to sing at the top of her voice. Jen smuggled the remains of the picnic up the stairs.

"If she sees we haven't eaten this, she'll be on our case. I'll hide it in the bin," she whispered.

They disappeared into their bedrooms to change. Emily looked longingly at the bed, and wished she could just curl up and hide away from the world. Sadly, this wasn't an option, so she showered and put on her favourite cream silk dress. Her mum had made it for her after seeing the design in a magazine, and Emily felt especially proud every time she wore it.

Memories of the day they had bought the material unexpectedly flooded back into her mind - Emily and her mum, on one of their regular shopping binges that lasted all day, with lunch at her favourite restaurant. It had been such pure and carefree fun, free of any worries over money or new babies. Her mum had been trying on hats for her friend's wedding - sending Emily into fits of laughter, most of the time - until she put on a white broad-brimmed straw hat, designed by Dior, that looked so stunning everybody in the shop stopped to admire her. A rather good-looking man told her she looked like a film star, causing the woman he was with to walk off in an almighty huff. Now, so much in Emily's family had changed, and in such a short period of time. There was a baby brother or sister on the way, and Dad had just lost his job. She doubted if things would ever be as happy as they were then.

Emily stared at her reflection in the mirror. The girl looking back appeared to be a stranger to her now, and she began to wonder who she really was. The reality in which she found herself that night seemed almost surreal, with Emily feeling as though she belonged more to Deeron's world than this mere mortal one, trying to be all sensible and ladylike. She quickly decided, however, that she had to pull herself together, as to act strangely around Martha would only cause trouble. Running her fingers through her hair as she tweaked it into place, Emily noticed that the end-of-term bags had gone from under her eyes, and the outdoor life had given her a healthy glow. This was astounding, considering she'd almost been frozen to death only a few hours before. Her hands were still cold though, and her fingers felt numb. Jen suddenly appeared at the door, wearing a pink halter-neck top and cropped denims. Her hair, now hanging free, framed her pale face as it rippled down over her shoulders.

"You look great," said Emily smiling, which was true even though she did appear as white as a ghost. Neither of them felt at all like being sociable, but you couldn't refuse Martha at the best of times, and the last thing they wanted right now was to be subjected to a barrage of questions. Emily sprayed them both with perfume, and they descended the stairs to face ordinary everyday life.

The meal was a grander affair than usual, with the table set in the dining room. Martha had invited Eric the farmhand and Nick to join them, and everyone seemed to be in a merry mood. Bill, having already been fed, lay on the warm patio slabs watching them all through half-open eyes. The aroma of garden herbs drifted in through the open door and mingled with the delicious smell of Martha's cooking, as Eric made jokes to Emily in his broad Birmingham accent about her being a "townie" who ate "micro chips and cubed cabbage." Martha soon appeared from the kitchen with a huge jug and some pottery mugs, leaving Eric to take on the serious job of pouring out the golden liquid.

"A sweet drop of ale," he announced, as though each syllable were important to the taste. He handed a mug to Emily. "'Ave a drop, it'll put 'airs on yer 'ed." Emily's face disappeared into the huge tankard. "Where's she gone?" he cried, looking under the table. "Oh no!" he yelled as Emily's face reappeared. "Put yow 'ed back in, chick, yow look better in there!" Emily nearly choked with laughter.

She was pleased that Nick was being friendlier, after the odd way he had behaved the first night they met. He was dressed very smartly, and wearing a starched-collar shirt so stiff that it looked like it was made of wood. Emily decided that he probably didn't dress up very often.

It was a delicious meal, finished off with strawberries and ice cream, followed by chocolate mints and coffee. After coffee, Eric asked Emily about her family. Emily appeared reluctant at first, thinking they'd all be really bored hearing about it, but everyone listened politely. Jen chipped in and told them about how their mums were old school friends, and so that was how they had come to be together this summer.

"I think mum invited Emily here as a way of getting the two of them back together," said Jen.

Emily twisted her napkin into a knot on her lap. 'What if that was true?' she thought. She had been so wrapped up in herself needing someone to talk to, that she hadn't even considered her mum might also need a friend. After all, with the baby coming and dad out of work, she could probably use a friendly ear. Emily felt annoyed with herself for not having understood this before.

"So what 'ave yow bin findin' to do in this wilderness?" Eric's cheery voice broke her thoughts. "I'll bet yow've bin bored to bits!"

"Oh no, we've been exploring the forest and having a picnic every day!" replied Emily, enthusiastically. Nick glanced a cold look to Martha, who began noisily to clear the table, almost throwing the cutlery into the empty gravy jug. Eric was used to Martha's moods and so chatted on, ignoring her.

"Yow should take Emily to see the village, Jen. Show 'er the church."

"Great idea," agreed Jen, who had actually already thought of this. "We can go tomorrow."

Martha's mood suddenly lifted upon hearing about the next day's deviating plan, and stopped clearing the table almost as quickly as she'd started. Eric grinned at Martha, and then turned to Jen. "Now, Miss Jen," he announced, getting to his feet and ceremoniously bowing. "Will yow play for uz?"

"Of course, Mr Eric," she replied, returning a curtsy, and then playfully pulling the napkin from under his chin. They all then moved from the table to the comfy armchairs in the lounge, to hear Jen play the piano.

How well she played! Her new friend's talent really impressed Emily. As Jen's music filled the room, Emily glanced round at everyone. Nick was slumped in an armchair, gently tapping his fingers and swaying his feet to the music. Emily could see now that his legs were too long for his trousers, and that he was wearing orange socks. Eric had collapsed onto the sofa, with his long legs sprawled out across the hearth. He held his tankard in one hand, and gently conducted the music with the other. His straw-blonde hair hung over his face, his eyes were closed, and he appeared to savour every note. Emily thought he was a lovely person, and good-looking too.

Martha sat with her hands neatly folded in her lap, smiling proudly at Jen. Emily suddenly realized that it was Nick, Martha and Eric who were Jen's true family, as they were the ones who spent the most time with her, and who both encouraged and guided her. Jen's mum and dad were, it seamed, simply too busy either arguing or trying to find themselves to take much notice of her.

Emily closed her eyes, letting her mind drift back to Deeron's Hall, where she imagined herself dancing the deer dance in a dress made from golden leaves. The deer were all around her, swaying their heads like a corps de ballet, as she danced with the grace and ease of an ice skater. Then, positioned in arabesque, Emily stood poised and light as a feather, as though supported by an invisible partner. 'Will this be how I dance', she wondered, 'when I dance for Deeron?' The sound of applause jolted her back into the sitting room.

"Oh well done, Jen!" praised Martha, with a beaming smile.

"Brilliant, cherry'ed," congratulated Eric. "Gets better every time I 'ear yow."

Emily looked around. Nick had gone. The patio door was wide open, and the evening breeze gently brushed the curtains. 'How rude to leave before it was over! What a strange person he is,' she thought. Eric gallantly bid them all goodnight, and went off to do a last check on the farm before "turnin' in". Jen and Emily went to the kitchen to help Martha.

"You should see this kitchen sometimes, when the whole family's here," said Martha to Emily.

"The whole family isn't here very often though, is it!" muttered Jen, sarcastically.

"Now, now." Martha put a comforting arm around her. "It'll all work out, you see." She turned to Emily. "We've had such lovely times here, in this kitchen." Martha now had what Emily's mum would refer to as her talking hat on, and although she was really too tired, Emily sat down politely at the kitchen table to listen.

"Your mothers," continued Martha, "were just like the two of you, here in this kitchen." Suddenly, both Emily and Jen were interested.

"What were they like when they were girls?" asked Jen.

"Just like you two are now. Miss Rosemary was dark as a raven like Emily, and Miss Meg was just like you Jen, with long blond hair all the way down her back. When I look at you two, it's as though I've gone back in time."

"Was Nick here then, and was the farm much the same?" asked Emily.

"Oh yes, things don't change much here in the country. We still do things in the old way, like the baking and the brewing. The only new additions here are Bill and Eric."

"And the dishwasher!" quipped Jen.

"Oh, thank the Lord!" Martha clasped her hands in mock prayer.

"What sort of things did they get up to?" Emily was eager to hear more about her mum.

"Your mum was quite an artist, you know."

Emily stared at Martha, suddenly quite shocked. "No, I didn't know."

"Oh yes, very good she was. She gave me a picture. I've still got it somewhere, hang on…" Martha disappeared into an alcove, and quickly returned with a framed painting. "There!" she announced, placing it on the table in front of Emily. "Strange subject…"

Emily looked down at the picture. She could feel Martha's sharp eyes piercing the top of her head.

"…But well painted, wouldn't you say?" Martha sat down opposite Emily, waiting for her reply. Emily felt a wave of astonishment rise inside of her, so swallowed hard to try and gulp it down. The picture was of a lake. Only not just any lake, but *their* lake in the forest! A huge stag's head hovered above the water and stared down into his own reflection. Emily spoke through clenched teeth.

"Yes, it's… really good," and slowly slid the picture towards Jen, trying to prepare her for the shock. Jen covered her mouth to suffocate a gasp. Martha's eyes darted from one to the other, scanning their faces.

"Quite an imagination…" she probed.

"Yes… amazing," stumbled Emily.

"Er…what did my mum do while Rose was painting?" enquired Jen, trying to divert the subject topic.

"Go off on long walks. Be gone for hours she was, just like you two." Martha's voice suddenly became icy. "And sit in the study for hours. Hours on end..." She paused. There was silence. They heard the clock ticking.

"...But mostly they were noisy, messy and usually late for supper, just like you two!" Martha started to laugh, causing Emily and Jen to join in, both relieved that the tension had been lifted.

"Now come on, take this hot chocolate up to bed with you. You must both be dead beat." She beckoned them out of the kitchen, and up the stairs. "Nighty-night, sleep tight."

"Goodnight," said Jen and Emily together, as they both wearily climbed the stairs to bed. At the top, Jen hung over the banister and listened, until she heard the kitchen door click shut.

"My mum never once mentioned the forest, or the lake!" she whispered to Emily. "If ever I wanted to go for a walk in the forest, she would say, "Well, Nick says it's overgrown and that you could get lost." And all the time she knew! She knew about the lake, and the deer!"

Whether Jen's mum actually knew about Deeron and the magical world was far from certain, but the painting was too near the mark to be simply a coincidence. It seemed highly likely that Martha knew something about it too, but they couldn't know how much without asking her, and that could lead to all kinds of trouble. They both decided to basically act dumb about it, and so prevent Martha from banning their days out. Nothing was to get in the way of helping Deeron and the magic stags, so the trip to the church was agreed, as it would help to keep her off their case for tomorrow at least.

"Remember," Emily stifled a large yawn. "Deeron said we should rest."

"Night then," Jen gave Emily a hug.

"Night-night," Emily hugged her back.

Although exhausted, Emily went to her bedroom window to gaze upon the dark forest. "My mum, an artist," she whispered. "I never knew that!" She fell into bed and closed her eyes, and thought about Deeron and his strange and wonderful deer, somewhere deep in a forest in another world. She tried to imagine Smolder Bagot, but the frozen dead-white faces came into her mind. She gripped the pillow, and waited for her stomach to stop turning over. The sad eyes of the stags were the next image, and she suddenly felt an overwhelming fear of what she and Jen had let themselves in for. There had been no doubt at the time that they should help, and so it was best to go along with that. Anyway, they had promised now.

Thoughts of Deeron's Hall, and the warm glow of the candlelight, put her at ease once again. In her mind, the image was so real that she could smell the wax burning, and taste the honey drink on her lips. A warm golden haze then wrapped itself around her, while a ball of cold white light bounced far off into the distance. Emily quickly drifted off into a deep and peaceful sleep, leaving her chocolate drink untouched and slowly going cold.

Antlers in the Church

*B*oth girls awoke late the next morning, but as there was no hurry to be off into the forest, they began with a late breakfast. Afterwards, Emily decided that it was probably a good time to write her weekly letter home. She began,

> *Mum & Dad,*
> *It's really great here, and I'm having a lovely time.*

She stared at the page. It didn't even begin to explain the time she was actually having, plus it read almost word-for-word the same as many of her previous letters. Also, she guessed that things wouldn't have improved much at home either, which made her feel guilty for enjoying herself at all. To end the letter she settled for,

> *Missing you, wish you were here.*

> *Lots of love,*
> *Em.*

This made her feel even worse because she hadn't had time to miss them, and the last thing she wanted was for them to be here! It wasn't because she didn't love them, it was just that they would never understand the mission to help Deeron.

The village was only a mile away, so they decided to walk rather than wait for the unreliable bus. The day was blustery, with a damp chilly air and grey clouds hanging menacingly overhead, so it was a good day to be doing something different. As they walked along the road, they heard the forest rustling in the breeze, seeming to call to them.

"See you tomorrow," said Emily, quietly. She gazed at the open space, fields, woodland and farms that they passed on their short journey. Hidden in the forest was a strange magical world where deer understood humans. 'Quite something really,' she mused to herself, 'as half the time, humans don't even understand each other.'

The deserted village looked dreary in the stormy light, made worse by the glistening damp on all the houses along their route. Some were thatched with white-washed walls, while others had slated roofs and wrought-iron gates. All of them had pretty gardens that opened out like colourful fans along the crooked high street. They walked across the village green, passing by the local pub that gleamed from fresh coats of black and white paint. After making a steep climb to the top of the road, they followed a high red brick wall, behind which stood an imposing Victorian house.

"That's my school," muttered Jen, with more than a hint of disgust.

"Oh wow!" gasped Emily, clambering up to sit on the wall. "It's… amazing!" She struggled for the right words because it actually made her own school seem like a scrapyard. "It does look a bit like Dracula's Castle, though!" she teased.

"It is!" scoffed Jen.

"You must love it here, really."

"It's all right, I s'pose," she replied, swinging off the gate. "It's school! Who cares!" Emily examined the red stone walls and the arched stained glass windows. It had the air of importance about it, of privacy.

"Wish you could come here, Em. It would be more fun."

"We'd never do any work, you and me together!" laughed Emily.

"You could come and live with me, that'd be good."

"There's just one problem," replied Emily, eying the school sign. "It's an Independent School For Girls. You have to pay to come here, don't you?" Jen kicked a stone along the ground.

"Yeah, but if you're clever or musical you can get a scholarship, then you don't have to pay." Emily didn't consider herself to be especially well equipped in either department, so this wasn't very likely to happen.

They arrived at the church, in the highest and oldest part of the village, overlooking the green and the school. The tiny stone interior was beautifully decorated with lilies and tall green ferns, all combining to fill the air with a fragrant scent. On the far wall behind the font, Jen spied the very thing she had brought Emily to see. Hanging on brass hooks were six pairs of antlers, beautifully carved from wood and looking convincingly like real ones. Jen peered at the brass plaque on the wall, and read it out loud:

"Horn Dancer's Antlers. Traditionally used by dancers to grant good luck and fertility over the forest."

"These are the ones they use in the dance," she explained. "They collect them from here and dance with them all over the parish, holding them above their heads pretending to be stags."

"Wow!" gasped Emily, "Do you think they're heavy?"

"I doubt it," replied Jen, "'cause they run and skip about with them."

They both sat down on a pew and stared up in amazement at the antlers, as it all began to sink in. These antlers belonged to a tradition called the Horn Dance that went back centuries - nearly eight hundred years, according to Deeron - and was the reason both Deeron's herd and his forest existed at all. Now, thanks to an evil being called Smolder Bagot, this same tradition was threatening their very survival. Deeron had explained to them both how power created at the Horn Dance each year collects inside the Golden Light of Goodness, and passes to the antlers of the six magic stags in his magical world. Now, with Smolder in possession of those antlers, that power goes to him, and this would soon result in his inevitable victory over Deeron in his quest for ultimate power and supremacy over all the forest and the magical world. To prevent this from happening, Emily and Jen have just five days until the next Horn Dance to retrieve the magic antlers from Smolder's Castle. The task ahead daunted them both, although Emily also wondered if Smolder's theft of the antlers was why so many bad things were occurring in the mortal world, like wars and famine.

"I wish we could stop this Horn Dance from happening," pondered Jen, quietly. "Then Deeron would have another whole year to recover the magic antlers from Smolder." Suddenly, she leapt to her feet, making poor Emily almost jump out of her skin. "Let's take them! Steal them! We'll hide them in the graveyard!"

"Jen, are you nuts?" replied Emily, suitably aghast. "We can't steal them! That's theft, and we're not thieves. Besides, can you imagine Martha's face if the police turned up at the farmhouse? And what about your parents? I tell you, mine would go ballistic if…"

"Okay, okay," butted in Jen, rather sheepishly. "Bad idea."

Emily got up and walked towards the door. "Come on, we mustn't meddle with the plan anyway. We'll just have to do as Deeron asks, and hope that he can do the rest."

Jen followed Emily to leave. As Emily pulled open the large wooden door, Jen spied a man in the churchyard. "Oh, no!" she whispered, jumping back behind the door. "It's Nick!"

Emily peered over Jen's shoulder to see Nick hunched over a grave, tidying the flowers.

"What's *he* doing here?" Jen sounded quite disgusted at seeing him there.

"Tidying a grave, by the looks of it," proffered Emily. Jen pulled her back behind the door, as it was obvious to her that

Martha had sent Nick to check up on them, and she didn't want to give him the pleasure of reporting back. She set off down the aisle to a black velvet curtain at the back of the church, which she knew concealed a rear entrance. She threw back the curtain, grabbed the iron handle and tried to turn it. "It's locked!" she exclaimed.

"Well, he'll just have to see us then," shrugged Emily. "Does it matter?"

"You bet it does!" snapped Jen, her eyes fired with determination. "Come on, we'll hide." She ran back to the front of the church and up a narrow spiral stone staircase just by the entrance, which led to the bells and clock in the spire plus an annexe set slightly above the eaves, used mainly for lighting repairs and cleaning inside the church.

"Come on, will you!" Emily was dragging along behind, thinking this was all a waste of time. They made it to the annexe just as Nick came in through the arched doorway. The stone platform made a perfect place to spy on him, as he made his way down the aisle. His shoes made a scraping noise on the stone floor - *clip-clip-clip* - until he stopped at the antlers. He stared intently for a moment, and began stroking them gently with his rough, working hands. Then he turned to the font, and cupped his hands in the water. He carefully carried it to the antlers, and threw the water over them. Emily and Jen watched as he did this over and over again - *clip-clip-clip*, then *drip-drip-drip* - until both the antlers and the floor were soaked. He was so absorbed in this ceremony that Jen realized he wasn't looking for them after all.

Finally, he leant over one set of antlers and caressed them tenderly as if it were a child, or someone he loved. Jen was amazed, as she had never known Nick to be gentle, not even with Bill. Slowly, he turned away and walked - *clip-clip-clip* - to the back door. Drawing back the curtain, Nick turned the handle with ease, disappearing into the daylight that poured in from the graveyard. The door closed softly behind him.

"That door was locked! I'm sure of it!" whispered Jen in dismay.

Emily and Jen remained crouched and hidden, just to make sure that Nick wasn't going to suddenly reappear. After a few minutes, Emily got to her feet, rubbed her knees and exclaimed,

"Right, I'm out of here!" She scurried down the stairs, closely followed by Jen, before they both then crept gently out of the door like a couple of housebreakers. The sky outside was dark, and rain began to fall heavily. "Typical," muttered Emily, in mild disgust.

They ran as fast as their legs would carry them, jumping over puddles but still managing to get soaked to the skin. The moment they opened the farm gate, Bill started barking loudly to announce their arrival to Martha. She was horrified at the state of them - yet again - and ran to the cupboard to fetch dry towels.

"You're wet enough to flood my kitchen!" she cried, poking the fire and stirring it into action.

With a change of clothes, a glowing fire and a hot cup of tea, they recovered soon enough. Supper was eaten at the kitchen table, while Martha went off to exchange knitting patterns with her group in the village.

Storm, Storm in the Forest!

After supper, Jen took Emily into the study to browse through her parents' collection of old books, in the hope that they might learn something about the Horn Dance. Emily loved the study, with its musty old books and leather furniture. Scouring the bookshelves, she imagined herself to be a detective like Sherlock Holmes, about to expose a hidden legend or reveal some secret passageway behind the bookcase. The shelves were loaded with books on all sorts of subjects, most of which she didn't understand, although there were some on poetry that she liked the look of. The wording on the spine of a large fat green leather volume soon caught her eye however, perched upon a high shelf.

"Look Jen, *A History of the Traditions of Staffordshire*. This could be good." Emily stood on a chair to try and reach it but could barely touch the book with one finger, so instead began to pluck at the base of the cover to try and prize it from the shelf. Dust specks rained down upon her as the book eventually lost balance and crashed onto the floor.

"Eurghh!! What a state!" exclaimed Jen disgustedly, but Emily was far too absorbed in wondering what the book might contain to notice.

"Wow, this book is so old!" She knelt down and carefully opened the ragged and torn-edged book cover where it fell, to reveal the yellow-stained pages within. A musty smell engulfed the air as each page displayed a spidery print that seemed to glow from the paper, as though it was crying out to be read. Skimming through the chapters and pages, Emily could see that the book contained a mine of information about Staffordshire. "There's a section on the woodlands of Cannock Chase here, Jen," she added.

"Oh, I've been riding there!" said Jen excitedly, kneeling down to join her.

"Rich pasture land, divided into dairy farms..." Emily read aloud some of the text that appeared alongside old grainy pictures of neat farms and beer barrels from the Brewery at Burton upon Trent.

"That's Lichfield Cathedral," said Jen, pointing to a picture on the opposite page, before also reading the caption below it. *"The oldest spire was destroyed by Cromwell's men during the Civil War.* Wow, I never knew that."

"I knew it was the birth place of Samuel Johnson," added Emily, "as we did him at school." Turning more pages, something else stirred Emily's senses - the smell of pipe tobacco. She recognized it at once because her granddad used to smoke a pipe, and the sweet woody-aroma lingered everywhere he went. A fond image conjured itself up in her mind, of him sat in his favourite rocking chair pouring over a newspaper, with his glasses perched on the end of his nose. Years ago someone else had opened and read this book, and she wondered if that person had been like him - studious, gentle and kind.

"Look!" Jen screeched directly into Emily's right ear, making her jump. "It's the Horn Dance!" Sure enough, on the open page was printed a photograph comprising a village green and some people dancing with antlers, held up above their heads. Just below, a smaller picture displayed the antlers hanging in the local church. "It says that the antlers never leave the parish. If only the real ones had never left Deeron's herd."

"And here," continued Emily, turning the page, "is a map of the forest!" The print was frail and faded, but they could just spot Deerbrook winding its way through Needwood, and Huntswood which was marked by clusters of pine trees. "And that must be our lake!" Both girls were now completely enthralled.

"And that's our farmhouse!" Jen shrieked once more. "Wow! How old is this book?" Emily quickly flipped back to the first pages in order to find a publishing date, but the print was simply too pale.

"Can't make it out, I'm afraid," she said, disappointedly. "Ooh, I have to get up! I've got pins and needles." Emily stood up and began hobbling around the room.

"Deeron said that it had been years since their lives were peaceful," pondered Jen, fumbling through the book herself now. "So, do you suppose this fight between him and Smolder goes back a long time?"

Emily by now was stamping her feet down on the floor, trying to return some feeling to her legs. "I dunno," she replied, somewhat dismissively. "Er, maybe. Why?"

"Well, if it was, say, thirty years ago, someone at the Horn Dance then could still be involved with it now, right?"

"So?" Emily flashed Jen a quizzical shrug in-between stamping.

"So," she replied, getting up off the floor, "it shouldn't be difficult to trace whoever organizes it today, and we could ask them if they'd ever felt anything strange at the Horn Dance!" Her eyes now sparkled with excitement. "That would tell us…"

"Jen," interrupted Emily, incredulously, "are you mad? Are you seriously suggesting that we knock on someone's door, and…?"

It was Emily's turn to be interrupted this time, as a combination of rain suddenly hammering viciously against the patio windows and howling from Bill in the kitchen, cut short her tirade. Emily turned towards the wooden glass doors to see what was happening, just as Jen grabbed her arm.

"Em…look!" Emily followed Jen's stare to the bookcase. A thick dark shadow was slithering out from underneath the lowest shelf, and slowly climbing up the wall like a giant spider. The figure grew in size as it moved, spreading like black ink on blotting paper. At first it resembled a cloak, but soon transformed into an enormous set of antlers, coming to a standstill in the middle of the wall and then simply hanging there, motionless.

Both girls jumped in terror as a lightning flash engulfed the room, followed very quickly by an almighty crash of thunder that shook the farmhouse. A second lightning bolt then followed almost immediately after, this time causing one of the patio doors to literally explode and shatter glass onto the study room floor! Jen dived down behind the nearest leather chair, pulling Emily with her. Both then pressed their bodies hard up against its high back, utterly incredulous at what was going on around them. Emily saw, out of the corner of her eye, the shadow antlers on the wall suddenly move. Now even larger and darker than before, they were clearly heading towards the bookshelves. Emily clenched her eyes shut, dreading whatever was about to happen next.

Thud! Vooom! Thud! Vooom! Thud! ... The antlers had begun plucking books from the shelves and hurtling them into the air! Great heavy atlases, along with bird books, Latin texts and thin dog-eared paperbacks; all were cascading down from the bookcases and crashing onto the floor, sending clouds of dust everywhere. As they hit the ground they instantly ignited, propelling bursts of flame upwards through the dust storm that was rapidly engulfing the study. Emily had by now covered her ears with her hands and was trying to breathe through her sleeve, whilst keeping her eyes firmly clasped shut. Jen, however, was half-peering over the armrest with a combined sense of fear, wonderment, and more than a little disappointment at Martha's housekeeping skills. 'How could she have missed *that* much dust?' was oddly Jen's first thought. She too covered her nose and mouth with a sleeve, but by now she could barely even see Emily who was squeezed up next to her.

STORM, STORM IN THE FOREST!

Apparently not content with even this much destruction, the antlers, upon emptying the bookcases, then began scooping up the burning books and throwing them about the room, setting fire to curtains, cushions and a pile of newspapers. Jen darted back behind the chair for cover, as burning missiles flew over their heads. The room was now filling with smoke and flame - they had to get out!

Jen screamed to Emily, "We've got to get out of here!" She pulled Emily up off the floor and they raced across the room towards the patio doors. Bill was barking and frantically scratching now in the kitchen, unable to reach them as the door was latched. Emily grabbed the door-handle and threw it open.

"Come on, Bill!" they both cried together. Bill, tail wagging furiously, scurried out and they all ran into the courtyard.

The situation outside unfortunately wasn't much better than that which they had just fled. The storm was now a tempest and raged harder than ever, combining a deluge of rain with icy blasts of wind coming from the direction of the forest. Jen raced off to the tractor shed, followed closely by Emily and Bill. It was a relief to close the door and be out of the downpour, for the moment at least.

"Smolder Bagot, you just wait!" yelled Jen between coughs. She wiped her face with her sleeve. "We've got to go and see if the deer need our help."

"Deeron told us to stay away, remember?" replied Emily. "He said Smolder might be watching us, and he obviously is!" Both girls were trying to remove dust and rain from themselves. Bill, by far the least concerned, shook himself, yawned and lay down on some straw.

There didn't appear to be too many choices at this stage. The house wasn't safe, and there was little point in staying in the tractor shed all night, so finding Deeron seemed to be the logical thing to do. That was after finding some waterproof coats and sensible footwear first. Jen remembered that Martha kept some sacks of old clothes for her favourite charity

63

somewhere in the tractor shed, so began rummaging around trying to find them.

"Here they are!" she cried, triumphantly. They both rooted through the bags.

"These'll do me," said Emily, banging off the dry mud from a pair of walking boots.

Mindful of the fact that dusk would soon be upon them, Jen climbed up onto the tractor to look for the torch Nick normally kept in the cab. "It's not here!" she muttered, disappointedly. As consolation for not finding the torch, she decided to perform her favourite trick of sliding down the wheel-arch of the tractor and jumping onto the floor. As she did so, her foot landed on something cold and hard.

"Ow!" she cried as she peered down to see an object like a bone. "Oh Bill, you are disgusting!" Bill half-opened one eye but was far too comfortable to be bothered to investigate. Gingerly, Jen scraped away the straw covering the mystery object, and tried to pull it out from under the tractor. "Give us a hand, Em. It's something horrible that Bill's brought in."

As they tugged away at the bony thing from under the tractor, it dawned on them that it was actually something much bigger; huge in fact, as they brushed away more of the straw covering it. A set of antlers began to appear, with another and then another, until they had all six sets on the ground in front of them.

"Somebody must have brought these here!" exclaimed Jen, who at this moment could be excused for stating the obvious.

"What *is* going on?" Emily felt overwhelmed by the strange events that were all happening at once.

"Let's get to Deeron's Hall," replied Jen, heading quickly out into the farmyard. "That's where we'll find the answers." She let out a piercing whistle. "Come on, Bill! Get out of there!"

As they both ran along the road towards the forest track hotly pursued by Bill, neither had any idea of what they were going to do. Emily kept thinking about Deeron's instructions to stay home, and hoped that they weren't going to make things worse. 'At least it's stopped raining,' she thought mockingly, although the fading light of the day worried her. Bill nuzzled her hand as he finally caught up with them, and the three explorers ventured down to the lake, ankle-and-paw-deep in mud. A blaze of lightning flashes suddenly illuminated the sky and forest, stopping Jen right in her tracks. Down the bank and to her left, she glimpsed a tiny animal stumbling awkwardly through the bracken.

"Did you see that?" she shouted back to Emily. "Down there… a fawn! It's hobbling! I think it could be injured!" Emily sadly hadn't seen anything, as she was still some way behind leant up against a tree, nursing a stitch. "You townies!" quipped Jen, sarcastically. "Come on!" She ran off into the ferns, closely followed by Bill. Emily did her best to catch up but her feet slid from under her, sending her tumbling down the bank, with bracken slipping through her fingers as she frantically tried to grab it.

All three reached the bottom of the bank - one way or another - and sure enough, peering out from behind a tree, stood a tiny honey-coloured fawn. Spying Emily and Jen, the young doe wobbled forward on its frail legs to greet them, her coat glistening with rain as her sad eyes melted their hearts.

"Isn't she adorable!" whispered Jen, as she knelt down and gently wrapped her arms around the young doe's neck. The fawn instead wriggled itself free of Jen's embrace, and staggered off towards the trees.

They all raced after her. First was Bill hot on her trail, followed by Jen and lastly Emily. Although the young deer certainly appeared wounded, she still moved fast enough to make it hard for the girls to keep her in sight, and they were certainly glad that Bill was with them. They ran over a rickety makeshift bridge, crossing a loud rushing stream. On and on they pursued her, going deeper and deeper into the forest. It was already quite dark, and they had absolutely no idea where they were.

Unbeknownst to them, a large white cloud had gathered above their heads and was following them furtively. By the time anyone realized the cloud was there, it was too late to take cover. Emily looked up, and bursting open like a split carrier bag, the cloud suddenly deposited millions of pine needles straight down on top of all three of them!

Bill spun around howling, and tried to run back towards Jen, but was engulfed up to his neck almost instantly. The girls tried to take cover under nearby trees, but the carpet of needles was so thick it was like trying to wade through glue! There was no option but to stay where they were, and in seconds they were completely covered.

Emily had crouched down as the needles buried her, and was only just able to breathe. She tried to stand up, but the weight above her was too great. Instead, she threaded her hand slowly sideways through the pile until, miraculously, she felt free movement. Moving her arm from side to side, she then managed to make a hole big enough to gasp for some air. Nervously, she continued to work the hole with her arm, soon creating a tunnel big enough to squeeze her other arm through, and then wriggle herself out of. Emily emerged, choking for air and covered in needles. These were no ordinary needles either, for they were much longer than normal and covered in a sticky paste like tree resin. She brushed her eyes and studied the dark sea of needles spread before her.

There seemed to be something trembling beneath the needles, just ahead of her. Deciding to adopt a breaststroke-like movement, Emily waded over and plunged a hand down. Frenetically, she scooped handfuls of needles and threw them aside. Eventually, a head appeared. "Jen!" she cried, as her friend emerged, coughing and spluttering.

For a moment, they sat where they were, bewildered, exhausted and covered in sticky needles. Jen whistled to Bill. There was no sign of him. She grabbed the tree they were both leant up against and pulled herself to her feet. Panic stirred in her throat. "Bill!" she yelled. "Bill, where are you?"

As they scanned the thick dark carpet of needles, Emily caught sight of the fawn staring at them through the trees. She ignored it for now, as the most important thing was to find Bill. They stumbled over and through the needles, yelling his name and straining to see any sign of him.

Jen was becoming increasingly distraught, and tears were soon rolling down her face. Then, suddenly, Emily caught sight of a light spot among all the needles. She scrambled over to investigate, and to her joy discovered Bill's tail. "He's over here!" she yelled, frantically scooping the needles away. Once Jen had arrived at the spot, they both very quickly dug him out. Poor Bill was dazed and exhausted, but alive. They both gave him a hug and checked him over for injuries. He recovered quickly enough, growling angrily as soon as he spotted the fawn.

"How come it wasn't buried with us?" asked Jen, not expecting an answer as they all eyed the fawn turn and run a little way along the footpath, just beyond the huge mound of needles. It then stopped and turned back, seeming to pause as though waiting to see whether they would follow. Emily, Jen and Bill remained still, precisely where they were. A few moments passed, after which the fawn returned to its first position, turned and then ran along the path once more, coming to a halt and waiting again.

"I've got a bad feeling about this fawn," said Emily, coldly.

"You mean, like... it could be working for Smolder?" asked Jen, whispering. It was obvious when you thought about it, as after all, what would a genuine young fawn be doing wandering around the forest on a night like this?

"We're not going with you!" shouted Emily with defiance. "Go and tell Smolder that!"

With Emily's words still resonating throughout the forest, the fawn suddenly transformed into a weird-looking grey goat with black horns. Its eyes glowed red and sparkly now, like a small set of traffic lights. It lowered its head, pounding the ground with its front hoof as it did so, and then, replying in a simpering, slithering voice, said, "You can tell him yourselves if you like."

Bill barked and growled angrily, causing Jen to grab his collar to prevent him from charging.

"Come with me," the goat attempted to sound reassuring, "and you will see for yourself. Your feeble Deeron cannot win, and I will show you proof of this!"

"We're not going anywhere with you, and that's final!" Emily then quickly turned to Jen, whispering, "Come on, let's get out of here." All three clambered to the edge of the needle mound, and jumped down onto the forest floor.

"*Sis a flung!*" the goat hissed, producing a noise that both felt and sounded like an arctic wind blasting across barren ice-sheets. Emily tried to run, but her legs seized up almost immediately. She turned to Jen, who was just the same - they were stuck! The sticky resin substance that coated the needles was now on their skin and clothes, and had quickly hardened.

"Ha-ha!" the goat laughed. "Now what are you going to do?"

"Run a…way," gasped Jen, trying to grab her legs and pull them along, but this only resulted in her hands becoming stuck to them as well, trapping her further. The more they tried desperately to move, the harder the sticky substance became. Bill charged round, barking frantically.

"I can also see," the goat snarled angrily, "that I'm going to have to shut that dumb dog up as well… *Sis a fl…*"

Before the goat could finish its curse, Bill was face to face with it snarling viciously, rolling the whites of his eyes and flashing his strong white teeth. He looked terrifying! The creature backed away alarmed, and pounded the ground with its hooves trying to intimidate Bill in return. Bill kept the pressure on, all the time growling and edging forward, forcing it back into the trees and towards the bank. With one last pathetic whine the goat turned, ran down the bank, and was gone. Instantly, both girls were released from the spell, causing Jen, who was all twisted up by her attempts to run, to collapse onto the ground.

"Thank heavens," gasped Emily with relief. "I really thought we'd had it."

"Thank Bill!" exclaimed Jen proudly, picking herself up and looking around for him. They both ran over to Bill, who was still scowling and scanning the forest in case the goat returned. Jen hugged him for being such a brave dog. "What on earth was it, Em?"

"Well, I guess it was one of Smolder's army, or maybe even Smolder himself. Deeron said that he could already enter our world remember, so we really shouldn't have followed it. Now we don't have a clue where we are."

Emily felt annoyed with herself for not having been wiser in the first place, as their situation was about as bad as it could possibly be. Darkness was now well upon them, and they hadn't any idea where they were or how they could reach Deeron, or even return to the farm. They were almost certainly being watched, and they were most definitely in danger.

"Em, I've just thought. When we went to Deeron's Hall before, it was the dance that took us."

"So?"

"So, let's try it again."

Emily didn't feel much like dancing at this point, but as she couldn't think of an alternative herself, anything was worth a try. They found a spot where the path opened out into a small clearing, and Emily began to circle around, albeit half-heartedly.

"Was this what I did before?" she asked, blankly. She began to turn on the spot, holding her arms above her head to make antlers. "Oh Jen, this isn't right…" She was desperately in need of some encouragement.

"No, that's it!" Jen decided to join in and offer some support. "Come on Bill, stay close!"

Although Bill immediately began jumping up, barking excitedly and alternately chasing his tail, both girls tried hard to engross themselves in what they were doing. It took a while, but eventually they began to dance properly, gathering speed and height as they spun-and-jumped, and spun-and-jumped again. Round and around just like before, jumping higher and higher, and imitating the stags they had seen on those first trips to the forest.

A brilliant white light suddenly shot down from the sky, right behind Jen. It hit the ground like a lightning strike, and exploded into countless tiny threads that spun around Emily's, Bill's and her own feet.

"Jen, quick!" screeched Emily. "White light-threads! Don't let... Whoa!" The threads instantly lassoed their feet and hauled all three, upside down into the air!

"Hey! Get off me, you vile..." Jen was frantically trying to pull the threads from her feet and ankles as she was being hoisted upwards, but they were impossible to loosen, and freezing to touch. Bill growled and bit angrily at his, but even he couldn't cope with so many, and the fact that they had gripped all four of his paws. They further taunted him by pulling at his tail. As the three ascended, what looked like ice sheets began to form around them. In less than a minute, they were suspended upside down and in mid-air, inside a giant ice cube!

"Now what!" Considering their predicament, Jen's response was surprisingly bold and gutsy. She appeared to be more peeved than anything else, and at any other time Emily would have been quite taken aback by this. Right now, however, she had other things on her mind, and was concentrating on a yellowy orange blur on the other side of the ice wall beside her. From experience, Emily guessed this to be golden light-threads, which was great except they were still being suspended at halfway-up-a-tree height, upside down!

On the outside of the cube, a thread of golden light was indeed beginning to burn its way through the ice wall like a blowtorch. It was becoming alarmingly obvious to Emily that in seconds they would all plummet to the ground, pursued by a torrent of water. Jen saw it too, and braced herself for the crash landing, as the white light-threads around their legs and paws, finally, … snapped!

"Ayrooww!!" Bill let out a haunting howl as he, Jen and Emily nose-dived towards the ground. Just as they were about to impact, a golden hand flashed into view! Travelling at incredible speed, the hand dived directly beneath them and literally scooped them up, both breaking their fall and hauling them clear of the cascading deluge from above. Then up, up into the air they went, flying high through the forest once more.

A freezing cold wind blew in their faces, while long icy fingers stabbed at them from all around, just as before when they'd taken this ride. Only this time, the hand started rocking from side to side and rolling them around in its palm, like dice about to be thrown. Bill, on this his maiden voyage, was not amused at being poked and thrown about, and tried to snap back at the ice prodders with his teeth. This was all to little avail, however, as there were just so many of them. The hand, perhaps sensing trouble, clenched its fingers around them, and in moments, they were sealed inside a dark, golden fist. Then it dived; down and down, so fast it felt as though they were in freefall.

"Oo-er!" cried Jen, anxiously. "Em, I feel sick…" Jen's courage seemed to suffer a momentary relapse, probably due to her stomach now feeling as though it were many miles away from her. She grabbed hold of Bill for comfort as he whined, softly. Nobody could see anything.

After what felt like a time span to test even the most robust constitution, the diving finally ended and normal flying resumed. The hand then released its grip to reveal a gentle green glow all around them. Glancing through the cracks between fingers, Emily realized that they were now flying through the tunnel of what must be a vast cave! The walls whizzing past them were made of rock, with glistening trails of water clearly seen trickling down the sides. She remembered having read something about algae in caves that gave off light.

This particular cave was barely wide enough for them to travel through, but the hand made a seemingly effortless job of navigating every twist and turn.

They moved on swiftly, coming soon to an opening, whereupon the hand glided up for a short distance, and then - *whoosh!* A blast of air hit them head-on as they ascended into the night sky once more. Dotted above them were countless bright stars, with a new moon rising in the distance. Compared to that tunnel, darkness had never before seemed quite so appealing.

Jen, seeing Bill rather enjoy the air blasting through his fur, relaxed a little herself and turned round to peer through a gap in the hand's fingers with Emily. Up ahead, they could see snow-capped mountains reaching up to the sky like rocky cathedrals. As they drew closer, Emily noticed giant faces hewn from the rock, each with their mouth gaped open, looking as though they had once cried out for help and were instantly frozen solid.

"Oh no!" cried Emily. "Not this again!"

"What's wrong?" asked Jen, who up until this point had been gazing at the stars, trying to identify Orion's Belt. "Oh…" The hand flew cautiously in-between the rows of heads.

Suddenly a face leapt out at them, with the speed of a toad snatching at insects! In a split second, before the hand could do anything, they were captured inside a giant, granite mouth! Now in total darkness, the hand's fingers rapidly closed around them again, more tightly than before. Emily, Jen and Bill could barely move at all now, as the hand prepared to defend them against whatever assault was to come. The hand flipped over, so that its fingers were curled under.

Now in the shape of a fist, the hand quickly began bashing the sides, ceiling and floor, trying to smash a hole through their cave-like prison. Rolling around like dice in a tumbler, Jen, Emily and Bill felt themselves smash against a hard wall, over and over, as the fist seemed to apply itself like a battering ram to the inside of the frozen head! Adopting a different attack, the hand then spun around and pounded away at another area, never relenting in its ferocity. They tipped, rocked, blasted, spun… and then suddenly, they were free!

The fingers quickly opened, allowing Emily to glance back as they fled at an incredible speed. She could see that they had escaped through a now smashed and hollow eye! The frozen face gawped a vacant, damaged and motionless stare back at her as they sped away. In seconds, the face had diminished, and in a few more moments was lost completely from view.

"That was close!" sighed a greatly relieved Jen, as she righted herself. "Wandiacatum's no place for laughs, is it?" Emily didn't answer, for she was too busy feeling sick to her stomach.

The hand soon resumed its normal position and travelling speed, as though sensing that danger had now passed. After a while they were able to look down again, and Jen soon recognized up ahead of them the frozen lake and clearing where they had landed before. The hand slowed down, and after circling a few times gently descended once more onto the bed of dry leaves. Emily, then Jen followed by Bill, jumped down from the hand.

"Thank you," whispered Emily, as they watched the hand float gently off into the night sky. With a bright full moon to thankfully guide them, Emily led the way along the same path she and Jen had followed, after having met Deeron for the first time. Venturing deep into the forest once more, it wasn't long before the same elaborate spires of Deeron's Hall could be seen towering above the treetops.

The doors to Deeron's Hall were open, so they peered nervously inside not knowing what to expect. Everything looked very different, as the hall was full of animals of all kinds. There were rabbits, squirrels, badgers, and owls, with Emily even spotting a few foxes. Many of them were injured, and the deer were busy bathing wounds and saying comforting things to them. The fawns were doing their bit to help by carrying round bowls of food and goblets of drink, while

Deeron played a gentle lullaby on his flute. His eyes wandered across the room to the three cold and damp explorers, standing at the entrance.

"Our brave friends are here!" he called, excitedly. "Their dance has brought them to us again. Welcome, come and join us." They made their way wearily across the leafy floor towards him.

"We have seen awful things this night," he explained as he greeted them. "A terrible storm raged here and many animals were injured, with many more driven from their homes. But we will be strong, for we shall see far worse than this before the battle is won. When dawn arrives, we shall leave to begin our long journey ahead, towards the fight against evil." Deeron's antlers glowed in the firelight, and the leaves from his cloak glistened.

"Is there anything we can do to help?" asked Jen.

"All is well," he replied, placing his hand upon her shoulder. "We are skilled in caring for the injured. Besides, you three look as though you need to rest yourselves."

"Deeron?" asked Emily, a little reticently. "When can we meet the magic stags?"

"Tomorrow," he replied, softly. "But first, let us take nourishment, and then sleep."

Emily, Jen and Bill joined Deeron at the table for supper, whilst the deer ate nearby. Large bowls of hot steaming soup were provided, with wedges of brown bread, washed down with the delicious honey drink. Bill wasn't too keen at first but he was soon persuaded to eat, by hunger and the fact that the only alternative was the deer's diet of fruit and nuts!

As they ate, Emily described to Deeron what had occurred in the study of the farmhouse, and how the replica sets of antlers from the church had strangely appeared under the tractor. Jen also mentioned the strange goat disguised as a fawn - complete with an elaborate retelling of the pine needles incident - followed by their subsequent journey and eye-opening revisit to Wandiacatum.

"There are forces of good and evil at work here," he pondered, thoughtfully. "Someone in your world is trying to help, while that creature with horns was most likely one of Smolder's younger guards. Smolder's army is largely made up of mountain goats, many of which possess large and swept-back horns. He probably watched you leave the farmhouse, and sent a guard to follow you. Because he has the magic antlers, Smolder's guards can now shapeshift, which means they can change into any creature of the forest. By turning into a fawn the guard instantly had your trust, but you were wise to see through the deceit and defeat his plan to capture you."

Before long, everyone lay down on the warm leafy floor to sleep. Staring upwards, Emily noticed deer heads carved into the long wooden beams above her. In the firelight, they seemed so real that she was sure they were smiling down at her, but Emily's head soon began to spin with the enormity of the task ahead. Desperate to catch some sleep, however, she turned onto her side and tried to relax, but the awful frozen faces of Wandiacatum kept haunting her mind.

Jen's thoughts were of the farmhouse. What on earth was Martha going to say when she saw the state of the study, and then realized they were missing? Jen had visions of her phoning the police, quickly followed by Emily's parents. "Oh no," she thought wearily, "this is just too awful. Think of something else…" The trouble was, there really was nothing else she could think of to make her feel any better. Her body ached from being bashed around in the golden hand, and she longed to get on with the journey now, for she feared she might not have any courage left by the time morning arrived. Bill had already fallen fast asleep, leaving Jen to suddenly feel very alone. 'I just hope we're brave enough to go through with all this,' she thought, sombrely.

Gently, the soothing glow of the fire wrapped itself tenderly around them all as they listened to Deeron's deep-rich voice sing a lullaby.

"Pass the cup of golden honey,
Remember when we sang this song,
Time holds us in dark November,
All the spring and summer long.

Hear the crackling of the fire,
Grant a wish to one and all,
For tonight we all will slumber,
Safely here in Deeron's Hall.

Hear the trees when they do whisper,
Pass the wonder of it all,
For in the darkness we remember,
Unhappy tales from Bagot Hall.

Give us the strength to stand alone,
Grant us the wisdom to fight as one,
For at last tonight we know,
How our battle will be won.

Pass the dancing of the flames,
Fill us with her fiery power,
Time holds us in her stillness,
Ere we meet our magic hour.

Then hear the dancing master calling,
Let your courage rage and roar,
For this day will end in triumph,
Safe within our home once more."

"Sleep, now... sleep," the fire seemed to whisper, softly.
Emily and Jen both sank into a deep and restful slumber.

A Crow called Elderash

"Pack up the goblets and plates, please. We'll need to eat on this journey. Has anyone seen the rest of the cloaks?"

Emily sat up and rubbed her eyes, unsure as to whether the scene in front of her was a dream or was actually real. Prior to this summer holiday, she couldn't remember having ever before seen ordinary deer, let alone ones that spoke and packed luggage! Yet here she was, not only awakening beside them but also finding herself in a magical land where such behaviour was completely normal.

Jen began to stir beside her. "Ooh, I do ache," she groaned. "This floor's like concrete! What I'd give to be back at the farmhouse…"

"Morning," said Emily chirpily, deciding to ignore Jen's moans.

The place in which they found themselves - the Great Hall - was now a makeshift hospital, with furry heads peering out from under blankets. Some wore bandages while others had eye patches, but even those animals stared in bewilderment at the image before them.

The stag dispensing the orders was the same one that had appeared from behind the dissolving golden hand, on their first trip to Deeron's Hall. Now close up and in the early light of dawn, his coat colour shone more reddish-brown than golden, rather like a polished conker. What really gave him away, however, were those unique and unmistakable steel antlers. He was obviously very high-ranking and important within the herd, as the others obeyed his commands without question and went about their duties in a very calm and orderly fashion. On the far side of the hall, a group of does and tiny fawns watched eagerly while the hustle and bustle continued, until the steel-antlered stag suddenly reared up onto his hind legs, announcing,

"Make way, make way! Deeron comes!"

Deeron entered, wrapped in his cloak of golden leaves. Four... no, six young deer followed him. As they drew closer, Emily and Jen both spotted the tiny stumps on each and every head, where antlers had once been.

"The magic stags!" whispered Jen excitedly, as they both quickly stood up and desperately tried to tidy themselves in the few seconds they had left. Bill trotted over to join them.

"Good morning to all," smiled Deeron, addressing the entire hall, before beckoning Emily and Jen to join him.

"These are our new friends, the Wandiacates," he informed the deer, "who are going to help us in our quest to retrieve the magic antlers. Emily and Jen, let me introduce you to my six magic stags."

"First, this is Tamhorn," a dappled grey stag stepped forward and bowed. He had a shiny grey and white coat, with brown polished hooves.

"Blythe," continued Deeron, gesturing to a deep-red stag who bowed politely but kept his head held high so as to obscure his stumps.

"Fole, and Folly," two silver stags stepped forward. They both had sweet comical faces with white circles around each eye, making them look as though they were wearing spectacles. Jen and Emily beamed adoringly at them both.

"Which one's which?" whispered Jen to Deeron.

"I'm Fole and he's Folly," they both said quickly and together, looking at each other, and causing Emily and Jen to burst out laughing. They still didn't know.

"Hay," announced Deeron, "and Leif!" His voice swelled as he introduced his last two stags, both coloured a beautiful bronze. They elegantly dipped their heads to one side in a gesture of friendship, before gracefully gliding into line alongside the others.

"Many more will also be joining us on our journey," he continued, "and there will be plenty of opportunity for you to meet them all along the way. But for now, let me finally introduce Arog." The steel-antlered stag trotted over to join them, allowing both girls to finally put a name to this face. Emily could also now see just what it was that had appeared different about his eyes the first time they'd met; one was coloured opal-cream, whilst the other shone an emerald-green. "Arog is going to lead us on our journey to Smolder's Castle, and he is my second in command."

"Welcome!" Arog smiled and bowed, while Deeron carefully placed over the shoulders of Emily a cloak of golden leaves, followed by the same for Jen. As both girls gazed approvingly at their new garments, Arog announced, "Now, if all is well, Deeron, I should like us to set off."

With final preparations completed, the determined army began to file out of the hall. Proceeding through the arched doors, Jen felt a cold wet nose nuzzle her hand. Bill had joined the procession.

"Bill, you're the bravest dog in the world," she whispered, "but I don't think you can come on this trip." Jen's words, however, appeared to cut little ice with the bravest dog in the world, who simply bounded off ahead in his usual investigative fashion, seemingly intent upon joining the convoy.

"Looks like Bill's made up his own mind on that one, Jen," laughed Emily.

"He always does," shrugged Jen disappointedly, although privately she was glad that Bill was coming, for she'd only miss him otherwise.

Once the last of the troops had finally filed out of Deeron's Hall, the great doors closed behind them, causing Emily to feel a knot tighten in her stomach. "I wonder what's in store for us on this journey, Jen?"

"We can't know, can we?" she grinned, excitedly. "I mean, how amazing is this summer!"

The procession advanced swiftly, their progress made all the easier by a rising sun which quickly dispersed the final remnants of an early morning chill. Deeron and Arog led the group, followed by a few stags - one of which Jen had learned was called Fauld - while they in turn were followed by the six magic stags. Emily and Jen walked along behind them, while at the rear was an assortment of does and stags, most of whom were carrying provisions and supplies to sustain them on their long journey.

As they walked, both girls chatted while Emily casually kicked leaves into the air. "My granddad believed in fate," she began, deciding to link her arm through Jen's. "He said things were set out for us in life. I never really understood what he was on about, but it's as if this forest has been waiting for us to arrive, knowing that we would come here one day."

"My gran also used to talk about stuff like that. But if it's true, that means whatever you do, you can't change your life. So like, I could become a world-famous pianist without ever practising."

This didn't sound quite right to Emily. "I don't think it works like that, Jen. I think it's just with places and people. You still have to work hard to make things happen."

"Well I'm not risking it," smirked Jen. "I'll keep practising, just in case." They both laughed.

"Is that what you want to be then, a famous pianist?" asked Emily.

"Yeah, I love playing and it would be great to be famous and wear beautiful dresses for concerts. What about you?"

Emily simply shrugged, as she didn't think she was particularly good at anything. She usually achieved C's and

D's in exams at school, and while her teachers liked her, they often said that she was a scatterbrain. Dancing was the only thing she really liked doing, but that cost money, and she was going to have to get a job as soon as she was old enough to help pay for classes, especially now that her father had lost his job.

"What about dance? You're a lovely dancer," said Jen, encouragingly. "So graceful." Emily suddenly felt a tiny surge of pride upon hearing this, but simply gave Jen a soft smile. After a few moments, Jen asked, "What do you think about this magic power Deeron mentioned? This Wandiacate thing?"

"Hmm," nodded Emily, "I've been thinking about that. I'd never say this to anyone else, but I've felt a sort of strangeness before when I've been dancing. Not at my dance school, but other places like the garden, or out on walks."

"What do you mean, strangeness?"

"Well… it's a bit like the ground starting to spin, as if the world was whizzing around me. I'd have thought I was mad to even dream that dancing could conjure something up as amazing as those light-threads, though. I had no idea that was possible."

Jen continued to ponder in silence for a while as they walked on. Deeron had said they would see many things on this journey not meant for their eyes, and she harboured a silent dread of what that might mean. As for being able to create goodness just by dancing, if she'd been told just a few weeks ago that she could create magic at all, she would have found lots of exciting uses for it. First on her list would have been trying to persuade her mum and dad to get along with each other, but now she had experienced the White Light of Evil, she knew there were far greater forces affecting everyday life than people could possibly realize. There was no telling how this might all work out. Emily harboured her own fears about the trip, but the sight of Deeron's army of deer marching determinedly onward somehow gave her strength and optimism.

Farther on, the group came across a small clearing in the forest. In the middle stood a vast oval stone table, supported by four white beech tree stumps. All of the surrounding trees were completely stripped of their bark and leaves, while on the ground lay nothing more than a dry brown earth platform with withered roots poking up through the dirt. Deeron called the party to a halt, and refreshments were quickly prepared. "Come along, you two," he smiled, as he stroked Bill. "Bill's already tucking into his."

"This place is weird!" exclaimed Emily. "What is it?"

"It's called Smolders Slip," explained Arog. "He comes here whenever there's a full moon to practise his magic. One of his tricks is to spin the wind into a gigantic ball, and send it rolling down the valley into the forest after us. The first time he tried it he didn't get it right, and ended up stripping all the foliage from these trees and turning the ground dry and barren." Arog tried to laugh, but it was hard to sneer at such a senseless destruction of nature, even if it was at Smolder's expense.

The deer all knew that the most insulting thing they could do to Smolder was to use his magic slab as a table to eat off, so that was precisely what they did. General jeers of approval rang out as the picnic was laid, with everyone grateful for a drink and some rest. Jen smiled at the sight of Bill sitting with the stags. 'What an amazing dog he is,' she thought, proudly. One thing was certain; Bill was never going to go back to being an ordinary farm dog after this!

Tilting her head back as she sat perched up against a tree, Jen glanced upwards at the bare branches above. On the end of one branch sat an enormous and very black bird. Jen stared transfixed for a second or two, as she couldn't quite decide what sort of bird it was, given that its size was about the same as an eagle's, but its appearance was dishevelled and unkempt. 'Eagles are beautiful...' she mused, before deciding, 'that's not an eagle! It looks more like a crow!' The bird stared down at her, completely motionless, with its shoulders hunched up, as though stalking prey. Then suddenly, it blurted out in a squawking, croaky voice,

"Get Deeron!"

The sound, or rather noise, alerted everyone, and Deeron arrived swiftly at Jen's side, flanked by stags. "Who are you, and what do you want?" he demanded.

"I am Elderash, Smolder's messenger," it croaked. Elderash then jumped down onto a lower branch, to just above Deeron's head-height. "I come to you with a proposal…" He paused, leaning slyly over towards Deeron, and with one eye peering into his, added, "a deal."

Deeron glared right back at him, only this time in anger. "We don't, nor will we ever, make deals with Smolder. Now clear off!"

Elderash arrogantly leaned back upright onto his branch, and attempted an unruffled and business-like feather shuffle. Dust, twigs, and goodness knows what else billowed out from his mangy wings and bedraggled body. Undeterred, and apparently not the least bit concerned for his appearance, Elderash decided to pompously observe an upturned claw as he retorted,

"You might, when you hear what it is."

"Are you deaf as well as vile?" roared Deeron, forcing Elderash to veer backwards on his branch. "I said, clear off!" More grot and clouds of filth detached themselves as Deeron bellowed his demand head-on, made all the worse by Elderash frantically flapping about, trying to regain his balance.

Having retrieved his stability, Elderash suddenly appeared worried. His body language altered completely, from austere and demanding to pathetic and pleading. He began to make pitiful begging-motions with his wings as he blurted out, in a high-pitched and obviously fearful squeak,

"Give me the Wandiacates, and you can have your antlers! All six!"

Deeron hollered even harder at Elderash now, forcing ever greater plumes of dirt and debris from his wretched, soiled body. "Be gone with you! And tell Smolder that we do NOT do deals with the likes of him or you!"

Deeron's vocal assault had caused the branch Elderash was perched upon to finally snap, plunging him rapidly towards the ground. Elderash quickly spread his enormous wings and took flight, just before he and the barren ground below collided.

"You're making a big mistake!" cried Elderash, as he swooped overhead. "I offer you one last chance. Give me the Wandiacates, and the war is over!"

Arog moved to Deeron's side. "You heard what Deeron said, Elderash! THERE IS NO DEAL!"

Elderash circled above the tree line, keeping a keen distance between him and everyone else. It was now impossible to see him due to the sunlight blazing down and rendering only his silhouette visible. "Arog, I remember you from long ago," he croaked, pathetically. "You were stupid then, and you're stupid now... and still a coward!"

Elderash continued circling round and around, squawking various threats and insults. As he did so, his looming shadow appeared to grow ever larger over the party below, until the sky was almost completely blackened out. A dark and now gigantic silhouette cast itself over the ground, shrieking again and again,

"Give me the Wandiacates! Give me the Wandiacates!"

The noise became excruciating, having increased along with Elderash's shadow and evident size. The ground then began to shake, causing fruit, goblets and whatever else remained of the picnic to fall in all directions, while gigantic tree roots shot up from out of the earth, wrapping themselves around the deer's feet and binding them to the spot. Emily and Jen clung onto the edge of the shaking table, trying to lift their feet off the floor and so avoid the roots. Bill dived down on top of a root near to Jen and bit hard into it, but was flung backwards as the root whiplashed him off. He landed upside down on the ground, with goblets and plates piling on top of him.

Emily suddenly looked up, as something dark caught her eye veering straight towards her. "Oh no!" she cried. "Jen... look out!"

Elderash swooped down with his claws outstretched in front of him, aiming them directly at Emily and Jen! He was now perhaps thirty times his previous size and could easily have grabbed, or even eaten, them both. Jen almost passed out witnessing this enormous creature hurtling towards her, open-mouthed and with outstretched fully extracted claws. Deeron ran over and leapt up, attempting to stab the bird with his antlers as it lunged towards its desired prey. Elderash quickly pulled up abandoning his descent, moments before being struck by Deeron. He circled around again to attempt another attack.

Slowly and calmly, Arog picked up a branch and began to gently brush the table, chanting,

"From wind & from fire,
From ashes & mire.
May all that is good, and is true,
Be away with the likes of you!"

Elderash shrieked a pain-riddled cry as Smolder's stone table split, straight down the middle!

"Be away with the likes of... YOU!" demanded Arog again, pointing the branch now directly at Elderash. Instantly, the bird froze solid in mid-air, then shrank back to his original size as he plummeted to the ground. The roots that had lassoed the deer, and still had hold of Emily's right leg, withered and disintegrated. In the time it took for Elderash to fall, everyone was free.

Smolder's messenger fell down dead onto the split table in front of Arog, causing everyone to look up from where they were and stare at him in complete amazement. "What's up?"

he asked, grinning. "Are you so surprised that I know a little magic of my own?"

"Thanks be to all that is good that you do," replied Deeron, "or we might have lost our precious Wandiacates."

Jen and Emily walked over to where Arog and Deeron were standing. Both simply gawped at the dead bird on the ground, aghast and completely horrified. After a few seconds, Jen asked in a slow and confused voice,

"Why would Smolder want us so much that he'd be prepared to return the antlers?"

Deeron, sensing her fear, placed a hand upon Jen's shoulder and squeezed. "We know," he replied, "that Smolder would never return our antlers for anything, but it may simply be that he believes capturing you as well will further enhance his powers in the mortal world."

"And will it?" asked Emily, casting him a piercing stare.

"I really don't know," he replied, with a gentle sigh.

Jen returned her gaze to the deceased Elderash, and visibly shuddered. 'What if Deeron had agreed to the deal?' she thought, 'What would have happened to us then?'

Emily placed a comforting arm around Jen, and gave her a gentle hug. "We *can* trust them, you know," she whispered. Jen nodded doubtfully, and hugged her back.

"I know," she replied, trying to force a smile.

"We had better leave this place," said Arog, "in case Smolder sends us another 'messenger'."

Deeron agreed, and instructed the deer. Many were busily gathering together what was left of the crockery, while Bill played his part by scurrying around picking up the goblets and dropping them into a sack.

"Would you like a ride, Jen?" invited Blythe. "You look very tired… climb up." Jen put her arms around Blythe's neck and lifted herself onto his back. It was wonderful to rest her feet.

"Come along, Emily!" called Tamhorn, trotting over to her. "I'll give you a lift."

Emily likewise climbed up onto his back, and then they all departed. It was wonderful to view the forest from up high, and observe the long trail of deer stretching both ahead and behind. Bill too could also be seen, running in and out of the strict marching line. They really did look like an army, proceeding through the forest despite all the dangers at every turn.

"Are you alright up there?" called Tamhorn after a while.

"Great!" came an enthusiastic reply, for Emily knew this was a moment in her life she would never forget.

While they walked, Deeron thought long and hard over what had just happened. He had never considered the possibility that Smolder might be able to somehow exploit the Wandiacates' power for his own ends. Of course, he couldn't know for certain whether or not this was achievable, but there seemed to be little doubt in Smolder's mind, and this worried him greatly. Although Smolder's 'deal' was so obviously a sham, the fact that he wanted the Wandiacates at all only added to Deeron's concern. Could he, with both girls as prisoners, actually corrupt the Golden Light of Goodness? Deeron could not bear to imagine the catastrophe that would befall them all were Smolder to possess that degree of power.

Yet here Deeron was, about to place the Wandiacates right inside Smolder's Castle - undoubtedly the most dangerous place of all, running the greatest risk that they would be caught. But, what could he do? Without the magic antlers back they were finished anyway, and no matter how hard Deeron tried, he could not think of a single alternative to having the two girls inside that castle. It was simply a chance they would all have to take, including the Wandiacates themselves. Deeron knew his plan was dangerous, and that he was gambling with many lives.

As the day wore on, the air turned even colder. They eventually came across a clearing, where Deeron announced they would rest for the night. The marching herd dismissed and wearily dispersed. Only Arog remained standing.

"Deeron, we still have much forest to put behind us. There is precious little time to rest," he pressed, determinedly.

"My brave and loyal friend, be still!" answered Deeron kindly, but with equal intensity. "If we do not rest, we will not have the strength to fight our enemy when we confront him. Nourishment and sleep will make us rise tomorrow like the sun; golden and fiery!" He placed a brotherly hand on Arog's mane. Arog gave a subtle, conciliatory smile and slumped slightly, as though suddenly realizing his own tiredness.

Having stopped at last, Emily realized just how incredibly tired she was, even after having been carried for half the day. Her legs were numb with cold now, and she watched eagerly as Deeron lit a fire. Relieved of the load they were carrying, the deer settled down to rest. Arog walked amongst them, doing a head count and checking for injuries. Fortunately there were none, and in no time at all they were feasting on nuts and fruit around a roaring fire. There was great happiness and optimism, which surprised Emily considering who it was they were due to face.

Hay carried round goblets of honey drink. When he came to Emily and Jen he winked, and whispered, "I shall be very handsome when I get my antlers back!" They both giggled, shyly. Fole and Folly began prancing around too, showing off until they almost fell into the fire, and forcing Arog to order them to behave. Bill sat with the stags, enjoying every minute of his newfound importance within the group.

Later, Arog began to sing. His deep-rich voice seemed to stir the flames of the fire, creating a delicate visual accompaniment. Emily watched his bewitching form through the flames, wondering once again whether this was real or a dream. He sang about his world, and their home in the forest.

"I'll tell you tales of long ago,
When peace reigned in our woodland home.
When golden skies sent summer rain,
To grant us wealth, to heal our pain,
We were safe within our world to roam.

I'll bring you word from far away,
Where evil deeds were dreamt and done.
Where wicked spells were made and cast,
To hold us tight in autumn's grasp,
Where love was lost, and hatred won.

I'll sing of battles bravely fought,
When war was hard to understand.
Of Wandiacates who came to see,
If their dance might be the key,
To grant us peace in Deeron's land."

The fire crackled softly as Arog sang, and gradually the deer, Bill and the two girls fell fast asleep.

World of Dreams

$\mathcal{E}$mily awoke to the sounds of the night. Something had disturbed her, but she couldn't make out precisely what it was. An owl hooted somewhere in the distance as the fire crackled gently, while other unknown strange and far off sounds occasionally pricked the air. She blearily gazed up to see a few guards tending the fire as they kept watch. Next to her, Jen was fast asleep. It was Emily's turn to feel lonely this night, and start to ponder on what the days ahead might bring. She quickly decided, however, that she was far too tired to spend the night worrying, so closed her eyes and tried to think pleasant thoughts to coax herself back to sleep.

As her eyelids closed, she felt a tug at her sleeve. She opened them again to see the dark figure of a person wrapped in a cloak, knelt down close beside her.

"Come with me," the figure whispered hurriedly. "I have something to show you."

It was a woman, and although the hood of the cloak obscured her face, Emily was sure she knew that voice. She got up, curiosity getting the better of her, and decided to follow as the cloaked figure guided her out of the camp and into the forest. After all, she had to find out whose voice that was, as the name was on the tip of her tongue.

"Keep up! You must keep up!" the figure kept repeating. Emily was finding this almost impossible, due to the speed at which the guide was moving as she appeared to glide effortlessly and in silence across the forest floor. Emily's pace wasn't helped much either by the ground below her feeling weirdly spongy, and it lying hidden beneath a thick carpet of mist. Worst of all, however, was the fact that Emily's legs were simply not responding to demands to go faster. At all costs, she knew she had to stay in sight of her escort.

"Stop!" the cloaked guide suddenly ordered, forcing Emily to an abrupt halt. "Come here and look."

Emily moved over to where the woman was standing, and gazed into a wide-open and sunken glade. There was nothing there especially to see, only space and empty blackness. Besides, she still hadn't worked out precisely who this cloaked person sounded like, or was. A hand suddenly grabbed Emily's shoulder.

"Eek!" The shock caused her to jump up and around, to face whatever horror awaited her. It was Jen! Emily exhaled loudly in relief, and wondered whether her heart was still beating.

"I thought I'd never catch you," gasped Jen, trying to get her breath back.

"I thought you'd just killed me," retorted Emily dryly, holding her chest as she tried to calm her own breathing.

"Who are you?" Jen asked the cloaked figure. There was no reply. "Em, who's…?"

"There, look," demanded the guide, taking no notice of either Jen's presence or her questions, but continuing to point towards the same spot.

Her breathlessness having subsided, Jen was now herself taken aback upon hearing the guide speak for the first time. She recognized that voice! She couldn't be sure, but it sounded somehow altered or different in some way. She tried, but just couldn't put a name to it, or even fathom what it was that made the voice sound different.

"Look hard, and you will see," the guide directed again, still pointing into apparent nothingness. Neither Jen nor Emily really heard the words said to them now anyway, as they were far too busy desperately trying to put a name to that voice!

It was like an itch that had to be scratched, or a puzzle where you're so close to cracking it, but there's one solitary piece still left to solve. Emily had the name on the edge of her lips; and Jen, well this was really starting to bug her, as she was usually good at these things, and besides, it couldn't be anyone from school, which really only left celebrities and rela…

"LOOK!!" Emily and Jen heard this word clear enough, as their attention was seized with all the force of an explosion! Every muscle inside both their bodies locked rigid, as though they had suffered an electric shock. For one thing, it had been said in a very loud and stern manner, but what had most arrested their thoughts was that the word had been spoken directly inside their heads! It was just like someone blasting a foghorn, directly in the centre of your brain! Their vocal brainteaser vanished without trace.

Both girls peered into the darkness as ordered, trying to discover any kind of shape beyond or beneath the murky black. As they stared, a thick creamy fog gathered in the centre of the glade. The guide blew gently. Almost instantly, the vapour appeared to shimmer and then repeatedly ripple out like a pebble dropped in water. As the ripples dissolved, so too did the haze to reveal a gigantic and ugly wooden fortress.

"This is what I have brought you here to see," their cloaked guide whispered. "Smolder's Castle. It must be destroyed, but be warned; Smolder may be in there, and he will stop at nothing to prevent you from taking the antlers."

"Where are they?" asked Jen.

"In a chamber underground. He has magic protecting them so you must be very careful. Your dance will weaken his powers, but he has many guards and informants."

"How do we get in?" asked Emily. "It looks impossible."

"Come, I will show you."

They followed the guide as she glided off down the bank, thankfully slower now. As they proceeded towards the castle, Emily craned her neck to look up at the great log walls, towering so high that the roof could not be seen. It was more like a prison than a castle.

"What if he catches us now?" asked Jen, nervously.

"He cannot, for in this moment of time there is no 'now'. This is your world of dreams, and Smolder has no means to enter it, even with all his magic."

"You mean, we're in a different time?" enquired Emily, a little nervous herself now, as well as confused.

"There are many worlds and times in which you may be. Your waking time now is the magical world, but you come from the mortal world. Deeron occupies your world of adventure, while in your world of dreams, well, all and anything can be here."

Emily and Jen followed her around the castle, expecting to find a door or drawbridge. All they could see, however, were solid walls of towering tree trunks. There was no way in.

"Here!" the guide instructed, pointing to a pile of white stones on the ground, covered over with bracken. "This is the entrance which Deeron marked last time he was here." Jen and Emily moved the stones to one side, to reveal a wooden-slatted hatch that lifted with ease. The ghostly guide dropped down the hole.

"Come," she called. "It is safe!"

Jen climbed in first after her, quickly followed by Emily. Some steps descended to a passageway that in turn led to a round opening, shaped like an air-vent or funnel. The hole was black and slippery, and you could not see where it went. The cloaked woman disappeared down it.

"Oh well…" sighed Emily, and jumped in feet-first after her. Jen closed her eyes, took a deep breath, and did likewise. She was feeling pretty claustrophobic by now, but there was no way she was going to be left behind.

They both slid down a twisting circular tube at frightening speed, completely unable to stop or even slow down. After a few too many rollercoaster moments, especially for Jen, they came to an abrupt and bumpy stop by landing on top of each other inside a pitch-dark tunnel. Emily tried to get up, and thumped her head on what appeared to be a very low ceiling.

"Ow! Jen, move your foot, I... oow!" She bumped her head again, this time on a side panel. Emily painfully began to realize that the tunnel they were in now was so narrow they had to crawl along on their hands and knees. They were grateful that at least they could still see their guide, due to a misty haze of light now silhouetting her cloak.

"Watch out for those tree roots! Don't let them grab your ankles!" the guide anxiously warned, as they proceeded along the passageway. This was certainly easier said than done since they couldn't even see the roots, let alone avoid them!

Eventually, the tunnel led to an opening and access into a long wooden-panelled corridor, lit by burning torches hanging from both sides. Emily for one was thankful just to be able to stand up and walk again, and at least now see the dangers around them. After pausing briefly to adjust to the light and dust down, they made their way along the corridor.

On and on, through an apparently endless underground labyrinth they went. As they walked, they noticed that alongside each torch was an arched door, one after another, all made of wood and all identical. Emily thought it looked like some vast medieval office block for some hideous government department, like the Ministry of Torture or the Guild of Village Executioners. She imagined that behind each door there sat a faceless person in a drab office, shuffling files. The very thought of it made her shiver.

"Stop! See this door," their guide commanded briskly. "It is the entrance to Smolder's White Chamber. This is where he contacts the White Light of Evil, and ingratiates himself to it. Never enter this room. If this door begins to open, run!"

"But how will we know?" complained Emily. "It looks exactly the same as all the others."

"These corridors all run in circles, so you will find it eventually. Each time you pass this door you will grow weaker, and move closer to danger."

"That's reassuring," a sarcastic Jen quipped, quietly.

They walked on a short distance further along the corridor, until the guide stopped abruptly once more, by yet another identical door.

"This door," the guide pointed directly at it, "is the entrance to the Stone Chamber. Behind it is where the antlers are kept. Examine it closely. One of you touch it, please."

For Emily, this was all beginning to look impossible now. There seemed little point in touching a door that was indistinguishable from any of the others, particularly when she couldn't even determine which part of the corridor she was in. How would they ever navigate their way back here? And how many times could they pass that last door until they got caught? She sighed, and, not wanting to appear defeatist, touched the door.

Incredibly, the moment Emily's finger touched its wooden panelling, the door instantly turned to stone - solid grey stone, with a glint of granite that sparkled in the light of the naked flames all around them!

"Whoah," Emily jumped back with surprise. "I wasn't expecting that!"

"Way to go, Em!" Jen's eyes shone with wonder.

"Only with your dance can this door be found," the guide said flatly, in direct contrast to Emily and Jen's astonishment.

"Can't we just go in there now, get them and be done with it?" Jen asked, impatiently. "After all, he's not here to stop us."

"No!" the guide snapped back angrily. "You cannot take items from the world of dreams and place them into the world of adventure. These things do not transfer. It must be done in the world in which they exist. You have to know this. Do you see?"

"The world of adventure," sighed Emily, rather deflated at the thought of having to run, crawl, fall, walk endlessly, *and* probably bang her head, all over again, *as well as* find their way back here.

"Is this clear?" the guide repeated.

"Yes, I understand," replied Emily.

"Well I don't…" muttered Jen, softly.

"How will we know what to do?" asked Emily, who hadn't counted on actually having to physically take the antlers.

"Your dance will help you. Remember this, and remember all I have told you."

Emily turned and stared up at the door, trying to find some distinguishing mark or difference that would help her to identify it. There was none. She sighed yet another deep sigh, and wondered how on earth they were going to find their way back *in* to the corridor avoiding the *last* door and *yet* find *this* door and *then* get the antlers *out* from behind it *and* get them back up all those passageways and tunnels *without* getting stuck or caught by Smolder *or* his army. The phrase "This is nuts!" had already entered her thoughts on more than one occasion this holiday. This was another. And as for dancing down there, the very idea was ridiculous!

"Hey, wait!" cried Jen, interrupting Emily's silent lament. Their guide had continued along the corridor, and was now some distance away. They both ran after her, Emily's head still full of unanswered questions.

"Please wait," she called, as they ran. "We still don't know how to get in there!"

"You have your dance… that is the key," she called back. "We have spent many years searching for those with the power to enter Smolder's Castle, and you both have that gift. We weren't sure at first, but we now know for certain that you are Wandiacates."

"Will you be here to help us?" called Emily, panting out of breath and still some distance away, but desperately trying to catch up.

"No," she replied. "I cannot, for I have been here too many times and failed. I can only come here now in my world of dreams."

Jen and Emily continued to run after her, past many more doors and along the labyrinthine hallway, until finally they caught up with her standing by the ventilation shaft they had used to first enter the corridor.

"Once Smolder is destroyed, I shall never come here again," she said very calmly, and also rather kindly for the first time. "Now, I must leave you."

The cloaked guide's figure suddenly began to melt into a white, hazy fog. To Jen, it looked like the very same fog through which they had seen Smolder's Castle in the forest. Also, the shimmer and ripple effect that dissolved it appeared again, as the cloaked outline faded into nothingness.

"Please don't go!" Jen begged. "How will we get back to Deeron?"

There was no reply, but as the figure faded away almost completely, a face suddenly assembled itself from the faint misty outline. Emily and Jen could both make out round features, with a hair-bun on top and a broad, wide smile.

"Martha!" they cried together.

"Martha, Martha!" muttered Emily. "Don't leave us Martha, don't... Mar..."

"It's okay, Emily. Emily..." she heard a gentle voice, and opened her eyes to see Leif smiling down at her. "You were just having a dream."

Emily sat up and rubbed her eyes. Jen awoke at the same time, and they both simply stared at each other, completely dumbstruck. There was no need for either of them to speak, for they both knew that they had been there together in the world of dreams, inside Smolder's Castle. Emily wrapped her cloak around her shoulders, and sighed. "I just don't know what's real and what isn't anymore." Slowly, they both got to their feet.

"Breakfast!" Jen excitedly sniffed the air, as she spied the food set out on a fallen log. "That's real!"

Emily stared for a moment, observing the bizarre sight of many deer, a dog and a young girl, all eating together at a log table in a forest. She wasn't completely sure whether even this was real, but hunger carried her over to join them, all the same.

Smolder's Tricks

$\mathscr{A}$ fragile sun peered faintly above the horizon, illuminating the camp in a silver hazy mist which seemed to dampen further the spindly smoke trails, rising from the dying embers of the fire. The deer were already packing up and preparing to move on. After breakfast, Emily threw some water over her face and then attempted to coax her cold, stiff muscles into action. Jen ran her fingers through her hair, wishing for all the world that she had brought a brush with her. Emily spied the dappled coat and kind face of Tamhorn, peering at her through the trees.

"Good morning, Tamhorn!" she greeted him.

"Good morning, Emily. I see the cold has gotten into your bones as well."

That was true enough. Emily couldn't remember having ever before felt so stiff, not even after a really tough dance class. To warm up, she decided to walk to the edge of the hill, not far away, and view the sun rising from across the valley. Tamhorn joined her, and they both stood for a moment in the sunlight, quietly surveying the landscape as it swooped down to an idyllic-looking piercing blue lake. Emily pulled her cloak tightly around her, still fighting off the early morning chill.

"There lies our destination," said Tamhorn, pointing a hoof. "That is where Deerbrook meets the river."

"Is Smolder there?" asked Emily.

"I believe his castle is somewhere near there, but it's covered in an invisible fog he created. Even up close it remains hidden, and he'll see us long before we manage to get anywhere near him."

"How come?"

"Because his powers are very strong at the moment, due to him having the antlers. Many trees are forced to watch for him, while some animals will act as lookouts and informants, afraid of what he will do to them if they refuse."

"Why, what does he do?"

Tamhorn hesitated to answer, as he gazed upon Emily's young face. "I'm sorry to have to tell you, but he turns them to smoke. Then he makes the smoke work for him, inside his castle. After all, the only wildlife you've seen so far were the wounded in Deeron's Hall."

This was also true, although she had heard animal sounds in the night, and had of course had the dubious pleasure of meeting Elderash, but he was Smolder's messenger anyway.

"That's what he does," sighed Tamhorn. "He either enlists, or imprisons. Sometimes, he kills. It's said that his castle is more like a prison."

"Oh!" Emily gasped, placing her hand over her mouth. Suddenly, it had become all too clear what lay behind those doors in the endless corridor, which both she and Jen had witnessed in the dream.

"Yes," she murmured. "I'll bet it is." The imagery of the previous night remained firmly imprinted in her mind.

"Good morning," a voice behind them announced. Emily was glad for someone breaking her thoughts.

"Good morning Arog," replied Tamhorn, warmly. "Are we ready to move on?"

"Almost." Arog stood beside him and pointed across the valley. "We'll need to cut down the side of that slope, and make our way along the edge of the forest. It's a harder route but we'll be shielded from view, which will hopefully buy us time before we're noticed."

Emily gazed down to where Arog was pointing, to a part of the valley that resembled a cauldron full of swirling cloud and mist. An image flashed into her mind of them all ending up in a foggy brew at the bottom of a very deep gorge, which was a far from cheerful prospect. Determined not to make herself feel any more anxious than she was already, Emily cast the mental picture aside. Besides, it looked like a lovely walk down there, with forest and heathland decorating their path.

"Are you well rested, Arog?" Tamhorn turned to face him.

"I'd feel a whole lot better if I'd been sleeping on the leafy floor at home, thanks."

"That makes three of us, then," a jovial Tamhorn replied, turning to Emily for vague approval.

"And how have you survived the night, Emily?" asked Arog, turning towards her. Emily didn't really want anyone to know how she felt, as the dream had left her feeling both exhausted and worried. If it were true that they faced many horrors ahead as well as great danger, then the reality of this expedition was turning out to be even more frightening than she had originally thought. Composing herself, she managed to force a smile and simply answered, "Oh, I'm fit enough, thank you Arog, but I do think we should get on."

"You are very brave," he replied, kindly.

Emily briefly glanced into Arog's opal-cream and emerald-green eyes. Something about him - besides his appearance, of course - marked Arog out to be special amongst the herd, although Emily couldn't quite put her finger on what is was exactly. Whatever it was, Emily thought, Deeron had doubtless put him in charge for a very good reason.

With the announcement made that the party was ready to leave, everyone returned to their position in line. Arog joined Deeron at the head of the procession, whilst Tamhorn regrouped with his fellow five magic stags close behind. The remainder of the party then followed, with Jen, Emily and Bill bringing up the rear this time. As they walked, the mist began to clear, empowering the sun to adorn their path in a gentle golden light, and with it returning hope to the group once more.

"We shall soon be there!" called Arog, cheerfully. The sound of hooves clomping through the bracken seemed to inspire music in him, for he began to sing at the top of his voice.

"Dance, dance for Deeron,
Dance like the Deer,
Wake our forest from her slumber.
Fill our hearts for evermore,
With the joy your dance will conjure."

Emily found her feet playfully responding to the rhythm. She began to skip instead of walk, while Bill darted about in front of her. Jen also found the rhythm infectious - *be-dum-be-dee-dum, be-dum-be-dee-dum* - so much so that she completely forgot about how tired she felt, and joined in with Emily's skips.

Very soon, the two of them were creating complex rhythms of their own. This was then followed by altering and swapping around the emphasis of each one, all running on top of the heavy-hoofed *be-dum-be-dee-dum, be-dum-be-dee-dum*. All in all, it actually had quite a military pulse to it, and introduced a determined spring into the line. The sunrays beaming down upon them now shone in glorious intensity, and seemed to decorate and embellish their already spectacular march. The previous night's chill had become a distant memory, with everyone in the group now feeling pleasantly warm. Emily dropped her cloak from her shoulders and let it drag along the ground, as she and Jen continued their gambol.

Curiously, Emily suddenly felt instant and intense heat. Jen had obviously felt it too, as she had stopped dancing to grapple with her cloak that refused to come undone. Even Bill glistened in the heat. Emily glanced up ahead, wondering if any of the others were also feeling it. To her horror, she saw great steam clouds billowing up the path, looking like some vast travelling geyser or runaway steam train, only minus the train. With alarming speed it moved towards them, spewing out great surges of steam and hot air. Chaos and confusion had by now erupted at the front of the party as the deer tried to come back up the slope. This was made all the worse by the path itself suddenly becoming unstable.

"It's boiling!" yelled Deeron. "The Lake's boiling over. Get back, get back, or we'll all be stewed alive!"

Deerbrook Lake no longer resembled the twinkling postcard scene at the bottom of the valley. Now it resembled an overfilled pot that was bubbling over and swelling a thick hot fog towards them! Vision was drastically reduced as steam scolded their eyes and skin, whilst mud and earth from above began to slide down like treacle on a pudding, making retreat all but impossible. The deer slipped and crashed helplessly, both into each other and the avalanching trees. It was as though a combined earthquake and volcanic eruption had just taken place!

"Emily! Help!" cried Jen, who was fast slipping down the slope. She had turned around to see where Bill was, and lost her footing. Emily quickly grabbed Jen's arm, and tried to pull her back up the hill. This proved to be hopeless, as her feet simply slid in the mud as well, resulting in the two of them tumbling down uncontrollably towards the boiling water! Fortunately, Fauld was in front of them and saw what was happening. He rammed his antlers hard into the ground to try and break their fall. Jen crashed into him first and, grabbing an antler with one hand, caught Emily's arm with her other as she plunged past. Around them, mud began bubbling and spitting, while thick clouds of steam soaked them to the skin.

"Thanks Jen," wheezed Emily, trying to clear the steam from her eyes. "And you, Fauld!" The noise from the boiling lake, and the landslides going on all around them, was tremendous now.

"Thank me later!" Fauld shouted back, above the apocalyptic din. "Try to get back up the slope… quickly!" By shifting his antlers and weight around, Fauld helped Emily and Jen to their feet, just in time to see Bill slip down the hill to the right of them.

"Bill! Bill!" cried Jen, in a desperate panic. Without thinking, Emily threw herself towards him and made a grab for his collar, to hopefully break his fall.

"I've got him!" she yelled, grasping Bill's collar for all her might. She then frantically tried to gain either a foothold or a handhold of something - anything to prevent them from falling any further. Bill thrashed about with all four paws, but it was useless. They both started to slide down the slope towards the rising, deadly lake of steam.

Jen lunged across towards Emily, with both arms outstretched as far as she could. She managed to grab Emily's foot just before she and Bill slid out of reach. By a combination of sheer luck and a rather nifty balancing act by Fauld, Jen's right foot had become hooked over one of his antlers. Her five toes were now all there were preventing all three of them from careering down the slope and being boiled alive!

"Bill! Here, Bill! Come on… climb up! Climb, Bill!" Jen, with the one hand that wasn't holding onto Emily's ankle, beckoned Bill to walk towards her, and climb up onto Fauld's antlers. Bill, gingerly at first, managed to maneouvre himself up above Emily and crawl along her side, and then likewise alongside Jen. Once Bill was safe, Fauld dug his legs and antlers in hard again, shifting his right rear leg out closer to Emily and placing his hoof just beneath her stomach.

"Fall onto my leg, Emily!" he shouted. Emily did as she was told. With superior strength, and by what seemed like little more than a flick of his hoof, Fauld catapulted Emily upwards to just above his antlers. She landed right beside Bill.

"Me too, now!" cried Jen, who was dangling quite perilously now from about two toes. Emily quickly grabbed her leg and an arm, and pulled her up. As soon as she was safe, Jen put her arms around her beloved pet. That had almost been the end of Bill.

Deeron's voice struggled to be heard above the chaos and noise. "Hold tight! Dig in! Dig in!" he yelled, but the herd were sliding ever closer towards the boiling mud bath, and apparently couldn't make any sense of his instructions.

Emily looked around. To her right she saw a large rock jutting out from the slope, quite nearby. She hadn't noticed it before, but probably due to all the tons of earth and trees cascading down, it had now become more visible. It looked rather like the figurehead of a ship, and to Emily appeared to offer their only salvation right now.

"If I could only get over to it," she muttered to herself, "I could then call the deer to safety." Getting to her feet was impossible right now, so Emily crawled along on her hands and knees. Using one hand to grab bits of bracken for stability, she dragged Bill by his collar with the other. "Follow me!" she yelled to Jen.

They cautiously made their way towards the rock, shuffling along on a thin crust of barren earth beneath which was now a gurgling river of mud. Their passage felt increasingly wobbly and unstable, while the heat from below oozed ever upwards. As the rolling earth slipped away, newly exposed clusters of rock dug into their knees and hands, but at least gave them something solid to grab hold of.

With surprising speed, they arrived at the base of the rock, glistening hard and grey in the swirling steam. Just as they reached it, the brittle skin of solid ground upon which Emily and Jen knelt suddenly collapsed, plunging them both up to their waists in mud! Bill was just about keeping his nose above it, although his body was sinking fast. Lurching forward, Emily thrust her free hand towards the hard surface of the stone for all she was worth. Nothing. She tried again, but her body simply refused to follow.

In actual fact, Emily was sinking. Her legs, thanks to the mud and both her and Bill's weight, were dragging them downwards into the sliding swamp. She couldn't let go of Bill, but what could she do? She desperately needed her other arm to have any hope of getting out of this. If she didn't make it, no one would.

As if answering her call, Bill lurched forwards and sprang into action. He began frantic doggie-paddle movements, first to upright himself, and then to try and move closer to the rock. Mud was splashing everywhere but nobody cared, least of all Emily.

"Go on, Bill! Good dog, that's it, keep going!" Jen kept up the encouragement, and it seemed to be working. Spurred on by his determination, Emily managed to get her hand behind and beneath his body in the mud, and basically push him upwards.

"Up Bill, up!" yelled Emily, as Bill's paws scraped wildly around the surface of the rock, trying to find some grip. His front paws seemed to have it, while all the time his back legs continued to scratch about below mud level, desperate to achieve the same. Suddenly, it looked as though he had some footing! Bill was climbing! Up, up, …

Covered in mud and soaking wet, Bill reached almost halfway up to a rocky ledge, slipped, and then slithered helplessly back down! Emily, with Jen who was now alongside her, raised their hands to try and break his fall.

"Got him! Push Jen, push!" Having prevented Bill from falling all the way back into the mudbath, he continued to scratch about trying to regain some traction. Fortunately, the girls now had something solid beneath them to stand on, and pushed as hard as they could. Bill altered his direction, now deciding to head for a lower jagged outcrop. He scrambled, they pushed… and success! Bill was up on the rock!

The main platform of the rock was impossible for the girls to reach, while the ledge that Bill had scrambled onto was now all muddy and wet, offering no opportunities for climbing. Jen waded down and further around, looking for a better surface to come up. She felt beneath the mud with her foot, and found a small protrusion just big enough to gain a foothold. Bill by now was up at the top, looking down and barking encouragement as Jen heaved her soaking mud-clad body onto the rock.

"Here Emily!" she yelled. "Over here! There's a footing!" Emily waded round to where Jen was now climbing, and felt for the same step-up. Once Jen reached a suitable ridge, she stopped to offer Emily some guidance and a helping hand. Emily carefully followed Jen's footsteps as they continued to ascend, realizing that Jen had probably done rock climbing before. Very soon, Jen and Emily were on top of the ridge with Bill, safe for the moment at least.

Thankfully, many of the deer had heard Bill's barking, and were now making their own way towards the rock. Moving unsteadily among the patchy mounds of dry earth and rock, they nevertheless travelled fast as earth continued to collapse and roll away down the slope past them. Unlike the army, however, the six magic stags appeared very nimble, navigating easily across their stepping-stones whilst neither sinking nor slipping at all. They reached the rock way ahead of the others, but then fell into trouble. Their hooves provided no grip on the stone, and one after the other, they all slid helplessly back into the mud.

"Come on!" yelled Jen, who had climbed down to reach them and was trying to grab a stump, a clump of fur, anything to pull them up onto the rock.

"Let me through!" The shouted order came from behind the magic stags, but whoever it was could not immediately be seen. Beneath the thick foggy steam, Jen could just make out a stag jumping from rock to rock towards them. It was Arog! Obediently, the magic stags manoeuvred themselves to allow their leader through to take control. One powerful swipe of Arog's head wedged his steel antlers deep enough into the rock to take his weight, and allow him to haul his body up onto the ledge Bill had used. Jabbing his hooves firmly into the stone, he was then able to lower his antlers down to the stags. "Grab them with your teeth," he commanded. One by one, the six magic stags dangled from Arog's antlers by their teeth as they were lifted onto the rock. Just one last jump, encouraged by Jen, and they were up on the flat ridge with Emily and Bill. Following Arog's example, the other stags mounted the rock in the same way, with each one then lowering his antlers to assist a doe. Finally, with the entire army standing wearily aboard the rocky platform, they looked like a crew of shipwrecked explorers, until Arog suddenly realized that the captain of the ship was missing.

"Deeron!" he yelled desperately, scanning the devastated landscape for any sign of him. Panic began to break out amongst the army as they stumbled about the rock, calling his name.

"There he is!" cried Leif, pointing to a set of antlers poking out just above the mud, barely a hair's breadth away from the lake's edge. "We need something to haul him up, quickly!" Leif looked around for anything to help keep Deeron afloat, while Arog moved to the closest ridge on the rock to try and find a way to reach him.

Behind them, on the highest point of the rock, stood an old and very large oak tree, towering high above the devastation. Its upper roots lay naked and exposed by the landslide, but its deeper ones lay well embedded into the rock.

"Those roots!" shouted Purbrook, pointing a hoof towards the uncovered stems. "We can tie together lengths to make a rope!" The army of stags immediately got to work, separating the upper exposed roots from the tree. Some began breaking them with their sharp teeth, while others including the does scraped the roots free from the rock with their hooves. They moved quickly and diligently, with further instructions given out by Leif and Blythe.

"Quick Jen, we can do this," said Emily, grabbing the first lengths of root to be cut. "You tie those, I'll do these, and then we'll tie yours and mine together." Everyone worked as fast as they could, all aware that they could lose Deeron forever, at any moment. Arog continued to shout down to him, trying to keep his spirits up and inform him of what they were doing. Even Bill played his part, collecting up and carrying over to

Jen and Emily the freshly severed roots. Both girls worked incredibly hard, developing blisters on both hands in no time, as they continued to knot and pull the root stems together.

All the while, mud, debris, trees and loose rocks continued to cascade down the slope towards Deeron and the boiling lake. The noise was incessant, and it was difficult to see any farther than a few metres away. Arog struggled to maintain sight of Deeron through the sodden haze of steam continually rising from the lake. He wondered how on earth he was coping with all the hot vapour and boiling mud, and quietly despaired at the thought of each sighting being potentially the last.

"Here!" shouted Jen across to Fauld, who was also supervising the root breakers. "This should be long enough. I just hope it holds." Leif scrambled over to quickly observe their handiwork.

"Well done, girls! This looks fine. Right, tie that end to the tree, and I'll try to lasso Deeron." Emily went to help the stags secure the tree end, while Jen followed Fauld to the rock's edge. They stood for a moment at the periphery, trying to locate him. "Where is he? I can't see him!" shouted Fauld, despondently.

"Over there!" cried Arog from his lower vantage point, pointing to an area at the water's edge, obscured by steam and wreckage. Amongst the chaos, some trees had shunted up against one another as they had tumbled down the slope, creating a line of logs that floated on the mud. It resembled a haphazard half-built bridge, or some logging ready for transporting across water. Something, maybe a rock, was preventing them from falling straight into the lake. But where was Deeron? As Jen and Fauld tried to peer through the thick mist, they could just make out some movement at the lake end. It was Deeron!

He had managed to manoeuvre himself onto the logjam, and was now crawling slowly up it. He was still some distance away, and the logs only extended to about one third of the way up the slope to the rock, but at least he was out of the boiling mud.

"If only those logs would just stay where they are," said Fauld to Jen, "he'll be okay. For now."

Fauld launched the root-rope with his antlers, high into the air, in Deeron's direction. It landed, but came down short of the logs! Even if Deeron scaled all the way up the log line, he still wouldn't reach it.

"It's too short!" cried Arog from below. "More slack!"

"More slack!" repeated Fauld, turning to those at the tree end. "We need more rope!"

"There is no more!" called back Blythe. "We've used the minimum possible!"

Emily quickly scanned the area again to see whether there was anything nearer the edge that they could anchor to, but there was literally nothing else.

"Untie the rope," said Blythe, reluctantly. "We've no choice." Emily did as she was asked, and removed the rope from around the tree.

"Emily and I could lengthen the rope with more roots," suggested Jen to Fauld, trying to be helpful.

"There's no time for that, Jen," he replied. "Those logs won't hold for much longer. We need a solution, now!"

"I've got it!" exclaimed Blythe, excitedly. "You stags, come with me. You too, Emily." Blythe commandeered four army stags - Purbrook, Booth, Grindley and Lupin - and led them with Emily to the middle of the rock. He arranged the stags in a circle, all facing each other, and directed them to intertwine and lock together their antlers. When in place, he turned to Emily to thread and tie the root-rope securely around them.

"These stags can be our anchor!" he enthused. "We can create slack by moving them closer to the edge, as needed." Fauld and Jen joined him and Emily. "When Deeron has the other end, we can haul him up!"

"Good work, Blythe!" congratulated Fauld. "We can also use mine and Arog's antlers to guide the rope and ensure it doesn't catch on the rocks. I'll let him know what we're up to." Fauld scurried back to the edge of the rock to inform Arog of the plan, while Jen and Emily hauled up the rope, ready for it to be re-thrown.

The four hooked stags shuffled closer to the edge while Fauld, just as before, prepared to relaunch the rope. With a force many times greater than his small slender frame would suggest possible, he cast the rope high into the air, aiming as accurately as he could for the area where Deeron was last seen. Because of the steamy mist that had now enveloped and engulfed the entire valley, nobody on the rock's top platform could see the logjam any more, or really anything below a few metres or so. They waited anxiously for Arog to report from his lower vantage point as to whether they'd been successful or not. They waited... and they waited...

Then suddenly, an almighty jolt shook the four interlocked stags, and started dragging them towards the rock's edge! Instantly they fought to steady themselves and adjust their footing, opposing this unseen force for all they were worth. The situation rapidly became a full-blown tug-of-war, as other stags quickly moved in front of them to help take up the weight and add further resistance. Yet still they staggered, compelling Fauld to order even more stags to lock their antlers in with the main four, and stand fast against the weight beneath. They shook again, and then finally stood firm.

The call from Arog was short, loud and unequivocal. "PULL! We've got him!"

Anyone who wasn't already pushing or pulling was now, as everyone played his or her part in saving Deeron. Jen and Emily ensured the rope, guided from below by Arog, stayed free and didn't become caught or snagged anywhere. Jen was also quietly praying to the root-rope - "Please don't break! Pleease...!"

The stags fought for what seemed like ages, slowly yet steadily hauling Deeron up from the wreckage of what had been an idyllic valley, towards what was now a vertical and barren cliff. Throughout their endeavour, the noise, mudslides, destruction and billowing hot steam continued unabated.

Fierce gusting winds then suddenly appeared as Deeron neared the top, forcing Jen to stumble as they all struggled to steady the rope. The resulting shift of steam allowed Emily, who was guiding the rope closest to Arog, to witness the disaster beneath. The tranquil and pleasant path they had followed earlier that morning could no longer be even imagined, let alone seen. Everywhere was total devastation, and it was all down to Smolder.

"I can see him!" was the cry from Arog that concentrated Emily's mind. "One more pull... keep going! That's it... he's up!" A loud cheer rang out as Deeron, now firmly on the rock, slowly made the last small ascent up to the top, with Arog close behind.

"My friends! I cannot tell you what a joy it is to see you all again, and thank you with all my heart for your hard work in saving me." Deeron stumbled and appeared wounded, but was at least now out of danger. They all moved a safe distance back from the edge, as more rocks and debris tumbled down around them.

"Are you hurt, Deeron?" asked Emily, speaking for everyone as concern was clearly etched upon every face.

"I'll survive... really, I'm okay. We are all safe, and that is what matters," he said, forcing a smile whilst fumbling with the root-rope still tied around his waist. He patted the trunk of the tree. "Many thanks to you as well, old friend," he whispered.

A piercing, high-pitched whining noise suddenly began to fill the air, compelling the deer to rock their heads from side to side, as every eardrum felt fit to burst! Emily and Jen cowered down covering theirs, while Bill tried to cover his with his paws. Then, just as quickly as it had started, the incessant din stopped.

"What was that?" cried Jen, prodding an ear with her finger.

"Smolder, I should think," replied Deeron. "We must remain on our guard. I feel he is very close."

Everyone watched as steam from the valley lifted up high above their heads, and floated away like fast-moving cloud.

The rock beneath their feet then began to vibrate, as a sorrowful moaning sound rose from out of the earth. The noise sounded like sobbing and became increasingly intense, just as though someone was buried deep down and was crying out to be freed. The earth pulsated with the moaning, until Emily could bear it no longer. In an apparently hypnotized state, she stepped off the rock, fell and sank up to her waist in mud.

"No Emily, come back!" yelled Fauld, jumping down after her and snatching the hood of her cloak with an antler. "It's Smolder trying to trick us!"

Emily just gazed ahead, deep in a trance. Fauld held onto her tightly, preventing her from falling any further into the mud, while the others helped pull her up. Emily was transfixed by the image of six ghostly antlers, hovering in the sky. She was sure they were calling to her from a desolate and lonely world. "I'll come," she called, weakly. "I'll come and rescue you."

"Hahahaaaaaah!!!!!" a piercing laugh shrieked from somewhere up the valley. "Come on then, Wandiacate! Come and get them!"

"Oh no, no! Go away!" she yelled, covering her ears. The taunt seemed to awaken Emily, as she found herself back up on the rock being comforted by Jen and Deeron.

"You see," explained Fauld, "just how easily and cruelly he torments us. You must never listen, Emily, nor follow his call, or you will be captive in his world forever."

"Smolder will try and trick each and every one of us whenever he can." Deeron turned to them all. "So we must all be on our guard, for ourselves and each other. But right now, if we are ready, we must proceed. We have no choice but to cross the water."

No one had the energy to speak, but all nodded in agreement. Whatever supplies had survived or could be salvaged were collected up, and final preparations made to move on.

"We shall have to climb back up to the top," instructed Arog, gesturing to the highest point behind them. "We'll follow the path through the forest and along the ridge, until it drops down nearer to the river over there somewhere. There's no path and precious little on the ridge, so it will be difficult but at least we should avoid any further mudslides."

Arog was right about it being difficult. Because of the landslide, the slope was now a rock face. Progress was slow for everyone, even the deer who were strong and agile, and used to climbing in different parts of the forest. Emily soon felt exhausted and was filthy from all the mud, while her hands were sore and blistered from both the rope and scaling the rock.

"Is it much further, Em?" called Jen, who was slightly behind her.

"No, we're nearly there," she replied, sounding surprisingly optimistic considering she actually had no idea.

"This is the top!" yelled Arog, just ahead of her. Emily felt relief beyond words.

They were now back in the forest again, and walking through masses of brambles covered in thorns. These were no ordinary brambles, however, and nor were they ordinary thorns. For one thing, the brambles lay everywhere, and for another, they scratched and lashed out at everyone who passed, even trying to wrap themselves around hands, hooves and feet. This made progress very slow and also painful, causing deep scratches and trickles of blood to soon appear, especially on Jen and Emily. Holding them back for each other to pass didn't help much either, as the moment they were touched the brambles grew at an astonishing rate. Poor Bill was having terrible trouble, as his paws kept getting stuck due to him being smaller and nearer to the ground. He struggled to even see them before they lashed him in the face.

"Follow us, Bill," said Jen, pulling him towards her. "We'll try and flatten them for you." This was a good plan but rather slow, and Arog soon became impatient.

"Do keep up, everybody!" he shouted back down the line to them all. "We're losing time!"

Jen felt annoyed at Arog's insistence, as it was all right for him with his strong coat that seemed to repel the thorns from scratching him. Also, the brambles were no match for his big steel antlers that like a scythe cleared his path, as he swung his head to and fro. The ground immediately behind him was clear.

"Follow me," directed Emily, leading Jen and Bill into and behind Arog's path. At last they were able to make faster progress. Everyone else, Deeron included, was having a much harder time.

Finally, Arog stopped and waited for the rest of the party to catch up. When everyone was assembled, he gestured to a path leading down to a glistening lake far below.

"Right, we go down this way," he said.

"He's got to be joking!" whispered Jen, for the slope the path ran down appeared to be many times steeper than the last one, and it was almost a sheer drop at the bottom to the water. Many deer also peered down with varying expressions of reluctance and fear, while others fixed their disbelieving gaze firmly onto Arog. Bill let out a nervous little whine.

"Why are we going this way, Arog?" asked Tamhorn, seemingly speaking for everyone.

"Because the forest splits from the lake after this point," he replied. "If we go on, we'll be travelling away from Smolder's territory, not towards it, and will end up in open ground which will make us easy prey for our enemies."

Arog knew exactly what he was doing, and the others trusted him implicitly. The deer nodded approval, and set off one by one tentatively along the steep path. Deeron waited at the top to see them all down.

"Try going backwards," he advised, when it came to Jen and Emily's turn. This proved to be the safest way, especially as you couldn't then see the scary drop into the water below. Bill found it easier to trot down sideways, and was pleased just to be able to keep up with the others. The does and stags slid down on their front legs, only needing to dig their hooves in quickly at the bottom to prevent them from falling into the water. After a while, everyone was safely assembled at the edge of the lake, unable to believe their luck at not having broken their necks.

"Well done, everyone. Good work!" exclaimed Deeron, as he descended the slope to join them.

"Right," said Arog, resuming command. "There's a line of raised stepping stones that cuts through this water somewhere, and we need to find them. It used to be right here, but it looks as though Smolder has turned the lake around to confuse us."

The shoreline around the edge of the lake was smooth and able to be walked upon, making the search easier for the moment. Jen observed the bare and sparsely clad trees nearby which seemed to contrast with such healthy-looking, glistening water. Beneath their feet, the ground squelched like a soaked brown carpet. Just above the lake, a mysterious mist hovered. It was impossible to tell at this point whether it was steam or frost.

"It's here!" called Arog, from further up the lake. "We go over this way!"

Arog led them to the narrowest point of the lake, where flat stones were visible through the clear water. Booth was the first stag to step in, but as his hooves touched the water, he shuddered and howled.

"Oh no!" cried Deeron, looking dismayed. "Is it still boiling?"

"N-no Deeron, it's f-f-freezing!" Booth stood in the water, shaking uncontrollably.

Emily thought he looked so funny, standing there shivering. Even Arog couldn't help but laugh.

"Come on," he smiled. "It won't kill us."

Fortunately, it wasn't very deep, so they were only frozen up to their knees! For Bill, of course, it was far worse because the water came right up to his stomach, but it at least offered them all an opportunity to wash off the last remnants of mud from themselves. It was such a relief for everyone to finally reach the other side, where they all then tried to reawaken their frozen limbs. Emily was convinced that she would never feel her feet again, never mind dance on them!

The group rested for a time, gazing across the water at the steep trail they had just left behind. Emily instead decided to look the other way at the climb yet to come, wondering how much longer this journey would ultimately last. She sighed, and glanced up at the sparse line of trees waiting to greet them at the top of the valley. Then suddenly, something caught her eye - a flash of bright light, followed by another, and then another, pulsating out from behind the treeline.

"Oh, look!" she called, pointing upwards.

"What?" Arog quickly turned around. "What is it?"

"Oh, it's gone," she faltered. "I thought I saw light coming from behind those trees."

Arog appeared to be neither amused nor concerned, giving her an icy stare before coldly adding, "We've got enough to worry about, without you imagining things!"

Emily wished she hadn't said anything at all now. It was true that she could have imagined seeing something, as after all, she was frozen and exhausted, but it looked real enough at the time. Arog was obviously in a pretty bad mood right now, and he didn't get Emily's vote when he was like this.

They trudged wearily on, ascending once again to the top of the valley. It was a long hard climb, and no one had the energy to talk. The deer were tired, and many stumbled as they went. Bill curiously had by far the most zeal now, scampering off ahead as usual and glad to be in charge of his feet once more. He stopped periodically to wait for the others to catch up, and barked triumphantly when he finally reached the top. The party managed a tired but grateful cheer. The way ahead now thankfully appeared to be flat for the moment at least, affording them all some time to get their breath back and give their legs a bit of a rest.

As they journeyed on, the number of trees around them gradually increased, until they eventually found themselves walking in thick forest once more. The trees stood heavily laden with dark coppery leaves of every shade and shape, while many began to drop as they walked along beneath them. The scene was rather stunning, if you could forget that it was actually summer.

"This reminds me of Christmas," said Jen happily, enjoying her walk through a picture-postcard landscape.

"Christmas! Where on earth will we be by Christmas?" muttered Emily, suddenly horrified at having to confront their unknown future.

"Well, I'll tell you one thing. If we're not home by then, Martha'll have the whole country out looking for us!"

"If our dream was true," muttered Emily, "she already knows where we are." Tamhorn suddenly trotted up to them, deciding to make small talk.

"Our journey is easier for the moment, thank goodness," he said.

"Yes. Isn't the forest lovely?" replied Jen, smiling.

Tamhorn and Emily stopped, staring at her in astonishment.

"Lovely?" gasped Emily, "It's either dead or dying!"

"Well, I mean the colours," she stumbled, trying to qualify her remark. "They're nice, that's all. And those new trees over there, they're not dying, are they?"

Tamhorn gave Jen an understanding smile. "What makes the forest beautiful, Jen, is balance, such as seeing each season flourish and to observe the many changes from one period to the next. The colours around us are rich, but without summer's growth the new life of spring will die, which in turn means that this autumnal landscape will never return. Everything here in the forest is relative, with each part reliant upon another to create the whole. After all, what joy is there in nature's decline if we never see her burst into life again?"

"Wise words, Tamhorn," said Emily, softly.

"Do you remember Lord and Lady Bagot?" asked Jen, suddenly realizing how daft her comment was, and wanting to make the most of an opportunity to get some answers.

"Well," replied Tamhorn, "a little, but not much."

"Did they live like royalty?" pressed Jen, "And were they…?"

"I'm sorry, Jen," he interrupted. "Arog knows the history of the Bagots better than anyone. He is the one to ask."

"Is there something different about Arog?" asked Emily, becoming inquisitive herself now, until realizing the obviousness of her question. After all, none of them were exactly ordinary, were they? "It's… well, it's just that he seems to be more special than the rest of you," she stumbled.

Tamhorn smiled a knowing smile. "Oh yes, Arog is special alright. I don't know what we'd do without him really, although we may just find out soon enough."

"Why, what do you mean?" asked Jen.

Tamhorn drew closer to them both, and whispered. "Arog has said he plans to leave us when this is all over."

"How come?"

"Well," he replied, with a resigned shrug, "Arog has had to fight many battles in his life, either with Smolder or with armies allied to him, and has seen his own herd and land destroyed. When Smolder took our antlers and imprisoned Deity, Deeron asked Arog to join forces with him so that they might beat Smolder together, and both hopefully get back some of what they had lost. That was some time ago now, of course, while since then we've lost many more battles, and Smolder's power has only increased against us. I think that Arog has probably just had enough, but thanks to you two agreeing to help, he's decided to give it one last go against Smolder."

"Great," sighed Jen. "So no pressure on us to get the antlers back, then?"

"Whatever happens, Jen," replied Tamhorn, with his usual kind smile, "Arog will leave us."

"But that's awful," exclaimed Emily, with a look of shock. "For all of you, but especially Deeron, to lose such a trusted member of the herd!"

Tamhorn nodded. "That's life, Emily. Anyhow, Arog is really interesting to talk to about the forest and the Bagots. Get him talking when he's sat down by a fire. He'll tell you some wonderful stories."

Jen glanced up ahead, and spied Arog deep in conversation with Deeron. She wondered whether she would ever get the chance on this journey to sit down and chat by a fire with either of them. Just at that moment, the party came to an abrupt halt, and an excited whisper passed through the herd. All eyes quickly fell on Deeron.

"We shall camp here," he announced, "so that we are well rested for tomorrow, when the Wandiacates will dance and we shall face Smolder." Jen turned to Emily and gulped hard.

"How will we know when and where to dance, Deeron?" asked Emily, plunging into worry herself now.

"We must wait until we receive a signal," he answered calmly, although neither specifying the type of signal nor when or from where it would come. "We'll then head for a place called Marsh Valley, which is at the very edge of the forest. Once there, I shall ask you both to dance." Emily half smiled to Deeron as though she understood, although in reality she was as unsure as ever.

"We must leave this path," Arog now began dispensing orders. "And set up in those trees over there. Follow me." Everyone dutifully began trailing along behind him.

"Em," whispered Jen, grabbing Emily's arm. "What are we actually going to do tomorrow?"

"It'll be fine, Jen, don't worry," smiled Emily, trying hard not to reveal her own anxieties. "We'll do what we've always done, when we've danced before by the lake. Deeron knows what he wants, and he'll tell us if it's wrong. We just have to do what he says, that's all."

"Okay... I guess," she replied, sounding especially doubtful.

"Come on," said Emily, cheerily. "Let's help make a fire."

The Wandiacates Dance

As darkness fell, cold damp air began to snake and wrap itself around them. Emily and Jen sat propped up against a tree, with Bill in between, trying to get warm. Jen suddenly sneezed, and then followed it up with a sort of groan as she blew her nose.

"What's up?" asked Emily.

"Oh, nothing," she replied, sniffing loudly. "I was actually thinking about those antlers under the tractor in the barn. Without them the Horn Dance can't happen, so we might have more time than we thought."

Everything that had happened at the farmhouse seemed a lifetime away from them now, although it had actually been only a few days before. However, unanswered questions remained from back then, such as:

1) Had Martha or Nick stolen the antlers from the church and hidden them under the tractor?

2) If they had, why now? Why hadn't they done this to help Deeron before?

If the dream was to be believed, Martha had previously visited Smolder's Castle and had failed to retrieve the magic antlers. This was proving to be a hard fact for Jen to swallow as in all the time she had known Martha, Jen had only ever seen her leave the farmhouse to shop, visit her knitting-circle friends in the village and go to church on Sundays. She didn't like strangers very much, she rarely trusted the telephone, and would most certainly never go near a computer.

Jen and Emily both gazed into the darkness, mulling over the uncertainties. The night possessed a kind of strange, eerie stillness that, under normal circumstances, would compel anyone to retreat back inside and huddle up by the fire, behind closed doors. Sadly, these weren't normal circumstances and this just wasn't an option right now.

"I just don't get *how* Martha could be in on it," whispered Jen, deliberating further. "I'll bet he knows, though." She gestured towards Deeron, as he approached them carrying two large goblets and a bowl of water for Bill.

"Here you are," he said, cheerily. "This should help warm you up while we wait for the fire to get going."

"Won't it give us away, though?" asked Emily, having pondered on this very question as she and Jen had helped build it.

"Oh, I rather expect Smolder already knows where we are," he replied, "so we might as well be comfortable." They watched him walk back to Arog, who was crouched down near to the now well-alight and quite substantial pyre, staring intently into the flames.

"Arog's quite nice, really," said Emily, gazing at him. "I think he just gets a bit snappy at times."

"Well, he is the boss," said Jen, taking a sip of her herbal drink. "And he's got a lot of responsibility. I bet he knows better than anyone what's in store for us, when we get to wherever it is we're going."

As night closed in, the fire looked increasingly inviting so they moved themselves nearer to it, ending up as close as they could possibly get. Bill's nose almost touched the flames.

"Don't you dare get singed, Bill!" Jen warned him.

The flames quickly rose so high that they appeared to brush against the black starless sky, while the smell of charred wood penetrated through the camp. The deer passed around enormous leaves filled with berries. They didn't look particularly appetizing, but tasted delicious nonetheless. Even Bill liked them.

Soon, with their stomachs full and feet thawed out, the adventure once again didn't seem quite so bad after all. Everyone was exhausted and so lay simply gazing into the fire, each lost in his or her own private thoughts. Deeron took out his flute, and began to play softly. Before long, many were drifting off to sleep.

Emily, hoping to succumb to sleep herself, looked at the deer through her tired, half-open eyes. Arog lay on his stomach, with his hooves folded neatly under him. His eyes were closed, but his ears twitched to every sound, and she was convinced he must really be awake. Fole and Folly lay side-by-side and facing each other with their hooves touching, looking like a reflection of one another. Tamhorn had edged as close to the fire as he could; his ears and hooves twitched as though he were disturbed by dreams. Sleeping in the shadows away from the fire were Leif and Blythe. Grindley and Lupin lay either side of some does and younger stags, while Fauld and Purbrook lay nearest to her, Jen and Bill. 'How brave those two were today,' she thought. 'Their quick thinking saved Deeron's life.'

On the opposite side of the fire lay another carpet of hooves and antlers; it was almost impossible to tell who was who. She spotted Booth, looking like a dark red bundle and folded up like a sleeping cat; and there, glowing in the firelight, were the bronze hooves belonging to Hay. 'How brave they all are,' she thought, before falling into a deep and dreamless sleep.

Just before dawn, Emily awoke from the cold to find Bill's dozing head resting on her leg. Not wanting to disturb him, she gently pulled her leg towards her so that she could stand up. Bill of course was instantly awake and disturbed Jen, who sat up startled.

"What's up?" she sniffed, rubbing her eyes.

"I'm sorry, it's just that I can't sleep. I'm too cold, so I thought I'd go for a walk."

"I'll come." Jen slowly got to her feet, while Bill began wagging his tail excitedly, anticipating an early morning stroll up for grabs. As they tiptoed away, Arog opened his one emerald eye and watched them as they disappeared through the trees.

After a while, Jen stopped to gaze up into the darkness once more. The sky looked really weird as no moon or stars could be seen, just an endless blackness that seemed to hold them in like a ceiling.

"I wonder how mum and dad are getting on," she said still gazing upwards, as if suddenly confronted by thoughts of the other world and all its problems, doubtless waiting for them if and when they returned.

Emily didn't answer but instead thought for a moment, as she suddenly struggled to confront the fact that another world existed alongside this one. To her, their situation kind of resembled one of those novels where people go off to another land and later find out that time had stood still all the while they'd been away. She tried to put this into words, but what came out seemed rather inadequate, both to herself and to Jen.

"If time is standing still at home, how would we know? I mean, we can't ring them up and ask, because if time is standing still, they won't know, will they?"

"What *are* you on about?"

"Oh, I don't know. It's just that I can't imagine ordinary life going on all the time we're here, doing this. People sleeping in ordinary beds, watching TV and eating normal food."

"No, nor me really."

Bill started to whine. "It's alright Bill," whispered Jen, stroking his head. "We know you're not ordinary." They carried on walking, with Bill running off ahead as usual.

"It's a bit spooky out here," said Emily a while later, trying to force a light-hearted laugh whilst nervously scanning the area. "It's worse than Halloween." At that moment, Emily heard a thud behind her, so quickly turned around to see Jen spread out on the floor. She sat up, staring at Emily in utter disbelief.

"What are you doing down there?" she asked, more mystified than concerned.

"I was just leaning up against that tree, and it moved!" Emily fell into a fit of laughter, and leant up against another one herself for support.

"Oh, right! You're trying to tell me that just 'cause..." *Thump!* Emily likewise collapsed onto the ground.

"It... It moved as well!" she exclaimed, incredulously. "Like, suddenly it wasn't there. Unbelievable!"

"Doesn't hurt though, does it? Just like falling on one of those really thick crash mats in gym class. They're great fun!" Jen got up, and leant against another tree. *Thump!* Down she went.

"Now me!" laughed Emily. *Thump!* One after the other, Jen and Emily repeated their stunt many times over, collapsing into hysterics every time they hit the floor. With all the commotion, Bill had become more and more excited and begun chasing his tail.

"Shush," giggled Emily, suddenly realizing the noise they were making. "We'll wake the deer."

Jen covered her mouth with her hand to try and stifle her laughter, and then leant against a tree again. It moved, but this time Jen remained standing.

"Aha!" she giggled. "I was ready for you that time."

"This is a really spooky forest," whispered Emily, opening out her cloak like a huge bird. "I'm a spooky old tree!" she laughed, swirling around and dancing about. "A spooky old tree, that's what I be! Whooo!'

"Stop!" Jen's voice suddenly sounded very serious, as she pointed to an area behind Emily. "Look!" Emily turned to see bursts of flashing and brilliant white light pierce through the trees up ahead of them, seeming to come from somewhere much farther away. The strength of every beam was nevertheless intense, as each one sliced high up into the dark and starless night sky like a shining blade. A soft and fairly distant crackling sound could also be heard.

"Hey, that's what I saw before!" cried Emily softly, remembering the put-down she'd received from Arog upon mentioning it.

"Wow," flinched Jen, squinting as she raised a hand to protect her eyes from the powerful blasts of light. "Those flashes are strong! What do you think it could be?" She turned away, and began some repeated blinking to try and refocus her vision.

"Wish I knew," replied Emily, adopting seriousness herself now. "From the looks and sound of it though, I think we should warn the others."

"Right." Emily and Jen both raced back to the camp as quickly as they could, with Bill safely in tow.

Their somewhat noisy return created some initial panic amongst the slumbering herd, to the extent that some deer struggled with untangling their antlers and hooves while still half asleep. Arog rose calmly upon hearing Emily's explanation, and spoke to Deeron.

"It seems it is time for us to move on," he said quietly, kicking earth onto the fire to extinguish the last dying embers.

"Yes," replied Deeron, calmly. "It would appear that way."

"Don't you want to see it?" questioned Jen, showing some irritation at their apparent lack of concern. "It's the flashing lights Emily saw yesterday, only this time there are…"

"We know what you have both seen, Jen," interrupted Arog, "and it means that we are near Smolder's territory."

"So," Emily tried to recollect the previous night's discussion, "now we have to find a valley, right?"

"Yes, that's right; Marsh Valley," replied Deeron.

"And then we dance?" asked Jen, revealing a sense of fear in her voice.

"And then we dance," confirmed Emily, said as though each word imposed a dark judgment upon them.

Wearily the deer lined up, and began to trudge through the forest once more. As daybreak arrived, their path led them through a mass of huge stinging nettles that towered high above everyone's heads, and appeared both out of place and out of proportion with everything else. Worst of all, though, were the stinging hairs on the leaves that were much longer and thicker than normal. They didn't confine themselves to stinging only when touched, either. They also launched themselves at the army, like darts!

Everyone suffered, including the stags and does. The hair-darts flew at them from all directions, penetrating clothing, fur and skin as they injected their nasty stinging payload. It was impossible to see them in the faint light of dawn, but everyone certainly felt them. They kept moving as fast as they could, and followed closely behind Arog as he hacked away at the nettles with his huge sharp steel antlers.

Poor Bill was almost beside himself with pain and discomfort, howling every time a hair-dart hit. Jen tried to minimize his torment by having him walk in-between her and a doe, but it sadly made little difference. Deeron gathered up some dock leaves for Emily and Jen to rub into their sores, although this didn't help much either as more hair-darts kept attacking far faster than they could treat any existing wounds. All they could do was plod miserably on.

At last, an open clearing beckoned before them where the nettles gave way to long grass and a tiny lake, with a wide bank sloping down into an open valley behind. A treeline stretched into the distance either side of the vale, seeming to almost touch the large and jutting cliff-top ridge at the end. Beyond the cliff, all that could be seen were vast mountain peaks, for as far as the eye could see. They were now at the very edge of the forest, and staring into Marsh Valley.

Without thinking, a few deer became so excited at seeing water they ran and dived straight in, jumping and prancing around.

"Stop that now!" commanded Deeron. "Return to order at once. Somewhere around here lies Smolder's Castle, and he is bound to be watching us." The deer obeyed immediately, and looked rather ashamed at having behaved so naively. Deeron turned to Emily and Jen.

"Now, the plan is that we lure Smolder and his army out into the valley," he explained, "so that the two of you can enter his castle unseen. After you've danced, go with the magic stags to Fox's Drift where you should all be safe from harm. Tamhorn knows the way and the castle is near there, although you'll have to find the entrance to it yourselves."

"So how do we do that?" asked Jen, with a mild look of dread.

"Look for a pile of white stones," he explained, "for they mark an underground entrance. They'll probably be covered over with bracken and leaves by now, but you should soon..." He stopped, realizing that Emily and Jen were both staring at eachother in astonishment. "What's the matter?" he asked, sounding concerned.

"Oh... nothing," replied Emily dismissively, trying to sound as though she meant it. "It's just reminded us of something, that's all. A pile of white stones - got it."

Deeron hadn't the time to probe any further their behaviour, even if he'd wanted to. "The antlers are in a chamber some-where underground," he continued, "so you'll have to use your powers to find them. If anything goes wrong..." he hesitated, "... I mean, just in case, return to the Hall as quickly as you can. Tell the deer there to leave the forest immediately and elect a new leader. You two must return to the clearing where we first met, and wait for the golden hand to appear. You will both then be returned to your own world. It has all been arranged. If Smolder manages to take our magic stags..."

He paused to observe the loyal Hay, the comical Fole and Folly, and the courageous Blythe, Leif and Tamhorn. Gathered around them were all the brave does and stags that had also fought loyally in his army. Failure was just too awful a scenario to contemplate, forcing Deeron to leave his last comment unfinished.

"So Wandiacates," he resumed his official, businesslike manner. "It is now time for you to dance."

"Oh heck," whispered Emily.

All was still. The army had spread out to form a large surrounding circle, while all eyes gazed hopefully upon them, waiting for the magical and amazing dance to begin.

"What if it doesn't work?" asked Jen, self-doubt now clearly etched upon her face.

"Dance, Jen. Just dance," replied Deeron, soothingly.

Emily knew it was down to her to take the lead, but felt glued to the spot. Even though she'd danced in front of others and on stage many times before, this was a terrible ordeal to overcome. She felt incredibly vulnerable, standing there with all eyes and expectations placed upon her shoulders. Luckily, Jen had an idea and began beckoning to the deer encircling them.

"Dance with us!" she pleaded. The deer looked initially confused, returning puzzled looks both to each other and to Deeron. Their leader simply smiled his approval, and the deer obligingly began to sway their heads. Arog then began to sing.

"Dance, dance for Deeron,
Dance like the Deer,
Wake our forest from her slumber.
Fill our hearts for evermore,
With the joy your dance will conjure."

Emily picked up the rhythm of the song and swayed along with the deer, letting her arms take her from side to side. She closed her eyes, and tried to use her imagination. She pictured herself in a beautiful long dress made from golden silk, and imagined an audience smiling in admiration.

"Dance-now-Emily, dance-now-Jen." The army began chanting an accompaniment to emphasize a more intricate, underlying rhythm - *bee-dum-bee-dee-dum, bee-dum-bee-dee-dum* - as Arog kept repeating the words. Emily danced with all her heart, using every muscle in her body. She turned, twisted, glided and jumped. This, she knew, was the most important performance of her life. She reached out her hands to Jen and they skipped together, round and around, within the circle of stags. Bill pushed his way through the deer to join them both in the centre, and playfully ran along behind.

Hay, Leif, Tamhorn, Fole, Folly and Blythe then combined to make an inner circle of magic stags around the dancers, while Arog, Fauld and Deeron remained with the army in the outer circle. Then, both circles began to rotate - the outer going anti-clockwise, while the inner rotated clockwise. As they turned, the deer stomped the ground with their hooves - *stomp-stomp-stomp-stomp* - now stressing the 4/4 time signature. Golden light appeared all around them, rapidly growing in strength as both girls' dancing developed, expanded and evolved.

Very soon, the scene had become a kaleidoscope of magic, dance, music and light. The combined sound of stomping hooves, rhythmic chant, song and movement penetrated far into Marsh Valley ahead of them, and Bagot Wood behind. The immediate area around them was also now becoming bathed in a sea of piercing golden light with Emily, Jen and Bill at the very centre of it.

BANG! Suddenly, a streak of white light shot down from out of the sky. It hit the ground dead centre within the inner circle like a missile, causing Jen, Emily and Bill to be literally blown off their feet. The magic stags, although unharmed, had stopped moving. They stood momentarily shell-shocked from the blast, appearing unsure as to what to do next.

"Keep moving!" yelled Deeron from behind them.

Emily pushed herself up slowly, trying to assess her body for injuries. As she got onto her knees, a noise like a low-pitched whooshing sound directly above her head distracted her. She looked up and saw, spinning just above her head and within the inner circle's radius, a kind of frosty-white mesh or huge cobweb! It was checked with millions of tiny square holes like fishing net, and at each corner there was tied a large block of ice. It spun low and fast; so low that it prevented either her or Jen from getting back up onto her feet. Emily instinctively fell back down onto her front, suddenly aware that being hit by one of those blocks would be the end of her.

Quick-thinking Bill had already crawled out from under its span, and was making his way towards the outer circle that was still moving. The magic stags had by now regrouped and were starting to rotate again, but movement was at best haphazard due to the ice blocks spinning fast and close, directly at a stag's head-height! Jen very slowly was following Bill's example by crawling on her front towards the edge of the circle, and hopefully out from under the reach of the net.

Thud! The four ice blocks suddenly smashed into the ground, pinning Jen and Emily to the floor underneath the icy mesh. They could barely move their heads enough to then see both circles of rotating stags, lifted up off the ground! In seconds, Deeron's entire army was several metres above the forest floor, and still spinning! Worse still, they were speeding up. The kaleidoscope of magic had become a carousel of hell, as it spun round ever faster and completely out of control. Emily was desperately trying to pick at the frost net ensnaring both her and Jen, but each thread was as sharp as razor wire. They could only look on in dread as their friends endured unimaginable horror under the power of the white light.

After perhaps thirty seconds, the spinning suddenly stopped very abruptly, as though an emergency brake had been applied. The deer in each circle shunted hard up against one another, and momentarily were left just hanging above ground. Dazed, giddy and confused, they all looked fearfully down at the forest floor, and the distance between them and it. Before they even had time to contemplate what fresh misery could possibly befall them next, whatever it was that had them suspended in mid air, promptly vanished!

Terrified screams rang out as the deer one by one, like a collapsing circle of dominoes, plummeted towards the hard barren earth. A thud like an earth tremor shook the land as both Deeron and Arog hit the ground last of all. Jen gasped in alarm, and both girls anxiously scanned the devastation for signs that the deer were okay. They could see shocked and injured faces looking up at one another, and then gazing around with frightened eyes as a shrill howling laughter filled the air.

"We have *got* to get out of this net!" Emily began kicking the razor-sharp icy mesh trapping both her and Jen in an outburst of fiery rage, as her emotions finally boiled over. She felt anger, concern, powerlessness and fear, all rolled into one. Her desperation to help the deer was paramount, but her desire to show her utter revulsion for Smolder Bagot came a very close second.

"Do you really think you can beat me, Deeron?" A voluminous, hissing voice radiated from somewhere along the valley. "Well you can't! Not now, not EVER!" Deeron was busy seeing to many of the stags' injuries that had been sustained from the fall, and confirming just as Fauld had reported, that the magic stags were indeed mostly unharmed. He barely bothered to even listen to Smolder's latest rant.

"Break, damn you! Break!" Emily was really giving the frost net what for now, by trying to wrench it apart with both feet. Jen had also joined in with the somewhat rash and brutal approach adopted by Emily. Fortunately, it was beginning to pay off as parts of the surrounding mesh fractured and crumbled, with larger chunks even breaking off in places. Both girls' legs were strong from all the walking and dancing they'd been doing, and Emily especially had become more and more incensed by their capture.

After some more prolonged pulling, twisting and striking - *Boof!* The frost net shattered! Billions of shards of ice exploded dramatically into the air and scattered themselves into the wind, over both the girls and the surrounding area.

The ground shook again, harder than before. This time it was like a full-blown earthquake! Dark thunderclouds rolled about menacingly above, while fork lightning slashed from east to west, right across the sky. Everyone at this point held their breath as they waited to see what terrible punishment was next to be unleashed against them.

"Dance again," called Deeron to them. "It's our only hope. Dance again, you must." Emily and Jen, both covered in splinters of ice, were now back on their feet. Emily picked up two dead branches from the floor and gave one to Jen.

"Copy me!" she yelled, above the din of thunder and lightning, wind and earth tremors. Emily held her branch up to her head as an imitation antler, and began to turn on the spot, rising up onto her toes and then sinking down to the ground.

The injured deer, encouraged by her bravery, started to sing again. The magic stags, some of whom were limping and still dazed, quickly reformed their circle around the two girls and began slowly to rotate. The dance was alive once more! Emily swayed, turned and spiralled, creating her own choreography whilst letting the dance conjure its own special magic. She jumped high into the air, landing softly through her feet. Gaining confidence, she even managed to pirouette across the desolate, lifeless earth. Jen copied what she could, while Bill came out from the bush he'd been hiding under and leapt repeatedly, high into the air.

"Hahaaaaah!" the piercing voice yelled again. "Want a partner to dance with? Then dance with this!"

A stag's head suddenly flashed abruptly and dramatically into view, directly in front of them and right inside the magic stags' circle! Probably ten times the size of a normal head, it hovered just above the ground and appeared to be made of ice. This was no soft and friendly image either, like the one they had met before by the lake. This stag snarled and growled like a rabid attacking dog, while it flashed huge pointed teeth that more closely resembled stalactites in a dank cave. Its enormous mouth opened so wide that at one point, all Emily and Jen could see was a white tunnel leading to a set of icy tonsils. Both girls thought they were about to be eaten!

"No!" screamed Emily, backing away and then colliding with the magic stags' surrounding circle.

"Get lost!" yelled Jen, jabbing her branch into the gaping mouth. Instantly, the ice stag grabbed her stick in its teeth, chewed and then spat out wood chips onto the floor, right at Emily's feet. It was all too alarmingly clear that Emily was the one in most danger now, as the head manoeuvred itself between her and Jen, and leered ever closer. Emily was stuck, and had nowhere to go!

"Dance, dance for Deeron,
Dance like the Deer,"

The deer sang on, as the largely rebuilt outer circle now also began to turn. Bill, displaying a great deal more courage than he had with the frost net, began jumping up from behind and biting at the ice stag. The stag lashed out with its huge frost-white antlers, fending off Bill's attacks with apparent ease. Jen also tried jabbing at it again, this time with Emily's branch that she'd dropped. Both showed incredible daring, trying repeatedly to divert the ice stag's attention onto themselves and afford Emily some means of escape. But it was hopeless; this thing could see everywhere!

While all this had been going on, something else was occurring on the forest floor, right beneath their feet. Although some of the billions of fragments of ice from the exploding frost net had melted while others still blew around, many had remained hold of whatever it was they'd landed on. The melted ones, instead of disappearing, were running together as tiny water flows forming puddles. The puddles then ran together to form larger ones, all the time moving closer towards Emily and the lecherous ice stag. Jen suddenly saw tiny things jumping about at her feet.

"Eurgh!" Jen had a serious dislike for anything flea-like, and began frantically trying to beat them away with her stick, whilst Bill continued to take potshots at the ice stag. Jen soon realized that it was the ice particles that were moving and that, curiously, they were bouncing off of and away from her and towards Emily. Flakes on the ground and those still flying about in the air, all suddenly amassed together and converged upon her!

For Emily, it was like having her very own personal snowstorm. In moments she was covered from head to foot, and yet still they kept coming! The melted puddles had by now all gathered around her feet, and frozen solid again. Emily was not only being covered in ice now, she was also becoming entombed!

As if this weren't enough, the ice stag's head then appeared to turn itself inside out! A giant tongue flew out of the stag's mouth, whereupon the ice stag seemed to morph into more of the same, engulfing itself completely! Suddenly, all anybody could see was a giant tongue poised over Emily, trapped in a frost-bound version of a birdcage.

The tongue lassoed the top of Emily's enclosure, and flung it high into the air! Emily closed her eyes as she shot upwards at terrific speed, far faster than anything she'd experienced before. Then, after a few seconds, the speed levelled off. She opened her eyes again, but could do nothing other than gaze down in abject horror at the image far below her. The deer, Jen and Bill were now tiny miniscule dots. In barely a few more moments, she could hear and see nothing.

Albus Carcum

After a time, Emily's eyes registered a brilliant white light. She tried to judge how long it had been since she last saw Deeron, Jen and the others disappear into the distance. She couldn't be sure. She wasn't sure either whether she'd been awake, asleep or even unconscious during that unknown period. In fact, she didn't even know whether or not she was still inside that infernal ice cage. One thing was certain, however; Emily was petrified. This was not being helped by the fact that all she could see was white - no perspective, no definition, no distance - just pure white.

She felt herself spinning, as though she were dangling on the end of a long thread, like an insect caught in a spider's trap. Emily was feeling bad enough from all the cold and flying motion she'd just had to endure. This new mental picture of her predicament was far from useful, so she decided that it would be best not to think of anything remotely to do with spiders right now. She wondered instead where on earth - if that was the right expression to use - she was.

Suddenly, Emily's stomach rammed upwards, into her chest. Inextricably, she went from feeling just bad to abysmal, *seriously* abysmal. But wait… was she falling? Was she? How could she be sure? After all, the only thing telling her anything right now was her stomach. She could see no movement nor, really, feel…

BOOF! Emily hit something, hard. It was probably a good thing that she hadn't seen it coming as her body was quite relaxed, so she'd instinctively crumpled up and rolled on impact. She took it all rather well really, given the circumstances.

"OW!! Ooh, my… What…" Emily, a crashed heap buried underneath a cloak of golden leaves, moved slowly onto her front, just enough to tell her that, well, things could probably have been much worse. So far as she could tell, she still had two arms, two legs and most of the rest, but her stomach was going to have to get back to her later. Also, she'd bumped her head somehow, so decided to just hold still for a moment and allow the pain and dizziness to subside. Whilst waiting, other impressions of her surroundings were being assessed:

1) She was on solid ground, once more.

2) She could, sort of, see again.

3) This place was cold, and windy - intensely windy.

"Oh, my head!" With the effects of the fall now slowly receding, Emily moved a cautious hand up to examine her bruised and battered skull. A sizeable bump was there all right and no mistake, but all in all Emily thought she'd been astonishingly lucky. With her returning faculties registering ever-plummeting degrees of cold and a noisy buffeting wind, Emily lifted the rim of her hood to peer out from underneath the mound of cloak, Wandiacate and ice.

A violent blast of searing, sub-zero air hit Emily squarely in the face. Its penetration was colossal; this wind felt as though it would freeze instantly anything in its path! She ducked down beneath her cloak again, just as fast as she possibly could.

"This is ludicrous!" she said aghast and out loud, as she huddled tightly underneath her cloak. "I'm in the Arctic! I am actually *in* the Arctic! How am I supposed to get anywhere here?" A sharp, piercing sense of loneliness and fear grabbed her consciousness. After all she'd been through, was this how everything was going to end?

Something began happening to Emily's cloak of golden leaves, right on top of her. The leaves were beginning to glow and, better yet, give off heat. The effect began slowly, but quickly spread to involve every single leaf on the cloak. As each leaf was interwoven and multilayered, its defence from the outside freeze was felt, by Emily anyway, to be almost instant. It was as though someone had plugged the cloak into a mains socket, and just like an electric blanket, it was simply warming up.

"Golden light-threads!" Emily shrieked with joy, still crouched beneath the cloak. "Am I glad to see you!" She couldn't actually see the threads, but could feel the very same energy and goodness that both she and Jen had sensed on their many encounters with them. Emily felt relief beyond words that something, anything, was there with her to help protect and hopefully guide her in this ice-aged arctic wilderness. And actually, it was now really rather snug under there.

With restored vigour, Emily's thoughts returned to the battle against Smolder, and the fact that she must somehow facedown whatever ordeal lay beyond. Slowly, she manoeuvred herself up onto her feet, maintaining a tight hold of the inner edges of the cloak. As she arose, Emily wrapped the cloak closely around her body, keeping her head bowed low. By now, she could both feel and hear the full force of the air bashing against her small frame. It was like standing in the path of a wintry hurricane! She could even see the wind rushing past her, containing as it did millions of particles of ice and snow whipped up along the way. Emily struggled hard to retain her footing, as she was buffeted on all sides.

The heat and light from the cloak suddenly increased manyfold; so much so in fact, that it penetrated right through the garment to the outside. A bright warm golden glow radiated all over Emily, illuminating her like a beacon. The physical effect of this was no less dramatic either, as she noticed air currents veer sideways and around her. The golden light seemed to be fighting back by somehow altering Emily's aerodynamic shape. The cold she could also barely feel now, while the noise of the wind had dropped significantly.

It reminded her of when she'd travelled before by car on a cold stormy day - she'd known the wind was there, but personally couldn't feel it. For the first time, Emily felt as though she could at last stand up properly.

Standing upright, Emily surveyed the landscape. A vast open icy plane stretched out ahead, to either side, and behind her. Barren, desolate and empty. Wind and ice. No ridges, slopes nor snow-capped peaks. Just flat, white, empty infinity. Desolation, in its purest form.

Emily stood for a while, simply trying to take in and deal rationally with this latest and extreme incarnation of Smolder's evilness. Where should she go? Should she walk forward, or backwards? Should she go anywhere? Was there even such a thing as direction here? Where is here? Emily quickly decided that these questions weren't going to achieve anything, except to probably confuse her and undoubtedly depress her. So, she decided to walk; not along any particular route, just walk. She wrapped the cloak tightly around herself to feel its warm golden glow - without it, she knew, she'd be finished in seconds.

After a while, Emily stopped walking. She'd just remembered something. Things had only ever changed after she'd danced. Not always for the better, mind - rarely, in fact - but it had changed. So, why not try it now? Besides, short of losing her cloak of golden leaves, she really couldn't see how her situation could get much worse than it was already.

Placing a few cautious steps, Emily tried to feel her way back into dance. This was far from easy, given her circumstance and location. For one thing, she felt severely restricted by the fact that she couldn't use her arms, due to there simply being no way that she was going to release her grip on the inside of the cloak; less still, poke her arms out from underneath it! Hence, things got off to a leisurely start.

Emily decided that it might be better to try dancing a jig, or maybe tap dance, than stick only with ballet. She didn't know much of either, however, having only seen Irish folk dance on TV, and barely mastered even the basics of tap. However, 'practise pays' was her ballet teacher's favourite saying, and so...

Emily, alone in an arctic wasteland and lit up like a lighthouse, slowly began to dance.

"1-2-3, 2-2-3, 3-2..." Emily counted out time for herself, whilst trying to recreate something she'd done in a tap dance class a few years before. Although stumbling in places, she persisted in trying all the time to become more fluid and consistent in her rhythm. She concentrated hard but found the going pretty tough, especially since her feet felt like blocks of ice. Also, the air currents, though now considerably less, were still powerful enough to veer her off balance. Regardless, Emily persevered and actually began to find the whole thing rather enjoyable. She'd never before even considered the possibility that tap dance could be fun. If nothing else, it took her mind off the reality of her situation.

Emily had become so absorbed, she hadn't noticed a sound being carried in the wind. It was light at first, and what with her hood being up plus the golden light protection, barely detectable anyway. It was getting louder though, and probably nearer.

"Tir-na-no'g, Tir-na-nana..."

Emily suddenly stopped dead. The sound was very close now, and unmistakable. It was a choir, singing! Emily was excited beyond words.

"HEY! I'M OVER HERE! HELP!" She looked round, in all directions. Nothing. The choir and phrase continued.

"Tir-na-no'g, Tir-na-no'g..."

"HELP! OVER HERE! HELP! WHERE ARE YOU?" This was awful! She could hear beautiful angelic voices, but see absolutely nothing other than this blasted empty, worthless, freezing hellho…

"Hello Emily."

Emily almost collapsed to the ground in shock. A voice - a woman's voice - spoken so near, as if to come from directly in front of her, but with no person there. And so… pure.

"Er… hello. Who are you?"

"I am Deity." Emily knew that name. Deity? Of course! Deity, Goddess of the forest! Deeron had spoken of her early on when they'd first met, and how her capture was why the forest was forever locked in autumn, and slowly but surely dying.

"Deity! It's so great to hear you." Emily suddenly felt rather humbled to meet a goddess no less. "Are you alright… I mean, harmed?"

"I am as well as can be expected, thank you," the voice replied. "My powers are low, and I so ache to return to my forest. Your being here brings me such joy, however. To have come through what you have, and to make it here alive; you offer us much hope, Emily."

After all the loneliness, cold, fear and self-doubt, Emily felt a modest surge of pride. She wasn't going to let it get the better of her though, and quickly returned to the subject in hand.

"Er, do you know where 'here' is?" she asked.

"You are in Albus Carcum," replied Deity, "or 'white prison'. This is the land of the White Light of Evil, and the ultimate force behind Smolder Bagot. It is here that the lost souls are imprisoned, and like slaves are condemned to help whoever is decreed to further evil throughout our worlds."

Emily, of course, knew only too well about the lost souls and their frozen faces. She'd seen them, been attacked by them, and had nearly even been eaten by one of them. She

shuddered at the thought of those experiences, but was curious
to know more about the White Light of Evil though.

"How can this White Light of Evil force a soul to do
anything?" she asked.

"A soul is only truly free when either it is pared to a naturally
chosen material being, or it evolves and sheds forever its
physical form," replied Deity. "At any other time it is in *fluxus*,
or unsure as to its destiny. Part of my role as forest keeper
involves guiding upon death the souls of animals, trees and
plants towards their future path. By abducting me, the White
Light of Evil can easily capture *fluxus* souls. Once caught, a
face is embodied in stone and ice in Wandiacatum, imprisoning
each one completely. With command over their energy, they
are then compelled to fight against good in the never-ending
battle that rages constantly throughout Wandiacatum. Good
is converted to evil, right converted to wrong, generosity
converted to greed. The power that is generated goes to
Smolder, and as more forest dies and more souls are captured,
evermore energy is harnessed to generate evermore of the
same. It becomes a self-fulfilling cycle of annihilation..."
Deity's voice trailed off, becoming suddenly distant.

The pause gave Emily a chance to try and absorb some of
what had just been said.

"So," she stammered slightly, "the faces in Wandiacatum
didn't really want to attack us, but were forced to by the White
Light of Evil in order to help Smolder, right?"

"Yes," replied Deity. "The souls have no control over
anything they do anymore. That is why they appear so
tormented and traumatized."

"But that's terrible!" Emily felt awful. She'd always
assumed that the frozen heads were just as cruel as Smolder
was himself. She hadn't even considered that they might be
being controlled against their will.

"What about you, Deity? Does the White Light of Evil have
a hold over you?" Although this was a serious question, Emily
didn't have the slightest doubt over Deity's integrity.

"No, Emily," she replied. "My soul can never be captured, because it resides in so many different places. I only ended up here because I failed to see behind Smolder's black magic and deceit. In the forest, such treachery is unthinkable."

"But if your soul isn't trapped, why can't you escape?"

"My powers are so weak here, and I cannot conjure any golden light for no goodness exists anywhere. Albus Carcum is evil immortalized in ice. It is the sum of all worst places, and a land from which escape at this moment is impossible."

"Great. So how does me being here help anything?" Emily's voice contained more than a hint of concern.

"Because you *can* escape," replied Deity, sounding upbeat once more. "You possess far more Chiron than Deeron or myself had ever dared to imagine. You see, Emily, you should not be here in Albus Carcum. Even Smolder cannot survive this place, and I am certain he would not have wanted you here, beyond his reach and with every chance that I might find you. Yet, you are here and alive. What is more, you have brought with you into this land of evil the Golden Light of Goodness. That is so important, for it means that you not only summon the golden light from your dance, you also carry it within yourself. It protects you, and will guide you ahead. You, Emily, have the means to defeat Smolder."

"Oh," was all Emily could think of to say, lost deep as she was in her own thoughts. She'd wondered off and on about this whole Wandiacate-thing quite a bit. Ever since, in fact, Deeron had first told both her and Jen that they had it, whatever 'it' was exactly. She knew, of course, about this Chiron - well, sort of - but had something now changed? Did she possess more Chiron than normal, assuming there was a 'normal'? Was she now basically invincible, and regardless of what Smolder subjected them to, safe from harm? This scenario hardly concurred with these past days, where she'd encountered pretty much every negative feature life had had to throw at her. Emily felt far from indestructible, that was for sure. And what about Jen? Does she carry the light with her as well?

"Okay," Emily tried to summarize her thoughts. "I have the golden light with me, and that's great 'cause I wouldn't last a minute in this deathzone without it. But, what's changed? I mean, can I just walk into Smolder's Castle, grab the antlers, walk back out, find Deeron and then go home?"

"Sadly no," replied Deity. "Nothing has altered as drastically as that. You face an opponent every bit as formidable and wicked today as he was yesterday. There are many obstacles left in your path, and much danger also. Your journey will most likely become more treacherous from now on, as Smolder will undoubtedly find out about your visit here, and your meeting with me. This will anger him greatly, and he will seek to exact revenge upon us both. "

"Wonderful." Emily sighed away her sarcastic remark, as waves of frustration and disappointment swept over her. In all fairness, to be standing alone as she was in an arctic desert and be told that things were about to get worse, would test even the most stubborn of characters.

"So what's the big deal about me being here, then? That I can survive it?"

"Well, survival is certainly one part of it," replied Deity, sounding like her mum in one of their 'but-life-isn't-fair' discussions. "However, let me show you something else."

A large, wide-angled and golden-coloured block of light suddenly shot upwards out of the glacial ground, barely a few metres in front of Emily.

"Wow!" exclaimed Emily, almost literally bowled over. "Hey, that's impressive!"

"You see, Emily, because you have brought into Albus Carcum the golden light, I am now able to use some of my powers again."

As Emily's eyes adapted to the radiance, she began to make out moving images inside the light. It was rather like a projector beam in a cinema, except this was way more powerful. The fact that there was no screen seemed not to matter one jot, as the images shone crystal-clear. To Emily, the image looked as though it were three-dimensional, rather like a hologram. She could suddenly see an image of a tree lined and muddy slope, falling away to meet a valley below. Down in the valley, a battle between two opposing armies was raging. Emily could just about identify antlers, goats and deer.

"What *is* this?" Anxiety was now evident in Emily's voice.

"You are watching the battle between Deeron and Smolder begin."

"Oh no! But I have to be there, to help them!"

"No, Emily," replied Deity, firmly. "Your task is to retrieve the magic antlers before the next Horn Dance, and return them to whom they belong. You cannot become involved in this battle. Deeron and his army will manage. You must take advantage of Smolder's distraction and enter his castle at the earliest opportunity. Time is running out."

"But where's Jen, and Bill?"

"They are safe, and waiting for you near the castle's entrance." Another image appeared alongside the battle scene, of a girl and a dog sat by a tree in autumnal woodland.

"Oh, thank heavens!" Emily was at least relieved to see them again, apparently nowhere near the fighting. "All right, Deity," she sighed, as if having reached an agonizing compromise. "So how do I get there?"

"Dance into the light, Emily, and I will take you to them."

With her mind now refocused entirely upon the task set ahead, Emily simply did as she was told and danced straight in. No buts, what-ifs, or how-do-I-do's passed from her lips. She even appeared to forget where she was, as she threw back her cloak and performed a first-rate pirouette into the holographic beam. It mattered little, for she left Albus Carcum just as she had entered it - in an instant.

Smolder's Castle

*Th*ud!

"Shush! What was that?"

"Ooh! Pff…" *Rustle.*

"No, stay! Good boy, good… Bill, stay!" Pulling for all his might against Jen's manic grip around his collar, Bill excitedly sniffed the cool dusky air. The long yawning shadows of the forest were finally giving way to the onset of darkness, and an eerie stillness of night. Jen was crouched down behind a tree at Fox's Drift, trying desperately hard not to conjure up in her mind the ten worst possible things ever that could, and probably were, right behind her and just down the slope, making all those muffled moaning noises.

"Hmm… pfff… pffooh!" *Rustle-rustle.*

"Ooer, I don't… No, Bill! Bill!" Curiosity, having decidedly got the better of Bill, coincidentally made a mockery of Jen's frankly lax dog-control skills. Now free from her grasp, Bill sped off down the bank in hot pursuit of whatever it was that lurked there. Jen stayed firmly huddled behind her tree, cursing under her breath about Bill's indiscipline, in-between wondering for all the world what she was doing there, what she was going to do, and where on earth Emily was. More rustling, sniffing and various assortments of groaning noises ensued. Then, barking.

"Woof!"

"Bill!" commanded Jen through clenched, angry teeth. But… that was odd. She'd just called him yet heard the same word, albeit muted, coming from behind her at the same time, like some freaky echo effect. "You don't get echo in forests!" she thought to herself, so decided to try again.

"Bill!"

"Woof! Woof!"

"Jen! Pffooh, pffeurgh!"

"Who's there?" Jen was wary, in case it was Smolder or one of his minions, trying to trick her. Besides, who else would say something like 'pffooh' a lot?

"It's… pffooh…peurgh! It's me! Jen!"

"Emily?"

"Woof!"

"Yes…pffh… help!"

Her concerns instantly forgotten, Jen climbed out from behind her tree and clambered down the bank. She quickly caught sight of Bill, with his head buried inside a huge mound of leaves, bracken and twigs. He was whining and digging ferociously.

"Em? Are you in there?" called Jen, rather nonplussed at the situation in front of her, as she regardless began shifting dead foliage alongside Bill.

"Pff… yes!" came a stifled reply.

"Hang on!" Jen worked urgently now, recklessly rummaging and throwing aside great clusters of leaves, and whatever else stood in their way. The heap was massive, and Jen knew that they had to find Emily as quickly as possible, as she was certainly to be short of air. Jen and Bill knew only too well what being buried was like; both had barely survived the earlier pine needles incident in the forest.

"Em? Emily!" hollered Jen, repeatedly. No reply. Pile after pile of foliage was scooped up, scraped away and thrown behind. More calling. Still, no answer. Then, at last, Bill found a wrist.

"Woof!" Bill grabbed the wrist in his mouth, and proceeded to drag out an arm. Jen, alerted by his bark, grabbed the attached hand.

"Pull, Bill! Pull!" There was no time to worry about how this might be feeling at the other end of the arm. They just both pulled, for all their worth. Very soon, Emily's head appeared, and then her upper body. Grabbing both arms, Jen managed to finally pull her clear of the stack that by now was dangerously close to collapsing back on top of them.

Emily lay on the ground, motionless and with her eyes closed. Before Jen could even react or try to revive her, Bill purposefully barged past and rapidly began licking Emily's face. Quite dramatically, Emily suddenly sprang into life.

"Pfff… pffOOH… PFFFEURGH!" Emily sneezed, gasped and coughed all at the same time, propelling clouds of twig, dust and leaf forward, most of it straight into Jen's face.

"Charming," was all Jen could think of to say as she disgustedly picked bits off her, as though each one were contagious.

"Thorr… ATTCHOOO!" Emily sat up panting desperately, trying to get air into her lungs. After a few moments, her breathing lightened enough for her to speak, sort of. "Eurgh-yuck! Thorry, Jen. By wreckon I've shwallowed half that bompost hea… ATTCHOOO!"

Jen supplied a much-needed tissue. "If that was an apology, I forgive you," she joked. "You're alive, otherwise… Anyway, what were you doing in there, and where have you been all this time? You've been gone all day!"

"Balbus Park… ATTCHOOO! Yeurgh! Bits-up-by-nose! Pffeurgh!" Emily repeatedly blew her nose, while attempting to clear bits of twig and leaf from her face and hair.

"What park?" Jen by now had taken off her cloak and was shaking it ferociously, convinced there wa a spider, or some such other 'thing', inside it. Bill had already super-shaken himself well and truly clean, and was now enjoying a well-earned scratch on top of receiving congratulatory pats from Jen, who was privately feeling daft for having doubted his actions.

Emily stood up, her airways at least clear again. She stared at her dishevelled form in utter dismay. "Look at me, I'm filthy! Why did she have to dump me in there?"

"Who?"

Emily began prodding about her waist, looking for her liquid carrier. "Jen, have you got any water? I must have lost mine in the Arctic."

"Sure, here." Now completely baffled, Jen passed Emily her bottle. "Look, Emily, what's been going on? What's all this about the Arctic now? And where's this Albert's what's-his-name's park?"

"Albus," corrected Emily, as she swallowed large gulps of water, spilling some over her face to try and clean off the remnants of debris. "Albus Carcum, it means 'white prison'. It's where Deity is being held."

"How do you know that?" Jen's eyes suddenly lit up with interest, having at last heard a name she recognized. "Did you see her?"

"Not exactly, no," Emily took another swig of water. "I did meet her, though. Very nice person-er-ality, and mega helpful. I wouldn't be here without her, actually." Emily glanced a rather disappointed look over to the semi-dismantled leaf stack. "Bit of a let down to have been dumped in there, though. S'pose she thought it was the softest option…" Her voice trailed off, as she consumed yet more water.

"Look, I'm not getting any of this!" Jen was becoming quite cross at Emily's lack of a coherent explanation.

"There's no time to explain it all now, Jen," said Emily calmly, still dusting herself down. "With Deeron and the others hopefully keeping Smolder busy, we've got to enter his castle as soon as we can…" she briefly paused, looking around her. "I thought Tamhorn and the other magic stags were supposed to be with you," she said, staring intently at Jen. "Where are they?"

"Oh," came a deflated reply, as Jen recalled the events of her day. "Fauld came to get them, as they were needed for something at Marsh Valley. They wouldn't tell me what for, but it couldn't have been anything good for Deeron to have to risk putting them so close to Smolder."

"No," sighed Emily, remembering all she'd seen in Albus Carcum. "So we've got to hurry, as this could be our only chance to sneak inside and get the antlers."

Jen still had a multitude of unanswered questions, but thought better of asking them. "Okay," she replied, "so how do we find it?"

"Well, in our dream Martha showed us the castle by taking us to a sunken glade. I guess we should try and find that again."

"But that could be anywhere!"

"Deity said you were close to the entrance, so we can't be far. Come on."

"Whatever," she sighed, following along behind.

Emily led the way back up the bank, and past the spot where Jen had concealed herself only minutes before. They followed a narrow path through tall pine trees, and over ground covered by large thick tree roots. Bill bounded off ahead as usual, sniffing intently for any discernable scent. Both girls repeatedly stumbled, as it was hard to watch out for the roots and navigate their way. Night was well and truly upon them now, with only a slow-rising, tired and dull old moon for any illumination. As darkness fell, so too did a layer of silken mist likewise descend, gathering at waist height as it meandered in between the high trees.

Emily kept thinking about Deeron and all the stags and does, and what they must be going through. Were they hurt? Were any dead? It was all too awful to contemplate. She couldn't talk to Jen about it, as she didn't want to worry her; and besides, it would simply take too long just explaining how she knew. Emily resolved to herself that she must concentrate only upon her and Jen's role in all this, and find the castle as fast as possible. Failure was simply not an option.

Thump!

Emily spun round quickly, to see Jen lying spread-eagled and face down on the ground.

"Ow! Blast these roots!"

"You all right, Jen?" asked Emily walking over, and helping her back onto her feet.

"Oh, I'll survive... probably," replied Jen, angrily.

Emily suddenly gazed about at their surroundings, as if startled by something. "The castle's here," she said.

"Hey? Where? I don't see anything." Jen likewise scanned the area as she tried to soothe the discomfort in her ankle by rubbing it. It all looked the same as ever. Aside from the fact that it was dying, the forest looked like a typical autumnal woodland landscape really.

"I don't see anything either, but somehow I know it's here."

The pain in her ankle distracted Jen. It wasn't reducing as per normal, and she began to wonder if it was going to be a problem to walk on. Bill had returned to investigate the commotion and was now sniffing it suspiciously, making her even more concerned. Carefully, she lowered her foot to the ground, and cautiously placed some weight upon it.

"Oh great, it still hurts!" Jen let out a long, exasperated, and frankly rather melodramatic sigh. "Now what?"

"Look!" Emily pointed to a spot, directly up ahead of them. In between some trees, the moonlight appeared to shimmer in the mist, rippling out repeatedly just like a pebble dropped in water. As the ripples and vapour dissolved, the light revealed a gigantic, tall and ugly wooden wall.

"Smolder's Castle!" they both said together, their eyes transfixed upon the image-within-an-image in front of them.

"This is really freaky," said Emily, excitedly. "Like some kind of... mirror fog. It must have been you sighing, Jen. That must've allowed us to see behind it."

"Wow," said Jen, initially underwhelmed, as she pondered on its significance for a moment. After a few seconds, she added, "Hey that's really cool, I never knew I could do that!" Jen had come to the conclusion that this was pretty impressive stuff.

"Sigh again or blow or something, Jen, and let's see if we can find the hatch." Emily decided to encourage Jen's new found talent, as having her sounding upbeat again was definitely preferable to her being a mope.

"What are we looking for?" she asked, blowing close to the area where the wall had appeared. Her ankle injury was quickly forgotten.

"A pile of white stones," replied Emily, "covered with bracken or leaves, probably."

Both girls scrutinized the scene for anything that looked vaguely familiar. Although Deeron had reminded them - to their great surprise - about the white stones, the rest had still been just a dream, albeit a shared one. Trying to remember the finer details of it, especially after the days and events that had since passed, was proving to be a real challenge for both of them.

Jen pursued the line of the fortressed wall. Repeatedly, she would exhale air and wait for the ripple effect to subside, then examine the scene and move on. If she thought avoiding the roots was bad, that was a picnic compared to this. In effect, they were trying to negotiate two different places at once, not really sure of which one they were actually in, at any one time. It was a bit like having to find your way across a busy street whilst simultaneously walking through woodland. All done, of course, in the dead of night.

"Ooh, the ripples really hurt your eyes!" Emily averted her gaze, as she was starting to feel quite dizzy.

"It's here!" whispered Jen, catching sight of the stack of stones just up ahead, partially obscured by bracken. They moved closer, and both agreed that it was what they had seen in the dream. Emily crouched down and began removing the bracken and stones, ably assisted by Bill. Jen hovered about nearby, apparently pondering something.

"What if Smolder's in there though, Em? We're not in a dreamworld now, and we know he wants to capture us. He could even kill us."

"We have to try and get the antlers back Jen, especially as we've come this far. Besides, I'm sure he's kind of busy right now."

"But how can you know?"

Emily stopped what she was doing and stood up. "Look, Deity showed me Deeron and the others, facing Smolder's army…"

"But we should be helping them surely, because…"

"No, Jen," replied Emily, firmly. "We must stick to the plan, otherwise we'll miss the Horn Dance, and Smolder will win whatever happens. You have to see the bigger picture here. This fight isn't just about Deeron and the magic stags; it's about everything you see. The forest, trees, plants and wildlife will all die if we fail. So we mustn't fail, and we won't, but we need to keep faith; in ourselves, in Deeron and in Deity."

"Deity? But how's she going to help?"

"I don't know yet, but she said that some of her powers had been returned to her and I'm sure she'll help. Trust me."

Jen thought it all through for a minute. She still didn't like it, but right now at that time and in that place, what was the alternative? Even if she had wanted to turn around and return home, Jen hadn't the first idea of how to achieve it; and anyway, she didn't want to go back, she wanted to help. Jen wanted to help Deeron, Arog and the magic stags, the forest and the animals, the plants - all of them. She was just… well, scared.

The truth was, Jen secretly loathed tunnels, dark rooms and enclosed spaces. Smolder's Castle - quite considerately, she thought, in her usual sarcastic way - contained all three. Before in the dream, it hadn't seemed to bother her much, probably because she wasn't actually physically there. In the here and now, of course, the real McCoy stood before her - tall, dark and terrifying. To Jen, it resembled a coffin more than a castle.

She caught sight of her beloved Bill, loyally removing twigs and fallen branches from around the stones. Playing his part, and conquering his fears. 'He doesn't like dark places, either,' she thought, recalling the time when, as a puppy, Bill had got himself stuck behind the cellar stairs. It had taken an entire day to get him out, and it was several years before he would go anywhere near the cellar again. 'Just look at him now,' she thought. 'I want to be that brave, and I am *going* to be that brave. I am going to be as brave as Bill.'

"All right, Em," said Jen, finally. "You seem to know a lot more about all of this than me, and I do trust you. So, let's go."

"Thanks, Jen. Let's." They both resumed taking off the stones and bracken, to access the wooden hatch below.

"How do you suppose Smolder gets in?" wondered Jen. "Does he fly?"

"No idea," replied Emily. "I guess there must be a main entrance around here somewhere. After all, the place is huge." This was no overstatement, judging solely by the height and length of the wall they were closest to at the hatch. Also, both of them could remember the endless corridors inside. That image alone made Emily shiver. She seriously wasn't looking forward to actually going in there.

With the stones now removed, Jen sank her hand down to pull up the door. As she knelt to get closer, her foot slipped in the mud, becoming wedged between the rising hatch and the surrounding hole.

"Eeiiyyy!" she cried, in obvious agony.

"Shush!" hissed Emily, worried that someone might hear.

Jen was sorry for having yelled out, but pain was shooting up through her body. "It's stuck!" she whispered, wincing back the urge to scream again. Emily plunged her hand into the hole and grabbed Jen's leg. As she pulled it out the slatted door creaked opened, and the entrance to Smolder's Castle lay before them. Jen rubbed her throbbing foot, as they both stared down into the hole.

"Terrific," grumbled Jen, quietly. "That was my good foot…"

"Come on," said Emily, determination etched in her voice. "If we think about this any more, we won't have the nerve for it."

Emily descended the ladder, followed by the ever-confident Bill, and lastly Jen. Once in the passageway, they walked to what looked like a ventilation shaft at the end. Both Jen and Emily knew that this was as far as it was safe for Bill to venture. Jen grabbed, hugged and fussed her best furry friend in all the world.

"You stay here, Bill. Good boy. Warn us if anyone comes." Bill whined, softly. "Good dog. We'll be back soon, don't you worry." Jen kissed his head. It was all rapidly becoming too much for her, and tears began to well in her eyes. She didn't want him to sense her fear, but Jen knew that she may not return, and this could be the last time she would see her treasured golden retriever ever again. Bill simply licked her face, lovingly.

Once Emily had likewise given him a great big hug, and Jen had stopped crying, they said their final farewells to Bill, jumped feet-first into the vent, and were gone. Bill, all alone now in the dark passageway, crouched down below the vent and watched, listened and waited.

Just as before in the dream, Jen and Emily slid down a winding, circular tube at breakneck speed. Just as before, they were unable to slow down or achieve any means of control. Just as before, their descent ended in an effective pile-up at the bottom. Just as before, that is, except this time Jen had gone first.

"Argh! Emily! You're on my head! Get… off!" Emily fumbled desperately to right herself, situated as she was upside down, facing her feet, with one arm wedged between her back and the floor, within a small, narrow, pitch-dark square tunnel. Oh, and on top of Jen's head. Because of the total absence of light, Emily couldn't see which way Jen was lying. She managed to collapse to one side, luckily falling onto wooden board and not more of Jen.

"Sorry, Jen. Are you alright?" she asked, as she continued to grapple with her position.

"I hate this place!" came a very angry and muffled reply.

"So do I, Jen, but this is our only way in, and we have to keep moving."

"But we can't see, Emily! I can't move if I can't see, and I CAN'T SEE!"

In this deeply oppressive, narrow, squared and utterly black tunnel, Emily quickly realized the seriousness of Jen's words. Through everything they'd encountered so far, she had never heard Jen speak like this before; in such a frenzied, eerie, resolute and yet petrified voice. Emily was fighting her own phobias down there, but now she was going to have to find a way to deal with Jen's as well.

"Look Jen, we're almost at the corridor… we're so close! Just hold on… you've got to keep it together!"

"But I can't move!"

"Yes you can. Take slow, deep breaths and…"

Right in the middle of Emily's frantic attempts at trying to prevent Jen from basically losing it altogether, both her and Jen's cloaks instantly and simultaneously burst into golden light! Suddenly, they could see each other again. After their eyes had adjusted to the light, both could observe clearly the wooden-slatted tunnel they were in. It actually appeared wider than it felt.

"Oh, thank God! Light!" exclaimed Jen, in nothing less than absolute relief. She began to move again, shuffling her body and garments into a more comfortable position.

"I'll second that," retorted Emily, exhalation fairly surging from her voice also. She had felt panic well-up inside of her, just trying to calm Jen. What on earth would they, could they, have done inside this tunnel having both gone to pieces? She shuddered, and tried to put it out of her mind. "How do you feel? Better?"

"I think so… just give me a moment." Jen was trying to slow her breathing down, a trick she'd found useful in the past, usually just before a music exam. It helped to calm her, as did focusing on a single point in the tunnel, while telling herself that everything was fine now that she could see again.

"This isn't the first time golden light-threads have come to the rescue, is it?" said Emily, in a throwaway comment sort of way, although she was actually thinking about Albus Carcum at the time. In the post-pandemonium, the fact that Jen wasn't aware of what had gone on there had somehow escaped Emily's mind. She was beginning to think of that event almost fondly now, compared to this tunnel.

"Nor the last, we hope." After another minute or so, Jen said, "Okay, I'm ready. Let's get out of here."

Emily and Jen crawled slowly along the tunnel, with Emily leading due to her having ended up facing the right way. They had remembered to watch out for the tree roots, and thanks to the golden light they weren't exactly hard to spot. The roots slithered along the tunnel walls like snakes, wrapping themselves tightly around loose slats, and poking in and out of gaps and holes above, below and to the sides of them. Even the noise they made sounded like they were hissing, as they scraped across and around the wood of the tunnel. If they weren't disturbed, however, they didn't seem to know that Emily and Jen were there, which was certainly a relief for Jen who was still on tender hooks. It was tricky to avoid them, though. They were everywhere!

As they crept along, Emily reflected on how much her life had changed since meeting Jen. Here in this magical world, you couldn't run away in fear or simply clam up and wait for tomorrow to arrive. There was no time for this. You simply had to make a decision and then get on with it. This world was all about action, about getting things done. If she came through all this, Emily thought, she would never be afraid of anything again. She certainly wasn't going to allow that school bully, 'Javelin-Julie', to throw insults at her any more, that was for sure.

After a while, the tunnel led to an open vent. Emily cautiously peeked out, glimpsing down along the long wooden-panelled corridor, brightly lit by burning torches hanging upon both walls.

"We're at the corridor!" she whispered to Jen, close behind her. "It looks safe… hang on…"

Emily pulled her legs round in front of her, and jumped down into the corridor as quietly as she could. Just as in the dream, alongside each torch she saw a door, one after the other, and every one identical.

"Okay, it's clear." She beckoned to Jen, who promptly jumped down and landed with a soft thud. "I remember these walls and torches," she said, gazing around as Jen stretched and dusted herself down, "but I don't remember how we found the stone door. Anyway, we'd best not hang around here. Let's follow the corridor. We might remember something."

"Right."

Emily and Jen travelled along the seemingly endless corridor once more, only this time for real. They passed door after door, and torch after torch. They saw no one and could hear nothing, except for their own gentle footsteps and a constant, low-pitched hum. After a time, Jen asked, softly, "These doors can't all lead to rooms, can they? I mean, how many does he need?"

"Stumped if I know," she whispered back, casually. "Maybe he collects things… nothing nice, I'm sure." Emily thought it best not to mention her previous day's conversation with Tamhorn, and her realization of what actually lay behind all these doors. She felt the exact same dislike for the place as she had in the dream, although she hadn't remembered her 'Ministry of Torture' metaphor. "Let's rest here a mo'… my feet are killing me."

"Don't joke, Em. This place gives me enough grief as it is." They stopped and both leant up against the wall, as Jen asked, "Wasn't there something about these doors in the dream? I'm sure Martha said something, but I can't for the life of me remember what it was."

"No, me neither," replied Emily, sighing the words away more out of deep thought than despair.

Tired and completely bewildered, Emily stared hard at the door right in front of her. Had they really been told something about them? It was impossible trying to recollect a dream days later, as for all they knew, Martha hadn't actually said anything and it was all just their imaginations running away with them. Emily could sort of remember feeling a cold sensation somewhere, but… was it here? Was it in the tunnel? Was it even outside? Whatever 'it' was, it was mostly hopeless.

Unfortunately, in all this intense deliberation, Emily had failed to detect the door just behind her, and to the left, move. Slowly and silently, the door cracked open, and a creamy-white line of mist gently flowed out onto the floor of the corridor. Resembling a miniature fast-moving stream unbeknownst to anyone, it then began to wrap itself many times around Emily's ankles, like a predator stealthily surrounding its prey and calmly preparing to pounce.

And pounce it did. Instantly, the line of mist hardened into rope and pulled with tremendous force, literally pulling Emily's feet straight out from under her.

"EEEEEK!" she screamed, more out of shock than anything else, although her landing was far from painless, as she slammed down hard onto the floor.

"RUN!" was Jen's instant reaction, and she took off down the corridor. Emily tried to scramble to her feet and run after her, but crashed back down again from all the force and tension of the rope. She really was caught, and no mistake. Jen, suddenly realizing the gravity of Emily's situation, stopped and began running back towards her. For Emily, things were quickly becoming worse, as she felt herself being dragged towards the door!

"Hold on!" yelled Jen. "Give me your hand!" She lurched forward to grab Emily's arm. As she did so, a thick tree root she hadn't seen on the floor wrapped itself around her leg, anchoring her instantly to the spot. Screaming, she kicked and stamped on the root with her other foot, then tugged at it with her hands. Free quite quickly, Jen then lunged towards Emily again who was disappearing rapidly past the now fully open door, and into whatever lay behind it. Jen grabbed her sleeve, and pulled for all she was worth. It was hopeless, however. Emily was being dragged away, and Jen simply wasn't strong enough to do anything about it.

"Oh Em," she gasped. "I can't do it!"

"Go!" yelled Emily. "Find the antlers!"

"No way, I'm not leaving you!" Jen now had her feet wedged up against the doorframe, trying desperately to prevent Emily's upper half from disappearing into the thick soupy blackness of the room.

"It's no use, Jen! Go and find the antlers! Please!"

Thick white smoke now billowed into the corridor from the room behind the open door, making it impossible for them to even see each other, although Jen still had hold of Emily's arm, just. Regardless, Emily was still sliding helplessly into the room, and towards her fate. Jen could do nothing, other than feel her grip around Emily's wrist loosen… and then finally, break. Moments later, she heard the door click shut. Jen was now all by herself, alone in a smoke-filled corridor.

"Emily! Where are you?" Jen frantically ran her hands along the wall, trying to find the door. Because of the smoke, she couldn't see anything, and neither could she find the door. It had disappeared completely, leaving only flat wall.

"I'm here!" came a reply, but instead of the sound coming from behind the wall where she thought the door should be, it appeared to come from far off along the corridor.

"I can't see you, Em! Where are you? The door's gone!" Jen strained to hear anything from along one end of the corridor, and then the other. Dense, impenetrable smog kept building up around her, almost pinning her to the wall.

"Don't panic! Just listen to my voice! I'm here! Listen! Here!" Jen not only couldn't see anything, she also now struggled to work out which end of the corridor Emily's voice was coming from. Sound was bouncing everywhere! One word sounded close, and then suddenly far off. Then, sound came as though it were from one end of the corridor, and then instantly from the other. It was impossible to know where she was.

"I can't see you!" Jen was really beginning to fret now, and wondering what on earth she was going to do.

"Jen! Find the antlers! You've got to find…" Emily's voice trailed off into the distance as it faded into silence, and then, nothingness.

A Moth called Nocturne

"Oh Em, where are you?" cried Jen softly, as tears welled up in her eyes. She remained huddled to the same wall Emily had only seconds before disappeared behind. The smoke was now so thick that Jen was finding it difficult to breathe, even with her hands cupped over her nose. Suddenly she felt very alone, frightened, and entirely at a loss over what to do or where to go. After all, what could she do? She couldn't see! How on earth was she going to find the antlers?

Rubbing her eyes, Jen suddenly realized that she was neither entirely without sight nor completely alone. A dark shadow loomed through the smoke just a little way off down the corridor, and began moving menacingly towards her. The instant she saw it, two bright red laser-like eyes pierced through the smoke and shone directly into hers, momentarily blinding her. At that second, fear gripped Jen's stomach like a wet towel being wrung out dry. Without pausing to even contemplate any other options, Jen turned and blindly ran as fast as she could, away down the opposite end of the corridor. Unfortunately, she didn't get far, as fright combined with the smoke had disorientated her. She crashed hard into the other wall, and collapsed onto the floor.

Jen couldn't see, could barely breath, and now had to endure pain shooting up through her body. Something was stabbing her in the back, and pinning her down to the floor. A cold wet hoof then slammed down hard so close to Jen's hand that she cringed in terror, petrified that her fingers were about to be stamped on! She craned her neck to see the two penetrating red laser eyes stare down from directly above her. She also managed to make out two enormous curly horns on either side of a goat-like head. Jen quickly decided that this had to be one of Smolder's guards, and she was now caught - hook, line and sinker.

"Get up!" it hissed, loudly. Jen's captor prodded her viciously in the back with what Jen reckoned to be its other hoof. Aching and still in pain, she tried to slowly get up, but was impatiently and unceremoniously dragged to her feet by the hood of her cloak. "Smoke! Work!"

What happened next was a rather staggering sight, even for someone as petrified as Jen. The all-engulfing stagnant and stilted smog in the corridor suddenly rushed together, as though hit by some immense force of wind. Like sand whisked up in a desert storm, the smoke surged rapidly around a single point, whereupon it appeared to instantly congeal into a thick solid clump around Jen's, and her captor's, feet. In barely a few seconds, the entire corridor was completely clear of smoke once more, just as when Jen and Emily had first exited the tunnel.

Without even a moment to consider what was happening, Jen felt a jolt, as though the floor had been pushed upwards. Glancing down, she realized she was no longer standing on the wooden corridor floor at all, but instead suspended up off the ground by... smoke! Then a sudden lurch forward, and *whoosh!*

Jen found herself speeding off along the corridor aboard some bizarre ball of solid smog, with her and her captor balanced precariously in the middle. To Jen, it felt like a cross between downhill skateboarding and riding on a magic carpet, although she'd actually experienced neither. Also, the journey was light years away from being enjoyable, and less still controllable. Jen kept her eyes shut as much as she dared, as the smog ball rocked, tilted and swayed recklessly along. More than once she lost her balance and fell against the guard, forcing her to open her eyes and see door after door and torch after torch whiz past. The goat-guard's body was absolutely stone cold, not like a living creature at all. Not only did its complexion look like marble, it felt like marble as well! The smog ball suddenly veered upwards like an elevator, through some kind of chute or shaft. Moments later it levelled off, and then abruptly stopped. Jen was forcefully shunted off the smog ball and through an open entrance into another corridor.

"Walk!" the guard hissed at Jen. He turned back to the smog ball. "Smoke, go!"

The smog ball obediently disappeared. The guard then repeatedly prodded Jen in the back with his horns, hastening her quickly onwards. Jen walked as fast as she could but it was far from easy, given that she still ached and the floor seemed to be covered in some kind of slippery mould, as well as rotting leaves. The walls of this corridor were also wooden, only here covered in a sickly green slime. Jen felt freezing, while in the air hung a dank musty smell of decay.

"Stop!" he commanded after a few minutes of walking, or rather sliding. Two huge arched stone doors to the right of them suddenly swung open. "In!" The guard ordered, prodding Jen forward.

Jen stumbled into a large hall, grimly lit by the dull glow of a few burning torches. An obviously damaged and filthy candle chandelier hung in the centre of the room, with some sort of ivy enmeshed around it that trailed all the way down from the roof to the ground. The floor was covered with sticks, branches and twigs, while the walls were coloured a stained and once velvety red. Anonymous rickety paintings, impossible to see beyond their frames due to being caked in soot and dirt, hung messily about its walls. On the opposite side of the room, a fire blazed within an enormous hearth, surrounded by large copper buckets. Above the mantelpiece was draped a faded tapestry of deer grazing in a forest. To Jen, it looked like the neglected remains of a once grand room in a stately home, of the kind reserved for banquets and special occasions.

Apart from the soft crackling of the fire and torches, the room was still and silent. Then suddenly, the noise of loud snapping twigs from behind her caused poor Jen to almost die of fright! Something, someone, was lurking, concealed in darkness behind one of the open double doors. Jen instinctively turned round, only to endure the instant stab of the guard's four sharp horns, digging into her side. The pain momentarily distracted her, but not enough to stop her from trying to glimpse this skulking prowler. She couldn't see anything, however. It was pitch-black back there.

"GET... OFF!" In an instance of bravery combined with infuriation at her treatment, Jen pushed away the guard by grabbing at its horns. Sadly, it proved to little effect, as the guard remained steadfast and refused to budge.

"I found this, my Lord," the guard instead blurted out, obviously in fear of whoever or whatever lay in wait behind the door.

'Lord?' thought Jen, trying hard to keep her head together whilst continuing to scan the darkness for any advance warning on what was to come. 'Who would they... could they... was it? It must be! SMOLDER!'

Out of the shadows limped the most bizarre creature Jen thought ever imaginable, let alone possible. Had she not seen it for herself, she would never have believed it. Into view hobbled something that, on first impression, appeared to be part-man, part-goat and part-stick insect. Jen gawped in horror and more than enough fear, at the contorted creature veering towards her.

Its overall appearance was clearly that of a man, but a man so twisted, so warped and so wretched, that neither nature nor accident could possibly lay claim to such gruesome affliction. Whatever, whoever, lay behind this contortion possessed the hand of evil - pure evil. Arms and legs appeared first. Tall, rigid and stick-thin, Smolder moved as though he lacked both elbow and knee joints. Then, into the dim light came his body, a body so inhuman as to be more like that of an upright goat's, being as it was round at the stomach and with a narrowing ribcage. The fact that this torso also supported manlike shoulders made Smolder appear all the more menacing.

Finally, into Jen's field of sight ventured a head, by far the scariest of all Smolder's foul features. With a long protruding chin, a flat nose and skin drawn back so tightly across his face and forehead it looked like cling film, Smolder was indeed an eerie sight. His ears were tiny and pointed, and there were no eyebrows to speak of. Receded smoke-white hair, visible only at the back of his scalp, curled upwards and around like horns on either side of his skull.

Worst of all, however, were Smolder's eyes, a hypnotizing white colour with red streaks of bloodshot and deep black rings instead of pupils. They ably demonstrated, above all else, Smolder's wicked use of power and the danger Jen was now in, for the instant his eyes fixed onto hers, Jen felt a monumental pounding inside her head as though a freight train were travelling at full pelt, right through the middle of her brain! In moments, she was suffering the migraine of all migraines. As someone who barely ever suffered headaches, Jen was woefully ill prepared for such agony. She immediately closed her eyes, covering her face with her hands, and collapsed onto the floor.

Fortunately, now that Jen's eyes were closed, the pain subsided almost as quickly as it had begun. She was nevertheless left feeling groggy, wondering for all the world what had hit her. As she gradually picked herself up off the floor, Jen could hear shrill laughter all around her. One thing at least was now abundantly clear - to look Smolder directly in the eye was one big mistake.

Once their hilarity had died down, Smolder continued to sneer at Jen, obviously gaining immense satisfaction at witnessing the pain he could inflict upon her. For as he knew, such suffering could only mean one thing - he had a Wandiacate.

"A-hah! So, I was wise to return from the battlefield," he hissed as he gloated over her, hobbling about as he did so. "I knew something was being planned, but I never thought Deeron would be so stupid as to send me his Wandiacates. This will make my power greater than great!" Smolder turned to his guard. "Where is the other one?"

"It… it… g-got away, Lord."

"IDIOT!" Smolder shrieked in instant fury. "Find it immediately, or I will turn you to smoke!"

"Yes, Lord." The guard grovelled pathetically to his master. After a few moments, he asked, hesitantly, "What shall I do with this one, Lord?"

Smolder veered closer towards her, causing Jen to stand up quickly. Through the dim light, she could now glimpse more clearly his ugly face, which was also covered in dry mud. He really was a revolting sight. Jen was careful not to gaze upon his eyes again, however.

"What are you doing here?" he hissed. As he spoke, the most terrible smell poured out of his mouth. Jen thought she was going to be sick!

"Mind your own business," she snapped back, defiantly.

"Deeron has perished," he said, scornfully. "They are all dead, and in just two more days I shall reign over this forest and all the land beyond! There is only one more thing I need to make me Supreme Lord, with power over all worlds forever! Do you know what that is?" he snarled.

Jen said nothing, but instead stared directly at Smolder's hideous body, desperate to avoid making any eye contact. She had a pretty good idea of what he was talking about, though.

"Wandiacates! Wandiacates!" Smolder was suddenly screaming in a weird and frenzied way, all the time flapping his stick-like arms about whilst teetering from one leg to the other. He looked like a wooden string puppet gone berserk! Jen maintained her gaze, not daring to look at his face. Although in any other situation Smolder's actions might have been hilarious, in the here and now Jen suddenly felt even more frightened, if that were at all possible.

"You!" he hissed at the guard. "Put this one away, and go and find the other!"

The guard instantly grabbed Jen's cloak in its mouth, and pushed her forcefully towards the pitch-black area behind the double doors, precisely from where Smolder had first appeared.

"Hey! Leave me al… Whoa!" Before Jen could even finish her rebellious remark, she felt the floor below her suddenly vanish! A short fall, followed by a heavy thump, and Jen found herself hurtling along what she could only assume to be a tunnel, again. Given her speed, it was probably a blessing that she couldn't see anything.

Zoomph! "AIYIEEH!" ***Thump!*** *Rustle!* ***Clonk!*** "OW! Ooh, my…"

The finale to Jen's latest jaunt along one of the many chutes, shafts and tunnels that both adorned and interlinked the many walls, floors and corridors of Smolder's castle, was an especially loud affair. It ended with her lying face down - as ever, in a pile of leaves - nursing yet more bruises and scrapes, in a dimly lit square room about four metres wide. Looking up bleary-eyed from her crash landing spot, Jen was at least glad to be able to see again, and be away from Smolder for the time being.

She stood up slowly, and brushed away the leaves from her clothing and hair. She looked to find the shaft or hole through which she had obviously fallen, but could see nothing except solid walls, floor and a ceiling, all coloured a dirty stone grey. Feeling about, she wondered whether there might be some secret passageway or concealed door somewhere. All Jen could feel was cold solid stone. There wasn't even a door! How could she get anywhere if there wasn't a door?

"Em, where are you?" she called, anxiously.

What was left of Jen's earlier determination, garnered at the entrance to the castle, ebbed away like a leaf upon an ocean wave. It had been some time now since she'd last seen Emily, and Jen was beginning to lose hope of ever seeing her, or indeed anyone, again. She looked around the room for something to sit on. It was almost as disgusting as the derelict hall she'd just left, in this so-called castle. There were a few overturned barrels, and some copper buckets.

She sat down on a barrel in the corner and thought about Smolder's words, and all that had happened. What if he was telling the truth, and Deeron, Arog and the herd were all dead? The last time Jen had seen them, both armies were about to face each other to do battle. After Emily had been launched up high into the air in an ice-cage by that stag/tongue thing, Smolder's army had begun appearing in the valley below. Deeron with his army then moved out to oppose them whilst Tamhorn led her, Bill and the five other magic stags to Fox's Drift. There they'd all waited for most of the day, up until when Fauld had appeared recalling the magic stags to the battlefield. Tamhorn had told her then to wait with Bill for Emily whom, he had assured her, was alive and unharmed. Now it seemed, they were all dead, she was imprisoned, Emily was who knows where, and Bill was left alone at the entrance. Tears began to well up in her eyes once more, causing them to sting from all of the grit and dirt on her face.

"What am I going to do?" she cried, softly.

For a while, Jen let the tears flow freely. There had been such optimism, such hope and courageousness along the way. It was hard to accept that they were now beaten and Deeron's wonderful herd was gone. Where were Tamhorn, Blythe, funny Fole and Folly, and the amazing Hay and Leif? Were they destined to be Smolder's prisoners as well?

Whilst Jen sat with her head in her hands, a wisp of golden smoke appeared directly beside her, coming inexplicably through the wall. When she finally noticed it, Jen immediately leapt up and ran over to the opposite side of the room, wondering if she was going to have to deal with fire now as well! More smoke continued to flow in, causing her then to wonder if, instead of fire, this was about to become a prelude to something more akin to the phantom antlers witnessed in the study back at the farmhouse, only here throwing buckets and barrels about the place! The thought of that terrible storm, and the subsequent events that had essentially led to her being precisely where she was at this moment, was more than Jen could deal with right now.

The smoke suddenly stopped pouring in, and gathered itself into a ball on the floor in the corner of the room. Jen stared at it closely. It seemed to have a face, like the moon does sometimes, causing her to feel less afraid.

"Can *you* help me?" she found herself asking.

The ball instantly rolled towards her, jumped up into the air, and began to ricochet around the room. Jen watched in amazement as it bounced from the floor to the wall, over and over again, as though someone were standing there hitting it with a bat. As it bounced, the ball increased in speed, until - *boof!* - it exploded in mid-air! Like a firework, fragments of glittering light then cascaded down onto the floor.

From behind the gleaming light-shower, suddenly appeared a bright golden moth! It flew towards Jen, who was still over the other side of the room, and hovered close by her at about head-height. She stood transfixed, as it seemed to radiate an incredible glow from its body. Not only its body but its wings also, that looked so delicate and thin as to be barely there at all. In fact, Jen only really knew something was flapping because light pulses could be seen scattering outwards from the moth's body as fluttering rays. Everything about this moth seemed exaggerated, even surreal; like a dream, in effect. It was almost too bright to look at, especially given the dull backdrop of the room/cell she was in. However, the shock of its appearance was not half as great as the shock of hearing it speak!

"I can help you," the moth said.

"Huh?" Jen had seen some staggering things already on this trip, but nothing could have prepared her for a talking moth, less still a talking moth with a young and forthright female voice!

"I SAID, I CAN HELP YOU!" The moth sounded seriously annoyed at having to repeat herself, seeing fit to exaggerate and italicize every word, loudly.

"Oh, er, that's... great," Jen didn't know whether to apologize, offer thanks, or go and stand in a corner, quietly. She quickly decided, sort of, upon a dismissive tact. "Er, what's your name?"

"Nocturne," the moth replied with evident pride and self-importance, but oddly no hint of her previous irritation. "Obviously, it's because I fly at night; although technically, here in Smolder's Castle it's actually impossible to tell night from day." Nocturne then proceeded to draw some truly stunning images in the air. Via incredible speed, aerial acrobatics and the golden light trails that followed her every movement, Nocturne drew animals of the forest: first a stag, then a rabbit, then a... giraffe?

"Of course, I've never seen a heron but I _know_ they look like this," announced Nocturne pompously, her self-pride fairly splattering itself across the room.

'O-kay,' thought Jen dryly to herself. 'Someone who likes to show how wonderful and clever they _think_ they are.' Jen's mild contempt for this type of character didn't preclude her from appreciating that she nonetheless needed Nocturne's help, and would have to tread very carefully with her. The face of Geraldine Dribbens, a so-called classmate, flashed up in Jen's mind, much to _her_ annoyance. 'Someone else who...' she growled to herself, but quickly erased it from her mind. The crucial thing right now was to keep Nocturne onside, and persuade her to make good on her offer of help.

"That's incredible," said Jen gushingly, trying desperately hard to mean it.

"I know," replied Nocturne, proudly.

Jen took a deep breath and decided to adopt, initially at least, some small-talk tactics.

"So how did you end up here? Are you a prisoner too?"

"Of course I'm a prisoner! Why else would I be here? I've been here ever since Smolder stole the antlers, and the first storms were sent to destroy the forest. I was actually blown in - awfully bad luck, really - but I fought Smolder AND all his army incredibly well..."

It was at this point that Jen's eyes glazed over, and she stopped listening to Nocturne's self-congratulatory, and no doubt somewhat embellished life story. 'How much of this am I going to have to put up with?' she lamented silently to herself.

"...Turned to smoke! Hah! They can't beat me! Now they even think that I work for Smolder! Me! ME!! Hah! I don't work for anyone. I'm far too clever for them! La-da-dee, dee-da-da-dum..." Nocturne began to fly-dance gently around the room in time to her own singing, in obvious bliss, while all the time leaving long golden light lines trailing along behind her. She was actually managing to be mesmerizing *and* annoying, both at the same time.

"Oh, and I just *bet* you're a musical genius as well," cursed Jen quietly under her breath, as she waited for Nocturne to finish her 'lap of honour'.

"Hmm? What's that you say?" asked Nocturne, still circling.

"Oh... nothing. Have you heard any news about Deeron and his army?"

"Not much," she replied, coming to rest on the edge of a barrel. "They're all alive, and fighting Smolder's army outside in the valley. That's all I know."

Jen was relieved to hear that they were at least all still in the land of the living, contrary to Smolder's evil boast. The news didn't exactly inspire great euphoria, however. How long could they hold on for against Smolder's powerful force? How old was this information, and where on earth was Emily? Jen had to escape and find her as soon as possible. She decided to try - not very successfully, alas - to casually manoeuvre the conversation back to escape.

"So how come you can turn back into a moth?"

"Oh, that's because Deity cast a spell before Smolder's power completely took over. She gave every animal from the forest the ability to change back into its proper form, in case any of us were turned to smoke. Smolder found out and so imprisoned Deity far away, assuming that would stop us. It did, for a while. Even our smoke turned from golden to white, just like Smolder's guards when he smokes them. But I can turn from white to golden, AND back again, AND EVEN into a moth whenever I choose, because I'm so clever..." Nocturne did a flaunting back flip mid-sentence, followed by a loop-the-loop, returning to her hover position at Jen's eye-line. "...And what's cleverest of all, is that Smolder doesn't even know!"

"Albus Carcum!" Jen suddenly blurted out, excitedly. "It's where Emily went, and she said she saw - well, met anyway - Deity. But the point is, she must have taken the golden light with her into Albus Carcum, and that's allowed some of Deity's magic to work again! I understand now what she was on about!" Jen had only been half-listening to Nocturne, but the mention of Deity reminded her of the conversation she'd had with Emily, just after she'd emerged from the leaf stack. The fact that Jen had understood next to none of it, then or since, had been bugging her for a while now, but suddenly it all made sense. She was actually rather pleased with herself for having finally grasped what had been going on, all that time Emily had been absent. Nocturne, on the other hand, looked most put out by this revelation, and more than a little aggrieved.

"Oh... really?" There was a pompous pause, as the moth attempted to compose a suitable reply that would adequately massage her now dented and somewhat fragile ego. "Well, it's POSS-ible, I suppose... though frankly, I consider my scenario FAR more likely. Anyway, there are THOUSANDS of animals in here that are smoke. Why can't they turn back? Besides, you Wandiacates really don't seem to get much right, do you? I mean, look at you! You're stuck in here!"

Jen gritted her teeth. "Well, so are you!"

"Me, stuck? ME!? ME!!!? I'll show you just how stuck I am!" With her words of indignance still resonating around the room, Nocturne shot upwards like a bullet, ramming slap-bang into the grey stone-like ceiling above!

"DON'...T!!" With her hands clasped to her head and a face full of horror, Jen was suddenly convinced that Nocturne, her only companion and lifeline right now, had just committed suicide by smashing herself into the ceiling! "Oh no!" She covered her eyes as she struggled to contemplate what she had just seen and stood frozen to the spot, aghast at the event.

After a few seconds, Nocturne's head popped down from out of the apparently solid-stone ceiling, just above the barrels, with a heated expression on her tiny face.

"What now!" she demanded, huffily.

"Oh, thank heavens!" exclaimed Jen, relieved beyond words. "I thought you'd..."

"What?"

"Well," Jen suddenly found herself grappling desperately for tactful words and means to describe what she actually thought had happened. "I just..."

"Yes?" Nocturne, it seemed, was not prepared to let this go and was impatiently requiring - nay demanding - some sort of an explanation.

"I just thought you'd left me, that's all."

"Don't be ridiculous! I said I'd help, didn't I? Tsk!" Nocturne tutted, and with that vanished back up through the ceiling.

"Sorry," she called back gently, followed by a huge sigh of relief. Jen looked up at the ceiling. For the life of her, she couldn't work out what was going on in this room. The walls, ceiling and floor all looked identical - same colour, texture, everything. Jen had already examined the four walls with her hands, and they were rock solid. So was the floor.

She decided to arrange a few of the copper buckets and barrels like steps, so as to try and reach the ceiling. The resultant makeshift structure felt, and looked, seriously rickety, but she managed to climb up and touch the ceiling with one finger… just. It was solid as well! This made no sense at all. However, Jen thought it perhaps wiser to consider her findings back down on terra firma, not balancing three metres up off the ground via two toes, hanging off the edge of a barrel!

Having successfully clambered back down, Jen pondered her cell and Nocturne's disappearing act. She knew that Nocturne could switch from smoke to moth and back again, but how could she penetrate stone? This was a question Jen simply couldn't answer on her own, and so she decided to sit back down on the barrel and wait for Nocturne to do, whatever it was, Nocturne was doing.

Seconds later, a rope dropped down through the ceiling directly in front of her, almost hitting Jen on the nose. She gazed at it, transfixed for a moment, as the rope glowed a most radiant rich golden light, seeming to come from within itself, running all the way along the cord. Jen put her hand out, wondering if it would be too hot to touch, but actually it felt quite cool. She gave it a small tug, hoping it was fastened to something at the other end. It felt solid.

"Come on!" Nocturne's huffy head popped down again through the ceiling, proffering insightful comment as ever. "A rope is generally used for climbing you know, not gawping at! Hurry up!"

"But how?" Jen was stood holding the rope, staring directly up at Nocturne's head.

"How what?" The tiny hairs above Nocturne's eyes rose, as she adopted a disbelieving, almost disdainful look. "Are you seriously telling me that you can't…?"

"No," interrupted Jen, guessing what was coming. "I mean, how do I get through the ceiling? It's solid to…"

"Put your hood up!" interrupted Nocturne back, and tutted again. "Tsk! Don't they teach you Wandiacates anything?" With that, she disappeared up through the ceiling once more.

"Not about this place, they don't," grumbled Jen quietly, as she grappled with the back of her cloak.

The prospect of banging your head on a stone ceiling was not something anyone - least of all Jen - would relish. Nevertheless, with her hood up and her eyes closed, Jen climbed the rope, slowly. She anxiously waited for the thump, followed by pain, but it didn't arrive. Instead she just kept on climbing, all the way up until she heard Nocturne whisper, "Stop!"

Jen opened her eyes and instantly shuddered in terror, clenching hold of the rope for dear life! Suddenly - at least it seemed sudden to Jen - there was nothing around her or, for some distance, below her. The shock of having gone from a small-enclosed supposedly solid room, to dangling high up in the air via a single rope, was not something anyone would necessarily take lightly.

Once her initial alarm had subsided, Jen realized that she must now be up in the rafters of the castle's roof. Looking directly above her Jen could see, a little higher up, the knot securing the rope around a long beam of wood. This made her shudder far worse than before - almost to the point of panic - as the stark reality of that knot, and the consequences were it to break, hit Jen's train of thought like a sledgehammer. She even let out an involuntary squeal - well, more of a squeak really - causing Nocturne to reveal both her position (just behind Jen's head), and a distinctly spicy example of her usual brand of charm and tact.

"SHHH! For Pete's sake, get a grip!" Nocturne, although whispering, managed nevertheless to emit quite voluminous levels of scorn. The irony was probably unintentional. "Sit down and be quiet!"

Sit? Jen, still hanging onto the rope for dear life, was now puzzled as well as petrified. Her position high up, looking out upon a vast area of roof and different-sized rooms, corridors and hallways below, meant that she couldn't see what was immediately behind her. Her hood didn't help much either.

The slope of the roof, combined with the lack of light, told her that she was close to an outer wall. Gripping the rope as tightly as it was possible to grip anything, she slowly dipped and twisted her neck to try and glimpse if anything was there. As she did so, the rope began to turn, and she with it. A rapidly growing sense of nausea in Jen's stomach was halted by the venomous sound of,

"Here!"

Perched on a thick wooden beam, running parallel to the one to which the rope was tied, sat the irritated and considerably peeved Nocturne. Grumpy though she looked, Jen was relieved beyond words to see her, on something solid and so near. In fact, all she had to do was rotate herself back to her original position, and basically sit down.

Once Jen had gently manoeuvred onto the beam, and convinced herself that the castle roof would most likely not collapse with the extra burden of her 7 stone weight upon it, she gradually felt confident enough to loosen her grip on the rope. Their vantage point offered a relatively safe and well-hidden bird's eye view of the entire area of the castle.

Looking out, Jen was struck by just how high up they were in relation to the floor below. It seemed as though one, perhaps even two, floors of the castle had been missed out or removed, and there were no windows anywhere. Because of this, it was impossible to tell precisely which floor she was looking at, although she knew for certain that it wasn't the same one by which she and Emily had entered the castle. There therefore had to be at least one other floor, probably underground. Thick, dank smoky air combined with many different pongy smells to waft slowly around Jen's head, causing her eyes to sting.

Eleven - no, twelve - rows of white stone-coloured square rooms, encased in a thick black outline, could be seen below. Those farthest and nearest to her were single rows, whilst the remaining ten were blocked into five double rows lying back to back, with corridors separating each block. These corridors connected via passageways, breaking up many of the longer double rows into smaller blocks. Along each corridor, Jen observed the same rows of doors and torches as she'd seen before with Emily, although the passageways were new. It reminded her of a crossword puzzle, or a maze seen from above. In reality, it more closely resembled a prison.

Some passageways contained a different room. These rooms were much larger than the others; perhaps four or five times the size, with none appearing to possess a ceiling. From her vantage point, Jen could see, in one of these rooms, golden light and smoke spiral up in the middle. It rose to a certain height and then seemed to plateau, filtering out towards the four walls, and changing colour from golden to white as it did so. It was quite an impressive sight, looking a lot like water going down a gigantic plughole, except in reverse, or a sort of cross between an electrical storm and a tornado, only in slow motion.

"Those rooms with the light and smoke," queried Jen, softly. "What are they?"

"Smolder's smoulder chambers, where he turns us to smoke." replied Nocturne, flatly.

The fact that golden smoke was still being converted to white - the fact that smoke was still being created at all - worried Jen, although it didn't seem to bother Nocturne one bit.

"So, how…?"

"Shh!" interrupted Nocturne. Suddenly, movement combined with a rattling of keys in the corridor just below them, alerted her.

"Quick!" the moth whispered, with glaring urgency. "Guards! Let go of the rope!"

Letting go of the rope was something Jen was seriously reluctant to do, given that it was her only known way back down. However, first-hand knowledge and repeated experience of Nocturne's brashness persuaded her to do as she was told surprisingly quickly. The instant Jen let go, the light of the rope suddenly began to shimmer and pulsate very rapidly, all the way up and down along the flex. Then moments later, it simply dissolved into thin air! In no more than a few seconds, the rope had completely vanished. Nothing remained - no cord, mark or indent. It was as though it had never existed. Jen's stomach sank.

Nocturne peered down intensely into the room from which they had just escaped. Although all anyone could really see from above was the stone-coloured ceiling, looking closely Nocturne could just make out two silhouettes moving about. Seconds passed, after which the clanging of copper buckets being kicked around the room could be heard.

"Hah! They're in big trouble now," whispered Nocturne joyously, as the guards finally left the room and proceeded slowly back along the corridor. "We ought to move…" The moth suddenly took flight, moving over to the opposite side of Jen. "Over this way, methinks!"

Nocturne's merriment was lost on Jen. She hadn't seen the commotion below, as that would have meant looking straight down directly beneath her, something she was resolutely against right now. She'd heard it though, and it was certainly not a sound to instill high spirits. Regardless, Jen now had to find a way, and the courage, to move along the beam.

"Come on!" snapped Nocturne, considerate as ever.

Jen decided that the safest way to move along the beam was to sit astride of it, and pull her way along. She was very mindful of the fact that Nocturne, although largely infuriating, had nevertheless got her out of that room as promised. Not upsetting her had to remain a priority. Jen shunted her way along, as quickly and quietly as she could.

After a while, Jen began to hear voices. They were distant at first, but became louder as she progressed along the beam.

"… But Lord, it was locked in!" Jen heard one trembling voice say.

"Then how did it escape?" shrieked another.

"I… I d-don't know, Lord," came a reply.

"Imbeciles!" the shrieker shrieked again.

By now, Jen had caught up with Nocturne who had perched herself within a suitable recess, conveniently set back into the shadows. She was looking down into the large hall with the candle chandelier, where Jen had had the dubious pleasure of meeting Smolder. Lo and behold, there was Smolder, and evidently not in the best of moods. Nocturne, on the other hand, could barely control her glee.

"IDIOTS!" screamed Smolder, as he angrily waved his long stick-thin arms about at two guards, who were standing just inside the double doors. They were receiving a severe verbal thrashing, no doubt because of Jen's escape. Smolder was so incensed, and basically mad anyway, that Jen began to wonder whether their punishment would ultimately remain that of the solely spoken variety.

She didn't have to wait long to find out. A trail of white smoke suddenly began to rise out of the top of Smolder's head! He looked as though he were about to explode, or else burst into flames. The guards instantly cowered down.

"No, Lord… please, we beg you!" one of the guards pleaded pitifully with him.

"Smoke!" commanded Smolder, as a hissing noise around him rapidly grew in intensity and smoke continued to billow out. Then suddenly - *Vooomph!* A bolt of white light shot across the room, hitting one guard straight between the eyes! The guard was suddenly gone, and a swirl of thick white smoke was all that remained. Then, as though sucked up by some giant invisible vacuum cleaner, the smoke shot off to the side of one of the double doors and vanished! It was the exact same area - pitch-black, where even the floor and walls could not be seen - from where Smolder had originally entered, and Jen had been shunted into just prior to landing in her cell room.

"Look," whispered Nocturne to Jen. "That room, fifth corridor." Jen counted down the long passageways she could see to number five, and scanned along the row. It was weird. In this corridor, only some of the rooms had stone-coloured ceilings, and then they stopped. The others after that had no ceiling at all, in fact barely any walls or floor either. What was there appeared to be wooden, and all in quite a serious state of disrepair. It was only when Jen moved her gaze along to the first dilapidated room in the row that she saw what was happening. The room was filling up with smoke, but instead of simply wafting about as you would expect normal smoke to do, it seemed to be solidifying along the walls and floor, while also creating a ceiling.

"Was that all it was in my room? Smoke?" whispered Jen as she continued to stare, utterly flabbergasted. She had felt the walls, the floor and even the ceiling of her cell, and was sure it had been made of stone.

"How do you think I got in?" tutted Nocturne, in her usual disparaging way. "Tsk! Not even I can get through stone… yet." She continued to spy on events below. Jen didn't bother to inform Nocturne that she had actually grappled with this very fact back in her cell room. That was one question answered, anyway.

Smolder had by now turned his anger towards the second guard, who was cowering on the floor. "I am sick of you as well," he said slowly, with steaming malice. "You've lost the one Wandiacate we had, and you still haven't found the other one!" Another bolt of light - *Vooomph!* The second guard was instantly turned to smoke, just like the first. His airy remains disappeared into the darkness beside the door, and the room in the fifth corridor gradually filled a whitish-grey, until all that could be seen there was a square, stone-coloured ceiling.

"You!" Smolder screamed at a third guard, standing on sentry duty just outside the double doors. "Go and find these Wandiacates before they get away. Do your job and get it right!" The guard nodded, and made off as quickly as he could. Smolder turned, and awkwardly manoeuvred his taught and inflexible stick-figure self towards the fire.

A small goat stepped into view from the corridor, pausing before entering the hall, presumably to gauge Smolder's mood.

"What news from outside?" he demanded abruptly without looking round, and in a tone that strongly advised against anything other than good news.

"The battle is over, Master," the creature grunted, obligingly. "Deeron and his army are overwhelmed. There is no escape now."

"Come here," ordered Smolder, and turned to look up at the tapestry above the hearth. The goat pattered over to join him.

"You see this picture?"

"Yes, Master."

"What do you see?" Smolder waited as the goat stared up at the faded embroidery, wondering what answer he was supposed to give.

"Er... deer, Master. I see deer."

"What else?"

Fear began to well up inside the goat. Up until now, he had been Smolder's favoured and most loyal protector, despite having failed to capture the Wandiacates in the forest once before while disguised as a fawn. He couldn't afford to make another mistake and so instead remained silent, waiting for his master to do the talking.

"You see that person there? That's me."

The goat stared at the image of a small boy, dressed in a sky-blue shirt and short brown trousers. He had an untidy mop of blond hair, rosy cheeks and a broad white smile.

"That's me," he repeated, sadly.

Then, just like the flick of a switch, Smolder's mood lightened, as though he had purposely erased something from his mind. "You see that man there?" he continued. "That's my father."

The goat searched the scene. There was a man holding out his hand to a fawn nuzzling his palm, among a sizeable herd of deer. Some were grazing, while others rested or drank from the stream. Had the goat been in anybody's company other than Smolder's, he would have openly volunteered the opinion that the scene was peaceful, and strangely captivating.

Looking closely at the young boy again, however, the goat was suddenly struck by what he saw. The smile on the young Smolder's face appeared to alter before the goat's very eyes. That broad beaming smirk suddenly looked artificial, while those brazen and exposed teeth belied a sneering and deviousness, which could almost be seen to harbour malevolence and evil intent. The longer the goat stared, the more distorted and twisted the image became.

Before him lay no embroidered portrayal of innocence, or some wayward youthful spirit. Instead, the image of a selfish, demanding and conniving child revealed itself. As his closest defender, the goat had often wondered, but would never have dared ask, about Smolder's disfigurement - the hows and the whys. Now he didn't have to. It had all become clear.

In the faded tapestry, Smolder was revealed to have consumed envy, greed, resentment and revenge from a very young age. Now they had consumed him, absorbed and devoured him; every part of him, mind and body.

"He loved them, Targot. More than he loved me."

The goat's attention was jolted back into the room, at Smolder's use of his name. For the first time ever, he found himself glancing warily at his master through distrustful eyes. The stick-like creature beside him was outwardly pathetic and weak, but Targot knew Smolder well enough to know where his power really lay, and just how deadly it could become. Lost in his own thoughts, Smolder continued to stare at the hanging embroidery. After a few more moments, he began to speak, although not to Targot.

"I shall be great," he hissed, still staring up at the tapestry. "I will prove to you that I am the greatest Lord of all time. I'll rule the Wandiacates, and they will dance for ME! The Golden Light of Goodness and the White Light of Evil will be mine! All mine! So you see, father, the mortal world I will also own, and any friends of yours had better fear for their lives!" He laughed wildly, rocking maniacally from one stick-leg to the other. Targot stood frozen to the spot, quietly petrified at Smolder's increasingly erratic behaviour.

Seemingly oblivious to his own bizarre outburst, Smolder then turned to Targot to address him personally.

"You have been loyal to me, Targot, and when this is over I shall reward you generously."

"Thank you, Master." Right now, all Targot really cared about was getting out of that hall and away from Smolder, as fast as possible.

"I need those Wandiacates! Go and find them! Use the Falx if you have to, but just find them!" Smolder seethed loudly, his anger never far from the surface.

"I won't let you down, Master."

"You'd be well advised not to." Smolder stared directly into Targot's eyes, as he made his thinly veiled threat. After what probably seemed like a lifetime for Targot, but what was in reality no more than a few seconds, Smolder calmly turned back towards the fire. Targot left the room, just as fast as his four hooves would carry him.

"Did you hear?" whispered Jen to Nocturne, excitedly. "They still don't have Emily! Where could she be?"

"How should I know? Right now, we need to get ourselves out of here," replied Nocturne urgently, now buzzing around Jen's head. "They're desperate to find you, and that goat knows his life is on the line. Heaven help us if the Falx are let in."

"Why, what are they?" asked Jen.

"Shhh, not here! This way, quickly!"

Nocturne gestured Jen back to a distance away from Smolder. Jen hadn't the time to maneouvre herself around 180° on the beam, so had to make do with travelling backwards. This proved to be awkward, as her cloak kept becoming caught underneath her, and splinters from the timber poked through her jeans. Nocturne, as ever, waited impatiently.

"Well?" Jen, having finally reached Nocturne's designated discussion area, was quietly fuming at having had to endure such a journey.

"Falx are warriors of the White Light," explained Nocturne, "who guard the outlands of Albus Carcum. They prevent souls from escaping, and golden light from entering. They defend to the death the White Light of Evil."

"So what are they doing here, then?" she asked.

"As Smolder's power increases, so too does the White Light's supremacy. They're here to help Smolder win the battle, but also keep an eye on him."

"How come?"

Nocturne gave a skyward glance and tutted, apparently despairing of Jen's grasp - or rather, lack of it - concerning current events.

"Tsk! Because they don't trust him, of course! Smolder works for the White Light of Evil, remember?"

Jen couldn't possibly remember, given that this was the first time she'd heard about it, although on reflection it made perfect sense.

"I mean, it's hardly a pact made in heaven is it? Just because..." Nocturne was in danger of blathering on off topic again, especially now that she'd taken flight and was spinning around Jen's head, annoyingly. Jen decided to try and 'nip it in the bud', as it were.

"No, sure... er, yeah, whatever."

Nocturne came to an abrupt stop and hovered, eying Jen suspiciously. Fortunately, she thought better for instigating further elongated proceedings. She continued.

"Anyway, up until now they've been roaming the forest, slashing anything and everything in their path. They do entirely as they please. They're mostly invisible, and totally lethal." Nocturne suddenly paused, for effect more than anything, staring straight into Jen's eyes, before adding, "They don't turn you into smoke, dear Wandiacate, they kill you."

"So why aren't they here already then, finding us now?" Although this latest round of bad news concerned Jen greatly, Nocturne's established tendency to embellish things gave her some cause for comfort, and further enquiry.

"Because Smolder doesn't trust them either," replied Nocturne. "Falx move about invisibly, although you're supposed to be able to hear them, and they can only be seen when they're hunting. Each one hunts by reflection, by first sending out a blinding white flare, just as it becomes visible. A sickle-scythe then appears behind the flash, ready to mirror anything caught up in the light back onto its shiny curved steel blade. If an enemy of the White Light of Evil is reflected, then that enemy is destroyed. It is said that the moment you see the blade, it's already too late. Not long ago, I overheard some guards talking. One said the Falx could kill Smolder if they wanted to. They help him outside as they further weaken the forest's defences, but in here they're an unknown force."

Jen pondered on this for a moment, as Nocturne's words reminded her of the flashes of light both she and Emily had seen the previous night in the forest. Were those flashes made by the Falx? According to Deeron, the lights seen at that time were merely a signal indicating that Smolder's territory lay nearby. But if it really were the Falx, did Deeron actually know? And what about Arog? Did he know about them, and of what they were capable? One thing Jen did know; to mention any of this to Nocturne would be seriously unwise.

"I doubt many Falx would want Smolder's image reflected on them," she quickly added, more as a throwaway comment and means to break the silence, than anything else.

"Couldn't say myself," retorted Nocturne haughtily, as she embarked upon some side-to-side aerobatics, "seeing as I've never ACTUALLY met him, because I'VE never been caught…"

"Hmm," Jen sighed away Nocturne's latest jibe wearily. "Perhaps it's time we moved on."

"Just what I was saying…"

Jen, now facing front and guided by Nocturne, moved further back along the beam to where another supporting timber jutted out at 90° towards the middle of the castle roof, passing directly over smoke-filled cell rooms, lit corridors and dark passageways. Numerous struts or pillars, running vertically from it all the way up to the rafters above, intersected along the way.

Nocturne obviously wanted to follow this route, but Jen had some serious doubts. For one thing, they'd be easier to spot from below, due to the light from all those burning torches radiating upwards. For another, it was rough and uneven wood, and looked as though it were covered in something revolting as well. Worst of all, however, was the fact that the beam was simply too wide to straddle, meaning that Jen would have to walk along it upright, with nothing either side of her onto which to hold.

"Come on, it'll be a doddle!" said Nocturne, cheerily.

"That's easy for you to say," replied Jen, throwing Nocturne a very stern look as she carefully pulled herself up onto her feet. Holding onto a rafter above her for support, she stood for a moment, sizing up the possibilities of actually walking along the beam. Although the timber itself was roughly the same width as her body, her height above the ground made it feel as if she were about to walk along a tightrope. The simple fact was that Jen had to move somewhere; she couldn't stay up there in the roof forever more. She had Emily to find, Deeron to help and Bill to retrieve.

"Look," proffered Nocturne, almost tactfully. "If you can make it past the third corridor, we can drop down into a room where we'll be safe, for a while anyway. Now, you've got two pillars for support along the way. I mean, even you can do that!"

"Thanks," answered Jen, barely noticing the insult. Her field of view was focused upon the ground below, and the distance between her and it. She closed her eyes, took a deep breath, opened them again and stared straight ahead.

"I have to do this… I can do this… the pillar's not far… I have to do this… I can do this… the pillar's not far," Jen kept repeating those words, psyching herself up to let go of the rafter above her, and walk towards the first pillar. Slowly, slowly she moved, taking tiny steps. Again, and again. Her right arm was now outstretched. One more step, and she'll have to let go…

Jen walked trance-like to the first pillar, which turned out to be further away than she'd originally thought. The experience caused her to grab the pillar forcefully when she reached it, while closing her eyes and letting out a huge sigh of relief. She took a moment to steady herself and her nerves, and absorb what she had done. She felt sick and shivered in fear, but resolutely did not look down.

"That's the girl!" exclaimed Nocturne gleefully, spinning rapidly just above Jen's head. "See, I…."

"Nocturne, not now! SHUT UP!" The very last thing Jen needed at this moment was one of Nocturne's 'I-told-you-so' lectures.

"Just trying to help!" Nocturne snapped back defensively, with more than a little hurt in her voice. She flew off ahead, presumably to sulk.

Jen fought hard to maintain her focus upon the second pillar now in front of her. She manoeuvred gently around the first, and prepared herself to walk once more. "All I have to do," she muttered, calmly, "is repeat exactly what I've just done and walk slowly, carefully and hold my balance. Easy."

Holding on to the first pillar behind her, Jen began timidly to move forward. One step… two steps… her fingers detached from the supporting strut. Another step, and Jen instinctively raised both her arms for balance, just like a tightrope walker. She paced forward again, again, again, aga… Suddenly, buzzing in her right ear.

"Oh, and by the way! If you ARE going to fall you'd be best not to do it here, seeing as you're directly above one of Smolder's smoulder chambers!"

"Wha...?" Jen's concentration collapsed like a landslide along a cliff edge. Her head instantly filled with indecisive and jumbled thoughts - should she go back? Should she make a run for the pillar? Should she...? Then she looked down.

Had Nocturne not disturbed Jen at the precise moment she had, Jen's left foot might have been placed on the beam more evenly. As it was, when Jen looked down and reminded herself of just how high up she was, she shivered in fear. Then she slipped.

"WHOOOA!" All Jen could do was cry out, and fall. With nothing nearby to grab hold of, and the manner of her slipping propelling her away from the very beam she'd been walking along anyway, there was nothing anyone - especially Jen - could do.

The fact that she had slipped turned out to be the sole positive in this whole incident. Had she fallen straight down, she would have hit only white smoke. As it was, Jen fell slap-bang into the middle of the room, right on top of golden smoke. Granted, golden smoke about to become white, thereafter to be a condemned and imprisoned servant to Smolder's ill intentions; but not white yet where she fell, not there.

Jen's fall was essentially just that - freefall, in fact. Her landing, however, was quite something else. The slo-mo golden-smoked tornado bent and twisted to absorb her weight and speed as she fell onto it, cushioning her fall rather like a trampoline. Similar except that there was no rebound forcing her back upwards. In reality, it wouldn't have felt that much different if she'd fallen onto a mountain of cotton wool. As Jen descended further, the golden smoke enveloped and wrapped itself around her, lowering her into the room; or rather, the chamber.

What Jen couldn't possibly have seen from her previous viewing position was the slow-burning compost - conventional enough looking, except for the surrounding barbed wire. What she couldn't possibly have detected was the putrid, acrid smell - enough to make anyone retch until their eyes fell out of their head. Finally, what she couldn't possibly have heard was the sound - the kind of noise that one could only describe as complete and utter bedlam.

Upon the conclusion of her landing, the golden smoke rapidly dissolved back into its original funnel-shaped rotating column, leaving Jen lying face upwards, directly on top of the smouldering compost. It was at this precise moment that her senses were bombarded with all of the above.

For Jen, the noise was by far the worst thing she had to endure in that compost. Even the severe, burning heat - lessened greatly by her cloak of golden leaves, although nevertheless felt in her lower legs, hands, feet and head - was preferable to this. Every possible animal sound from the forest could be heard: birdcalls, screams and cries, flapping and fluttering, barking, hooting, howling, mooing, braying, squealing, squeaking, scratching, galloping and even stampeding. All at once, and all intensely loud. If there was ever a sound that could kill, it was this one.

Jen knew she had to get out of there right NOW, whatever it took! She frantically fumbled about, trying to get on to her front, but her hands burned every time she touched the compost. Unable to see, she struggled to decide precisely which way was front. In the frenzy, the burning leaves started to shift underneath her. Jen began to slide, downwards and sideways.

"You!" Jen heard a yell - impossible to tell from whom and where - above the piercing, agonizing din. She didn't care. She was going to die in there if she didn't get out, fast!

"Smoke!" Another yell. Followed by, "Find her!"

Jen had now slid into something, possibly wire. She grabbed it to try and get up onto her feet. Pain instantly shot into her hand, with a sharp stabbing force. She couldn't stop and deal with this, or even think about it. The noise was beyond deafening, and she could barely breathe, and still couldn't see. Jen managed somehow to pull herself up, partially. Something caught her leg, causing her to trip forward. More pain, this time in her body, as she blindly rolled, but at least she could now feel solid ground once more. No longer was she on the compost.

"Smolder will smoke me if that Wandiacate's not found!" The hollering voice cutting through the din sounded near hysterical now, and alarmingly closer than before. "Search the compost!"

Jen, lying on her back, quickly turned onto her front to stand up and make a run for it, even though she could barely see. This very movement caused the hood of her cloak to flip up over her head automatically, providing an instant and near total protection from the overbearing noise. The relief was extreme and in itself quite shocking; so much so, that Jen was left momentarily baffled as to what had happened, and then why she hadn't thought of putting her hood up herself much earlier.

"Smoke! There!" The bellowed order, now so close as to jolt Jen straight back into her predicament, forced her to turn around and face the bellower. Even through her sore weeping eyes, she could make out just ahead of her a large shadowy figure holding a pitchfork. "Gag her! Gag her!"

Before she could even react, Jen felt something wrap itself around her mouth like sticky tape! She tried to grab it, but could feel nothing there with her hands. Horrified and confused, she tried to prize apart her lips but they remained stuck together like superglue, point blankly refusing to separate. Worse still, the tightness around her mouth was becoming evermore severe, as though something were wiring her jaw shut!

Now rapidly approaching total panic while the shadowy figure loomed ever closer, Jen retreated back towards the corner wall. With nowhere to go, barely any eyesight, and no way out, she felt trapped and terrified - mortally terrified. Stumbling back further, she failed to register information coming from her right hand, namely that the wall behind her had suddenly ended. The dark shadow was now so close, she could feel its breathe upon her other hand, which she'd raised in a futile defensive gesture. She cowered down, dropped backwards and fell…

When you go from being on solid ground one moment to freefall the next, you naturally want to cry out. Jen wanted to, but she couldn't. The fall didn't last long though, which was undoubtedly a good thing. More dead leaves and general forest foliage broke her descent, into goodness knows where this time. Jen lay still for a moment, trying to gauge whether what was underneath her now was also burning. Cold dry leaves told her that it wasn't. She tried to stare up through watery eyes towards the ceiling through which she had supposedly just fallen. The room around her began to spin, while her stomach felt as though it was turning in the opposite direction. It was no use; she simply couldn't muster the strength to climb out, or even deal with the very process of thought right now. Her body and self were just too weak. She collapsed back into the heap of dry leaves, and promptly passed out.

Freyar, Garrett and the Sarcastic Squirrel

$\mathcal{E}$mily had lain perfectly still on the floor and in silence for some time after awakening, waiting for either something to happen or for someone to appear. As it was, neither event had yet occurred, and she began to feel increasingly confident that neither would.

However, the only fact Emily knew for absolute certain right now was that she was lying in a small dimly lit square room, with dark greystone walls and floor, and a low ceiling. She also knew the floor was freezing cold, and that she could seriously do with getting up ASAP to warm herself, somehow. Lastly, she knew one of her ankles ached like crazy from having been caught, yanked and dragged from the corridor outside, by some unseen force with a rope.

At least, she thought the corridor was just outside, but how could she tell? She knew she'd been dragged from A corridor - indeed, THE corridor from which she and Jen had been separated - but she couldn't be sure precisely where that was, distance-wise. This dilemma stemmed from the fact that Emily thought she had continued to travel for some distance, after the rope around her legs had actually stopped pulling her. When it had stopped, there had been a brief pause of a few minutes, followed by a strange sensation of feeling moved again by some other kind of force. After that, she had bizarrely and involuntarily fallen asleep

Although it sounded crazy, this wasn't the first time Emily had grappled with the sensations of time and movement when no visual clues were there to help her. In fact, it was precisely because of her falling experience in Albus Carcum that she had thought she was moving at all. Fortunately, the impressions here were nothing like as severe as back then; nor the landing, thankfully. In this instance, it had all been rather smooth and relatively comfortable - a soft flow of air brushing through her hair and across her forehead, combined with a general sense of being... well, weightless, or elevated off the ground somehow. Various pongy smells seemed to pass by as well. There was also, of course, the added difference of being surrounded by pitch-blackness, as opposed to bright white.

So, Emily was somewhere; she just wasn't sure where. She sat up and gently rubbed her ankle in an attempt to stop it throbbing, whilst examining the room more closely. There appeared to be no door, no window, no anything. How did she get in there if there was no door?

"This can't be right..." she pondered quietly to herself. There had to be a way in, and also likewise a way out.

Emily stood up slowly, and gave herself time to test her ankle. Once satisfied that it was okay to walk on, she approached the wall nearest to her. She placed a hand upon it to try and determine if it really was made of stone as it appeared. It was freezing cold, just like the floor; so much so, that she could only maintain contact with it for a few seconds. The wall felt like stone, that was for sure, but Emily remained unconvinced. Somehow, there was something going on in that room, she was sure of it. She just couldn't grasp what it was.

Emily shivered, having been cold for quite some time. She wrapped her cloak tightly around her body. The recollection of Albus Carcum made her long for the warmth her cloak had given off there, when she had wandered across that arctic plain. She was certainly warmer then than she was now. She pulled up her hood, thinking that it might help, and attempted to warm her hands by the meagre flame of one of the torches, hanging on the opposite wall.

Then, something caught her eye. At one end of this wall, Emily detected the thin outline of what looked distinctly like a door. Distinctly, that is, except that this door seemed to be behind the wall. The wall itself appeared translucent somehow or see-through, just enough to make out the vague contours and no more. Also, usually with doors you have an outer frame, some hinges, plus a handle or latch. This door possessed none of these, instead appearing to be completely flat with another wall behind the semi-transparent one. Were it not for the barely visible lines, you wouldn't know there was anything there at all.

As Emily moved nearer to examine the door more closely, she was struck by something even weirder. She had already scanned the room pretty closely, and hadn't been struck by any of this then. How come? Granted, this 'door' wasn't exactly advertising itself by slamming about as though caught in a force 9 gale, but it was certainly visible. So why…?

Emily's train of quizzical pondering suddenly came to an abrupt halt. She'd remembered something. When she'd first looked around the room, her hood was down. Now it was up. Was that it? Her hood?

Slowly, and whilst standing directly in front of the door, Emily lowered her hood. The moment it became completely detached from her head, the outline of the door disappeared.

"What the…!" Emily gasped, in absolute astonishment. She knew, of course, first-hand just how amazing - lifesaving, in fact - these cloaks of golden leaves could be, but to be able to enhance or alter your vision, that was something different. VERY different. What other things might the hood allow her to see? Approaching guards? The whereabouts of the hidden antlers? Deity? In Emily's mind, the potential consequences of this were in serious danger of running away with her.

Regardless, encouraged by her discovery and with her hood back up, Emily wondered if she might be able to actually open this door. As there was no handle, knob or any other such attachment, she decided her best bet would be to basically place her shoulder up against it and push as hard as she could. To her amazement, the door swung open quite easily; so easily, in fact, that she almost fell into the new room. Reacting quickly in case there was anything about to jump out at her, Emily scanned the area. Actually there appeared to be nothing, other than yet another cold, dark and barren space, lacking even one torchlight.

A little deflated at this, and judging the first room to be preferable, Emily turned to leave. Then, in the weakest of light passing the open door, she suddenly caught a glimpse of a small pair of green eyes, blinking up at her from the farthest corner.

"Hello," she called nervously, and rather surprised herself. "Who are you?"

There came no reply. Instead, a second pair of eyes suddenly joined the first. And then another, and another! Emily reached back into her room and lifted a burning torch down from the wall, hanging just by the door. Now armed with light, and also a weapon just in case, she cautiously ventured back into the dark space to investigate who or what was there. As Emily moved forward, she heard the sudden pattering of tiny feet, and panic stricken squeaks.

"It's alright," she called softly, not wanting to alarm anything. "I won't hurt you, I promise."

Emily stood still, and the movement stopped. She gently swung the torchlight towards the area of the room where the commotion had come from, to see many pairs of tiny eyes gazing up at her. Slowly, she stepped a little closer, to finally see a huddle of terrified and trembling rabbits in the torchlight, all squeezed up against one another and the wall.

"Oh, I'm sorry," she said gently, "I didn't mean to frighten you. Really, you've nothing to fear." Emily placed the torchlight into a nearby wall holder, sat down on the floor in the middle of the room, and waited. Gradually, movement centred around the corner wall became calmer and more spread out until, one by one, Emily could see tiny eyes peek up at her as they nervously entered the glow of the torchlight.

"Come on," she called again, in her usual bright and friendly voice. "It's okay... really."

As the numbers around her increased, Emily could see that there were not only rabbits, but squirrels also. A few of the larger and less timid ones made their way to the front.

"You must be Smolder's prisoners, like me," she said, reaching out to stroke one of them as they congregated around her.

"Aye, that's right," said the largest rabbit somewhat suspiciously, as he made his way to the front of the group. In the role of apparently delegated representative, the rabbit adopted a rather austere and business-like stance. With a round stomach, a very broad North Country accent, and a protruding left foot that gently tapped the floor as he spoke, the rabbit continued. "There's many more o' us than's 'ere, and some's smoke already. So who are thee then, and what's tha' doin' 'ere?"

Emily had struggled with many things on this adventure, but she could never have guessed that accents would be one of them. All the same, she did understand the request for her name and an explanation, eventually.

"Er... oh, my name... er, Emily. I... well, I came here with Deeron and his army, who are fighting Smolder. My job was to find the antlers belonging to his magic stags, but somehow I became captured. I also lost my friend, and, well, here I am."

"Oh aye," the spokes-rabbit replied slowly, seeming to reflect upon Emily's story. After a few moments, and apparently satisfied, the rabbit's mood appeared to lighten. "Well, tha's welcome wi' us." he said, moving closer. "I'm Freyar." Two of the other larger rabbits, followed by a squirrel, also wandered nearer, choosing to stand in a line alongside him.

"Pleased to meet you," replied Emily.

"This 'ere's Garrett," said Freyar, turning to the rabbit nearest to him; "then there's Swift," pointing to the next rabbit; "and Pottle." the squirrel on the end was last to be introduced. "Guz wi'out sayin' there's more o' us, as tha' can see."

"How long have you all been here?"

"'Aven't a clue. We started keepin' count 'ow many times meals came, but it came so much that we gave up. Not that they feed us well, mind. Food's diabolical in 'ere, tha'nose."

"Do you know why you were brought here?" asked Emily, wondering if this information could shed any light into precisely where they were.

"For our good looks and charm, of course!" butted in Pottle the squirrel rather loudly, and in an absurdly pompous voice. "I mean it's obvious really, isn't it!"

"Sorry?" Emily was more than a little confused by this reply. Freyar glanced skywards, and groaned. Garrett interjected.

"Er, that is to say… er, well, as it were…" Garrett fairly stumbled over his words, "Young Pottle, Miss, he was just being… well, he does rather have a tendency to be…"

"Sarcastic!" interrupted Freyar angrily, throwing Pottle a fierce stare. "'Cause that's all 'e does! Drives me up flamin' wall, ah can tell thee! Tha'll get no change outer that one, Lassy. Best ignore 'im! Ah do!"

"Emily. My name's Emily." Emily was struggling to keep up with, let alone understand, what was going on around her. Her words, however, fell on large floppy deaf ears. Freyar was now in lecture mode, and had decided to get a few things off his chest.

"If ah've told thee wonce, Pottle," Pottle was now attempting to cower behind Swift, "ah've told thee dozens o' times. If tha's got nowt good t' say, say nowt at all! Yer nay big, lad, an' yer way nay clever! Yer just daft! 'Ear all say nowt, from now on! Clear?"

"Er..." Garrett, in his very polished polite English and unassuming tone, tried to recover the reigns of Emily's original question and regain some semblance of calm. "Well, er... we're here, Miss, because we tried to escape. We're actually in the smoke queue, as... as it were, at this precise..."

Suddenly, chains could be heard clanging outside, and hooves clipping against the floor.

"Quick, hide her!" whispered Swift, urgently. "It's dinner!"

The rabbits and squirrels rapidly assembled themselves around, in front of, and on top of Emily, disguising her as a huge fur ball in seconds. It was rather smelly underneath them all, but they meant well, and she was grateful to them for hiding her. After all, Emily wasn't sure that she was actually 'captured' as such right now, given her certainty about having been moved after the original rope assault had ended. Also, why would her captors have placed her in that room - a room with a door, no less - next to the smoke queue, without interrogating her first about Jen's whereabouts? Besides, if they had captured Jen as well, Smolder would now have everything he needed, so it really didn't make any sense that she was there at all.

Whilst Emily was contemplating all of this under a large bundle of fur, a loud clunk was heard, followed by a blast of light suddenly illuminating the floor around her. She couldn't see much, but it appeared to be coming from low down in the corner of the wall directly ahead, precisely where the animals had cowered when she had first entered the room. Something was thrown in, and it clattered noisily as it hit the ground. Then another clunk and the extra light vanished, leaving the dull torchlight as sole provider once more.

The instant the second clunk was heard, every creature dived off Emily and onto whatever it was that was thrown in. She had seen neither the hatch nor the opening, nor even the tray being thrown in, but from what she could now see, there didn't appear to be very much for any one person to eat, let alone one person plus many hungry animals. Also, what there was seemed to be being systematically looted by the squirrels, who were snatching way more than their fare share. Irrespective of the meagre supplies delivered, in that moment Emily's presence had been all but forgotten by everyone. Everyone, that is, except Freyar, who attempted to reinforce some sense of order into the group.

"Now then, brothers an't sisters," he called, "we 'ave a Wandiacate in't our midst, so we'd better 'ear plan for our escape." Every animal suddenly stopped shoving, barging and generally dive-bombing onto the food tray. They all then simply stared, directly and expectantly at Emily. Many of the squirrels continued nibbling, however.

"Er… how do you know I'm a Wandiacate?" asked Emily rather defensively, being as she was totally unprepared for such a request. Nobody had told her that as a Wandiacate it was also her job to hatch plots, surmise strategies and present proposals for breakouts, all upon demand. She had actually hoped that Freyar was going to ask the others to save her some food. Did they want diagrams as well?

"Well, guz wi'out sayin', don't it!" replied Freyar, rather gruffly. "Tha' must be, 'cause 'ow else could tha' enter this place? So come on then, out wi' it, what's t' plan?"

"Well," replied Emily, stumbling for the right words, "I haven't actually got one."

"Oh, she hasn't ACTUALLY got one!" mimicked Pottle, in another outlandish voice. As he did so, bits of nut spewed everywhere from his mouth, causing some of the nearby rabbits to complain bitterly. Further arguing, name-calling and other such loud bickering then ensued, mainly over the uneven distribution of the food tray, and Pottle in general. Freyar slumped, glancing wearily skyward again, and shook his head.

Now, let us remember what Emily has been through. She is tired, bruised and very hungry. She has lost Jen, is lost herself, and happens to consider mockery unfunny at the best of times. To be repeatedly ridiculed by a bunch of rodents who consider her presence there to be of no greater importance than to rescue them is, frankly, akin to pushing all the wrong buttons, so far as she is concerned.

"Alright then, so what's your plan?" retorted Emily, sharply. "After all, there's plenty of you, and you've been here long enough to think something up, surely!"

Much jeering and squeaky laughter came from both around and within the food tray, as though the very idea of them doing anything for themselves was simply ludicrous. Emily was becoming more heated by the moment, until Freyar stepped in to try and calm things down.

"Na'then, na'then" he called, gesturing for some quiet. "This 'ere Lassy's right. Why, it's as plain as day that we're in't majority round 'ere tha'nose, so we've got t' pull together t' find escape, or else be stuck 'ere 'til smoke comes. I'll not be 'avin' that! Nor will the rest of yer, so come on!" There was a pause, punctuated by zero movement from anyone, and complete silence, until Freyar asked quietly, and a little shyly, "So, er… what's the plan then, Lassy?"

"Emily," corrected 'Lassy' again, through gritted teeth. She was beginning to regret having entered this room at all now, and they weren't exactly the brightest bunch to have to deal with. After all, what was required was pretty obvious. "We need to look for any hole or opening that any of us can squeeze through, or else make bigger. Anything that you can see on the floor, walls or ceiling."

"Oh aye, right," muttered Freyar, approvingly. Then, adopting a loud and commanding voice, he said "Well off yer go all of yer, and no kippin' nor fightin' on't job neither!"

With enforced vigour and restored order from Freyar, combined with the fact that the food tray had now been ransacked bare anyway, all the animals set to work to find a way out of the room. The obvious place for Emily to start was with the hatch, except that when closed it was impossible to see. No markings or indents were visible from the inside at all, not even via close examination by Emily using torchlight.

"Oh aye," nodded Freyar sagely, casually observing Emily searching along the wall, and no doubt seeing an opportunity to delay his own involvement. "Ah noticed this before, tha'nose. The others, well they don't pay much 'eed to such things - too busy trashin' tray an' all - but me, well," he paused, as though about to reveal something of deep significance, "not to blow me own trumpet, tha' understands like, but when ah see 'atch open, food chucked in, then 'atch go, ah think "Well, that's clever is that 'atch. 'Ow'd they manage that, then?" Nowt remains after, tha'nose, nowt at all. Tha canno' even see owt with glasses! Now young Swift 'ere, 'e was..."

"Ooh, hang on..." interrupted Emily, suddenly remembering what had allowed her to see the door. Freyar's musings had barely been heard anyway, much less understood. "Let's try this." With her one free hand she grappled with the hood of her cloak, eventually managing to pull it up over her head.

The instant her hood was up, Emily could see a square hatch in the bottom left-hand corner of the wall. Like the door, it was only visible by its faint outline, and seemed to be behind the wall she could actually see. Also, just like the door, the stone wall appeared translucent, allowing her to see it.

"It's here! I've got it!" she said, excitedly.

"Gerraway! Ah canno' see owt." Freyar scanned the wall in vain.

Emily knelt down to get a better view, and to see if she could access the hatch. It was only when she was this close that she could see what was happening to the wall. For one thing, it was moving, and for another it seemed to have literally turned to smoke! Great long trails of dark grey matter that once resembled stone now swirled slowly both around and into themselves, from one end to the other. The wall remained vertical and flat, as though the smoke were contained behind glass or some such other unseen surface. It reminded Emily of a time back in the forest when she was staring down into the lake, and noticed something slither about underneath. That made perfect sense of course, peering into a lake, but this was a vertical wall she was looking at. She propped up her torchlight, and decided to touch the wall with her finger to see if it still felt cold.

The moment Emily's skin touched the wall, the smoke closest to her finger instantly recoiled, dispersing itself rapidly well away from the point of contact. It behaved like a frightened animal, or fast-moving shoal of fish fending off a predator. In its place remained a gaping hole, allowing full access to the hatch, which appeared to be part of another, this time wooden, wall.

"Whoa…" exclaimed Emily, in a rather understated and yet thoroughly bewildered tone.

"By 'eck…" added Freyar, in much the same way. Neither Freyar nor any of the other animals could observe the smoky translucence of the wall; only Emily was able to see that. What they could see now, however, was the hole in the wall and the hatch.

Although mindful of the fact that a guard could be just on the other side, Emily decided to give the hatch a gentle push to see if it would open. No such luck - it was locked or bolted somehow on the other side. Even after a harsh shove, it still refused to budge. This was a pity, as Emily reckoned she could just about squeeze through that hatch.

"It's no good," she said, sounding tired and deflated. "I'll never get this open, it's bolted on the other side. We need to think of something else." The kneeling down was starting to hurt anyway, so she withdrew her hand back from the hatch and sat down. As soon as her hand was clear of the wall, smoke rushed back in to fill up the hole instantly, forming a translucent mask over the hatch once more. While Emily sat pondering the stubborn resolve of the hatch, Freyar continued to stare agog at the wall.

"Bah gum, Lassy," he exclaimed, almost overcome by what he had just seen. "In all mah days, ah've ne'er seen owt so clever as that! 'Ow'd thee do that, Lassy? 'Ow? Thee must tell if tha'nose, tha'nose!"

"Emily," came an obviously heated response. "Freyar, my name is Emily!"

"Tsk! Oh aye, right…" Freyar gave another skyward glance, having forgotten yet again. "Sorry. Not so good wi' names, me."

"So I gather… anyway, that particular how is not important right now. The how we need to know is how we can open that hatch."

"We could all dig, I should imagine," a young voice from behind Emily, proffered sheepishly. It was Garrett, surrounded by the others who had come to investigate Freyar's energetic nattering. "Then perhaps one of us could squeeze through and release the bolt, as it were."

"Good idea!" said Emily, excitedly. Although it seemed obvious, Emily hadn't really thought of this bunch as the physical sort. Turning to Freyar, she asked "How often does the guard come?"

"Ee nor' often enough, an't no mistake," he replied, with a sigh and despairing glance towards the now barren food tray on the floor. "Er… ah'd say now 'e's bin, we'll be positively gaggin' before 'e comes again."

"Quite a long time, then?" queried Emily, a little sarcastically.

"Aye."

"Then let's get to it. Now Garrett, you dig…" Emily's delegation of tasks came to a rapid and chaotic halt as every rabbit, with the exception of Freyar, instantly dived for the wall and began digging for all he was worth. Worse than the fact that they were digging everywhere along the wall - everywhere that is, except under the hatch - was that they were trying to dig through stone as well!

"No, no! Stop!" she yelled. The rabbits obligingly paused, staring up at her with a blank expression upon each and every face. Emily could see that he hadn't misjudged this lot after all. "It's no good scraping at stone, is it? Look," she reached forward to touch the wall, "when I do THIS the stone disappears, which allows US to get underneath the hatch to the dirt below, so that YOU can dig. See?"

"Oh… absolutely, as it were," said a suspiciously confident-sounding Garrett. A few of the other rabbits nodded, vaguely. Freyar, as ever, looked despondently skyward.

"EXCEPT," added Emily sharply, guessing that they were all about to pounce on the hatch, "ONLY two of you can dig at a time, so you'll have to work in shifts, while the others move earth into next door."

"Got it. Right," said Swift, who appeared to take charge of roster duties. "Willow and Nib, you dig first!" Two rabbits instantly dived towards the hatch and set to work burrowing with notable enthusiasm, creating a pile of earth behind them in seconds. "Now, Tibbuck and Arrow, you move their pile." Two more rabbits began scraping Willow and Nib's pile behind them. "Padlow and Barl, you're next…" and so on, until a long line of rabbit pairs had been established, each moving the pile of earth in front of them to the pair behind, running all the way to the door at the back of the room.

Everyone was involved, including the squirrels who helped ferry stones, twigs and other larger objects. When the front two rabbits became tired, they moved to the back of the line, leaving the two behind them to take over at the hatch, while everyone else moved up a position. Emily had to admit that Swift was handling the soil removal very well, even if it was rather messy. Throughout the dig, she kept her hood up and her hand pressed against the wall. Garrett remained close by to monitor progress, and no doubt stay clear of the clouds of earth and dust now steadily engulfing the room.

Freyar declined the offer of a place in the line due, he said, to a bad back. Instead, he sought to make himself useful by patrolling up and down the effective chain gang, proffering such helpful advice to the troops as,

"Gerron wi'it, Magro!" and,

"Ya gret puddin' 'ead, Kapsin! Dig lad, dig!"

It wasn't long before Garrett's head popped out from beneath the hatch and, covered in mud, announced to Emily, Swift and Freyar that they were almost through to the corridor outside, albeit with a slight hitch.

"Thing is," he explained, enthusiastically, "we've dug through to the wooden floorboards in the hallway outside, but our chaps are having probs in the final push, as it were." Freyar, never one for Garrett's army-like talk, sighed and adopted a decidedly disdainful look. Garrett nevertheless persevered.

"Well, we've managed to make a teensy-weensy hole and can now observe, as it were, the lock fastening the hatch closed. However, it's barely big enough for the smallest here, and some of us, as you WELL know Freyar, are of the… well," Garrett emitted a soft, slightly embarrassed and light-hearted kind of laugh. "Ha-ha, I mean physically speaking, as it were… well, some of us are a little on the… well, the LARGE side, as…well, as well you know, as it were." Freyar was by now ready to explode.

"Thee speak for tha'self, Garrett! Ah manage! Always 'ave! Just 'cuz ah'm…"

"Guys, please!" interrupted Emily, as diplomatically as she could. "Can we just concentrate on getting out of here? We don't have time for squabbles. Now, Garrett, you say the hole is barely big enough for the smallest here. Are you saying there is somebody who can squeeze through?"

"Well, yes indeed, but…"

"But what?" demanded Freyar, suspiciously.

"Well," replied Garrett, hesitantly, "the only one actually here small enough is, well… Pottle, as it were."

"Lummin 'eck! 'Eaven 'elp us ahl if Pottle's ar best 'ope! Thee may as well thro' in't towel raht now!" Freyar shook his head, as much in disgust as dismay, and began walking back to where some of the rabbits were still finishing off, having seemingly given up on the whole thing.

"Look," Emily hastened after him, trying desperately to sound positive and recover some remnants of both the plan and the meeting. "He should be okay. After all, all he's got to do is climb through the hole and release the bolt. That's it! He can manage that, surely!"

"Huh!" grunted Freyar, not bothering to stop or even turn around. Garrett shrugged, and resumed directing tasks underneath the hatch.

"Oh he can manage it alright," mused Swift, casually gazing after Freyar's departure, "but Pottle's far from reliable, and he badly let us down in the forest. Freyar won't trust him again because of what happened."

"Why, what did happen?" asked Emily.

"Well," began Swift, with a soft sigh in his voice, "just before Deity was taken prisoner, some rumours began spreading through the forest, about how animals had been captured and ended up here, inside Smolder's Castle. Few believed it of course, but others like Freyar and Garrett began to wonder, especially as friends and relatives would go missing, often without a trace. Then the trees started dying, and so a group of us, led by Freyar, decided to try and make it to Huntswood, where we had heard things were better. We got as far as Deerbrook but couldn't find anywhere to cross, as Smolder's guards were everywhere and the river where we were was too wide."

"So how did Pottle ruin anything?"

"When it was dark, Freyar sent Garrett to look for any point where we might all be able to cross. Pottle went with him, as being the smallest in the group he could easily crawl through the reeds undetected. They got to a distance upriver when they stumbled upon a hidden lone guard. Garrett quickly made up a story that both he and Pottle were working for Smolder, patrolling the reed beds looking for escapees. The guard as good as believed him until Pottle opened his mouth, making some sarcastic remark about the guard's job. They were promptly detained, and a search was mounted. They found the rest of us soon after. Freyar has never forgiven him."

"Oh," was all Emily could think of to say in response, as this put a whole new light - or more accurately, shade - upon the situation. The simple fact remained, however, that there was no alternative or plan B to fall back on here. If Pottle was the only one who could fit through that hole, then it had to be him to unhook the latch.

"Okay, look," she began, adopting her now well-honed dispute-settling mode. "The chances of there being a guard on the other side of this hatch are thin, but if there is anyone out there we can't escape this way, so we're no worse off than we are already. If there isn't a guard there, Pottle can hardly give the game away to anyone, can he? Basically, we don't lose anything by him going out there, trustworthy or not."

"Well no, I suppose..." answered Swift, slightly lost in the argument.

"Right then, Pottle can undo the latch but he must be made to understand that he says absolutely nothing to anyone from now on."

To that end, Garrett made the suggestion that Pottle, for the time being at least, be confined to speaking out loud only after having been given special permission by either Freyar or himself.

"It worked frightfully well for us chaps in the trenches," he explained with quite some enthusiasm, and more than a little nostalgia. "Any soldier who strays from the line, well, he needs to be shown the error of his ways by discipline and example! You know, I'd go so far as to say I think this could be the making of young Pottle, as it were."

"If it shuts 'im up, ah've nay complaint," replied Freyar, coldly.

Pottle was thereafter given stern instructions from Emily, aided by Garrett, on how to unhook the latch. He was then given even sterner orders from Freyar on what to do - and more importantly, what not to do - if anyone was out there. Freyar could be quite an extraordinarily harsh leader when he wanted to, and these were extraordinary circumstances. The fact that he held Pottle responsible for them all being in the predicament they were in now, did not go unmentioned either. Pottle listened dutifully, and ventured only an occasional nod.

The truth was, that deep down Pottle was actually a good squirrel. He didn't actively seek to upset anyone or cause trouble - far from it - he just couldn't stop himself from making daft, insulting or sarcastic comments sometimes, usually at the most inappropriate moment. He regretted it afterwards of course, but would always do the same again regardless. It was simply his way.

"In order to facilitate an advance upon the enemy," enthused Garrett, explaining 'tactics' to Pottle at the hatch, "once in the lower chamber travel due east, whereupon, at approximately o' two hundred seconds later, you'll intercept said excavation at precisely twelve o'clock."

"'E means, the 'ole's above yer 'ead!" interrupted Freyar, brusquely.

"Er, well, precisely, as it were. Now then," Garrett quickly resumed his air of a military chief dispensing orders. "Remember, prior to exiting, to ascertain enemy positions, and, whence forth identified, plan and execute means for the disengagement…"

"Flamin' 'eck, Garrett! For 'eaven's sake, man!" Freyar, now close to the end of his tether, turned to the thoroughly bewildered-looking Pottle and continued his instruction in a rather more concise, and significantly louder fashion. "Na'then, you! Tha Listen 'ear! Get out there an' open 'atch smartish, and mind thee doesn't louse it up! Clear?" Freyar's large round face loomed down in fiery anger, millimetres away from the sarcastic squirrel's miniscule head. In no sense could Freyar's intentions be misunderstood were Pottle to snarl this up. He nodded, terrified. "Then gerron wi'it, lad! Move yerself!" Pottle dived down into the freshly dug tunnel beneath the hatch, just as fast as his legs could manage.

From a tiny hole in a dark corner of the floor just outside in the corridor, popped an even tinier squirrel's head. The first thing that struck Pottle was the light; way more than he'd been used to, having been confined to the dark cell room for so long. As his eyes slowly adjusted, he began to make out a long straight passageway ahead of him, with door after door and torch after torch separating each wall into identical blocks for as far as he could see. Pottle was staggered and more than a little frightened, causing him to cower somewhat back down into the hole. To a squirrel of the size he was, everything looked gigantic and rather intimidating at the best of times, but here it was made all the worse by the total lack of anything to run up, forage through, hide behind or climb inside of. This place was naked and barren, and seriously uninviting for any animal, especially a squirrel. Pottle quickly decided that this Smolder person/thing must be several bags short of a full load to want to live here! What's more, he'd have fun telling him, if he ever got the chance.

Eventually satisfied that the stillness and almost total silence - except for a low hum - would continue, Pottle crept out of the hole and into the corridor. The hatch was directly above his head, and he could easily see now the latch at the top holding it closed. 'This'll be a cinch,' he thought, convincing himself that an easy job done would ensure his return into Freyar's good books. It was all beginning to feel like a gift, until he caught a glimpse of the guard just behind him.

Pottle froze dead to the spot, his mind frantically assessing all he had done since poking his head up from the tunnel, for anything that might have given him away. Fortunately, he'd done very little, except climb quietly out of the hole and dream about being Freyar's best pal again, not that he ever was before. Of course, if he'd paid a little more attention to the task in hand and simply looked behind him, he'd have seen the goat standing there; and standing he was, although he wasn't moving. Actually, he didn't appear to be doing anything at all, except drooping his head down close to the floor, and making a soft rumbling noise.

Pottle stared more closely, and could see that the guard's eyes were closed. He was asleep! The guard was actually asleep! And snoring! Pottle at first felt strangely let down by this, failing completely to see the potential advantages of a slumbering sentry for the purposes of a breakout. 'Just how useless a guard do you have to be to fall asleep on the job?' he brooded to himself. Then, a devilish and mischievous grin formed across Pottle's tiny face, combined with a swelling urge to creep up and yell something loud and, needless to say, sarcastic in the guard's ear. That, or else kick him squarely on the behind. After some deliberation, Pottle decided that the latter option would probably be less effective due to his own physical size. Besides, his strength lay in his vocal chords.

To Pottle, a dare - any dare, even one self-imposed - was like a large pile of hazelnuts; he just couldn't resist the temptation. With both the gagging order and Freyar's third-degree lecture already long since forgotten, Pottle crept slowly forward, mentally refining his 'Wakey-wakey!' punchline whilst poised ready to deliver it at full throttle. Just then, coming from the escape hole now behind him, he heard a "Psst!" sound. He looked down to see two rabbit's eyes peering up at him. It was Garrett.

"What's going on, as it were?" called up Garrett quietly, with an air of impatience. "The chaps are becoming restless, don't you know... er, permission to speak, as it were!"

"Wha...? Oh... er, nothing, nearly there..." replied Pottle whispering, his attention reverted back abruptly to the official mission, that of opening the hatch and speaking only when authorized. He suddenly felt himself grappling with a serious dilemma, as, for Pottle, the lure of conveying some witty remark - as he saw it - into the right ear of a dozing goat was intense. However, Freyar's anticipated fury, combined with the thought of letting everybody else down - again - appeared to win through, for the moment at least.

Pottle scrambled up the side of the protruding hatch door to the top, and along to the latch in the middle. It was fairly stiff to move and took some effort on his part, especially for a squirrel with his slightness of build, but after several tugs and some persistent picking, the latch flipped upwards and the hatch door fell, with Pottle perched atop of it. He jumped off just before the door hit the floor flat on with a *boof!* sound, followed by a cloud of dust that instantly engulfed the air. Amongst the general haze of grot now both covering and surrounding him, Pottle could make out Freyar, Garrett and the partial head of Emily, staring back at him through a neat square hole in the wall.

"WE'RE…" Freyar, having immediately seen the guard, slapped his paw over Nib's mouth who, in a flurry of rowdy excitement, was about to shriek to the group, and quite possibly the entire castle, that they were free, which in truth they were not.

"Nay a sound!" hissed Freyar in a scalding whisper. "Any of yer!" He turned back to observe in silence the dormant goat, with Garrett, Emily and a few of the others. The guard suddenly appeared to be affected by the dust, sniffling and twitching his nose quite wildly, and causing him to lift his head. It looked as though he were about to sneeze! Then… the urge having thankfully passed, he merely lowered his head once more and resumed his inactive position. Emily, for her part, was just mightily grateful that someone had seen the guard, because she hadn't. She was still waiting for her eyes to adjust to the light even now.

"What do you suppose he's, um, doing precisely, as it were?" queried Garrett, in a soft-clipped undertone voice. Pottle had by now rejoined them, completely covered in dust and looking like a ghost. He was about to blurt something out, but suddenly remembering the gag rule, began instead to make bizarre eye and body movements whilst pointing towards his mouth. Freyar eyed him with barely concealed contempt.

"Gerron wi'it, permission t' speak!" he murmured.

"He's asleep!" whispered Pottle, animatedly.

"You sure?" asked Freyar.

"Positive! He's barely moved since I left the tunnel, and he snores! Listen." Everyone obligingly eavesdropped on the guard for any confirming sounds of shuteye. A soft, occasional and breathed rumble could be heard from across the passageway.

"See?" grinned Pottle triumphantly, still covered in dust.

"Ah canno' 'ear owt," said Freyar disappointedly, as he scratched the inside of one ear.

"Well you know, there's POSSibly something there, as it were," pondered Garrett deeply, committing a level of scrutiny probably better suited to a court of law than a breakout.

"Who cares!" snapped Emily, with as much urgency in her whispered voice as impatience. "He's dead to the world! Let's go!"

"Oh, aye," nodded Freyar quickly. "The Lass… er, Emily's right, tha'nose. Let's gerroutter 'ere. Quietly!"

One by one, every animal, aided by Garrett and Pottle, climbed gingerly through the hatch into the corridor, and stood silently along the opposite wall under the watchful glare of Freyar. Surprisingly it all went off rather well, except for one incident where Magro managed to trip himself up and fall over quite spectacularly. All eyes anxiously converged upon the sleeping guard as he hit the passageway floor with a dull thud, but the sentry luckily remained still and steadfastly aslumber. Emily exited last of all, making it through the hole with barely millimetres to spare. She took her time and moved slowly, all the while keeping a close watch on the guard. As she crept back up onto her feet, she had the brainwave of closing the hatch behind her so as to allay any suspicion from the guard once he woke up. This would hopefully result in their escape remaining undetected for quite some time.

Emily scanned each end of the passageway, trying to decide which way to go. The logical route would be to go right, and so avoid walking past the siesta-loving sentry, but she just wasn't convinced. The corridor was dead straight that way, meaning that if the guard woke up they'd easily be seen. Going left at least offered a bend in the hallway not far away, but for all she knew it could be a dead end beyond. On top of that, she still had Jen to find, the stone door to locate, and then remove the antlers from behind it. Oh, and she had to find an escape route for Freyar and his mob as well! Emily was hungry and exhausted, and the work had barely begun.

She made the decision - left - and signaled as much to everyone. Freyar raised a questioning eyebrow, while some of the others formed decidedly worried expressions on their faces. However, left it was, and so they began to slowly and silently tiptoe past the sleeping goat. Emily led the way, followed by Freyar, Garrett and the others.

Had Pottle not been consigned to the back of this procession, things might have gone very differently. It had always been the case that he'd resented being last in anything, but Pottle's mood had darkened throughout the cell room exodus, largely because no one had shown any direct appreciation towards him. This was now a cause of deep and intensifying rancour, that after having singularly, as he saw it, saved the day by opening the hatch, there should be no gratitude nor praise, nor even any recognition of his stunning bravery or of a job well done. Worse, Freyar had made no attempt to make amends for the many times he had wronged him, nor even removed that ridiculous no-talk rule! Pottle seethed, resentful and angry, at the very end of the line.

Idling past the guard, he recalled how insulted he'd felt that even this dismal excuse for a watchdog had failed to witness his glorious moment of... Then, where bitterness suddenly peaked, temptation took over once more - the temptation to throw a spanner in the works, to upset the applecart, to give everyone a piece of his mind.

Walking calmly and resolutely towards the guard's right ear, so immersed was Pottle in actually thinking about revenge, when he reached his tiresome target he couldn't remember what it was he was going to say! His earlier honed and ultra-refined sarcastic punchline had gone completely. Suddenly mortified, and with rising panic, Pottle proceeded to blurt out at full volume the first thing that came into his head.

"…YOU'RE FIRED!!"

Pottle's ability to belie his physical size through his vocal chords was actually quite something, as his words cut into the near total silence of the corridor like a lightening strike, resonating far down both ends. Everyone within earshot lost at least one heartbeat as they were forced to stop dead on their tiptoes, momentarily stunned by the verbal explosion just detonated. As for the guard, he'd received his unofficial marching orders directly into his right ear, causing him to shudder up rigid as if instantly frozen solid, or electrocuted.

Emily glanced back just in time to see the guard begin to shake his head and grunt aggressively, obviously trying desperately hard to come round after his ear-splitting awakening. Precious time gains were slipping away fast, leaving them with only one option.

"RUN!"

Emily shot off along the passageway, pursued by what resembled a mad race of squirrels versus rabbits. The squirrels, naturally enough, were doing quite well and managing in the main to keep up, but the rabbits were struggling. Their tails bobbed up and down as they tried to run quickly, but were just too slow. Things probably weren't helped by Freyar's fiery tirade towards Pottle all the way along the corridor, screaming,

"Ah'll 'ave 'im! Ah will! Ah'll flamin' well 'ave 'im!"

Emily could very quickly detect the heavy and distinctive clip-clop steps of the guard, rapidly gaining pace behind them. She'd now reached the bend in the corridor, but it was all too obvious that they'd be caught in no time; and with who knows what ahead of them except probably more passageway and closed doors either side, she took the only possible course of action she could see. She yanked the hood of her cloak up over her head, and threw herself at the nearest door. To her great relief, it opened.

"In here, quickly!" she called, as the door swung inwards. Everybody scurried in after her just as fast as they could, and she stood poised ready to close it again the instant the last rabbit had bounded in. Barely a second passed between the door clicking shut and the thunderous sound of the guard's heavy hooves charging past in the corridor outside. They were safe, for the moment at least, but back inside a dark dusty room again, not that far from the one they had worked so hard to break out of. Emily felt a strange mix of relief combined with almost total frustration.

"Lummin' 'eck!" gasped Freyar, panting ferociously whilst clutching his chest as he propped himself up against the wall. "That were close!" Everybody suddenly glanced an anxious eye towards him, as if struck by what he had just said. After all, it was clear to anyone that Freyar was well past his prime physically, but the fact that he had been the last one through the door just before Emily had closed it, gave his words a deeper resonance. It may have been close for them, but it had actually been a hair's breadth for Freyar, and the fact was they had very nearly lost him.

Many glancing eyes, as if on cue, diverted away from Freyar and onto a corner of the room where stood a mortified, and very alone, Pottle. Anxiety was, from some, turning to anger, with many of the younger rabbits beginning to gang up around him. Suddenly, a very real threat presented itself of the scene descending into chaos, and probably violence. Garrett, as second-in-command, took the initiative and immediately stepped in-between Pottle and the looming crowd, which was just as well because Freyar was still gasping to get his breath back.

"Now then, that's enough of that," ordered Garrett, in his usual dignified but nevertheless firm tone of voice. "Back to order if you so please, as it were." The crowd reluctantly backed away. "Young Pottle here will answer for his actions, but in the proper way and NOT by mob rule." A few puzzled expressions fell upon Garrett, as few in the crowd appeared to know what the 'proper' way was, or that there even was such a thing. "Swift, both you and Scud are responsible for Pottle until either Freyar or myself say otherwise. Take him into custody please. We shall deal with his insubordination at a later time." This was actually clever thinking, given that Swift commanded respect amongst most of the other animals, while Scud was both the largest and undoubtedly toughest squirrel in the group.

Emily glanced around their latest residence with a sense of dismay. It appeared to be in an even worse state than the one they had just left, with dirty straw and various other kinds of grot strewn everywhere across the floor. Two barely alight torches hung on the wall, radiating a dullness that only added to the general air of neglect.

"Well, at least we're not prisoners any more," she said, trying hard to sound optimistic.

"Aye," added Freyar, apparently having at last regained enough of his breath to speak, briefly.

Suddenly, and quite unexpectedly, a young hesitant voice from amongst a barely visible and usually silent group of squirrels, chipped in.

"But... that means, no more food trays!" A stunned gasp filled the room. Every animal looked towards Freyar in varying degrees of horror, combined with an expectation of reassurance, and no doubt a solution. Freyar, vastly ill-equipped to cope with such demands, adopted the very same look and turned to Emily.

"By 'eck," he exclaimed, visibly stunned. "I ne'er thought o' that!" Loud and nonsensical gabble then began to fill the room, serving only to fuel a rapidly rising tone of panic. Once again, Emily was regretting ever having met this lot.

"Look," she said, her diplomatic skills now stretched to absolute breaking point. "Getting all worked up won't help anything. We should be able to find you all a way out of here soon, and there's still food left in the forest. Anyway, it hasn't been that long since you lot last ate. It's been ages for me, so everybody just calm down." Many of the animals, including Freyar, suddenly dropped their gaze, seemingly confronted by their own selfishness.

"Oh… aye, well, 'at's right I s'pose." Both the temperature and noise in the room lowered somewhat, although it was obvious that the general confidence of the group had been far from restored. Some scratching at the back of the room, followed by much sniffing of the air, quickly diverted the attention of all the animals. In moments, expressions of disgust over odour had taken the place of anxieties over food.

"What IS that smell?" several of the rabbits asked together.

"Oh I say… it is rather strong, as it were," exclaimed Garrett as only he could, although visibly taken aback by the offending fumes now apparently engulfing the room.

"It's coming from here," a tiny voice cried from the back of the room. "We've found a hole!" Many animals jostled to try and get a better view, but it was so dark back there almost nothing could be seen.

"Na'then, let's be 'avin' yers!" Freyar, now fully recovered, took charge again. "Clear way! Mind thee! Come on, move yerselves!" Attempting to clear a path, he made his way to the back of the room to investigate further, followed dutifully by Garrett.

Emily's thoughts had barely begun to return to matters of escape - such as how long she should wait until opening the door again - before this latest distraction appeared. As it was, she knew that some length of pause would be sensible, and, well, if it stopped them banging on about food for five minutes, she may as well go along with whatever it was that was occupying their minds, however brief that may be. It sounded to her like a mouse hole anyway, and she couldn't smell anything worse than normal. She lifted one of the torches down from the wall, and ambled behind Garrett towards the gap at the back of the room.

As she got closer, Emily began to detect the offensive stench. It was a heavy-burning industrial kind of smell, acrid and thick; something you'd expect to find around a chemical factory, not a castle. Bending down to take a closer look at the hole, she could see that the wall around it was damaged quite badly by fire. She placed her hand up against an area to see if it was still warm, but to her and everyone else's surprise, a sizeable part of the wall abruptly collapsed into the next room! The animals jumped back in fright, but luckily no one was harmed. Badly charred wood now littered the floor all around a gaping hole in the wall, but it at least meant that they could all now get through into the next room, should they actually want to.

"What's tha reckon?" asked Freyar, nervously. "Does tha think it safe?"

Emily stood for a moment, wondering whether it really was such a good idea to go in there. The smell told her probably not, but it was just possible that there may be access to other rooms or corridors. Besides, it wouldn't take that guard long to find them if he had even half a brain cell available, so… Emily swallowed hard.

"Let's see," she said soberly, taking a cautious first step through the gap. "It's probably best, though, that the others don't follow us. Leave them in here for now. Just bring Garrett with you."

"Aye… right." Freyar gave instructions to the others, and then both he and Garrett followed Emily in.

Were it not for Emily's torch, the room would have been completely dark. Quite unexpectedly, the first thing that struck her was noise seeming to come from above. She hadn't heard it at all in the other room, which was odd because it sounded like absolute bedlam. Also, the sound was heavily muffled, as though it had travelled quite some distance, or else been dampened considerably. Whatever the cause, she couldn't see anything that would give clues as to its origin. The smell of course was strong, but that too seemed to be coming from somewhere else, and not this room. Ultimately, it was just more weirdness in a very weird place, with little to be gained from wondering about it.

"Ouch!" Whilst pondering the futility of thought, Emily had walked into something hard and sharp. She lowered the torchlight to see barbed wire surrounding what appeared to be a compost heap, containing mainly leaves it seemed. It certainly wasn't something you'd expect to find in a room of a castle - any room, in fact - which made it all the more intriguing.

"Hey, come and look at this," called Emily to Freyar and Garrett, both of whom were standing by the entrance hole looking decidedly worried. Neither moved from their position, but instead just stood staring intently at her. "What's the matter?" she asked, a little annoyed at yet another interruption.

"Ee Lassy! T' sound!" exclaimed Freyar, his eyes wide open with anguish. "It's comin' from… from what d'yama call it! Thingy!" Freyar's level of distress and incomprehensibility was being matched closely at this point by Emily's bewilderment.

"Er," called out Garrett, seeing some need to intervene, "that is to say, as it were, the sound that one can hear - and doubtless too the odour - would seem to be coming from Smolder's smoulder chamber, as… as it…"

"O-kay," said Emily slowly, cutting in, trying hard not to shout herself but nevertheless be heard above the noise. Unfamiliar as she was with both the thing and its implications, she was eager for a little expansion on both. "So this smoulder chamb…"

"In t' smoke!" interrupted Freyar, his eyes wide with fear. "'E turns us in t' smoke! You an' ahl, Lassy! You an ahl!"

"Fine, got it… okay," said Emily placatingly, wanting desperately to calm Freyar down before he panicked everyone else. This smoulder chamber thing sort of chimed in with something Tamhorn had mentioned before in the forest, but there really wasn't time to explore it further now. She decided to adopt a reassurance tack. "But look, there's no chamber in here, is there? There's only a compost heap. See?" She shone her torch about over the barbed wire fence nearest her, and the leaves contained behind it.

"You know," began Garrett soberly, turning to Freyar, "she may rather have a point, as it were."

"Don't mean 'e canno' gerr'us tho, do it?"

"No, absolutely," agreed Emily, although not actually understanding what Freyar had said. "But it really seems to be okay in here, and we have to find a way out for you and your group. Right?"

Freyar thought for a moment, then added, a little haughtily, "Aye, well, thee should watch out, tha should. That's all ah'm sayin'. It's nay safe in 'ere, tha'nose, nay safe at all." Followed by Garrett, he cautiously made his way towards Emily and the barbed wire compost.

"Right," she instructed as they drew near, "we need to see if there's another gap into the next room on from this one, as all those we've been in so far were either damaged or else had a concealed door, so…"

"I say! There's something there!" butted in Garrett excitedly, pointing into the compost. Emily spun round fast and defensively, causing her burning torch to give a *whoosh* sound as it glided through the air in front of her. "A foot I think, as… as it… oh." Garrett stopped dead in his worded tracks, an unease having gotten hold of him yet again.

In that moment, Freyar's fragile resolve also disintegrated. He started moving back towards the gap in the wall, exclaiming fearfully,

"I told thee! I told thee! Tha'nose, I told thee!"

"It's okay!" Emily placed her free hand up in a 'stop' gesture to try and calm Freyar, who was about to make a run for it back into the other room. The mayhem that would have resulted from the rest of the group seeing his face at that moment didn't bear thinking about. "Really it's alright! Keep calm. There's no danger, just give me a second…"

Having stopped, for the moment at least, Freyar's brazen withdrawal, Emily moved round to where Garrett was standing. The moment she saw the foot her stomach sank, and an intense feeling of dread came over her. It was a human foot, and it wasn't moving. Nothing else was visible among the leaves by the dull light of her torch - just a foot. Although tormented by the thought of what she might find, Emily knew she had to look.

She scaled over the barbed wire and clambered slowly amongst the dry leafy compost towards the foot, ever mindful of the fact that if she dropped her torch now the whole place would likely go up in flames. This thought, on top of the prospect of what else she might find at her destination, made it a far from easy task to undertake. Nevertheless, she made it, and nervously brushed the leaves away from around the foot. It was when she saw the type of jeans covering the leg, and then the long cloak, that Emily knew to whom the foot belonged.

"JEN!" Her cry almost caused poor Freyar to die of fright, right there on the spot. Emily frantically searched about, quickly finding Jen's head, body and arms, all thankfully still intact. Her hood was pulled up right over her head, whilst the cloak itself, made of golden leaves, had blended in so well with the compost, she'd been impossible to spot in the gloomy haze. Not knowing whether she was dead or alive, Emily began to frenetically scrape away the leaves from around her, all the time calling,

"Jen! Jen! It's me! Wake up! Jen!"

Jen's eyes blinked and fluttered faintly, as she tried to come round. To Emily, she seemed very groggy, and didn't appear to recognize her immediately. She kept calling, as the bedlam above went on unabated.

"Jen! It's me, Emily! Can you hear me?"

Garrett stood at the edge of the barbed wire, cautiously intrigued as to what was going on. Freyar hovered about nervously, midway between him and the gap in the wall.

In a sudden burst of recall and energy, Jen's eyes lit up wildly with equal measures of enthusiasm and alarm. "MMMMMM!" was the sound that greeted Emily. Jen then tried to grab her, but was so tangled up inside her cloak she lurched to one side and fell back down again.

"Jen?" asked Emily, anxiously. "What's happened to your voice?"

"MMMMM! M-MMM-MMMM!!"

"I might venture," began Garrett, in his slow and intensely ponderous voice, "that she has been gagged," He turned round, expecting Freyar to be behind him. Seeing that he wasn't, and unable to locate him through the darkness, instead called out, "Wouldn't you, er, say Freyar… as… as it were?"

"'Ay?" a distracted, nervous voice replied. "Oh… aye, probably."

"Gagged?" demanded Emily. "How?"

"Well," replied Garrett loudly, although still firmly entrenched in his reflective mode, "no one's entirely sure, but it does appear to prevent the opening of one's mouth, as it were. I am further reliably informed that certain garden implements are also involved, but other than…"

"Fine! Whatever!" butted in Emily, not wanting Garrett to elaborate any further. She had to shout now, just to make herself heard through the ever-increasing racket surrounding them. "It doesn't matter for now! We need to get out of here! Jen, grab around my neck!"

Emily helped Jen up onto her feet, and they stumbled slowly together over the leaves of the compost. Jen was still weak, leaving Emily to support most of her bodyweight. Once clear of the barbed wire, Jen attempted to brush away some of the debris still on her. She lowered her hood, presumably to tackle the bits in her hair; it was then that the rising din from above assaulted her eardrums with maximum velocity.

"MMMMMMMM!! MMMMMMMM!!" Jen suddenly looked petrified, staring about her and above. Emily was momentarily flummoxed, not understanding what it was that had changed so quickly. Then she realized that Jen's hood had been protecting her from the noise all along.

"MMMMMM!!" she continued, her face far more animated than Emily would have ever thought possible, especially given her weakened state. "M-MMMM!! M-MM-MMMMM!!" She began trying to describe something in sign language, pointing above and then to the compost. Emily wanted to work it out for her, but there just wasn't time.

"I know!" shouted Emily, attempting to reassure her. "The smoulder chamber! But we have to move!" She hastened Jen to the gap in the wall, followed closely by Garrett. Freyar, needless to say, led the way.

Back in the other room, the deafening noise thankfully ceased. Emily could see that Jen was quite taken aback at this sudden mute effect, and began scrutinizing the gap in the wall. It was then that she noticed all the other rabbits and squirrels huddled together in the corner, and gave Emily an intensely puzzled look.

"They're Freyar's group," began Emily. Then, suddenly remembering, she added, "Oh wait, I haven't even intro…"

BANG! Introductions had not even begun when the door suddenly flew open with incredible speed. The force literally shook the room and startled everyone in it. At the door stood the now fully awake and, judging by his expression, severely irate guard. Freyar, who was nearest to the door at the time, bolted around behind Emily and Jen to where Garrett was, faster than anyone would have ever thought possible for him. Emily was left facing the guard directly. She instinctively raised her torchlight, like a shield in front of her. Fortunately, she had half-expected this, and although she didn't have a clue what she was going to do if it did happen, she was at least prepared.

For a few seconds, nothing happened and no one moved. Then, noise in the corridor - *thud, thud, thud* - sounding close and becoming closer. Then, emerging into view, alongside the guard, appeared something for which Emily could never have prepared herself.

"What the…" Emily's jaw nearly hit the straw-strewn floor as she clapped eyes upon a truly grotesque and terrifying 'thing' now standing in front of her. A deep feeling of dread, combined with an eerie fascination, began to well up inside her. She struggled for words just to describe it to herself inside her own head, never mind to anyone else - the sticks for arms and legs, the large shoulders above a football stomach, the jagged and plastic-like skull combined with deathly eyes. Was it a man? A goat? How could anything be so wretched and yet survive? The one thing Emily didn't need, however, was a name. She knew who this was, for there was only one person it could possibly be - Smolder Bagot!

"M-MMM-MM! M-MMM-MM!" Jen tugged hard on Emily's cloak, obviously wanting her attention very badly. So much so, that she forced herself into Emily's sightline, partially blocking her view of Smolder and the guard. Shaking her head vigorously as she pointed to her own eyes and then to Smolder, Jen repeated, "M-M-M-M-MMM! M-M-M-M-MMM!"

Smug, gloating laughter from Smolder and the guard began to fill the air, causing many squirrels and rabbits to suddenly scramble through the hole in the wall and into the next room. Many returned almost immediately due to the even worse noise in there, resulting in panic well and truly setting in. Emily understood Jen's message, however, not to look directly into his eyes.

"So," hissed Smolder, in a sinister mix of glee and anger, "I finally have the Wandiacates exactly where I want them! My power shall be invincible, and Deeron will be dead at last!" He began to move closer towards them, stumbling on his stick-thin legs. As he did so, he growled, "And I will turn these thieving vermin into smoke right now!"

"No," said Emily calmly, managing incredibly well to hide her fear at this moment, as she raised the torchlight high above her head. "Let's turn YOU into smoke!" As she spoke those words, Emily hurled her torchlight at Smolder. It landed almost directly at his feet, instantly igniting the dry straw lying around on the floor. Far from being alarmed, however, or even moving clear of the developing fire, Smolder simply laughed.

"Ha-ha-ha! You stupid Wandiacate! You can't burn me! Hisssssssssssssss!" Smolder hissed menacingly like a cobra snake, and glared at the rapidly growing blaze beneath him. As he glowered from left to right, the flames died instantly, seeming at once to submit to his overwhelming power. With a leering and gleeful sneer, Smolder then lurched nearer, his guard following close behind.

"Back in there! Go!" shouted Emily, quickly gesturing for Jen and the animals to move back into the compost room, as she herself began retreating towards the hole in the wall. As it was, the animals had already gone back in, evidently more fearful of Smolder than they were of the noise. All Emily could think of to do right now was get away from Smolder as quickly as possible, and maintain some distance. Beyond that, she hadn't a clue.

She grabbed the remaining torchlight from the wall, and scrambled through the gap behind Jen. The noise in there was truly deafening now, forcing Emily to yank up her hood. The compost where she had found Jen was now smouldering, while smoke was rapidly filling the room. Neither Freyar nor any of his group could be seen.

"Ha-ha-ha! Nothing can save you now, Wandiacates! Nothing!" Smolder stood at the gap in the wall, smugly observing Emily and Jen's futile attempts to flee. "You!" he turned to the guard behind him, "Get them onto the compost!" The guard obediently entered the room, followed by Smolder himself.

Suddenly, amidst all the din and terrible chaos, Emily could hear Deeron's voice.

"Dance, Emily. Dance."

He sounded so close that she peered about through the smoke, half-expecting to see him, but his voice seemed to be in her head only. Besides, she had her hood up, yet his voice was as clear as the summer sun. He spoke again:

"Dance, Emily. I beg you, dance."

Without further delay, Emily threw her torchlight into the compost and began to turn around on the spot, with her arms held high like antlers. Whilst the bedlam around her continued and the guard advanced nearer, Emily calmly swayed and spiralled, absorbed in the world of her dance. Jen saw her, and immediately joined in. Emily turned to face Jen, and without speaking, they began to dance a duet. Ceremoniously they stepped around each other to complete a full circle. Emily went up onto her toes as Jen sank to the ground, and Jen rose as Emily sank. They repeated this sequence three times, and finished facing each other. Elegantly they curtseyed to one another, entwining their 'antlers' and walking in a circle with their heads held high, just as the stags had done by the lake on that day in the forest.

Thanks to Emily's torchlight, the compost was now well and truly alight. Roaring flames licked the beams of the ceiling, but instead of the room continuing to fill with choking white smoke, golden smoke began seeping down from the smoulder chamber above, as the two girls danced on. As it descended, the golden smoke swirled and churned, appearing to consume the white smoke as it did so, while all the time becoming brighter and denser.

"Stop them!" screamed Smolder to the guard, but he had already stopped moving. He simply stared straight ahead, transfixed and unable to move, hypnotized by the dance.

"Stop this, I order you! I will burn you all, I'll…" Smolder hissed and spat, his words now ineffective and useless, as Emily and Jen whirled and spun around the blazing compost heap.

Emily began to jump, spiralling up and coiling down, like a flickering flame in the fire. Jen skipped around and then joined in with the jumping, her antler arms still held high above her head. Then, from various corners of the room, Freyar's group began to appear, also joining in with the dance! In no time, they were bouncing and jumping, leaping and spinning, throwing their furry little bodies round and around the compost heap, until the room had become a kaleidoscope of dance.

While everyone else danced, Smolder was suddenly faced with a large ball of golden light that surged out of the smoke. It developed quickly, and began spinning within itself like a gyroscope. Smolder, sensing danger, attempted to back away from it, but could do nothing to match the speed and agility of the radiant sphere. It spun over and around him, and then effortlessly lifted him up into the air! Once airborne, the golden ball began veering towards the compost heap.

"Stop this, I say!" he yelled, looking down at the blazing compost. "Fire, stop I say!" Regardless, the fire continued to burn, and the golden ball rose still further, dangling Smolder threateningly over the flames.

Emily's eyes searched the room. The smoke was thick, and it was difficult to work out where they were in relation to the hole in the wall. She was choking with the fumes, and her eyes were stinging so badly she could barely look up to enjoy the sight of Smolder being suspended in mid air.

"Find the hole!" she yelled, desperate to be heard above the ear-splitting din all around them. Fortunately, some animals did hear and immediately obeyed, tearing around the walls until the hole was found. Then, one by one, chaotically they dived back through.

Although there was thankfully still less noise in the other room, the smoke had gathered into clumps to create huge, frightening forms. Gaping mouths, a goat's head with bulging eyes, and figures of great pointed horns spun around and above, viciously jabbing at them repeatedly. As Freyar jumped through the hole once more, he suddenly found himself face-to-face with a grey smoky tongue slowly unfolding, seemingly about to wrap itself around him like a snake.

"Lummin' 'eck!" he gasped, backing away very quickly and inadvertently falling on Pottle, who was trying to hide behind him. Terrified, many animals dived into a far corner, ending up in a large heap of furry bodies.

As one of the last to leave the smoulder chamber, Emily dived through the hole just as fast as she could manage. As she did so, her hood became snagged on a burnt splinter of wood and lurched backwards off of her head. Instantly, a set of white horns loomed in front of her that appeared to have been sculptured from smoky glass. They were pointed like a blade, and looked very, very dangerous! Instinctively, Emily yanked her hood back up, and instantly the solid forms were no more. They had suddenly transformed into a misty white shadow, floating aimlessly in the air. Emily sighed with a large dose of relief, and turned to see where Jen was. There was no problem; she was right behind, also with her hood up.

Smolder's voice suddenly shook everything around them as Jen finally made it back through the hole. A giant yell came from within the smoulder chamber.

"*Siss-a-flu.. flun.. flung…* make tunnel NOW!"

As if in response to those words, every misty figure and shape spinning around them instantly dissolved back into smoke, and then formed something resembling a thick line of thread. Emily, Jen, and many of the rabbits and squirrels all watched nervously as the tube of smoke weaved itself with tremendous speed through the hole in the wall and back into the smoulder chamber. Just like a long tube of flexible pipe being pulled through by someone unseen, the smoke began to disappear from the room.

There was no time to lose. Smolder would doubtless soon be free, but the fact that all his forces were now preoccupied at least offered the group a window of opportunity. Emily turned to the animals.

"GO!" she yelled.

Garrett composed himself and rapidly took control of the evacuation. "Come along now… this way, as it were… single file, if you would be so kind…"

Everyone in the group moved quickly, and in very little time indeed they had all entered the corridor once more, with Garrett shepherding the last of the squirrels, followed by Freyar, Emily and Jen. Freyar had managed to adopt his now familiar 'What now, Lassy?' facial expression, ready for Emily as she stepped back onto the wooden floorboards of the torch lit passageway. There really was no need, however.

"This way, quickly! Just Run!" Without pausing to consider any other options - not that there exactly were many - they all raced off down the corridor, continuing in the direction they had been travelling after having first escaped through the hatch. Just as before, the squirrels were outpacing the others, but neither Jen nor Emily had ever seen rabbits move quite so swiftly as they did in that corridor. Even Freyar was managing to keep up. Emily kept an eye on him and ran behind, poised ready to scoop up and carry him if necessary.

The passageway continued to bend around to the left. As they hurried along, Emily wracked her brain for any idea as to how she could help Freyar's group. Then she remembered something from the dream both she and Jen had shared. Martha had said, "These corridors all run in circles…" although Emily was struggling to remember anything else either said or seen that night. Do they just follow it? What's the point of running in a circle? Their situation, once again, was beginning to look and feel desperate.

Abruptly, the corridor stopped bending, and suddenly ahead of them lay a straight passageway. The effect of this was dramatic, as everyone instantly applied the brakes. Rabbits and squirrels - and very nearly humans - all ploughed into one another.

"EeeK!" Several light squeals rang out as the rabbits hurtled into, and on top of, the squirrels, generating yet another furry splodge of bodies.

"Stop!" called Emily as quietly as she could, although it was rather pointless as everyone already had. As some animals began picking themselves up yet again, Emily scrutinized the passageway all the way along for as far as she could see. Something struck her as being strangely familiar, which was odd in itself, as every bit of corridor she'd been in so far looked pretty much the same as any other.

"MM-MMM! MM-MMMM!" Jen's urgent grabbing of her arm whilst pointing to the wall further down, and her attempts to say something, arrested Emily's thoughts. She turned to see what Jen was pointing at.

"The vent!" Emily almost shrieked with excitement, recognizing at once the ventilation shaft by which she and Jen had entered the castle. "Excellent! Freyar, this is your group's ticket out of here!" Some squirrels had already begun investigating the hole in the wall, as Emily and Jen made their way over to it.

"Oh aye," said Freyar, still on the floor where he had collided with Magro, and now preoccupied with his various aches and pains. He seemed remarkably underwhelmed, although no doubt relieved. "Well, I'll tell thee," he slowly got back up onto his feet, "I canno' say I'm nay glad tha'nose, 'cause this place…" he sighed and looked around him, shaking his head whilst gently rubbing his sore back. "By 'eck, Lassy, ah've 'ad enough! Ah've gorra gerrouter 'ere, we ahl 'ave!"

By the time Freyar had limped over to the air duct, both girls had all but completed the task of helping the other rabbits reach the hole, and the few older squirrels that needed a boost. Emily carefully lifted Freyar last of all, placing him gently into the shaft next to Garrett, who was busy dispensing orders to his 'troops'. Suddenly confronted with the reality that it was time to say goodbye, and probably the last time she would see Freyar, Garrett or any of them again, Emily felt a tinge of sadness and affection for them all. They might not have been the brightest bunch, but they had helped her escape, and even Pottle's shenanigans had ultimately led her to find Jen again.

And actually, all in all, they had been rather fun. She was going to miss them, of that Emily could be certain, more than she would really admit to herself for quite some time to come.

"Now, you have to go along this tunnel, and then up a shaft…" began Emily, as she affectionately picked a few bits of twig off Freyar. Garrett appeared to be performing some sort of impromptu inspection. "The shaft is quite steep, but it's wooden, so use your claws for gripping and you should be fine."

"Nay bother, Lassy," replied Freyar, still nursing his back, as he cast a cynical eye over Garrett's antics along the dark narrow tunnel.

"MMM! M-MM-MMMM!" butted in Jen suddenly, looking quite tearful as she proceeded to draw something, and then pat the air at waist height.

"Oh… Bill! Of course!" cried Emily, mortified that she'd forgotten. "Freyar, there's a dog at the top of the shaft. Tell him we're fine, and that we'll be with him soon."

"Gerron wi' thee!! Tha' what?!" exclaimed Freyar, with a look of abject horror on his face.

"No," she replied, as soothingly as possible, "he wouldn't hurt a fly, honestly. He's with us."

"Oh… aye, well," Freyar calmed down quickly, apparently convinced, and instead shuffled himself awkwardly. "Well, tha'd best gerrof wi' thee now then, an' find them antlers, tha'nose."

"Go easy on Pottle, won't you," she said, "and take care of yourselves."

"Aye, nay worries," Freyar gave a wry, resigned smile. "An' thee an' all." Garrett had already begun to 'move out' his troops, and so Freyar started to likewise wander down the long dark tunnel. "Thanks for all, Lassy!" he called, as they disappeared into black.

"Emily, Freyar. It's Emily!"

"Tsk! Oh aye… sorry!" came an already distant and echoed apology. And with that, they were gone.

Treasures of the Stone Chamber

Deep in Bagot Wood and late into the night, a fire crackled softly as Deeron fed branches of battle-torn trees to the flames. Sharing the meagre remains of their food amongst them, his army lay wounded and exhausted. They ate slowly so as to try and make it feel like a proper meal, but they all knew that this would be their last, for the rations that had sustained them since leaving Deeron's Hall were now all gone, and the forest no longer had anything edible left to offer.

Arog stared into the flames, and sang softly.

> *"Tho' my foes lie dead and wounded,*
> *This dreadful battle is not done.*
> *The earth beneath my feet is crying,*
> *To gain our freedom we must fight on."*

They had suffered heavy losses that day at Marsh Valley, but managed to hold onto what precious little ground they had won. In some of the fiercest fighting yet, and vastly outnumbered, Deeron had managed to hold back Smolder's army in the valley whilst Arog took a squad of their best fighters along a route towards Marching Cliff. Arog's plan had been to bypass their outer flanks and attack them from behind. This he achieved, rendering Smolder's forces outmanoeuvred and vulnerable. The piled bodies of slain enemy strewn across the battlefield lay testament to their minor triumph, but no one around that campfire felt even remotely like celebrating. They had lost many friends in this and earlier battles, and nothing less than the total destruction of Smolder and every last facet of his evil empire would in any way begin to compensate for their passing. This remained a distant prospect, however, and although Smolder's army had at last retreated, no one could be sure whether or not reinforcements were already on the way.

Fole and Folly gazed downcast both towards the fire and to Deeron, too exhausted and demoralized to even try and cheer things up. At least they had survived another day, as had their four magic brothers. They were wounded and shattered, but alive. Arog suddenly raised his eyes, gazing deep into the darkness beyond the light of the flames.

"At first light we must move from here," he said, decisively. "This is a dangerous place for us to be, and way too visible for Smolder's eyes."

Deeron observed him through the flames. Arog's fighting spirit had not left him, nor fortunately had his sharp mind or intrinsic knowledge of the forest. Deeron was overwhelmed with respect for his loyal warrior.

"How far do you think we are from Smolder's Castle, Arog?" he asked.

"We are close, I'm sure," he replied. "Three, perhaps four miles north of here, I'd say. We have little choice but to head in that direction, for Marsh Valley will surely be heavily fortified by now. Our tactics today brought us small fortune, but our options have diminished. And whatever happens, we need food and must find Emily and Jen. Without our Wandiacates or the magic antlers, we are powerless against him."

Deeron knew the truth of this, as did they all. Although no one dared utter what was playing on everyone's mind, the fact that Emily and Jen had been gone for so long was not a good sign.

Sleep did not arrive for anyone. It was far too cold, and there was noise in the distance like the crackling of another fire. They took it in turns to fetch wood and keep watch. As the night sky eventually succumbed to a new day, the fire was allowed to die away naturally while the herd prepared to move on towards Smolder's Castle.

The sound of cracking branches from within a thicket nearby alerted everyone instantly. Deeron picked up a huge branch and brandished it like a baseball bat, whilst Arog and a group of stags dipped their antlers down low, ready to face the inevitable onslaught of yet another day at war.

Crack! The sound drew nearer. *Crack! Crack!*
Woof!

Bill's golden head suddenly emerged from behind a tree. Seeing Deeron first of all, Bill joyfully ran towards him wagging his tail, in delight as much as relief. The herd was thrilled to see him, and a great deal of fuss was made of Bill at that moment. Both Deeron and Arog studied the forest landscape ahead of them, expecting Emily and Jen to hone into view at any moment, perhaps even with the antlers in their possession. But sadly, although anticipation was intense, the outcome didn't arrive. Deeron took a deep breath, and tried hard to hide his disappointment.

"What's going on, Bill?" he asked, patting Bill's head.

The fact was, Bill didn't know what was going on, even if he had been able to tell them. He had loyally remained at the entrance to the ventilation shaft as instructed to await his mistress's return, and much time had then passed. So much time, in fact, that Bill had become worried. He had no water, no food, and being left on his own in a dark tunnel forever-and-a-day was not his idea of fun. He had barked into the shaft, he'd sniffed around, but no one had come.

So, Bill had had to face a dilemma. He'd decided that he had two choices - either crawl down the shaft after them, or return to the forest and find the herd. As the first choice involved jumping into a dark narrow tube with eerie sounds and smells coming out of it, Bill chose the second.

His journey through the forest had been for the most part uneventful, although strange crackling noises were heard for much of the time. These sounds didn't appear, at least as far as Bill was concerned, to be a threat, leaving him free to scurry on alone, golden and conspicuous against the dark decaying forest.

Deeron stroked the golden retriever's head, and stared deeply into his eyes. Bill's inability to speak was no barrier to communicating with him, and his lone presence in itself signalled to everyone that they were needed at the castle. After a simple bowl of water, for that was all they had to offer, the army prepared to move on.

"Lead the way, my golden friend." Arog gestured Bill to head the group. He dutifully did so, and began following his own scent back towards the castle. Fortunately, Bill had taken quite a sensible route through the trees to find them, meaning that their passage was both swift and discreet. At least, that was until the crackling noise - previously thought to be a distant fire - drew near. Close by, it didn't actually sound anything like a fire. It was more like the sound of many vast swarms of insects whizzing by, all seemingly heading in the same direction. At first, the swarms appeared to be ahead of them, but they soon switched to buzzing around behind. Eventually, and worst of all, the sound emerged from directly above their heads, crackling and hissing ferociously loud and terrifyingly close.

"Stay together, and keep moving!" shouted Deeron to everyone. "And don't look! Keep your eyes fixed on the path!"

To purposely not view whatever it was that was buzzing all around them was far from easy, although they wouldn't have seen much if they had glimpsed, for the source of this noise was invisible where they were. However, up ahead in the distance, the army could not fail to notice intense flashes beaming through the forest and up into the sky. In the after light of dawn, these blasts of radiance looked like early morning rays of sun, caught on the blades of many swung swords engaged in battle. That this light show possessed a piercing, metallic quality was no accident, for these literally were flying blades - sickle-scythe warriors, slashing anything and everything in their path. These were the Falx, and it appeared that they too were converging upon the castle. Their presence seemed all the more threatening by the fact that the beams of light, shone out by them, were also being reflected off the mirror fog surrounding the castle walls.

Both Deeron and Arog already knew of the Falx, of course - although not by name - as those telltale flashes of light had often been relied upon in the past to tell them they were nearing Smolder's territory. Arog had first observed them shortly after the death of Lord Bagot, just as Smolder was beginning to create his own fortress from the wreckage of Bagot Hall. Word reached Deeron concerning mysterious flashing lights seen nearby those ruins, and a patrol group led by Arog was dispatched to observe what was happening. It was also then that Smolder's screeching spell words - *Sis a flung* - were heard in the forest for the first time. This 'chant' or calling to evil appeared to trigger the Falx into action, which would often involve attacking the surrounding woodland, and everything in it, with relentless ferocity.

What neither Deeron nor Arog could know, however, was where the Falx came from or how they were being controlled. Deeron had for some time doubted that they were directly obeying Smolder, essentially because they unleashed such wanton destruction and mayhem. Everyone knew that Smolder's ambition was to rule over the forest, not raze it to the ground, yet that was precisely what the Falx were doing. Deeron wondered if the White Light itself were not controlling them, and that they were only responding to Smolder's incantation to further the White Light's power, and not necessarily his. Deeron privately hoped that this was so, because he could foresee a situation in which this might prove useful. After all, it would mean that the Falx were the one thing in the forest which possessed more power than Smolder, and a time would inevitably come where their particular interests would separate. As both were driven by greed and evil, one would ultimately consume the other, and there were few doubts over who'd win that battle. Until the stags were reunited with the magic antlers, it was the best hope to hold on to. What privately troubled Deeron greatly, however, was the new prospect of having to somehow defeat the Falx, even if Emily and Jen did retrieve the magic antlers. Up until the Falx had shown up, their fight had been only with Smolder. Now, it seemed, they were also going to have to battle with the White Light of Evil itself.

The group continued onwards for some time, ably led by Bill's self-tracking skills. As their path wove its way in all directions, the monotonous sound of the Falx reduced to little more than a distant crackling once more. Due to the sun having climbed way above the horizon, the blinding light from around the castle also decreased, and was thankfully no longer a distraction.

"Let's leave this trail for a while to rest," suggested Arog. "We're near Bagot's Folly, if I remember rightly, which means we must also be close to the castle. This way, I think."

Stepping cautiously through stinging nettles and pushing aside tall brown ferns, Arog led the group to a secluded area not far off, set down into a small valley. As they approached, they could see a honey-coloured square building built of stone. It had the look of a small Greek temple, with tall round pillars standing boldly beside two large wooden doors.

"Wow!" gasped Tamhorn. "What's this doing here?"

Arog smiled fondly at the folly. "Lord Bagot had it built for his wife. A place for her paintings and tea parties, I shouldn't wonder. Fortunately, Smolder forgot about it when he destroyed the house."

Deeron mounted the steps, and slowly turned the heavy iron handle that secured the enormous doors. To his surprise, the doors creaked open quite easily, and so they all cautiously filed inside. The air that greeted them was musty and the room seemed dark and lifeless, but as sunlight began to flow in past the now open doorway, Deeron and the others quickly became aware of paintings hanging upon each and every wall.

"These are stunning," commented Blythe, as they all absorbed the artwork surrounding them, much of which appeared to consist of does and stags grazing contentedly in the warm sunlight of summers past. In one scene, a group of stags stared inquisitively out of the picture towards the viewer. Hay counted them - there were six in all - and closer inspection revealed that the painting was indeed of him and the five other magic stags, all there in the very same room.

The dry darkness had preserved their individual colours in the painting, and only vaguely had the passage of time penetrated any of the artwork. Beautiful blue-sky landscapes, reflected in lakes and rivers, jostled for wall space alongside scenic green and lush open valleys, dappled with brightly coloured forest flowers and tall strong trees greeting golden rays of sun. All of the deer in every painting appeared well fed, healthy and very happy. Everyone stared in silence for a while, at both their ancestors and themselves, and their beloved forest in better days.

"Hey, I look pretty good in oil!" quipped Tamhorn, jovially.

"Not as good as me, though," jibed Fole, joining in with the light banter.

Deeron found himself drawn to a different painting, hanging on the opposite wall. In contrast to the summer landscapes in the folly, this artwork's setting was atop a cliff face at night. Behind the rock face and far below in the background, vast boglands were depicted trailing way back to various rocky peaks, spurting upwards to meet a starry sky at the very rear of the picture. The light of the moon, seeming to come from behind the viewer, shone especially vibrantly. What struck Deeron most was not the setting, however, but instead the large painted golden shield situated on the rock face in the middle of the image. Seeming to absorb all the light around it, the shield radiated incredible energy. This was illustrated by it appearing to grow and expand rather like a sponge soaking up water would do. Someone was clearly holding the shield up towards the sky - as if in battle or defiance - but the shield bearer's face could not be seen. For that matter, neither was any opponent or aggressor visible either. It was a strange picture, in that nothing really appeared to be being said or expressed by it - except energy, perhaps - and yet it was so oddly captivating to view.

Deeron was about to turn away when he suddenly noticed, carved into a plaque at the base of the picture frame, some wording. He brushed away the dust and cobwebs to try and make out what was written there. It read,

When your enemy is seen on the left,
This shield, will it come to your right?
With words I decreed, such power will find thee.
Believe, you must, free your might.
Remember I told you so.

The words intrigued him, as they obviously related to the shield in the painting. The question was: what did it mean? Did it actually mean anything? After all, the words could just be a nonsensical riddle, whilst the illustration might be an artistic vision of that riddle, conjured up in the mind of the creator. Come to that, the whole thing could be no more than a play-on-words - a pun, in fact. Deeron searched for the artist's signature, but could find nothing.

Still engrossed, he thought for a moment, just as Leif wandered over and stood quietly alongside him. Also gazing up at the picture, he commented, quietly,

"That's a rather interesting painting... the scene looks like Marching Cliff, don't you think?"

Deeron hadn't really heard Leif's question, as he was too busy scolding himself for having wasted time musing over artwork. The Wandiacates were missing, and the antlers were probably still inside the castle. All were likely in danger. As it was, they would have to rethink their strategy for getting inside that place, at least to rescue Emily and Jen, and try again later for the antlers. Regardless, the very last thing Deeron had time for right now was picture puzzles.

"It's beautiful," he replied flatly, and walked back out onto the steps. Arog followed him.

"Arog," he began, once they were clearly out of earshot, "I think you should go on ahead, with Bill and anyone else you need, whilst we wait here. It's a bad idea for us all to arrive at the castle before we're sure of Jen and Emily's situation. If you can, find them and bring them back here. If they're captured, our only option will be to face Smolder again, and hope against hope that he's weakened somehow. Maybe when he's on the move, we may be able to head him off at Marching Cliff."

Arog knew that if Smolder had captured the Wandiacates, they would never make it as far as Marching Cliff, but he could see by Deeron's face that there was no need for him to say so. He nodded and returned to inside the folly, appearing moments later with Bill and Fauld.

"Have a hearty supper ready for our return," he smiled as they prepared to leave, knowing full well that there was no food left.

"Anything in particular you'd like?" replied Deeron, wryly.

"You'll think of something, Deeron." The trio began making their way up the bank and back onto the trail.

"Go safe!" he called as Bill, followed by Arog and Fauld, disappeared into the trees. He quietly feared for them, for he knew what they inevitably would have to face.

Back on the trail, the trio made good speed. Since leaving the Folly, it had been obvious to both Arog and Fauld that Bill was in a real hurry to return, doubtless anxious to try and find Jen. As the hatch honed into view, Bill quickly scurried over to it and peered in anxiously, poised ready to jump back down. Arog, however, had other ideas.

"No Bill, not that way! Back here, quickly!"

Arog and Fauld had taken cover behind a pile of stripped braches, bark and dead bracken, set back behind the treeline but within sight of the hatch. Bill gave a soft reluctant whine, but did as he was told and rejoined them. Arog's decision to take cover was due to the activity of the flashing light, which for the last mile or so of walking had become increasingly bright once more, and also louder. As they had drawn nearer, both Arog and Fauld had noticed a cluster of light some distance away, further along and to the right.

"What do you reckon they're up to?" asked Fauld.

"I'm not sure yet," replied Arog, watching intensely the goings-on up ahead. "Let's see what they do next."

As they continued to observe, it seemed that the frenetic flashing light clusters were simply disappearing into thin air after having gathered together. Also, many more appeared, but the overall size of the group didn't increase. Although Arog knew more about the Falx than anyone else in the herd, he didn't know a great deal. In actual fact, he didn't even know what they were called! But crouched down watching them now whilst simultaneously seeing and hearing them for the first time, Arog concluded that it must mean they crackle when they move, and flash light when they're stationary. Then, reminding himself that both he and Fauld were viewing them beside an invisible castle wall, surrounded by fog that mirrors everything around it, the reality of what was happening suddenly clicked.

"They're entering the castle!"

By a delicious twist of irony, Smolder's protectors were not only giving away the castle's position, they were also offering the tempting prospect of another way in. The trio carried on watching the proceedings.

"How come they're not detecting us?" asked Fauld, a little concerned.

"We're probably too far away," replied Arog, "and we're only seeing a reflection of them anyway. We'll have to wait here a while, until someone either comes out or goes in. That'll show us precisely where the entrance is."

"But how will we get through the fog?"

At that precise moment, inside the castle,

"*Siss-a-flu.. flun.. flung...* make tunnel NOW!"

Smolder, suspended above a blazing compost heap whilst trapped inside a gyrosphere of golden light, screeched his deafening demand to be rescued. His power was being tested to the limit now, with every last ounce required to save him. The white smoke, having abandoned trying to prevent the animals and Wandiacates from escaping, surged into the smoulder chamber and immediately wrapped around the golden ball, turning its light to black. A long tube of smoke attached itself, connecting the now dark sphere to the wall. The tube then expanded rapidly in size, pulling in more and more smoke from the four outer walls of the smoulder chamber like a gigantic vacuum cleaner. The white smoke was suffocating the golden light by constructing around it dense impenetrable smog, strangling its energy and weakening its force. Very soon, Smolder would be able to make his escape along one of the many chutes, shafts and tunnels that interlinked the many walls, floors and corridors.

Elsewhere in the castle, a lone and fear-filled goat couldn't fail to hear the shrill and chilling invocation. Knowing those words to mean that Smolder was in trouble, Targot also knew his own situation had just taken a nosedive. As Smolder's loyal second-in-command, it was he who had been tasked with finding the Wandiacates, and he had failed. He had also lied to Smolder about the battle being won outside - the truth was, both sides had suffered, but Smolder's army had sustained heavy losses during the previous battle, and had actually lost some ground. Now, with Smolder seemingly on the brink of losing everything, this could only mean that the Wandiacates were on the cusp of victory. For all he knew, they may even already have the antlers. A deep sense of dread began to well up inside him.

Targot's first thought was to run, out of the castle and as far away as he could manage. His reasoning, in as much as there was any, was that if Smolder were finished, he at least couldn't come after him. The White Light probably would, but he'd just have to take his chances. The sole advantage he could see was that he was on Terra (ground level), whilst Smolder was below on Solum (underground level). That at least afforded him a head start. Without pausing to even consider any other options, Targot ran.

He headed full pelt towards a rarely used side-door, which he secretly left unguarded in case he ever needed to use it. As he butted the door and it flew open, a blaze of light hit him square on, causing momentary blindness. Almost losing his footing as he tried to brake, Targot's despair sank even further. The Falx! He'd forgotten about them, and they were now entering the castle of their own free will. Worse still, they'd seen him, which meant that escape was now practically impossible.

As Targot's eyes adjusted to the mass of light ahead of him, including daylight, he began to make out half-moon reflections of himself suspended in the air. More kept flashing into view, whilst others disappeared, resembling some kind of bizarre strobe light show. Like steel-edged hanging C-shaped mirrors - a vertical bar at the top completing the sickle-like shape - slowly turning back and forth, the Falx were about as threatening as they possibly could be. Occasional glints of the sun's rays would catch the very edges of the swivelling crescent blade, blinding Targot's view almost completely. He knew that when Falx were heard they were invisible and moving; when seen they were silent, and still or rotating. Due to the huge number now in abundance, both sound and vision were being inflicted upon him at the same time. At any moment, one or all of them could strike, killing him in an instant. Trying desperately to think fast as more and more kept appearing from out of the forest, Targot grabbed at the first idea to enter his head - lie.

"So, you're here!" he said quickly. "Good, you're needed. The Master is under siege! Go! Seek the Wandiacates, and destroy them and the deer! Go, go now!" At the specific end of Targot's last word, the sound of the Falx immediately shot towards him like a rush of wind, and then ceased completely. As shocking and ominous as you could imagine that would feel, it was as nothing compared to what happened next. Perhaps a hundred Falx instantly flashed into view - in front of, around and behind him - encasing Targot within a gigantic circular wall of light and reflection! Every single one displayed a mirror image of his own face back at him on the C-shape of its blade, then scanned very slowly as it swivelled on its axis from left to right and back, seeming to record every hair upon his head. Had his situation not been so dire, Targot would have registered more of the experience, which was actually quite something given that he was surrounded by an almost heavenly blaze of light and image, albeit exclusively his own. Matters, however, rapidly became even more intense; he felt as though they were all trying to read his mind, or else were deciding whether or not to believe him. Standing there, frozen to the spot, Targot felt a depth of fear he never thought possible.

More moments passed, in which the only thing audible was Targot's heart, beating ferociously. Then, as if in sequence or by copy, the Falx rapidly disappeared, the whooshing of their electric-wasp sound indicating that they were all continuing to enter the castle, just as before. After barely a few more seconds, every last one of them had gone, leaving Targot alone, and still too petrified to move.

"Now what?" Emily sighed away the question, which was more directed towards herself anyway, given Jen's inability to speak.

"Mmm." Jen nevertheless attempted a reply, accompanied by a tired, almost indifferent shrug.

Both girls found themselves standing in exactly the same place as when they'd first entered the castle, with everything around them also just the same as back then. Torches were still lit either side of arched doors that were still shut, along a passageway that was still creepy. Emily lent with her back up against the wall, in-between the ventilation shaft and a very exhausted-looking Jen, and slid slowly down onto the floor. Jen remained standing and simply stared into space, almost delirious due to what she'd been through. Both were shattered, as hungry as ever, and equally dishevelled.

Their situation had mildly improved, in as much as they now knew where Smolder was and that he was being kept busy by the golden light, although they didn't know for how long. Apart from that, things seemed as dire as ever, and they were still no nearer to finding the antlers. It was obvious that they should make use of whatever undisturbed time they had left, but the question was: how? A few more minutes passed, after which Emily said,

"Let's walk. We might remember something from the dream. After all, we know the antlers are somewhere along this corridor."

"Mmm-hmm."

Emily and, following a little way behind, Jen wandered along the passageway for a second, or possibly even third, time. Emily could remember that the dream had felt real enough just after she'd had it, but right now it was so vague as to be debatable whether she'd simply dreamt that she'd had a dream! It was solely the fact that they'd both shared it, which had convinced Emily there was anything to gain from it at all. But, travelling along the corridor once more, for the life of her she couldn't recollect any of the finer details. One thing she did remember, however, was the very real event of being dragged into that room after leaning up against the wall, too close to a door. She wasn't going to make that mistake again. In fact, passing by every door, both girls eyed each one suspiciously, ready to make a run for it in case any opened.

Jen, for her part, was having a bit more success on the recall front, as she'd previously remembered that Martha had spoken about the corridors running in circles. In fact, it was when she'd first been captured and put aboard that mad smog ball thing, hurtling down this very passageway on her way to meet Smolder, that Jen had first recalled her very words. Also, when she'd been up among the rafters with Nocturne, looking down on the floor above them now, Martha's words had again crossed her mind, simply because the two floors appeared so different. Having walked now for some distance, it occurred to Jen that they must be close to completing a full circle, and expected to see the ventilation shaft reappear any minute. In-between scrutinizing each door, she kept gazing at the right hand wall, almost willing it to emerge, until something stopped her.

"Oh!" Emily suddenly collapsed forward onto the floor, managing to put a hand out just in time to soften her fall. Jen ran over to her, wondering what on earth had happened. Just as she reached Emily, the exact same thing happened to her as well!

"**MMMMM**!" Jen hit the floor with a heavy thump, only just avoiding falling directly on top of Emily. After the initial shock, both girls took a moment to right themselves, and then simply stared at each other in complete bewilderment.

"What was that? Are you alright, Jen?"

"Mm-hmm. Mmm?"

"I'm okay... I think," Emily rubbed her neck, and swung her head gently from side to side. "It's just I feel so... shattered." Jen began stroking the arm onto which she'd fallen and blinked slowly, looking as though she was trying to regain consciousness. Emily gradually got back up onto her feet.

"That was *so* strange," she began, still totally flummoxed as she looked around for anything that might suggest what had happened. "I was just walking as normal, when suddenly I collapsed! It was like, all my energy had ... gone, or something..."

"MM-MM-M-M-M-MMMM!" exclaimed Jen, pointing to herself with a heated expression on her face.

"Is that what happened to you?" queried Emily, offering Jen a hand and helping her back up onto her feet.

"MMMMM!" she nodded, emphatically.

"That's really..." Emily stared for a moment at the part of the corridor down which they had just walked. She then slowly directed her gaze towards the two doors facing each other, and on either side of her, which they had passed immediately before tumbling onto the floor. Memories began to return.

"I'VE GOT IT!" Poor Jen, still feeling groggy, nearly crumpled back onto the floor with fright. Emily, however, now seemed ecstatically alive. "Martha! In the dream! She said we'd grow weaker every time we passed a certain door. This door - well, one of these two, anyway - this has to be it!"

"MMMMM!" Jen nodded, in as much realisation as relief that they were finally getting somewhere.

"But she said something *after* that," pondered Emily, doing her usual walk-and-talk routine. "Or we *did* something that led us somewhere else. Can you remember what it was?"

Jen's eyes looked puzzled for a moment, and then tightened, as she tried to recall the events of the dream. After everything that had since happened, it was a struggle to remember anything of that night.

"Something happened... and she said something ... it was something like..."

"MM-MMM! MM-MMM!" Jen suddenly sprang into life. She moved to the next door down, along the corridor. "MM-MMM!" she repeated, pointing at Emily and then at the door, whilst brushing her hand along its outer surface. Emily seemed completely nonplussed at what it was Jen was trying to say, so she crouched down and quickly scrawled in the dust on the floor with her finger, one word. 'Stone'.

"Stone...? Of course, the stone door!" Emily's face beamed, as the final details of their shared dream at last came flowing back to her. "It turned to stone from wood, and Martha said, "Behind it is where the antlers are kept"! And..." she paused to recollect the precise words, "Martha also said, "Only with your dance can this door be found"!"

"MMMMMMM!" Jen gave Emily a big, long, exhausted hug.

"Okay... so the question now is: what dance?" Emily scrutinized the doors yet to be passed along the passageway, trying to figure out how best she could use dance to find the stone door. Then, something she hadn't been aware of before about the corridor suddenly struck her.

"Hey Jen, did you notice last time we were here, that *all* the doors faced each other?"

"Mm-hmm," Jen nodded.

"Weird, I didn't... it's given me an idea, though." Emily placed herself in front of a door and began dancing hops and turns, with the intention of travelling along the passageway to the next door. Jen looked on, intrigued by what it was she was trying to achieve. "No wait, that won't work..." She stopped, and pondered over it some more. Jen, seeing another possibility joined in, and by adapting a few of Emily's steps, appeared to have more success reaching her second door square on. "That's it, Jen, you're almost there! What if we add another step after the turn, and then touch the door... so it's 'step, turn, step, touch'?"

Jen tried it again, also widening her turn this time to give herself more balance as she lent forward to touch the door. Emily did the same thing, only back-to-back with her. Jen faced the left wall and so started on her right foot, while Emily faced the right wall and thus began on her left. They practised again and again, until they both began and ended at the precise same moment, in the same place, and each touching the door facing them at the exact same time.

"That's it!" screeched Emily with excitement, grabbing Jen for yet another hug. "Right then, ready?"

"Mm-hmm."

"Let's go after two." Emily glanced down to see Jen's foot poised ready to go, and they began their dance. "One-two…"

"Step, turn, step, touch," instructed Emily. "Wood. What about you?"

"Mm," came a glum reply.

"Okay. Again, step, turn, step, touch. Wood. You?"

"Mm."

"Step, turn, step, touch. Wood?"

"Mm."

After about ten doors Jen felt dizzy, and Emily began to lose faith in her plan. Still leaning back-to-back, they each gazed at the door in front of them.

"It's got to be a trick," whispered Emily to herself, bitterly. She took a deep breath. "Let's carry on for a bit more."

Jen was relieved to do so. The last thing she needed right now was for Emily to despair, especially as she couldn't even say anything comforting.

"Step, turn, step, touch. Wood."

"Mm."

"Step, turn, step, touch. Wood."

"Mm."

"Step, turn, step, touch. Wood." Emily waited for Jen's reply. "Jen?"

"MMMMMMM! MMMMMMM!" Jen grabbed Emily's shoulder, almost dragging her around. "MM-MMM!" She continued, pointing at the door, as Emily looked and immediately placed her hand upon it to feel the surface.

"Jen! You've found it!" Tears of relief began to well up in Emily's eyes. Her fingers told her, without a doubt, that this was stone - hard, cold, solid stone. After everything they had been through, to finally be standing in front of the very door behind which the magic antlers were kept, felt nothing less than an historic moment.

Emily and Jen continued to stare at the door, if only to acknowledge their achievement. Then, together they placed their hands flat against it and pushed, first gently and then with all their might. It was firmly closed, that was for certain, and no amount of pushing was going to open it. Emily thought hard.

"What's the answer to this?" she whispered, both to herself and to the door. Then, it suddenly occurred to her that up until now, every time she had needed to see through something or break out of somewhere, the hood of her cloak had supplied the means to do so. In fact, their hoods had saved both the day and their lives many times already, and there was no reason to suspect they would fail them now. Besides, she'd already managed to open a door along this corridor. Why not this one?

Emily threw up her hood, and Jen did the same. Instantly, they both became aware of writing engraved upon the door that had previously been invisible. In winding spidery letters, scratched into the stone, the inscription said,

Who are you?

"Emily and Jen," answered Emily, eagerly. Nothing happened.

"MM MMM!" Jen chipped in, as best she could. The door remained firmly closed.

"Hello. I'm Emily, and this is Jen," explained Emily, wondering if perhaps politeness might be the problem. Still, nothing happened.

Jen then tried writing her name on the door with her finger, while Emily did the same. They tried writing as Emily spoke. After that, they tried writing one after the other, and then together. Whatever they tried, the door point-blankly refused to budge. To have overcome so much, just to be stuck on the wrong side of a door, was the most intolerable thing imaginable. To make matters worse, from somewhere unseen down the long passageway behind them, came the sound of hooves moving fast in their direction.

"Please open!" cried Emily, now hammering on the door with the flat of her hand. "We're Emily and Jen... Wandiacates!" With that last single word, the door suddenly swung open. There was no time to lose, as Emily pushed the door inwards a little further and darted inside, followed closely by Jen who shoved it closed behind her. Finally, and at last, they were inside the Stone Chamber!

The room appeared bare except for a silver tree standing in the centre of the room, sparkling in the firelight of flickering torches hung about its walls. Perched upon the leafless branches of the tree, hung the six pairs of magic antlers.

"Oh, they're amazing!" exclaimed Emily.

"Wow!" blurted out Jen, gasping and then suddenly prodding around her mouth frantically. "Wha...? Hey, I can talk again!" Her invisible gag had vanished without trace, returning Jen's original speaking voice to her.

"That's wonderful, Jen! I'll bet the magic of the antlers did that!"

Emily and Jen stared at the antlers for quite some time. They were indeed amazing. Jen reached up to touch one pair, but then backed away, having suddenly changed her mind. A strong force surrounding them could easily be felt, but she couldn't yet know whether it was good or bad, so they both simply walked around the silver tree, gaping up at them. It was rather like being in a museum, gazing upon the treasures of some lost tomb or the spoils of a shipwreck. There were the dappled grey antlers belonging to Tamhorn, and deep-red ones that could only belong to Blythe. Also glistening in the torchlight, hung two identical sets of white and grey antlers.

"These must be Fole and Folly's," suggested Jen.

Lastly, the antlers of Hay and Leif radiated in the bronze and orange colours of the surrounding torchlight.

"So, what do we do now?" she asked.

"Well, we've got to get them out of here. Maybe we can hide them in the forest, until we've found Deeron."

"But we can't take them all out at once," reasoned Jen, "and none of them would get through that ventilation shaft anyway." They had no other plan for getting the antlers out, and things suddenly seemed as hopeless as they had back in the corridor. She reached up and lovingly stroked the bronze set, as they both pondered on what to do next.

The instant Jen touched them, golden light-threads began to pour out of the ends of her fingers and entwine themselves around the antlers. Rapidly they spun, weaving and twisting, and racing to engulf one set before moving on to another. Emily raised her hands up to touch the deep-red antlers of Blythe just above her. As she did so the very same thing happened, except that the light threads from her fingers shone a deeper gold, like an antique paint. The experience for them both felt the same, as though blood were rushing from their bodies and into the antlers. What really flowed, however, was a golden force. The antlers quickly absorbed the light, and began to glow from within. Slowly and gracefully, each set in turn then arose from its perch and floated off the tree, coming to rest forming a circle around it with Emily and Jen. Finally, as though it were the most natural thing in the world to do, the two girls and the antlers all began to dance.

Whoever instigated it no one could be sure, but dance they did, round and around the tree. Even the golden light joined in, rotating around both girls' feet and arms, making them feel lighter and more agile than before. It spun around their heads, crowning them like woodland goddesses, and radiated out from the antlers continuously. Whilst Jen and Emily twisted and stretched, the antlers dropped and then swooped up high, creating elegant moves all their own. When the girls jumped and spun, the antlers lurched and tilted, sometimes overtaking or falling back but always maintaining the seamless and equal flow of the circle. Most striking of all, however, was when the girls danced their deer dance, for instead of using their arms as imitation antlers, a real set would glide up to just above each girl's head, and then proceed to swoop and dive in exact harmony with her every move.

While this radiant kaleidoscope continued, golden light penetrated outwards through the floor and into the four walls of the chamber like floodwater, turning its grey-stone colour into bright golden yellow. In next to no time, every wall was completely covered; in fact, so much so that the light appeared to then slither down again like wet paint, causing a thick carpet of gold to accumulate upon the floor. Through the light's translucent haze could be seen the collapse of the chamber's walls. What had appeared as stone but was actually smoke now simply dissolved, disintegrating into nothing while leaving in its place bits of charred and damaged timber.

As they danced, neither Jen nor Emily could fail to notice the golden light also engulf the ceiling, resulting in some of the long wooden beams supporting the castle roof becoming visible way above them. Jen glanced up, causing her to visibly shudder as she realized just how high up she had been with Nocturne, and just how far she must have fallen. She quickly reverted her gaze back down into the chamber and instead concentrated on her dancing, as golden light spread out into other cell rooms and chambers.

Corridor by corridor, the entire lower level of Smolder's Castle was being dismantled, and returned to its post-fire state. Now that the Wandiacates and the magic antlers were together and dance had begun, the true force of the Golden Light of Goodness could finally emerge, as it penetrated through each and every artifice of Smolder's construction. As other walls, ceilings, floors and fake doors disappeared along the circular corridors and interconnecting passageways of Solum - the former cellars of Bagot Hall - what remained was shoddy and dilapidated wooden shells, just like the chamber Jen and Emily were currently in. Many of these 'rooms', however, appeared to exhibit some of the worst examples of DIY imaginable, and contained only the barest and most basic of a room's structure.

What was worse, most of the construction had been done using burnt bits of wood, remnants no doubt of what had survived the fire; the blaze that Lord Bagot had started soon after the death of his wife, just before Smolder killed him to then build this fortress of smoke.

Also left, dotted variously amongst the ramshackle shells, were scorched-black vertical pillars, before unseen but now appearing to support the entire upper - or Terra - level. As surrounding walls receded, several pillars buckled and snapped almost instantly, causing the skeletons of nearby rooms to likewise collapse. Large gaping holes in the ceiling appeared and then grew, causing debris to fall from the floor above. The noise alerted Emily who, although continuing to dance, tried to see what was happening. Other pillars nearby were clearly straining under the weight, and she quickly realized that the smoke must have played a far greater role in the castle than she'd thought. In fact, it had helped support the entire interior structure of the building, and without it, all that remained was essentially firewood. The consequences of this were obvious, and it threw her into a mild panic. Still dancing, she yelled over to Jen,

"This whole place is collapsing! We have to get out of here!"

"I know!" came the reply, lacking any suggestion of a ways-and-means that Emily had hoped for.

Just then, an incredible din - moving, running, scratching, climbing, flapping, screeching, whistling, hooting, barking - followed up by a phenomenal sight. Thousands of animals, large and small, appeared out of every dark corner of Solum, and raced towards the golden light! Each and every one was on the move, rising en masse out of the dungeons of a crumbling castle, all heading in the general direction of the floor above! Free at last of the shackles of Smolder's spells, and with little else to constrain them, along beams and up pillars they ran, or through flight they gained height and soared high. The wildlife of the forest, no longer the fake walls and scaffold of Smolder Bagot's empire, were returning home liberated.

"Look, Em! That's incredible!" Jen was really taken aback - as would anyone be - at the sight and sound all around her. Still dancing, it reminded her of a wildlife film she'd seen about migration patterns; yet, here she was, standing in the middle of a mass movement of animals! In fact, she was even causing it to happen! It was certainly a sight she would never forget. Nor would Emily, but right now she was too busy contemplating the deteriorating state of everything else around them. The falling debris from above was increasing, and sounding heavier and more structural than before. Floor joists were snapping, causing other parts of the ceiling to cave in. This was not a place to be. In fact, it was barely a place at all now.

"We still have to get out of here! Right now!" Just then, ahead of Emily in the circle around the tree, Hay's antlers began to glide up towards the gaping golden hole above, clearly heading in the same direction as the animals. Instinctively, Emily grabbed Leif's antlers directly above, and glanced over to Jen. Fortunately, she had done the same and grabbed Fole's antlers above her. Both girls were then effortlessly lifted off their feet and up into the air, followed by Tamhorn's, Blythe's, and lastly Folly's antlers.

"Hold on!" As they gently rose up through what was now a huge golden hole, Emily glanced back down. The view from above shocked her, as she was now unable to make out any of the corridor along which both she and Jen had only minutes before danced. The walls, doors and torches of the passageway were all gone, and so too had the wooden floor and much of the ceiling. What remained was debris, along with jagged and burnt pieces of timber. She could see smoke drifting up from smouldering wood. The scene was as though fire had ravaged through the entire floor, devouring just about everything.

Emily caught a final glimpse of what was left in the Stone Chamber. The silver leafless tree now stood drooping and twisted, apparently melting into the barren and lifeless earth beneath. The arched stone door, standing upright and alone with nothing either side of it, looked eerily like a monument left by a people long since past, or else an ancient headstone marking the burial of some fallen leader. For Emily, it felt symbolic that such a figure stood amongst the debris, destruction and desolation of Smolder's Castle.

Gliding up to Terra level, what greeted them was bedlam and absolute chaos. The golden light was continuing to surge along corridors, walls and floors at an incredible rate, turning back into animals the smoke contained within. Many of Smolder's guards could be seen trying to stop various creatures escaping, but it was all to no avail. Walls around them were disappearing, botched wooden structures were collapsing, flooring was caving in, and fleeing animals were everywhere.

As Emily and Jen rose up above floor height, Jen quickly spotted the smoulder chambers she had seen before, when up in the rafters with Nocturne. The difference between then and now was stark; instead of smoke plateauing slowly upwards and changing from golden to white, in every chamber there now spun a ferocious tornado, comprised of spinning golden light-threads! Emily saw it as well, causing her to briefly recall the day when they had first observed the deer dancing in the forest. On that day, they had also experienced light-threads and seen the golden tornado, but the whirlwinds in front of them now were bigger. Much bigger! Here, they appeared to constantly grow taller and wider; each expanding quickly to become a vortex of power and golden light, spinning so fast that debris was flung remorselessly in all directions. Nothing could stop the sheer force and energy that these tempests possessed, as they unleashed evermore destruction and mayhem.

Amongst the turmoil, Jen suddenly spotted a distance away, the candle chandelier with trailing ivy, shaking wildly above the hall where she had met Smolder for the first time. This was hardly something over which she cared to reminisce, however, and less still now. They had to find a way out, before the golden light consumed the entire castle.

"Look! Over there!" Thanks to a disappearing wall, Emily suddenly spotted daylight and what seemed to be an open exit, quite close by and to their right. She gently turned Leif's antlers in that direction and they seemed to respond, with all the other antlers following along behind. They were soon at the doorway, through which torrents of animals were already streaming. For Jen it came not a moment too soon, as white light beams began bouncing off the interior walls of the castle, like many intense flash bulbs going off at once. She didn't know what it was, but she guessed it probably wasn't on their side. Anyway, she was sick of this place - sick of the smell, the dirt and dust, and the glim shadowy light.

With nothing and no one to stop them, the antlers gracefully banked sideways like turning aircraft, gliding out through the doorway and into the daylight of the forest. The relief for both girls to finally be out of there was immense. The air was clear, the light of the day was radiantly supreme, and their mission was accomplished. They had the antlers, and the battle with Smolder Bagot would now be well and truly squared.

The antlers gently set the two girls back down onto the ground, not far from the exit. As they landed, Jen caught easy sight of a collection of stones nearby.

"Em, look!" she screeched. "We're at the hatch!" She ran over to it excitedly, calling all the way, "Bill! Bill! Come on, boy! Bill! Here, Bill!" Emily stayed where she was, making sure that all six sets of antlers were with them, and fearing that someone would have to go back down that hatch yet again.

"Woof!"

"Bill!"

"Woof! Woof! Woof!"

"Bill?" Jen turned around, realizing that the barking was coming from behind her, somewhere in the forest. As she did so, from behind a large pile of dead branches and ferns, appeared her beloved golden retriever. He galloped over to her, and she to him, reunited in joy.

EMILY & JEN DANCE FOR DEERON

"Bill! Bill!" Jen caressed and hugged him, while Bill licked her face. "Oh, I have missed you!" Emily gave a huge sigh of relief seeing that Bill was safe and sound, and they were back together at last. It was an emotional moment for them all.

"Friends! You made it!" From behind the very same pile of branches, came a voice. Emily turned, immediately catching sight of a welcome face coming towards her.

"Arog! Are we glad to see you!" Emily greeted him with a long hug, as Fauld trotted over to join the joyous reunion.

"And it thrills me beyond words to see you two," replied Arog, close to being overcome at the sight before him. "Alive, and having freed the magic antlers! Your triumph moves us closer to when Smolder and the evil supporting him can be defeated, once and for all. Really, I cannot thank you both enough for this."

"Hey, no problem! Any time!" said Jen jokingly, whilst still hugging Bill. They all laughed heartily, which surprised Emily, it being really the first time they had laughed about anything on this journey. Also, she suddenly noticed optimism in Arog that had been absent before. Apparently buoyed by their success in retrieving the antlers, he seemed genuinely upbeat now, as though part of a great load had been lifted from him. Emily gleamed in a surge of silent pride upon acknowledging this.

"What is more," he enthused, "much of what you saw in there will be crucial to us, as little is known about the inside of Smolder's Castle. Your knowledge can only help in our battle, after which Deity can return to breathe life back into this forest. Then, finally the war will be over."

"Whatever else you need from us, Arog," said Emily, "we'd be glad to help."

"I thank you," he replied, with deep sincerity. "For everything." The six pairs of magic antlers suddenly glided upwards, anticipating departure. "Come, my brave heroines," he said, joyfully. "Let us return to Deeron, and crown the six magic stags!"

Crown, Crown the Magic Stags

Deeron stood guard on the steps of the folly, continually scouring the surrounding landscape for any hint of a disturbance that might signal another offensive by Smolder's army. The crackling noise of the Falx, having reduced in intensity as they had neared the folly, was now no more, leaving Deeron undecided as to whether this was a good or bad thing. Either way, what he most yearned for right now was to see the return of Arog, with Emily and Jen safely in tow.

As hard as he tried, Deeron could not help reflecting upon better days as he continued to survey the surroundings - days when the nutty smell of autumn predicted the white cloak of winter; the hope of spring's freshness augured a warm summer sun; and when summer's rich fruit foretold a harvest of plenty. Now, what lay before him was a forest floor hard and brown, where the only growth was from nettles and thorn bushes that stung and tore into flesh. Trees were dying fast, and in time would fall to the ground, crying out one last time for Deity their goddess. But their calls would not be heard, as Deity was imprisoned. No living creatures remained in the forest now either, having either starved to death or else become slaves. Deeron knew that such a fate would not await him or his army, for Smolder would kill them all once the Horn Dance had passed. He glanced back towards the door of the folly behind him. The deer inside were silent. Their moment of frivolity had long since gone, and they were once again dispirited and fearful.

He sighed a deep sigh. Then, gazing back into the forest once more his eye was suddenly alerted to movement amongst the trees. Instinctively he reached down for a weapon, but stopped as a shimmer of golden light penetrated his vision. Deeron looked hard to try and see more - yes, it was definitely there, and moving towards him. The light ventured nearer, and appeared to gradually rise up from the ground, rather like a large golden balloon. Then, suddenly, golden radiance blasted upwards like the rays of a morning sun emerging above the horizon, and six sets of antlers honed into view. Glowing like warm friendly searchlights across the murk of a war-shattered territory, Deeron gasped as the realization of what lay before him finally sank in.

"They're back!" He yelled. "They're all back, and they have the antlers!"

Every deer leapt to their feet and scurried out onto the steps of the folly, to witness what each and every one of them had barely dared to dream - the return of the antlers to the six magic stags, and the beginning of the end for Smolder Bagot. Fole, Folly, Tamhorn, Hay, Leif and Blythe stood on the top step, afraid to move for fear of breaking the incredible magic that was finally bringing their antlers back to them. They were close, and now they could also see Emily, Jen, Arog, Bill and Fauld following along behind.

To their even greater astonishment, behind Fauld could be seen many animals and birds, all heading in the direction of the folly! There were squirrels, rabbits, foxes, badgers, magpies, blackbirds, - you name it - with more appearing to converge from other areas of the forest all the time. Before long, there were hundreds, perhaps even thousands, of creatures amassing behind the group like some vast army on manoeuvre. In fact, probably every living creature from the forest was now following the antlers. As the group drew closer still, the sky began to fill with insects and smaller birds, all swarming towards them.

As the antlers were the first to arrive at the folly, they hovered gently in the air to await the arrival of Emily, Jen and the others. Almost breathless trying to keep up, they in turn arrived with Arog, Bill and Fauld, as crowds of animals filled every space both surrounding and behind them. The birds and insects settled on the roof and ridges of the folly, on bare branches nearby and even on other animal's heads! Then, once the jostling finally died down, an almost deafening silence fell upon the company. Gradually, the deer occupying the lower steps parted to the sides, leaving only the six magic stags standing at the top and the hovering antlers at the bottom. All eyes went from the antlers to the stags, to the antlers and back again to the stags, full of anticipation that something was about to happen. After a few moments, all eyes then fell upon Deeron.

Deeron thought hard as to what he should do or say to reunite the antlers with the stags. Then he suddenly remembered a song that Lord Bagot used to sing when he was out in the forest tending the deer. The words were muddled in his mind but the tune was there, so he removed the flute tucked into his waistband and began to play. As sweet melody filled the air, Arog started to sing.

"Deep in the forest,
Where we made our home,
Six magic stags are free to roam.

They bring us joy and they bring us wealth,
They bring us peace and they bring us health.

Crown, crown the magic stags,
Keep them free and safe to roam.
Crown, crown the magic stags,
Keep us safe in our English home."

As the song continued, one by one each set of antlers was returned to its rightful owner. First, the grey-and-white set belonging to Fole gently hovered over to him, coming to rest just above his head like a golden crown. Second was Folly, who stood looking triumphant and proud like an athlete receiving his medal, much to the amusement of some of the other deer. Arog continued to sing joyfully while Deeron played, and urged others around him to join in with their celebratory song.

"... Crown, crown the magic stags,
Keep them free and safe to roam..."

After Folly, it was the turn of Tamhorn to be reunited with his set of dappled grey-and-white antlers. Next was Hay, followed by Leif, who each regained their almost identical set of bronze antlers.

"... They bring us peace and they bring us health..."

Finally, the deep-red antlers belonging to Blythe floated gracefully up to meet him, as the chorus lifted to the final rendition of,

"Keep them free and safe to roam."

As those last words were sung, Deeron played a fast high-trill on his flute, and all six antlers lowered down onto the head of their respective stag. Flawless and without a mark to show they had ever been removed, the antlers bedded back onto the rose stumps on each stag's head seamlessly. In unison, the magic stags then reared upwards onto their hind legs in triumph, causing the entire congregation to bow with respect.

Just then, a roar like thunder could be heard in the distance, and the steps of the folly suddenly began to shake. The ceremony was brought to an abrupt end as the ground around them also shook violently. Birds and insects immediately took to the air for safety, while other animals scrambled desperately for cover. In an instant, joy had been replaced by dread yet again, although not everyone was intimidated enough to run. As animals dispersed, Deeron and Arog both scoured the surrounding treeline for any signs of Smolder's army or the Falx, but no one came and nothing was seen. Then, almost as dramatically as it had begun, the thunder died and the shaking stopped. After the wonderful ceremony they had just witnessed, Emily felt quite deflated at the realization that the battle was not yet over, although she tried hard not to show it.

The magic stags, for their part, seemed remarkably unconcerned as they walked majestically down the steps to greet their young saviours. Everyone in Deeron's group then gathered around and stood in silence, facing their two heroines and a brave courageous dog.

"With all our hearts, we thank you," said Tamhorn, bowing his head low in unison with the other five magic stags. Then, in turn, everyone else in the group, including Deeron and Arog, also bowed and thanked the Wandiacates personally.

"We thank you, Emily and Jen." The phrase was repeated again and again, as each and every deer expressed his gratitude.

For both girls it was a proud moment, in recognition of having gone through so much, and arriving victorious at that time and in that place. Although the war had yet to be won, their mission had been accomplished, and for that they both felt a justifiable pride that was all their own. Even Bill seemed to bask in the glory. However, they were barely able to even taste their sense of achievement before the ground began to shake once again, and even more ferociously than before. The steps around the folly were now beginning to break up, whilst the folly itself looked as though it might topple over! Loud and vicious claps of thunder filled the sky, seeming to ominously predict what yet lay ahead. Jen was left momentarily wondering whether their success in retrieving the antlers had actually changed anything.

"Jump on board," ushered Blythe. Jen swiftly mounted, closely followed by Emily climbing onto Tamhorn, as everyone moved clear of the folly.

All eyes then returned to Deeron who, for the first time in his life, appeared to be rendered speechless. He stood, simply gazing upon his refreshed, invigorated and empowered herd, and could not help but feel a strong sense of emotion himself. Only minutes before, he had stood on those very steps and stared at despair, doubtfully wondering whether this time would ever come. Yet here he was, moments later, now enjoying that time. For Deeron, it brought home just how much his loyal army and new friends meant to him, and how important it was to keep faith and maintain hope. Sometimes hope is all you have, but so long as you keep hold of it, it's enough.

They had not yet won and were not at the end, and Deeron hadn't revealed to anyone his private fears about having to battle it out with the still all-powerful Smolder. But with hope having got them this far, and with it now in abundance all around him, he entrusted to his instincts the words he would choose. All around him the landscape shuddered, and thunder roared once more in the distance; Deeron remained oblivious to it all. After taking a few more moments to compose himself, he spoke.

"Friends! Now that the stags are reunited with their antlers, we possess a magical force once more! The battle is not yet over, and we face as formidable an enemy today as we did yesterday. But," he paused, "… our strength has grown, so now we move onward to the castle, and to win!" Loud cheers rang out above the earthly din all around them, and the newly fortified army geared themselves up for what everyone hoped would be the last and decisive battle with Smolder.

Arog, as usual, headed the group, leading the way back to the castle alongside Deeron. The six magic stags now resplendent with their antlers followed close behind, while the rest of the army took up the rear and side flanks. As they walked, Arog updated Deeron on what both girls had reported to him as they had all travelled to the folly together. The revelations concerning the castle's layout had given Arog some strong ideas for means to pursue the next stage of the battle. Also, the warning words of Nocturne as recited by Jen concerning the Falx and their deathly blades, whilst not entirely unknown, were still nevertheless worrying for them both. But at least they could now name the culprit. Of especial interest, however, was Albus Carcum - a place neither knew existed - and Emily's meeting with Deity.

Lastly, Arog described what had gone on at the castle entrance, and how he and Fauld had witnessed the Falx almost kill Targot. All the time Arog spoke, Deeron pondered deeply the possible reasons for what they had seen there, and what it might mean for them now.

"If Smolder has resorted to letting the Falx into his castle," began Deeron, trying to make sense of it all, "then he is either incredibly desperate, or else very stupid."

"He's both!" shouted out Jen playfully, enjoying her free ride on Blythe's back whilst casually eavesdropping on the conversation just up ahead of her. "And he's utterly vile to meet."

"I'll bet," replied Deeron glancing round, although still maintaining a steady pace. "And I hear you saw a great deal of the inside of Smolder's Castle."

"We saw pretty much all of it," chipped in Emily, slowly coming round from having briefly dozed off aboard Tamhorn's back. "There's not much left in there now, though. The place was falling to bits when we left."

"It is thanks to you both finding the antlers that the inside of his castle has collapsed," he replied, "and that the forest animals are free once more." Both girls gave each other a self-satisfied grin, and enjoyed a little more of the praise now heaped upon them.

"Do you think this will affect the castle's defences, Deeron?" asked Arog, thinking about how to navigate through the mirror fog.

"Perhaps, but there's no way we can enter now with the Falx inside, at least not all of us. Smolder will have to come to us instead."

"Do you think the Falx will protect him?" Arog had been grappling with the very same dilemma as Deeron.

"I honestly don't know," replied Deeron softly, with a sigh in his voice, "but we should prepare for that possibility. Right now, it's probably best if we head back to Marsh Valley. He's bound to see us from there."

"Where we first faced him?" Arog's face expressed a sense of disbelief at the plan.

"Yes," replied Deeron, solemnly, "and where we lost so many of our herd." A noticeable silence fell amongst the front of the group, as every deer within earshot recalled that dreadful battle, only the day before. The aim had been to distract Smolder enough to allow Emily and Jen to enter the castle undetected. This, everyone now knew, had been achieved, but at a price that had cost almost half of Deeron's entire army. Through boiling mud, bullet-like hailstorms and even ice-daggers, they fought valiantly with all the strength they could muster. Many friends and comrades had fallen on that battlefield and disappeared into the mud. Mentally revisiting the carnage was hard enough for any of them, but the thought of physically having to go back there was indescribable.

Jen and Emily also felt solemn at this point, for they had both seen some of the battle, but very different parts. Jen had seen the battle rage just before Tamhorn had led her, Bill and the other magic stags back into the forest to wait for Emily. Emily herself had only witnessed the build-up in Albus Carcum, and had yet to realize just how grave the outcome had been.

Deeron sensed that the optimism, shown only minutes earlier on the steps of the folly, was ebbing away fast through the ranks. He attempted to stymie the loss, and revive their confidence by some quick pep talking.

"Smolder may have won that battle, but we shall win this war! We shall right his wrongs upon the land where we fell, and return Deity to the forest to breathe a future life for us all! Our herd will flourish in peace, and never again shall evil reign over us! We shall consign Smolder to a footnote in history! Let us witness his passing, and ensure it is swift!"

"Hooray!" Loud cheers rang out amongst the troops, as vigour and confidence rapidly returned. They marched on, faster and more determined than ever, towards the open valley behind Smolder's castle.

"Jen, what happened out there in the valley?" asked Emily, scanning the herd to see who was missing.

"Oh…" Jen, suddenly feeling deflated yet again as images of the battle replayed in her mind, replied, "Well, I'll tell you what I saw…"

As they ventured further towards Marsh Valley, nobody in the group could fail to notice the far worse destruction of the forest closest to the castle. There, almost all the trees had been stripped bare - not only of their leaves and bark but branches also, standing alone and lifeless like rows of redundant telegraph poles. Many also had large gashes along their trunks, as though attacked wildly with axes. Splinters and fragments of tree lay strewn everywhere across the forest floor, as it became all too clear that something violent and ruthless had rampaged through the area. It was a truly depressing sight, seeing pristine woodland subjected to what could only be described as mindless vandalism. No one needed to ask the question as to who or what was responsible, however, as the culprit remained uppermost in everyone's mind, especially now as testament to their power lay all around. In the final battle with Smolder Bagot, the Falx remained the truly wild card, with no one really knowing of what they were capable, or more importantly, what could stop them.

Into Battle

*B*ack inside the castle, all that remained was total devastation. In place of the many rooms, corridors, chambers and tunnels there was now strewn charred, damaged, blackened and broken debris. Roughly two thirds of the floor on Terra level had either disappeared or else collapsed, with what was left appearing seriously rickety and unstable, and likely to go the same way. Everything else was just space - raw, empty and desolate - all the way to the four outer walls and roof of the castle. Falx buzzed about noisily and unseen overhead, like many swarms of pesky insects. The golden twisters that had sent debris flying like missiles across the length and breadth of the building were now silent and no more. Only the aftermath of their awesome and destructive power was left in evidence. Smoke hung in the air from several small fires having started, due to the once-hanging torchlights now buried beneath rubble. Elsewhere, the charred remains of the fire Smolder had started a long time before lay all around. Except for the remaining outer wooden fortress walls and roof, Smolder's Castle had been returned to its post-fire state as Bagot Hall - ruined, derelict and destroyed. The consequences of Smolder's own actions were left facing him once more, everywhere he turned.

Smolder stood surveying the scene on a surviving part of the floor, accompanied by a few remaining loyal guards. He seethed, incandescent with barely-contained rage at the devastation surrounding him. Smoke wafted out from the top of his head like a simmering pot about to boil over, while his face glowed a dark and fuming blood-filled red. Rocking from one stick-leg to the other, he muttered softly yet menacingly to himself under his putrid breath.

"You think you can beat me? I'll burn you all... I will have my revenge, do you hear? I **will have**...

MY REVENGE!"

Those last two words, screamed at full throttle, reverberated around the castle walls like an earthquake. Everything shook within it, whether flattened or else still standing. Another section of what was left of the floor collapsed down into the basement below, sending clouds of dust and soot up into the air. The noise of the Falx suddenly grew louder and more widespread, no doubt having been disturbed by the outburst. Smolder's guards stood locked rigid with fear, as his black-ringed and bloodshot eyes then veered upon them in deranged anger.

"Find me those Wandiacates! Find them and capture them at all costs! They will pay for this, and so will you all if you FAIL ME AGAIN!"

"Y-y-yes, Master."

"THEN GO! And find me someone to shut these Falx up!"

The guards dispersed rapidly, just as another guard entered from the opposite side of what was left of the castle, onto a different section of remaining floor. Across a sea of debris and smoke, the guard's voice barely penetrated the hanging veil of ruin, let alone the noise of the Falx.

"Master! Deeron's army and the Wandiacates are all heading for Marsh Valley! The stags are there also, wearing the magic antlers!"

"So," Smolder's mood suddenly switched from raging to scheming; in his mind, the prospect of another showdown with Deeron, plus the retaking of both the antlers and the Wandiacates, loomed. "They think they can destroy me now, do they?" He began hobbling about from one leg to the other as his mood swung yet farther, now towards delirium. His voice grew in intensity as he cried, with his arms outstretched, "They think I am finished because of this? Hahahahahah! This is NOTHING! I shall avenge this insult in their death, with any left alive rebuilding my castle for me! Then they too will die! Every one of them!" Smolder's eyes then caught sight of another guard, standing nearby. "You!" he pointed, having finally stopped staggering about. "Prepare my army for war, and find me Targot NOW! We shall meet them in the valley with the Falx, and we will win, decisively! GO!"

"Yes, Master." The guard dutifully disappeared. Smolder resumed his conniving as he stared vengefully across the devastation all around him. Barely moments later, Targot appeared nearby.

"I am here, Master."

"Targot!" Smolder's wild and hypnotizing eyes met Targot's like two launched missiles, as his wrath prepared to mount yet another assault. Targot jumped back, wondering what on earth was about to happen to him, while Smolder's face reddened once more and his head began to smoke. Through his deathly stare he grasped at Targot's very existence, while pointing towards the wreckage behind him as he screamed, "This is down to YOU! ALL OF IT! I've lost countless fighters AND my powerhouse is wrecked! You failed me, Targot, and for that you will PAY!"

"Y-yes, Master, I…" Targot's eyes remained locked onto Smolder's, as he stood rigid and unable to move.

"If I didn't need you right now to control these damn Falx, I'd have you propping up that WALL! FOREVER! Do you HEAR?"

"Y-yes, Master." Targot felt immense power continuing to linger over him, as Smolder's stare projected a sinister combination of contempt and fury. After what must have seemed like ages for Targot, Smolder reverted his gaze back towards the castle wreckage. A few moments later, he spoke in an eerily calm, almost murmuring voice.

"We shall battle again with Deeron and his army in Marsh Valley. The Wandiacates and magic antlers are also there. We shall retake them."

"Yes, Master."

"Take the Falx to Shallow Ridge, and wait. When we have recaptured the Wandiacates, I shall call a truce to discuss a trade with Deeron. This will be your signal to surround Marsh Valley with the Falx. Before sunrise, we shall withdraw via Marching Cliff, leaving the Falx to kill them all at dawn. Afterwards, we'll return for the antlers. Go now."

A ghostly silence briefly hung in the air, as Targot summoned up enough courage to speak.

"B-but, M-Master...."

"What?" From behind Smolder's mask of calm there now returned an ominous hint of menace in his voice.

"Dusk is now upon Marsh Valley, Master, and the mist is descending. Soon fog will settle, and the Falx will not travel as they cannot navigate or see."

A long sigh emanated from Smolder as he slowly turned to face Targot once more. Targot gulped in fear.

"So, as my second-in-command, what do you suggest?"

"Well, might it not..." Targot chose his words carefully, "be more useful to leave the Falx here in the castle, and capture the Wandiacates as you suggest. With the fog as cover, they can be held in the forest while we lure Deeron into a trap. We need only convince him that his precious Wandiacates are back inside the castle, and he will surely follow. Once inside, the Falx will kill him instantly. His army will quickly collapse thereafter I am sure, as without him they are little more than a ragbag of lost inadequates anyway. And the magic antlers will be yours, as will the Wandiacates."

"Hmm," Smolder began mulling over Targot's revised plan, appearing, initially at least, to quite like the idea. Targot, noticing this favourable response, decided to plug his plan further.

"You will have it all then, Master, and what you choose to do with Deeron's army is entirely up to you. You could have them killed, of course, or they could be used to rebuild your fortress. It would be your choice."

Smolder pondered over the proposal a little longer, while Targot stood motionless and silent.

"Alright," said Smolder eventually, albeit with a distinct air of suspicion. "We'll do this your way." He hobbled towards Targot. "If you succeed, we shall forget your previous carelessness that has led to the almost total destruction of my castle…" Close now, Smolder leaned towards Targot, almost touching faces, as his mood switched back in an instant to fiery anger. "SO DO NOT FAIL ME AGAIN!"

"I… I w-will not fail you, Master." Due to the vile stench of Smolder's breath so close to him, Targot tried desperately hard not to retch as he spoke. Smolder stared his contemptuous stare once more before finally turning away, much to Targot's relief.

"Prepare what troops we have left for battle," he ordered. "We leave as soon as darkness has fallen. I shall accompany you myself to ensure this plan is successful."

"As you wish, Master." Targot galloped away to assemble his troops, for what he knew would be the last and decisive time.

⁘ ⁘ ⁘ ⁘

Sat waiting in position behind Shallow Ridge on the edge of Marsh Valley, Deeron's loyal herd of deer rested. Along their path to this point, just behind the treeline on the far side of the valley, the group had passed Rains Gulley and chanced upon some food and water. There wasn't much, but what little they had was now shared amongst them. Beyond, dusk was giving way to the onset of darkness, tempered only by the light of the rising moon. A buildup of mist had begun in Marsh Valley, creating a thin blanket of haze that would undoubtedly cover the entire area before long.

Looking out from on top of the ridge itself, Deeron was grateful for having made it to this point, because from here the entire valley could be seen. Marching Cliff could also be observed from here - behind and to his right – and so too could Smolder's Castle, which was of course still invisible, but given away by the surrounding destruction of trees, even from this distance. However, Deeron knew that vision would soon be difficult for them all, and he hoped it wouldn't be much longer before their final battle with Smolder commenced.

"Thank heavens we have the moon and a cloudless sky tonight," said Arog, clambering up the rocky slope to join him.

"A subtle breeze would also have helped," replied Deeron, "as it would clear the mist and help us to see the advancing fog."

"I hadn't thought of that." Disappointment crept into Arog's voice.

"I'm sure she'll have it covered, Arog." Deeron turned to him and smiled. "Besides, we can't think of everything, can we?"

"True enough," reflected Arog, soberly.

The wait afforded them a brief respite, which was welcome since it allowed last-minute preparations to be made, while Deeron ensured that everyone was fully up to date with what was about to happen. Since entering Smolder's territory, their numbers had greatly diminished, with those who had survived now appearing war-torn and fragile. But right now, in this time and at this place, their optimism had never before been higher. A plan had been devised, and the stage was now set for their final confrontation with Smolder Bagot. That's not to say, however, that there wasn't some doubt amongst them.

"This is awfully risky, don't you think?" asked Purbrook, as he and Fauld sat together, both munching away on some dried grass and stale berries.

"Not a bit of it," replied Fauld, casually brushing aside Purbrook's concern. "Everyone knows what they're doing, so where's the problem?"

"Putting the magic stags so close to Smolder, that's the problem! What if they're discovered?"

"Oh ye of little faith!"

Fauld laughed out loud, causing Purbrook to feel suddenly belittled by his older friend. Purbrook looked up to Fauld as a kind of mentor, and to him at least these were genuine concerns, not simply scepticism or scaremongering. Their very existence relied upon the success of this plan, and more than enough pain, suffering and death had passed to at least consider the downsides more openly. Fauld, realizing that he may have overstepped the mark a little on rejecting Purbrook's fears out of hand, adopted a more conciliatory tone.

"Look, Smolder's powerbase is now badly damaged," he began, "and we know this will make him crazy for revenge, and all the more careless because of it. The very suggestion of a way in which vengeance can be his will lure him in hook, line and sinker. Now, I've known Blythe since he was this high," Fauld lifted a front hoof to just above ground level, "and I know he can spin a convincing yarn when he wants to." Purbrook gave a knowing chuckle. "So, try not to worry. It'll work, you'll see."

"Well, I certainly think the Wandiacates will manage, given what they've already had to contend with," conceded Purbrook.

"Oh, without a doubt," agreed Fauld, just as Arog passed nearby to where he and Purbrook were seated.

"How much longer do you think they'll be, Arog?" called Fauld after him.

"Not long now," he replied. "Soon enough, I'm sure. Fog will begin pooling into one area of the valley, and then we'll know they are here. When three barks are heard and the circle of fog splits into two, that is our signal to move. Rest while you can, and eat what's available. It could get rough out there, and we don't know how many there'll be." Arog then wandered over to see what was left of the meagre food rations.

"See?" grinned Fauld back towards Purbrook. "Even Arog thinks we'll walk it. No worries!"

"… Every last warrior on that battlefield! Fit or not, I don't care! They're no use to me otherwise, are they?"

"No, Master."

"Then get them! Meet us at Rook's Edge, and you'll all pay with your lives if you're late!"

"Yes, Master."

Except for the distant glint of torchlight through the trees up ahead, Emily and Jen could only hear Smolder's latest tirade, and for that at least they were grateful. The very LAST thing either of them wanted was to have to see Smolder Bagot ever again, and their position a distance away from the castle fortunately hadn't allowed them to. Just hearing his voice was enough to send a shiver through both of them, although it was far worse for Jen than for Emily. Jen stroked Bill who lay beside her, whilst Leif and Folly crouched low on either side of them all, as everybody waited for the sound and shadowy light to fade.

"I can't believe we're going back in there," said Jen, softly.

"Me neither," reasoned Emily, "but this is the plan we all agreed to, and so…" she paused, briefly listening and looking once more, before adding, "I guess we should get on with it. Ready, guys?"

"You bet!" said Folly, in his usual jokey tone.

"Absolutely," added Leif.

"Right then, this way."

Thanks to the Falx, finding their way back to Smolder's invisible fortress was quite an easy task now, and so Emily, Jen and Bill, accompanied by the two magic stags, carefully and quietly made their way towards it. Emily peered anxiously through the dark forest canopy to try and locate the clearing just in front of the castle, from where they had exited only a few hours before. Had it been necessary, the magic antlers themselves would have led them to the spot easily, but it wasn't long before they wandered upon familiar territory.

"There!" whispered Jen urgently, pointing through a row of trees. "I can see the hatch." The open hatch could indeed be seen, surrounded by the white stones and perched upright, apparently against nothing, just as they'd left it.

"Good," said Emily. "Right, you all wait here while I close it. It's unlikely I know, but the Falx may try to escape that way."

"Humph! Good luck to them an' all," grunted Jen quietly, as Emily sped off towards it. "Fat chance they've got anyway, getting through there." Jen grimaced as she reluctantly recalled the experience of when they'd first entered the castle. She felt quite bitter about those tunnels, for she knew she'd have nightmares about them for months to come. Folly appeared quite taken aback by her attitude, but Leif's reaction was more philosophical. Being older than Folly, he had a far greater instinct for what both girls had had to go through to retrieve the antlers, and knew it couldn't have been much fun in there. A brief outburst was the least to be expected. Regardless, nothing could diminish either stags' sheer admiration for the girls.

Jen had barely forced those tunnels from her mind before Emily returned, having already completed her task.

"Done. Right," she crouched down to where the others were hidden. "Now we have to find the side door and enter the castle. I know we said we'd check for any other doors that might be open first, but Smolder could soon be in the valley, so I think we'll just have to trust it to luck. Agreed?"

"I guess," added Jen, doubtfully, "but we thought the mirror fog would have gone by now, and it hasn't. How are we even going to find that one door, never mind any of the others?"

"Ah," interjected Leif, with an accompanying broad smile, "well that's where Folly and I come in useful you see, because thanks to our antlers being returned to their rightful place," he playfully glanced upwards, "we can now see through

Smolder's barriers again, which is partly why he wanted to take them from us in the first place."

"Oh wow," said a surprised Emily, turning to Jen and adding, "we didn't know that, did we?"

"Absolutely not," confirmed Jen.

"And you two can as well," announced Folly, with a big grin on his face. "All you gotta do is ride on our backs, and hold onto our antlers. Easy! Here," Folly pushed upwards on his front legs, whilst keeping his rear ones crouched, "jump aboard, Jen."

"Wonderful! Suits me fine," exclaimed Jen softly, climbing onto Folly's back. "My pins are killing me."

"Pins?" he queried, as Emily likewise climbed onto Leif's back.

"She means legs!" whispered Emily, as both stags lifted themselves and the girls up onto all fours. "Don't worry Folly," she joked, "it's just one of her country sayings, that's all."

"Better that than your townie talk," jibed back Jen with a smile, as Leif and Folly made their way out from behind the trees and fallen branches. "Come on Bill, and stay close."

Seeing the outside of Smolder's Castle again - this time for real - made both girls feel suddenly claustrophobic and uneasy, oddly more so than they had felt inside. Emily and Jen had, of course, already seen the castle in their shared dream, but up-close and vivid it appeared far more threatening now than then. Perhaps it was the sheer size and height of the place, or the thick vertical tree-trunk posts that made up the outer walls. Whatever it was, Smolder's Castle was somewhere you seriously wanted to get away from as quickly as possible, and about as uninviting as you could possibly get, which was, after all, the intention.

"Eiyew!" Emily screwed up her face in a look of disgust as they rode past. "What a place. It's even worse from the outside."

"I preferred it when it was invisible," mocked Jen, disdainfully. "Smelly dump."

They followed the line of wall along from the hatch, and soon came upon the side door from which they had earlier escaped. Leif and Folly stopped close to it. The door appeared firmly shut now, and Emily thought twice about trying to open it. Maybe it was the castle's aura, or the dark, or both. She just wasn't convinced. Something wasn't right.

"Let's move further along, and see if there's another way in."

"Do you think there's time?" asked Jen. "Smolder's probably at the edge of the valley by now."

"There's time." Emily seemed convinced, even if the others weren't.

"It does allow us," added Leif, constructively, "to at least check partially for open exits. After all, if the Falx escape, our entire plan will fail."

They continued on in silence, walking long lengths of wall surrounding the castle as it turned 90° corners and stretched off far into the darkness ahead of them. Jen tried to relate in her mind the distance travelled now with what she had previously seen from up in the rafters with Nocturne, to gain some idea of where they were in relation to the inside. Of course, she quickly grasped that this was hopeless, as the interior no longer looked anything like what she had seen then anyway. It was completely wrecked in there now, and she probably wouldn't be able to tell one end from the other.

Emily, realizing that they had passed the end of a wall twice now, figured they must therefore be roughly halfway around the castle. No more doors had been seen, leaving them all to wonder if there was any other entry point. All things considered, however, it did seem highly unlikely that for a building of this size, the only way in or out was either through a small single door, or else via a ventilation shaft!

By a combination of coincidence and sheer luck, Emily and the others got a swift answer to this puzzle in the form of a sudden crack of light cutting a pathway through the darkness, just up ahead of them. Leif and Folly stopped dead in their tracks as a huge semi-arched door could then be made out swinging partially inwards, quite close by. Five of Smolder's guards then ran out into the forest, and the door closed quickly behind them. Neither the stags nor Emily and Jen could have been detected in those few seconds, but it didn't stop them waiting until they were absolutely sure the guards had left. Emily was about to offer a typical 'Phew! That was close!' remark, but Folly instead blurted out,

"Did you see? That was Fole!"

"Fole?" asked Emily, completely confused. "Where?"

"One of the guards, the one at the back. I'd recognize those hoofs anywhere!"

"He's disguised well," added Jen, casually, "as he looked just like the others. Are you sure it was Fole?"

"One hundred percent."

"You're right, Folly," said Leif, having pondered on it for a moment. "That was Fole. In fact, it was probably Fole whom we heard Smolder order to go back into the castle and get whoever was left. Presumably, that's what he's just done, and so…"

"…The castle's now empty!" butted in Emily excitedly, before adding, more downbeat, "Except for the Falx, of course."

"Handy," added Jen, slightly mockingly.

"No, it's good," said Leif, correcting her sarcasm. "It helps us. This way."

He and Folly trotted off towards the large door, each with a Wandiacate riding upon his back. They stopped squarely in front of it, observing now in the moonlight two doors creating one giant archway. They all stared upwards for a minute or so, gazing upon each door's vast size. Emily wondered how they'd ever be able to open either of them, and whether it might not be more sensible to return to the side door and enter that way instead. Jen - never one for hiding her thoughts - nevertheless spoke for them all when she scoffed,

"How utterly absurd! Who on earth needs doors that size? Smolder must need a separate army just to open them!"

"If it weren't for the White Light of Evil," added Leif, softly, "he would, but they open automatically."

"How do you know all this?" asked Emily, sounding especially curious.

"Because of the Horn Dance," he replied, almost surprised at the question. "Each year, it creates a magic which collects inside the Golden Light of Goodness and passes to our antlers, making us stronger and wiser. So thanks to you two, our wisdom and power have also been returned to us, which in turn means that we're able once more to overcome Smolder's defences." Both stags crouched down, lowering Jen and Emily gently towards the ground. "Now, you and Jen must dismount us and pull up your hoods. Folly and I will shapeshift into guards, and then we'll be able to gain entry." As Emily and Jen moved clear of the stags to grapple with each other's hood, Leif and Folly instantly transformed themselves into goat guards, complete with a marble-looking complexion, large swept-back horns and laser eyes.

"Whoa…" Jen was shocked as she turned back towards them, now with her hood up thanks to Emily. "That-is-convincing," she said, slowly.

"Good, huh?" grinned Folly, in total contrast to the expression Smolder's guards usually wore.

"I'll say," agreed Emily, still sorting out her own hood, and feeling equally as spooked as Jen. "Just promise us you won't look like that any longer than you have to."

"Don't worry," Leif assured them, "we only need to take on this appearance to get the doors open. Come on."

With Folly and the two girls plus Bill, Leif walked towards the huge arched double doorway of Smolder's Castle. Just before they reached them, he turned back and whispered, "Say nothing, and stay close!" Both girls nodded, while Jen beckoned for Bill to heel beside her.

At the entrance, Leif and Folly stood apart, each facing a separate door. Their horns almost touched the thick vertical trunks of wood that had been used to build each of the gigantic semi-arched structures. In the darkness, neither girl could fail to notice both stags' eyes suddenly beam out penetrating red laser light. They then each in turn butted with their horns, slowly and one after the other, the door in front of them twice. As they did so, the laser beams ran up and down the length of each door and left smoke trails, as they appeared to burn into them. At the fourth butt, the doors swung slowly inwards and both stags wandered in through the gap, followed closely by Emily, Jen and Bill. As soon as they were all inside, both doors then jolted back to their closed positions very quickly with a deep thud. Jen gulped heavily.

Leif and Folly instantly shapeshifted back into their normal selves again as Emily and Jen gazed around, trying to work out in which part of the castle they now were. They stood in a long hallway, with an arched ceiling and torchlights hanging upon each wall. Half a dozen tarnished and broken chandeliers drooped down along its length, offering neither light nor even any decoration, given their condition. Many paintings, mostly portraits, hung variously and crookedly along both walls, with all of them appearing to be damaged in some way, whether by fire or neglect. Several lay on the sodden and rotten carpet, having fallen from the wall and remained precisely where they fell. It was a stark reminder of the now derelict state of Smolder's Castle thanks to Emily and Jen having retrieved the antlers, but all anybody was interested in right now was where they were, and how close or far the Falx were in relation to them.

"This way," whispered Leif, turning back to check all was okay. He and Folly then began to slowly walk down the hallway.

"Can you see anything?" called Deeron over to Arog.

"I'm not sure… hang on, give me a minute."

Standing at either end of Shallow Ridge, Deeron and Arog searched the moonlit landscape before them. The night was eerily quiet and still, and just as expected, mist had enshrouded

Marsh Valley in a sea of hazy-white from end to end, obscuring the ground now almost completely. To hope to see anything beneath this pallid soup would seem pointless, but Deeron and Arog both knew what they were looking for. They'd waited this long and would wait longer if necessary, but as the moon rose higher and more time passed, Deeron began to feel a tad uneasy. If what they sought didn't arrive soon, something had to be wrong, and this was their best and only realistic chance to beat Smolder. Deeron's plan had meant exposing both the Wandiacates and the six magic stags to danger, and it had been a far from easy decision to make. All the same, he had made it and he stood by it now, but the faintest whispers of self doubt echoed ever closer to his inner ear.

"I see it!" Arog's excited call broke Deeron's thoughts. "Over there, by Rook's Edge. It's fog, I'm sure of it!" Deeron diverted his sightline towards the area where he knew the rocky outcrop stood. Although Rook's Edge itself wasn't visible from this distance, he didn't need to search for long to make out a dark clump, increasing in size and moving slowly through the lighter and more reflective mist. Arog was right; it was fog, and precisely the kind they were looking for.

"Excellent!" Deeron felt a surge of relief upon seeing at last the fog formation advancing towards them, for it meant that his plan was working. "I was seriously beginning to doubt that this would work, you know."

"So was I," concurred Arog, "but all's well."

"So far," added Deeron, dryly. "Because now we must wait until the fog separates. Let us hope we shall be able to tell which mass of fog is which."

"Rest assured, Deeron," Arog sensed his nervousness. "We've got this far, I'm sure everyone will deliver."

At Rook's Edge, Smolder and every last surviving member of his army prepared to enter Marsh Valley. The fog was becoming increasingly dense, making it barely possible for anyone to see a hand, or hoof, in front of him. With many pairs of long penetrating light beams piercing through the dank and dark murk, Smolder's army managed to look menacingly ugly and intent upon revenge. Everybody, that is, except Targot, whose task it was to ensure that this plan succeeded where others had failed. Even through the fog, pressure was clearly evident upon his face as he detailed the plan for recapturing the Wandiacates.

"Deeron and what's left of his army are positioned behind Shallow Ridge, Master. We have managed to infiltrate his group, and our spy tells us he is waiting for a signal to attack us when we are in the valley."

"A signal?" snarled Smolder, "From whom?"

"Er," Targot hesitated. "That we do not know, Master, but we do know that the signal is a stag bark. When he hears three barks, Deeron's plan is to attempt to surround us in a pincer movement, probably coming from the treeline on the other side of the valley."

"This spy of yours," questioned Smolder. "Is he reliable?"

"Yes indeed, Master," he replied, almost gushingly. "A more loyal fighter to your cause you are unlikely to find." Smolder eyed Targot suspiciously, sighed, and then thought for a moment while simply staring into nothing. Targot looked away, wondering if he hadn't just oversold his 'loyal spy'.

"So," began Smolder, resuming his usual air of arrogance and supremacy. "We know our enemy's intentions. What are yours, Targot?"

"I suggest, Master," Targot quickly began sketching a diagram in the dirt with his hoof, "that we enter the valley as Deeron expects. He cannot have anticipated this fog and so his lookout is now useless, and there's no way he could see us advancing from the ridge. If we imitate the deer bark signal when we are here," he pointed to a centre position on his map, "and thereafter split into two groups, our fighters can lure Deeron's army deeper into the valley and away from the ridge. This fog is a gift, Master, for the only way our fighters can be tracked is from the light of their eyes. While Deeron is kept busy chasing laser beams, you and I along with a few guards can proceed unchallenged to Shallow Ridge via Marching Cliff, where we know the Wandiacates are hidden. Once we have them I shall order our forces to withdraw, leaving the rest of our plan to fall into place easily."

"Well then," snapped Smolder, officiously. "Give the orders, and prepare to move out."

"Yes, Master."

Targot swiftly dispensed his orders among the troops and then they all, upon Smolder's command, ventured out into the valley. They moved quietly and surprisingly quickly, given the bizarre and robot-like way in which Smolder moved. Before long, they reached a point roughly halfway between Rook's Edge and Shallow Ridge.

"This will do," said Smolder, turning to Targot. "Make the signal."

Targot did as he was told and barked three times, watching for Smolder's reaction from the corner of his eye as he did so. Fortunately, Targot's imitation stag barks appeared to please him, the evidence of which lay in a devious and self-satisfied smirk widening across Smolder's wretched face.

"Right," grinned Smolder. "Let's go."

"You three," Targot quickly turned to three guards standing together. "You're coming with us. The rest of you, carry out your orders, and remember we want them all alive." The fighters bowed their heads down low in allegiance and then hurried off into the dark murky night, while Smolder, Targot and the three guards began making their way towards Marching Cliff.

"Targot, you lead," demanded Smolder grumpily, as they set off. "Everybody switch off his laser eyes, now. They may see us advancing, even in this blasted fog."

"A wise move, Master," replied Targot, slyly. "Very wise indeed."

"Shut up, Targot."

"I don't recognize any of this," muttered Emily nervously, as she and Jen followed Leif and Folly down a long hallway inside Smolder's Castle. "Do you?"

"No, and I thought I'd seen it all from up in the rafters," replied Jen quietly, though sounding equally anxious. "Looks to me like an entrance hall, which makes sense I guess."

"At least the floor's still standing," joked Emily, dryly.

"Shh," whispered Leif, chiding them both for speaking.

They walked on, further along the hallway. Gradually, the distinctive and unmistakable sound of the Falx began to be heard, coming from directly up ahead. Little beyond the end of the passageway could be seen, except for a dull orange glow and rising smoke. Jen guessed that they were approaching the main part of the building she and Emily knew only too well, and it left her wondering in what kind of state it must now be. She also worried about how that might affect their ability to carry out the task Deeron had set them. Even though they had managed, against all odds, to achieve so much on this adventure, Jen was not feeling confident about this final encounter one little bit. In her mind, Nocturne's highly charged words kept repeating themselves, over and over - "*They don't turn you into smoke, dear Wandiacate, they kill you.*"

As they passed the sixth and final chandelier, the outcome of their achievements could once again be seen beyond the end of the passageway. A vast and dark space loomed before them, with barely any of the botched and charred wooden structures left standing. Not much of the floor remained either; in its place, large stacks of smouldering debris littered the basement floor deep below. As Emily, Jen, Bill, Leif and Folly stood at the very edge of this warehouse of wreckage, what quickly grabbed everyone's attention was not the scene below them, but the noise from above them. The waspish sound of the Falx was suddenly becoming louder and louder, like someone turning up a volume control. Also, flashes of light had begun, and were quickly becoming intense and more widespread. Emily felt her stomach sink like a brick, although she bizarrely began to wonder if this was how film stars felt when photographed outside premieres by all the paparazzi.

"Don't look at them, whatever you do!" shouted Leif, trying desperately to be heard above the angry din. Thanks to Arog's knowledge, however, and Nocturne's warning - earlier recited to the group by Jen - everyone already knew that the one thing you do not do is look at the flashing blade of a Falx. With the ever-increasing intensity of the blasts coming at them from all around, both Jen and Emily quickly grabbed Bill's collar, forcing him to face them. Jen then dipped her head low over him to prevent Bill from seeing anything, while Emily pulled both their hoods further up.

Standing side-by-side and just in front of them, Leif and Folly also dipped their antlers. The instant our two magic stags did so, their antlers began to emit a tremendous glow. At that same moment, both girls' cloaks also lit up into a golden radiance, followed by tiny light-threads suddenly appearing as if from nowhere. Then, from the tips of the antlers and the leaves of the cloaks, golden light-threads began oozing outwards, spinning rapidly and in copious numbers up into the air. With more and more constantly being produced, these tadpole-like threads then quickly became a golden veil just above their heads, deflecting the light away from them. The Falx tried to counteract by attacking in greater numbers and by firing extreme bursts of light into the veil, but the shielding held firm. In fact, the harder the Falx fought, the quicker the veil continued to grow, safely protecting both the girls and the stags beneath it while also beginning to contain the Falx above.

With amazing speed, the veil transformed itself to become a huge and expanding blanket, spreading out across the entire span of the castle by anchoring itself to all four walls. After a short time, both girls were able to safely look up, and see nothing except a warm golden glow above them.

"Good! That's worked," shouted Leif to them all, still competing against the noise. "Now we need to raise it up, and for this we need you both to dance again!"

Up on Shallow Ridge, the triple deer bark was clearly heard prompting a surge of activity.

"There's the signal!" called Deeron down to the others resting behind the ridge, as he and Arog continued to study the mist-engulfed and wide-open valley before them. "Now we just have to… wait, I think it could already be… yes, that's it! The fog has split into two!" He and Arog quickly descended the ridge to join the others below.

"Prepare to move out!" Arog immediately began giving instructions for departure, while Deeron took Fauld aside for a quiet word.

"Fauld, we need you to stay here on the ridge as lookout," he explained, "and let us know if you see either the Falx escaping from the castle, or Smolder returning."

"Oh," began Fauld, sounding rather disappointed. "But are you sure there isn't someone else who would be better suited for this?" He had hoped to play a more active role in defeating Smolder.

"No," said Deeron, flatly. "Your eyes and ears are better than anyone's, and in this fog we need the best there is to help us on the battlefield. Use repeated single barks if the Falx escape, and double barks if Smolder comes back."

"Will do," replied Fauld, having reluctantly resigned himself to the part. Turning to rejoin Arog, Deeron stared back into Fauld's eyes and, placing a hand upon his neck, said,

"Thanks, friend." Deeron wanted Fauld to know that this did not go unappreciated.

"For the rest of us, it's back to Rains Gulley," announced Arog. "Just as fast as we can!"

Led by Arog, the group made their way back along the edge of the valley. Fortunately, neither the mist nor the fog had penetrated beyond the treeline, meaning that the simple light of the moon provided enough illumination to retrace their steps. As Deeron ran along behind his army of deer, he wondered what they might be about to face out there yet again. They had, of course, previously fought Smolder's army in this very same valley, and sustained heavy losses. Deeron knew that Smolder had also suffered casualties - then and since - but he couldn't be sure of how many, or what powers Smolder still retained. What was crucial to their plan was to keep Smolder's army distracted, as much as possible and for as long as necessary. They absolutely could not fail, regardless of how many there were.

Very quickly, it seemed, they reached the dip in the path that led down to the gulley below. As the trail from here swept out beyond the treeline and into the valley, the terrain suddenly dropped quite sharply, causing the path to narrow considerably. Everyone, including Deeron, struggled to keep his footing, but slowly and carefully, they all managed to make their way down into Marsh Valley and the mist, with the gulley itself situated close by and to their left.

Although not especially long, the gulley beside them was wide and very deep, and not an area where you would wish to stay for very long. It was certainly not a place you would want to be around in fog or mist, given that its sides dropped away like cliff edges, but it was for this very reason that Deeron and his loyal herd stood alongside it now. As part of the plan to defeat Smolder, Rains Gulley had been chosen as the place to ensnare his army. With enough thick fog surrounding them and disorientation from Deeron's group, the hope was that Smolder's troops would lose their bearings and be easily led towards the gulley, where they would simply fall in. Once trapped down there they would be of little danger to anyone, but in order for this to work, the plan was for them all to spread out and basically lure them in. Arog, however, had another idea.

"Deeron, I'm not happy about us all going out there and being put in harm's way."

"Oh?"

"It just seems too risky, and we can't predict how they'll react. What if just Purbrook, Booth and I go into the valley and coax them in? You and the others can wait on the other side of the gulley, and help lure them towards it when we get near. After all, they're bound to capture you if they can."

"Well," he reasoned, "their instructions are to drive us away from the ridge, but I do take your point. They could decide to exact revenge if they managed to seize any of us."

"And remember, when we thought this plan up we didn't even consider the possibility of us having to battle with mist, let alone mist like this. One of us could just as easily fall into that gulley."

"True," conceded Deeron, soberly. He thought for a moment, pondering on potential outcomes, before adding, "It's risky just the three of you, and Purbrook's still a young stag. Are you sure he's up to this?"

"Absolutely, and he's about the fastest we've got on four legs. Besides, a few passes and they're bound to come after us."

"Then keep moving!" Deeron was emphatic. "Don't give them an inch, and do not enter the fog. That's an order."

Arog smiled, bowing his head in agreement. He trotted over to Purbrook and Booth, who were nearby. Then, after a brief discussion, the three of them galloped off into Marsh Valley, through silky-white mist and towards a large clump of fog heading their way.

Targot, Smolder and three of his guards continued along their path towards Marching Cliff, intending to ultimately reach Shallow Ridge and - so they thought - the Wandiacates'

hideout. Targot led the way, followed by Smolder, while the three guards spread out at the rear. The fog around them seemed thicker than ever now, with the result that Smolder frequently lost sight of Targot, and even the guards behind him. He was also struggling with all the walking, as they had travelled for what felt like quite some distance. On top of this, the terrain had started to incline sharply and become rocky, causing disorientation to set in.

"Targot!" snapped Smolder, aggressively. "We're still heading towards Marching Cliff when we should have forked off for Shallow Ridge by now. You should know this! Where are we?"

"We are near the Ridge now, Master," came a hushed, fogbound and unseen reply from up ahead. "We have already turned, and are closing in fast. A little farther, that is all."

"It had better be," he scolded, angrily. "Why the hell did you bring us this way? And another thing, all of you keep within sight of me! I can't see a damned thing!"

They walked on, across boulders and up ever-steeper inclines, until the rock suddenly flattened out. Targot's silhouette disappeared from in front of Smolder yet again, as he stumbled awkwardly onto the plateau. Angry, and now obviously in some pain, he searched around for Targot but could see nothing. He looked behind him, expecting to see the guards hone into view any moment, but none could be seen or heard. Not knowing how close Shallow Ridge was, Smolder was reluctant to call out and so instead whispered a viperous,

"Targot!"

No reply.

"Targot! Guards!"

No reply.

"TARGOT!"

No reply, nothing and no one came Smolder's way, except ever-darker dense and thick fog, which even the moonlight now struggled to penetrate. Smolder briefly switched on his laser eyes but they made no difference. He could see and hear nothing. Standing alone and feeling vulnerable for the first time, Smolder's mind festered over the situation in which he found himself. As self-proclaimed Lord of all the forest, this was about as far removed from what he had envisaged for his role as was possible to imagine. It should be he who ordered others to undertake such ridiculous journeys, not be forced to embark upon them himself! His second-in-command had persuaded him into this course of action, and he now found himself isolated and exposed. Smolder cursed Targot's very existence as he mumbled,

"If I ever get my hands on you, Targot, you and those idiot goon guards, I'll..."

His mood, far from pleasant even at the best of times, took a decided turn for the worse as he sensed that events were moving beyond his control. Frenzied panic welled up inside of him as questions bombarded his thinking - were Targot and the guards now dead, or were they simply captured? Had they even deserted, or had Targot betrayed him? Was Deeron's army surrounding him at this very moment, poised beneath the fog ready to unleash a torrent of revenge? Devoid of answers, and with no one to order away and find any, Smolder sensed for the first time something that he thought he could only ever inflict - fear. His army lay positioned somewhere on the other side of the valley, while the Falx remained within the safe haven of his castle, miles away and precisely where he should be right now.

Grabbing his attention, the air around Smolder suddenly changed from completely still to moving. As if from nowhere, it seemed, a cold wind blew up all around him, making the temperature drop from typical autumnal to winter in barely a few seconds. Far from being alarmed, however, Smolder instead appeared to be merely distracted. After all, it was he who controlled the weather in these parts. He whispered, angrily,

"*Sis a flung! Go wind, leave!*"
Nothing happened. He tried again.

"*Sis a flung! Go wind, leave!*"
Nothing happened.

Smolder was about to shriek out his well-used incantation for a third time when he noticed something. The fog. It hadn't moved. Even with an icy blast blowing through it, the fog stayed exactly where it was. This, combined with the fact that his magic powers now appeared to be useless, told Smolder he was in trouble. Deep trouble. Fully exposed to the plummeting temperature surrounding him, he realized that to remain where he was, or turn back, would be the end of him either way. His only option was to walk on and hope that Shallow Ridge was close by, where he thought he would still have a chance of capturing the Wandiacates. His wretched and contorted body throbbed intensely now, so much so that he struggled to place even one foot in front of the other. More frantic murmurings prickled the fog -
"*Move, damn you! Mov... argh!*"

With even his own body now appearing to defy him, Smolder's behaviour became more erratic still as extreme anger infected his mind. His eyes lit up a seething wild red hue, while dark black smoke poured out of the top of his head. He frenziedly walked - or rather, hobbled - forward, manic in his desperation to salvage something of the plan, whilst unable to see absolutely anything. The biting cold and ferocious wind dug into his already aching form, penetrating his joints and stifling nearly all movement. Reduced to literally dragging one leg in front of the other, Smolder willed himself on by mumbling and babbling many of his now worn out lines.

INTO BATTLE

"I shall be great... you will all pay for this... I shall be Lord of..."

Then, breaking through the near-total darkness, Smolder's eyes registered a single flickering light, just up ahead.

"Light! Heat!" In a state of delirious excitement, Smolder hauled himself towards it. What he found, perched on a rock, was a single piece of coal burning a brilliant white flame. Without pausing, he picked it up. Leering into the glow whilst trying to absorb some of its meagre heat, Smolder nevertheless gleaned a look of relief combined with self-satisfaction. "White Light!" he drooled. "I knew my powers would not fail me. Guide me to the Wandiacates!" With the blazing coal held out in front of him illuminating a narrow path ahead, Smolder salivated over his incredible luck. He staggered on, towards what he was now convinced was Shallow Ridge, and the hideout of the Wandiacates.

Quite close by, Smolder's eyes suddenly gorged upon a far greater vision. He stopped dead in his tracks as the glowing coal lit up an image that, for Smolder, could only be described as paradise. A little way up ahead, oddly magnificent in the slender light of the coal, shone,

"The magic antlers!"

Smolder's eyes were not being deceived, as before him actually appeared the antlers of Deeron's magic stags. There were only four pairs, but he hadn't even counted them. He simply stared transfixed, while all consumed at the good fortune bestowed upon him. The Wandiacates and the magic antlers, all within easy grasp! In his mind, to have lost almost everything and yet come through it victorious, was nothing short of genius. His genius, and he was the best there was. Better, stronger and cleverer.

More tantalizing than even this, however, was the beckoning prospect of reward for his brilliance - the reward of power, and to rule over all the forest in both worlds forevermore. Dazzling in their spectacle, and glorious in the supremacy they bequeathed, the antlers appeared as inviting to him as they were defenceless against him.

It would be so easy for him to take them now - Smolder lurched forward - it felt like the gift of all gifts. No one in his way, and next stop the Wandiacates - he dragged himself nearer - this would return him to the reign that was his true destiny. Victory would be his. Yes, victory would be his.

"Victory is mine! I shall rule over you all fore…."

Drifting now along the edge of Marsh Valley and immersed within dense fog, the soldiers of Smolder's army were not finding their task of tracking down Deeron's group easy. For one thing, the thunderous hooves heard running close by them were proving impossible to locate, due to the weird acoustics of the area. For another, the wisps of shadows falling variously around them hardly helped either, for as soon as one was seen it would disappear. Even their laser eyes could reveal nothing to them now, seemingly unable to cut through the heavy and intensely dark murk surrounding them. All they could do was trudge on regardless, consoled by the fact that the enemy at least had to endure the same conditions.

As it was, 'the enemy' didn't have to contend with any such thing. Not far beyond the cluster of Smolder's troops, the fluid fog enveloping them stopped almost flat on like a watery-sprayed vertical wall. It moved, shifted and drifted just as they did, to ensure their encasement held. Unable to see beyond their own horns, Smolder's army had no idea at all that only they were being affected.

Sure, the mist was an issue, but where Arog, Booth and Purbrook were it was actually quite thin, with the moonlight providing ample night vision. Also, Arog's revised plan of driving the cluster of fog towards Rains Gulley appeared to be working. The idea was simple enough: Arog ran from one side of the fog towards the other anti-clockwise, whilst Purbrook and Booth ran from the other side in the opposite direction. When they all met in the middle, either Purbrook or Booth would run on whilst the other two would return to roughly the same position from where they had started ready to go again, except that each time they veered closer towards the gulley. This was having the double effect of mimicking a larger number of troops, whilst pulling Smolder's army in. Just so long as they kept advancing along that line, Arog thought, they would all fall into the gulley easily.

Arog had just returned to his start position and was about to begin another run, when he heard a faint bark - a barely audible stag's bark - repeating again and again. The sound was coming from the direction of Shallow Ridge. It had to be Fauld! Arog repeatedly scanned both the valley and Marching Cliff, trying to locate the cause of Fauld's alarm. Then suddenly, in front of his eyes, something began to appear on the horizon, marking a dramatic shift in the battle - the castle itself. Booth, having completed another circuit, ran over to join him.

"What's going on?" he asked, unaware of what was happening.

"Get Deeron!" Booth nodded, and darted back towards the gulley with great speed. Arog stayed where he was, trying to figure out what on earth was going on. As for Smolder's army, still contained within the blob of fog nearby, they had all but been forgotten for the time being. Deeron appeared on the scene quickly, having also heard Fauld's faint barks and already begun making his way towards them.

"Deeron, the castle…" began Arog.

"I know," he interrupted, calmly.

"What the…" Because of his age, Booth had never before actually seen Smolder's Castle. Never before, but now he and the others plainly could, as the dense, vast and dark fortress stood before them. The mirror fog, which for so long had kept the castle invisible to everyone except the magic stags, was now evaporating in front of their eyes. It had been Smolder's own power that had created the mirror fog, and soon it would be gone completely. Arog gave Deeron a look of sudden comprehension, whilst Deeron glanced knowingly back.

"It's happened, hasn't it?" he asked, staring straight ahead while making no attempt to hide his astonishment. "It's actually happened."

"It has," replied Deeron, with a sober and resolute tone in his voice.

"Smolder Bagot is dead."

They gazed in silence for a few moments more as the final strands of mirror fog dissolved into thin air, and the realization of what they had just witnessed gradually sank in. For so long now, Smolder Bagot had stood at the fore of every disaster, catastrophe and calamity to befall Deeron and his herd, by persecuting their lives, homes and territory. He had caused immeasurable suffering, and cost countless lives through his all-consuming jealousy and wicked use of power. His screeching frenzied laugh, his wretched and contorted body; all lay in testament to his malice, corruption and evilness of being. Now at last he was gone, and no more would he fester upon their lives. It was actually a lot for the three of them to take in, causing them all to stand in silence for quite some time. Then Arog, suddenly distracted, looked behind him.

"Where's Purbrook?" he asked Booth, hurriedly.

"I don't... know," stammered Booth, peering around anxiously. "He'd gone back to do another run, I..."

"The fog!" butted in Deeron. "He must have strayed in. We've got to get him out of there, fast!"

"I'll go," said Arog, determinedly. "You both wait here." With not a moment spared to consider other options, Arog raced towards the thick mass of murk close by, and within a few short seconds had disappeared into the fog.

As he entered, the first thing that Arog noticed was the freezing cold, and the dense near-impenetrable wall of water vapour surrounding him. He stopped, making a quick mental note of his bearings before cautiously moving further in. Vision was practically useless now, and he knew that to become disorientated would be fatal. He moved slowly, all the while trying to hear or see anything that might reveal Purbrook's whereabouts.

Still nothing, and then - a short sudden flash - red, faint and fleeting, up ahead and not far off. Then another, and another - by the looks of it, several closing in on something. Arog manoeuvred his route so as to try and sideswipe them, which seemed to be the best course of action given that he couldn't know whether Smolder's troops had all stayed together, or were now spread out. He didn't even know how many remained, but one thing of which he knew he could be absolutely certain, was that Rains Gulley lay too close to even think about attacking from behind.

As Arog closed in, he began to make out four pairs of red laser eyes, scanning the ground ahead of them. They had heard or smelled prey - Purbrook, almost certainly - and it had to be only a matter of moments before they found him! Arog had to do something, and fast, and take a gamble as big as any he would ever dare consider. He raised his head and called out loudly into the fog.

"Purbrook!"

"I'm here!" came a frightened and anxious reply, a little further to the right. Instantly, eight laser beams shot directly towards Arog - most missing him - with a few shots deflecting off his steel antlers. He had wisely ducked down low immediately after yelling, and now poised ready to charge, rushed towards the red eyes.

Wham! Arog ploughed into them with all his might, knocking over and into the air like tenpins, the remnants of Smolder's dilapidated army. They were no match for his speed or his strength, and nor could they withstand such an attack from his uniquely strong antlers. Braking hard so as not to lose his position, Arog then rapidly veered around to where Purbrook's voice had come from.

"Purbrook!" he called again.

"Arog, thank heavens!" came a voice close beside him, followed by the sight of Purbrook's anxious, albeit relieved face, poking through the deep black fog. He was found.

"Are you hurt?"

"I'm okay."

"Good. Follow me, and stay close."

Arog led Purbrook blindly back along what he hoped was the route he had come in by, although he was ever mindful of the fact that as the fog was constantly shifting, it may no longer work. Whatever happened, right now he just wanted to create enough space between them and Smolder's army to at least buy some time. As it turned out, Arog's superior tracking skills led them almost straight back into the light mist of Marsh Valley, within sight of a waiting Deeron and Booth. Surprisingly quickly, it seemed, they were all back together again.

"You're both safe! Well done, Arog!" Deeron greeted them both with open arms.

"I'm sorry," a shamefaced Purbrook began, "I was distracted, and…"

"It doesn't matter. No harm's been done," cut in Arog soothingly, having no desire to see Purbrook beat himself up over it. "Just steer well clear of the fog from now on."

"I will. Thanks, Arog."

Just then, from out of the darkness and across the valley, barking could be heard again. All heads instantly turned towards the castle, as the reason for Fauld's signal - single barks now, and repeated - revealed itself.

Inside the castle, the now gigantic veil of golden light masking the entire roof like a ceiling, at last began to lift. Above, the Falx were being hemmed in, constrained between this rising horizontal plane of light and the rafters. With the power of the golden light passing through their antlers, Leif and Folly stood firm, battling to retain control as the Falx attempted again and again to break through the barrier. The more they tried, the stronger the golden light became, and the higher it rose. From the noise alone, it was obvious that the Falx were angry; the sheer force of power emanating from them, which was being buffeted so effectively, flashed remorselessly across the castle walls in testament to their rage.

Yet, just below this relentless combat, Emily and Jen were behaving as though the chaos and destruction all around them had simply ceased to exist. With arms raised and their little fingers hooked together, the two girls circled around and then bowed to each other in a mediaeval court dance. Swapping arms, they then did the same but in the opposite direction, repeating the sequence over and over. Then, just as they had done in the smoulder chamber, Emily went up onto her toes as Jen sank down to the ground. Through every movement of dance they performed, the force of the golden light grew ever more. Not even the Falx could now prevent this from happening, and nor could they match its strength.

From somewhere amongst the noise and bedlam of above, Leif detected a different sound he hadn't heard before. It was a striking, scraping kind of noise, like a cross between an axe chopping wood and a sword fight. As it became louder, so the assault on the golden barrier above them eased. The buzzing sound of the Falx had increased, although it now seemed more distant than before. Folly heard it as well.

"What *is* that?" he shouted over to Leif, whose face could only register puzzlement as he grappled with the same thing.

"I don't know!" was all he could think of to say.

The difference in tone and ferocity of the Falx had now become evident to Emily and Jen, who regardless were still dancing behind the stags.

"What's happening?" called over Emily.

From the edge of Marsh Valley where Deeron and the others stood, the outside view of the castle also now paraded brilliant white C-shaped blasts of light piercing the night sky, bursting up through holes being devoured into the roof. Like anti-aircraft searchlights switching off and on rapidly, giant white flashes launched themselves upwards like spears in ever-increasing numbers, as more holes appeared. As they all continued to watch events unfold, Booth whispered, anxiously,

"Oh no! The Falx are escaping!"

The Falx were indeed escaping, and in such a frenzied and destructive manner as to suggest they may also be aware of Smolder's demise. They were angry, that was obvious; angry at being cooped up in the castle, and probably also angry at having been prevented from helping him. Deeron's eyes tightened as he briefly pondered on various possible outcomes, but his mind was already made up. In fact, so far as the Falx were concerned, Deeron had decided upon the means for tackling them long ago. What he didn't know, of course, was whether or not it would work. Finally, the time had come to find out. He peered across the valley towards Marching Cliff, and noticed that the dense patch of fog seen earlier up around there had now completely gone. The shadowy yet clear and oddly resplendent cliff top ridge that greeted him now glistened almost beckoningly in the moonlight, leaving him in no doubt as to the course ahead.

"Now that Smolder Bagot is dead," he said sternly, turning to the other three, "I must travel to Marching Cliff and finally end this. We shall meet at the castle when it is all over."

"You're not seriously going up there to face the Falx alone, are you?" a startled Arog asked.

"I am," smiled Deeron, placing a hand on Arog's neck. "And you've been a powerhouse of reasoning and heroism throughout all of this, Arog." Deeron stared deep into his eyes, as he spoke, now earnestly. "You have anchored my thinking, second-guessed the consequences of all my decisions, and saved countless lives." Arog gave a humbled and slightly embarrassed smile, but reverted back to his concerned look very quickly.

"Almost everything we have done, and all that we have achieved, has been down to trust; of each other and ourselves, of our knowledge and our courage. Now finally, the time has come where you and the herd must trust me, and me alone, to overthrow the evil that remains. Lord Bagot placed in my hands a force. Now that our stags are free and Smolder is no more, it is time to test that force."

"But our only evidence that any force exists rests solely upon the words of a dying and desperate man. Do you really think this will work, Deeron?"

"I do."

"Well," conceded Arog, "if this force has your trust, then you have ours, no question about it." Purbrook and Booth both nodded nervously in agreement.

"I am grateful to you all."

"But in return, I should like your agreement for me to take you to Marching Cliff. We should face the Falx together, Deeron, and if nothing else you'll get there faster."

"But I don't know that the shield will protect you as well, Arog."

"We'll just have to trust it then, won't we?" Arog gave a wry grin.

"So we shall," Deeron smiled back in reluctant accord, knowing it to be futile to try and talk Arog out of it.

"Jump aboard," he beckoned, lowering his hind legs. Deeron climbed onto Arog's back, holding onto his large steel antlers for balance, as orders were dispensed for the other two. "Purbrook, you and Booth go back to Rains Gulley and get Grindley, Lupin and anybody else you need to finally trap Smolder's army. Fauld should soon be with you, and when you're done lead everyone to the castle." Arog turned to leave, before adding, "Oh, and…"

"I know," interrupted Purbrook, still rather embarrassed by the whole thing. "Don't enter the fog."

"Good lad." Arog and Deeron both smiled, and then sped off with tremendous speed into Marsh Valley itself, and ultimately Marching Cliff.

As they raced across the valley, Deeron marvelled at the pace at which Arog was moving, running more like a racehorse than a stag. Marching Cliff would be reached in next to no time, which was just as well given what was happening. The roof of Smolder's fortress was now largely destroyed, but glaring white flashes of light from the Falx continued to punch through the gaping holes and cracks they themselves had made. This was odd, as usually the Falx tended to move around whenever possible, and so disappear from view. With nothing whatsoever to stop them, it appeared that the delay was of their own making. Were they undecided as to what to do next, and perhaps mulling over strategy? Were 'they' even in control of anything? It wasn't long before Deeron found out.

Suddenly, and all at once, the light from the Falx ceased completely. Neither Deeron nor Arog had ever seen this before, but Arog kept on running flat out towards the cliff regardless. Then, a few moments later, bursting into the night sky above the valley and to the left of them, a gigantic and luminous manifestation emerged! Looking stark and austere against the black backdrop, an image of a cloaked and faceless manlike figure appeared. Silhouetted completely in white light the figure drifted, fading in and out of view as it did so. Deeron could clearly see the telltale twinkling of the light that made up the ghostly apparition now posing a threat. It was the

Falx generating this image, of course, but many more than he thought existed, and all now displaying a significant advance - they were able to simultaneously move and release their deadly discharge of white light, seemingly at will!

Weighing up this latest development as they sped along, another sighting then revealed to Deeron the contours of an object - also in light - held alongside the white spectre. Its profile showed what appeared to be a long vertical handle, leading up to a horizontal block at the top, curving to a tip. Suddenly, in a moment of pure clarity, Deeron realized just what it was that he was about to face. In this final showdown, the White Light of Evil itself was now controlling events, exuding maximum menace and power by uniting every C-shaped sickle Falx together as one. The White Light had created the ultimate harvester and chief of all cutters, in the shape of a master Falx - or more accurately, a Grim Reaper.

Very soon, Deeron and Arog reached the edge of Marsh Valley, and the rocky path leading up to Marching Cliff. By now they had completely lost sight of the reaper as their trail became narrow, steep and uneven, with large jutting boulders scattered variously in-between sections of pathway boasting a sheer vertical drop on one side. Even with Deeron riding upon his back, Arog still managed to scale the track effortlessly, and before very long they were on top of the rock on the plateau, and the summit of Marching Cliff. Facing back towards a spectacular view of the now-distant castle shadowed by moonlight, and the mist-shrouded entirety of Marsh Valley, Deeron and Arog began searching the night sky for the Grim Reaper once more.

"So what now?" asked Arog, as nothing and no one tainted the serene vista.

Before Deeron even had time to answer, the now much larger Grim Reaper suddenly flashed into view, coming from behind them and on their left side. As it rushed past, a bolt of light fired out from the tip of its scythe straight towards them! The light viciously blasted into the rock face barely a metre away, just as a massive rush of wind and noise - like an ocean storm meeting a plague of wasps - also ploughed straight into them. The shock and force caused Arog to rear up, nearly throwing Deeron off his back, he only managing to stay on board thanks to his strong grip around those steel antlers. As Arog fought to steady himself, Deeron suddenly realized why it was that they kept losing sight of the Grim Reaper.

"It's got to be on our left!" he shouted, trying to be heard above the din still going on around them. "Only when it's near us can we see it straight on! We have to know what it's doing, and maintain a sightline! For that to happen, it has to stay on our left! Keep moving, and watch closely! When it comes in, then turn to face it! Got that?"

"Okay!" Arog began to shift about and circle around. Deeron then quickly spotted the reaper flying far out across the valley, no doubt preparing to attack again.

"I see it! Stay on this angle!" Deeron was anxious that they shouldn't lose eye contact with it, even for a second. The wind, light and noise buffeted constantly now, increasing in intensity and literally battering them from all sides and angles. Arog had to fight hard to maintain his footing and their line, while Deeron amongst all the watching tried to precisely recall the words of Lord Bagot. The Grim Reaper's flight path took a hard right-turn as it arced around and began descending towards them, its aura and presence exuding both extraordinary anger and incredible energy. As it came in fast Arog turned towards it, and Deeron blurted out, as loudly as he could, Lord Bagot's words.

"With this shield, I banish from o'er these lands all that is evil!
Peace shall prev..."

Before Deeron could finish, the Grim Reaper swooped down and then glided up in an ominous and confronting gesture. Its size relative to theirs was now immense, but its sheer awesomeness of power was about to prove devastating! In an instant, the phantom reaper collapsed in front of their eyes, as every single Falx suddenly swung around on a single circular trajectory, and propelled itself with colossal force directly towards them! Like a vast shoal of fish moving in unison, but with the weight and strength of a hurricane, hundreds collided straight into Arog and Deeron.

"ARGH!"

Deeron was blasted backwards and clean off Arog's back, coming to land several metres away in a dip of barren rock behind him. Fortunately, he'd closed his eyes just as the Falx had lunged, and was bruised but otherwise unharmed. He looked up to see a white flickering trail dissolve into the night sky, as the Falx shifted their position and disappeared from view once more.

"This is hopeless!" he exclaimed, clambering back up onto his feet. Quickly limping back onto the plateau where he and Arog had been hit, Deeron began with, "Arog, we'll have to…" but never managed to finish the thought. Startled by the scene that confronted him, he collapsed onto his knees.

"AROG!"

On the cold and hard rock, lay a lifeless and unresponsive Arog. A wound to his side was made all the more evident by a pool of blood gathering nearby, but Deeron quickly feared that this was not the only injury to have befallen him.

"Arog! Can you hear me?" A quick check of his pulse, followed by a closer examination of his eyes - both open, staring vacantly ahead - told Deeron just about everything he didn't want to know.

"Arog! Speak to me!" he pleaded again, but no response whatever, appeared or was heard.

Waves of shock, guilt and despondency fell all over him, as Deeron struggled to think what on earth he could do to help his closest and most trusted friend, right now and in this place. He did another check of Arog's vital signs, but the fact that his opal-cream and emerald-green eyes were open at all bore evidence enough of what had happened. The Falx had got him, that was clear, and his pulse was now fading fast. Soon, Arog's very soul would be taken from him, and he would be lost forever.

From the left corner of his left eye, Deeron spotted a looming and newly reassembled Grim Reaper, not far away just above Marsh Valley. He stood up, knowing that come-what-may, he would have to fight on with the White Light, as to do otherwise would lose them both their lives and everything they had struggled to gain. Although deeply anguished over Arog's failing condition, there was no way Deeron was going to let that happen. Then, suddenly, above the tumultuous wind and noise, Deeron heard words -angelically spoken, and from a woman's lips - repeating, seemingly directly into his ear.

> *"Believe, you must, free your might.*
> *Believe, you must, free your might."*

"Deity!" Deeron knew that voice and excitedly called out to her, expecting to hear her reply. Had she managed to escape now that Smolder was dead? Sadly, Deity's voice did not return, and so Deeron was left trying to recall where he had come across those words before. His mind was cast back to the folly and Lord Bagot's artwork, and he remembered that those words were part of a riddle, which appeared on the plaque at the base of a painting -

> *When your enemy is seen on the left,*
> *This shield, will it come to your right?*
> *With words I decreed, such power will find thee.*
> *Believe, you must, free your might.*
> *Remember I told you so.*

- The VERY painting of the Golden Shield as portrayed in battle, being held up in defiance against an aggressor unseen. Held up, but by which hand? The right hand? Then it clicked, and Deeron knew what he must do to finally end this.

Maintaining his corner-eyed sightline with the Grim Reaper, Deeron walked out into the centre of the plateau. As he reached it, the reaper raced in, no doubt seeing another opportunity to attack.

'Believe, you must, free your might.'

Those words kept repeating inside his head. Deeron stood sideways on to his approaching foe - concentrating, watching and waiting. Angered by Deeron's apparent defiance, the now fiery-white reaper sank down low and then lurched upwards, even larger and angrier than before. For the very first time, lurking behind the hood of its cloak, the Grim Reaper now displayed a face. It was a haunting, skeletal face of fury and death, spitting out piercing white-hot flames from its mouth!

Without a single flinch or visible recoil to suggest even a solitary presence of doubt, Deeron turned head-on to face the Grim Reaper and held up his right hand in a stop gesture. As the reaper towered above with a look of contempt and hatred, Deeron bellowed once again the words of Lord Bagot.

"WITH THIS SHIELD, I BANISH FROM O'ER THESE LANDS ALL THAT IS EVIL!

Like a gigantic flamethrower, the Grim Reaper suddenly hurled bluish-white fire straight out of its mouth directly towards him! Normally that would have been the end of anyone, but the very fact that Deeron now showed such self-belief in being able to overcome the White Light, meant that the conditions were at last met for the Golden Shield!

The instant the rush of flames reached Deeron, golden light suddenly exploded out from his hand and blocked the fire from penetrating or moving any further. Coming from the centre of his right hand, the beam shone so intensely that the Grim Reaper appeared to be stunned, unsure as to what was happening. It reacted by simply launching more fire at Deeron, but as it hit, the golden light suddenly began to solidify in front of his hand, curving outwards on both sides. Far from attacking or destroying anything, the Grim Reaper's breaths of fire appeared to energize, expand and mould the golden light into the shape of an actual shield!

While the firestorm and torrent of wind and noise bore down upon him more ferociously than ever, Deeron remained standing firm and utterly resolute in his purpose. His resolve was unswayed; not because of Deity or Lord Bagot's words echoing in his ear, nor even because he had finally worked out what had been meant by them. Right now, Deeron's fearlessness in facing down the Grim Reaper was due entirely to the plight of his most loyal and dear friend Arog, for whom time was rapidly running out. Deeron wanted this finished and over with, so that he could attend to Arog's needs as soon as possible. With the Golden Shield now not only formed but also growing, Deeron delivered another tirade to the White Light figure looming before him.

"YOU WILL LEAVE! I BANISH YOU FROM O'ER THESE LANDS, WITH ALL THAT IS EVIL! PEACE SHALL PREVAIL HERE!"

The Grim Reaper appeared to be becoming increasingly frustrated, as a succession of lightning bolts, fired from the tip of its scythe, failed to break through the shield! Just like the fire, their only achievement was in making the Golden Shield stronger. An attempt thereafter by several Falx to attack Deeron as they encircled and swirled around him, also came to an abrupt end. With an absolute belief in both the might and supremacy of the Golden Light now flowing through him, Deeron goaded the White Light by staring directly at them all.

One by one, as each of these Falx swivelled on their axes to capture Deeron's features, all that registered upon the C-shaped blades was a powerful golden haze. As the light hit, every Falx in turn simply disintegrated, while more energy poured into, and brilliance shone forth from, the Golden Shield!

"GO! YOU SHALL LEAVE THESE LANDS, WITH ALL THAT IS EVIL!"

A raging tempest of fire, wind and rain now completely engulfed Marching Cliff, as the wrath of the White Light summoned up evermore-powerful swirling light combined with hurricane winds and torrential storms! The Grim Reaper blasted, shot and spat; it cursed, set upon and inflicted; nothing could break the steadfast will and determination of Deeron to face down whatever force or weapon was thrown his way. With belief as his protector and the Golden Light as converter of every evil force, the more the reaper pounded and pummeled, the stronger and more resilient Deeron and his Golden Shield became!

Finally, in a state of wild Falx-flashing fury, the Grim Reaper raised the scythe above and behind its head with both arms. The image now in front of Deeron was horrific! A furious skeletal hooded figure wielding a scythe like an axe, poised ready to strike it down on top of him! Deeron lost no time as, with the shield held up higher still, he roared,

"YOU SHALL LEAVE!! THIS-IS-MY-WILL!!"

As the very last word was spoken, the Grim Reaper slammed down the scythe with tremendous force! Deeron met the pointed edge of the blade with the Golden Shield. The instant they touched, the Grim Reaper exploded out sideways into millions of tiny pieces, as though it had literally been blown apart! The blast of the detonation was so enormous that

Deeron's head was knocked sideways, causing his eyes to close shut due to the incredible and intense flash of light. A gigantic backwards gust of air then followed the explosion, forcing Deeron's body in all directions. He thought for one terrible second that he would be blown clean off Marching Cliff, but the Golden Shield that Deeron held in his right hand remained in exactly the same position, while his feet stayed firmly wedded to the rock.

Then, suddenly, nothing moved - literally, nothing whatsoever moved. Everything stopped, locked in its position. At a standstill now stood the wind, haze and noise, along with every fragment, dust speckle and light trail. An eerily breathtaking calm punched its presence into a scene of formidable conflict and surreal chaos. Time itself seemed to freeze at that moment, as though someone had simply pressed 'pause' on a remote control.

Deeron couldn't move either, although he was alert. He opened his eyes and briefly gazed around him, marvelling at the spectacular vibrancy of colours, light streaks and still-twinkling splinters of the obliterated Falx. How much time passed was impossible to tell, before a thunderous rumbling began beneath Marching Cliff. Deeron could suddenly feel tremors beneath the rock rapidly flow up towards him, and then grow in intensity to earthquake crescendoes of noise and vibration! Unable to move, all he could do was wait until it stopped.

Deeron then realized that the Golden Shield, still held high above his head, was beginning to throb uncontrollably. Also, he quickly became aware of energy flowing through him, as every muscle in his body and hair upon his head began to quiver. Like the earthquake, the trembling reached a climax incredibly fast, causing Deeron to begin shaking violently. The sense of power rushing through him and down into the rock was truly awesome! He struggled to remain conscious, but managed to glance up just in time to see those elements suspended in mid-air, now being dragged towards the Golden Shield! Every component, in fact, of a demolished Grim Reaper, hauled in by an overwhelming force resembling a giant magnet. Each particle, every flame, burst of wind and even noise; all were being pulled into the pulsating golden light!

The shaking increased, to the extent that Deeron expected to pass out at any moment. The noise as well was sheer bedlam now, whilst the rock under his feet rattled close to destruction. Brilliant white and golden pulses of light raced through his body, sending shockwaves deep into the ground. With every passing second, Deeron found it harder and harder to hold on. From miles around he could be seen lit up like a beacon, atop an electrified Marching Cliff! The pulsations then grew even more. This was madness! He was going. Deeron could feel his senses failing. He couldn't hold on! He was… then,

Shumph!

He shuddered to a halt, and collapsed down onto the rock in front of him. Slowly, Deeron lifted his head just in time to see a faint golden haze gush out across Marsh Valley from the cliff, swelling into the woodland either side and beyond. Like some vast wave rushing over dry land, this transparent glow stretched for as far as the eye could see, as though the last remnants of the White Light were being swept away, or some giant protective blanket laid over the entire area. After just a few more seconds, the afterglow sank down into the earth beneath, petered out and was gone.

Badly shaken up but otherwise unharmed, Deeron cautiously glanced around as he returned to his feet. In the still and quiet of the night sky, nothing now remained of his clash with the Grim Reaper, including the Golden Shield. The air around him was empty, except for the early light of day slowly ascending in the east, gesturing towards an approaching new dawn.

Finally, the battle was over and victory had been won, but at a cost almost too great to bear. Kneeling down beside his lifeless body, Deeron tenderly stroked Arog as he wracked his mind for something, anything, which might help his fallen friend. Sadly, no matter how hard he tried, Deeron could think of nothing. He had been the first of his herd to witness a Falx attack, and knew of no way to treat a victim. Arog was far too large and heavy for him to carry, and by the time any help arrived, it would be too late. So soon after the enormity of having defeated the White Light of Evil, the cruel irony of Deeron's weakness now lay before him in the dying body of Arog.

Very gradually, a breeze had picked up all around Marching Cliff. Deeron only really noticed when, carried through the air, a faraway and distant echo became loud enough to be heard. It was a heavenly sound of choral singing, and although nothing could be seen, Deeron knew at once to whom those dulcet tones belonged. Deity the woodland goddess, now free at last, was returning home to breathe life back into her forest, and upon the lands of Deeron's herd!

> *"Tir-na-no'g, Tir-na-nana,*
> *Tir-na-no'g, Tir-na-nana."*

He stood up as the sweet sounding celestial song drew closer, very soon near enough to seem as though it were being sung directly beside him. Deeron once more expected to hear Deity's voice at any moment, as that was how they had always communicated, given that she had shed her physical form many years before. What actually did happen took Deeron completely by surprise, and with more than a little shock. From behind a dark and barely visible cluster of rocks nearby, stepped a tall and beautiful woman.

She was pale in complexion with a thin and fragile appearance, and sweeping blond hair rippling far down her back. From her long dress shone a sinuous golden light, seeming to shimmer from within. Deeron was left speechless by the stunning mystical beauty now walking towards him, as never before had he seen the Goddess of the forest.

"I cannot thank you enough, Deeron," she began, "for having saved my forest. It is to you that I owe a debt which can never be repaid." Before Deeron could even think of what to say in reply, Deity knelt down beside Arog and rested her hand upon his mane. Almost instantly, Arog's eyes blinked several times, then his head lifted from the rock and he rapidly scrambled back up onto all fours.

"What happened?" he asked, suddenly highly alert, as if having awoken from a deep sleep startled by something. Arog was completely unaware of the Falx attack, and equally nonplussed as to what was going on around him now. For Deeron, to suddenly see his loyal friend return from near-death to full health in seconds, rendered him lost for words yet again. He simply stared in disbelief as Arog stared back in confusion, exhaled a soft laugh as much in relief as joy, and said,

"We won, my friend! We won!"

Turning then to Deity, Deeron gently took her hand in his, and knelt down on one knee. "You owe me nothing, my Goddess, for it is with your help that Smolder was defeated. Without the fog, our plan could never have succeeded, and," he paused, casting a glance over to his alive second-in-command, "words cannot express my gratitude to you now for saving Arog. Your return to the physical world was because of this I know, and I speak for everyone when I solemnly thank you."

"Thank you, Deity." Arog said softly, considerably humbled by circumstances he was only now beginning to understand.

"You are most welcome, Arog, and you too, Deeron."

Just then, the sound of hooves clambering up over rock could be heard. Deeron stood up and turned round just in time to see two, three and then four sets of golden antlers, peering up just above the plateau floor. A few moments later, scrambling up onto the flat rock and clearly out of breath, appeared Blythe followed by Fole, Hay and Tamhorn.

"We saw the battle rage from Shallow Ridge," blurted out Blythe, panting furiously, "but I knew something was wrong. We ran as fast... Deity?" The four magic stags were truly taken aback, as they each caught sight of the woman standing behind Deeron for the very first time.

"Deity, let me introduce you to four of our six brave magic stags," a smiling Deeron beckoned her. Formal acquaintances were made, along with brief explanations.

Deeron, Arog and Blythe stood at the very edge of Marching Cliff, just in time to see the new day's first blazing ray of sunlight pierce up above the mountain peaks, ahead and in the distance. They all stared down over the precipice into the dark boglands far below, and the grave of Smolder Bagot. It was at this very spot where he had fallen to his death, causing each one of them now to reflect upon the harsh reality of their triumph. To be literally staring at loss of life - even Smolder's - was a hard truth to swallow, but he created this war from his own jealousy and twisted ambition, and now had paid the ultimate price. So many had been killed, many by his own hand, that to end the slaughter had inevitably meant an end to Smolder himself. The fact that each one of them had planned and played a part in the process by which he did die, was a cross they all would have to bear for evermore.

Fole, having wandered over with the others, eventually broke the long silence. "You know," he began, "if the real Targot hadn't deserted, and Arog and Fauld hadn't seen him leave, this plan could never have worked."

"It couldn't have worked if Emily and Jen hadn't retrieved our magic antlers, you ninny!" exclaimed Tamhorn, rather haughtily.

"Actually," butted in Hay, attempting to sound authoritative, "you're both wrong. If..."

"Lots of ifs," interrupted Deeron, with more than a hint of annoyance at the break in silence and seemingly pointless banter. Deity now stood alongside him and simply smiled, sweetly. "The plan did work, and that is all we need to recognize. Now, it is time for us to rejoin the others at the castle, and celebrate our good fortune and future prosperity once more."

Deeron led the procession down from Marching Cliff onto a little-used path that ran along the edge of Marsh Valley, leading back into Bagot Wood and towards the castle. In the crisp early morning sun he and Deity walked together immersed in conversation, while Arog and Blythe ambled a little way behind. Hay, Tamhorn and Fole sauntered happily along at the rear, eagerly discussing each other's role as guards in the deception and defeat of Smolder, whilst subtly embellishing their own bravery and performance. Tamhorn, suddenly recalling an incident inside the castle, shouted up ahead.

"By the way, Blythe. I've got a bone to pick with you!"

"Oh?" Blythe stopped and casually glanced round, as did everyone else.

"What were those kind words you used to describe us all to Smolder in his castle? Something like… 'Little more than a ragbag of lost inadequates', wasn't it?"

"Really?" queried Arog, with a look of disbelief and required explanation, turning to Blythe who stood beside him.

"Ah…" Reminded of the scene, a tired and weary Blythe tried to hide his embarrassment as he stumbled, "Well, er, actually it was all I could think of to say at the time."

"Thanks," replied Arog, disappointment etched across his face. "That makes it even worse!" Deity and Deeron both burst out laughing, quickly followed by Tamhorn, Fole and Hay, as poor young Blythe didn't know where to put himself, especially with Arog's insulted stare raining down upon him. It was, of course, all lighthearted joshing, and both their journey and carefree contentment soon resumed, basking in the rising heat of a new day.

Inside Bagot Wood, once the sunlight had begun to penetrate beneath the treetops, Smolder's castle again honed into view. Even from a distance, no one could fail to notice the severe destruction the Falx had wreaked upon the barren exterior of the late Smolder's fortress, in their desperation to escape. The damage done to the roof had resulted in much of the rest caving in, causing some wall sections to lean precariously and teeter upon the brink of collapse themselves. The two giant semi-arched doors at the front, now battered and decrepit with gaping burn marks along each length, creaked and groaned as both struggled to stay upright. With no magic power left to support their massive weight, it had to be only a matter of time before they too, along with everything else, fell to the ground.

As Deeron and the others entered the clearing, the uppermost concern for everyone was that Emily, Jen and the two magic stags had exited safely and in time. Even with Smolder and the Falx now gone, there was still an eeriness about the place, and the complete absence of happy and familiar faces was not what anyone had expected.

"EMILY!" Deeron called out, as he scoured the forest all around him. "JEN!" No response came.

"LEIF!" Deeron was beginning to worry now. Then, from just behind the treeline over to the right, came a voice with the words,

"Hey! What about me?"

Suddenly, giggling and laughter were heard, and then from behind a large mound of branches and leaves, popped the head and magic antlers of Folly. Deeron's anxiety quickly dissolved as, from behind Folly, the faces of Emily, Jen, Bill, Fauld, Purbrook and all the others gradually appeared.

"Friends! At last, we are all back together!" With expressions of joy and outstretched arms, the Wandiacates and Deeron's herd reunited once more. Jen was the first to catch sight of the radiant female standing behind Deeron.

"Who's that?" she asked animatedly, but Emily knew immediately.

"It's Deity!" Both girls were truly taken aback as they approached her, not only by her presence but also her beauty.

Deity, for her part, was eager to greet them with open arms and warm gracious words.

"You both have much to be proud of," she smiled, "in retrieving the antlers and helping to overcome the evil that has plagued us for so long. It is thanks to you that our forest can breathe again, and life will soon return."

"Thanks go to you as well, Deity," replied Jen, "for supplying the fog. The plan couldn't have worked otherwise."

"My role was tiny, and only made possible," she turned to Emily, "because you, Emily, survived the perilous journey to Albus Carcum, and brought with you the Golden Light, returning some of my powers to me. Without that, I may never have been able to escape, even now. You forever have my gratitude, and shall always remain deep in my heart." For the first time throughout this whole adventure, Emily appeared dumbstruck in facing up to her achievements, mainly because Deity had come to mean so much to her. As a friend, a mentor, and someone whom she not only admired but with whom she now also shared a special bond.

"You're welcome," was all she could manage in reply, fearing that her emotions might otherwise get the better of her. Deeron and his herd crowded around the girls, as everyone wished to show their appreciation for the two brave Wandiacates. Deity, however, chose the moment to utter some words of caution to everyone.

"Our good fortune is to be rejoiced, but it is vital we remember that the White Light has survived, and so shall it always. Many souls remain imprisoned in Albus Carcum, while the ceaseless battle between good and evil rages on throughout Wandiacatum. We must stay prepared in case such wickedness once more invades our land, and the magic stags need protecting at all costs. Never again must we allow the power of good to be stolen and corrupted for the pursuit of evil."

"We shall protect them, my Goddess," replied Deeron, solemnly. "Of that, you can be sure."

"Thank you, Deeron."

"We shall all soon return here," he said, turning to his troops. "We shall tear down the remains of Smolder's Castle, and in its place create a lake and haven for wildlife. The folly shall be preserved and restored to a scale of which Lord and Lady Bagot would be proud." Clapping and general nods of agreement spread throughout the group. "But for now, let us all head home, and celebrate together our survival and victory." Loud cheers rang out as all six magic stags reared up together onto their hind legs, in triumphal display.

"I too must also depart, Deeron," said Deity, with a caring smile.

"Must you?" asked Deeron disappointedly, hoping to change her mind. Before she could answer him, Emily cut in, pleading,

"You're coming with us, aren't you Deity? There's so much I wanted to ask you, please come." Deity took Emily's hand in hers, and gazed meaningfully upon her and Deeron.

"I thank you both, but I must return to my forest, as there is much work to be done. Many animals and plants need my guidance to help them through *fluxus,* and on towards their future path. You saw with your own eyes, Emily, what happens to captured souls inside Wandiacatum. They remain forever tormented and lost, unable to break through the barricades of Albus Carcum. Far too many have already been lost during my absence, and I cannot allow yet more to succumb to that fate. I hope you both understand."

"Of course," Deeron bowed his head in acceptance. "I completely respect your decision, Deity."

"Me too," added Emily, with more than a hint of reluctance in her voice. "I'm just sorry that we couldn't have spent more time together, and helped those lost souls as well."

"Maybe one day we shall," she smiled, as she stared deeply into Emily's eyes.

"One day," replied Emily softly, returning the smile; and with that, Deity suddenly evaporated into thin air, almost instantly. Remarkably, it took no one by surprise except Jen, who blurted out,

"What's happened to her?" A brief silence fell about the group.

"She has once more shed her physical self, Jen," answered Deeron, with a soft sigh, "and returned to her home in the forest." He briefly paused, pondering upon her departure, before quickly resuming his upbeat tone. "Come, let us also return home, to Needwood where we shall rejoice in our triumph!"

Along the path leading out of Bagot Wood and hitching a ride upon the back of Fole, Emily turned back and took one last look at Smolder's Castle. For the very first time, as it lay exposed in the morning sunlight of what promised to be a beautiful day, the fortress no longer appeared threatening. Instead, it looked merely derelict and defeated, and a blight upon a damaged but soon to be rejuvenated landscape. Jen, riding on top of Hay, also gazed back, prompting her to ask,

"Do you think we'll ever come back here, Em?"

"I don't know. Maybe. Right now, all I want to do is sleep... for a month."

"If only!" she exclaimed, quite melodramatically. "But after the celebration at Deeron's Hall, we've then got to make it back in time for the Horn Dance on the village green this afternoon."

"The Horn Dance!" cried Emily, horrified. "I'd totally forgotten about that!" Because of everything they had been through, the actual event that had marked the deadline of their mission - the Horn Dance itself - had escaped Emily's mind completely.

"We don't have to be there," said Jen, "but I think we should."

"Of course," agreed Emily. "But hang on..." concern suddenly rushed across her face. "It took us two days to get here! How on earth can we be back in time for this afternoon?"

"No problem there," came a voice from behind them both. It was Arog. "Our journey here only took us so long because of the route we had to take, plus having to deal with all the forces surrounding Smolder's territory along the way. With him gone and the White Light defeated, we're actually only a few hours away from Deeron's Hall now."

"I thought you knew all this," said Jen, turning to Emily and trying hard not to sound disappointed. "Deeron mentioned it at the start, remember?"

"I know," she cut in, "I just forgot, that's all. It's been a long night."

"Actually," quipped Jen, jovially, "it's been six nights."

"Yeah," Emily gave a weary smile, "that feels about right."

Safely here in Deeron's Hall

Word of victory had travelled ahead to Deeron's Hall, due to many of the freed animals having already journeyed through Needwood. Loud cheers rang out as the enormous doors opened, and the returning herd at last arrived home. A welcoming of food and drink was provided in the Great Hall, along with warm words and much excited conversation. Their homecoming was made magnificent by the sight of many families being reunited, but tempered by the memory of those who didn't make it back.

Looking on towards the many happy and joyous faces basking in the glory of success and the morning day sunlight streaming in, Emily and Jen lost all thoughts of tiredness and battle wounds for the time being. Everyone gathered to admire the six magic stags with their returned antlers, gleaming on top of their heads once more. Victorious and dignified, they would all doubtless have great stories to tell in time to come, of their long battle against Smolder Bagot and the White Light of Evil. As the girls drank their honey drink, both felt proud to have taken part in such a courageous expedition, and prouder still to have returned triumphant with the future now assured for Deeron and his herd. Clearly, the deer that had been left behind at Deeron's Hall had gone hungry in order to save some provisions for this special occasion, and goblets were somehow never left empty as they all ate, chatted and laughed.

After a great deal of talk, Deeron stood at his throne and beckoned for some quiet. "I would like to propose a toast," he said, raising his goblet as the deer congregated around him. "First, to Deity our Goddess of the forest, who helped in our defeat of Smolder, and will doubtless provide for us all while the forest recovers." Many either bowed their heads or murmured agreement. "Also, to peace in the forest and prosperity in years to come." More approving gestures were both seen and heard. "But most of all...." Deeron paused for silence to return, as he turned to face the three of them, standing nearby. "To our Wandiacates Emily, Jen and Bill for their courage, loyalty, and their magic dance which was key to our success. They have given us the greatest gift of all - freedom to live our lives. To the Wandiacates!"

"To the Wandiacates!" replied every deer in Deeron's Hall together, in an emphatic chorus to honour their brave friends from the mortal world.

"Thanks," was all Emily could think of to say in reply, feeling as she was now slightly embarrassed by the praise repeatedly heaped upon them. Jen, on the other hand, simply basked in the adulation via a wide self-satisfied smile that stretched right across her face, as she proudly stroked Bill to mark his brave contribution. However they felt, though, both girls knew that they would never forget the kindness and appreciation shown for what they had helped to achieve.

"As a gift to you both," said Deeron, "we would like to share with you the goodness that comes from the Horn Dance. Each year when it is performed, a little magic will be passed on to you, to help you both achieve your goals in life and be happy."

"Wow!" exclaimed Jen, turning to Emily with a look of wonder and excitement in her eyes.

"We don't know what to say, except thanks," said Emily more sensibly, as she fought frantically against her tiredness to assemble something approaching a speech. "But you, Arog, Blythe, Fauld, Tamhorn, the others - you all deserve just as much praise as we do. We played our part, that's all, and we're both just glad that it all worked out. Besides…" she paused, staring apprehensively at Jen as she tried to sound believable, "we had a great time, didn't we Jen?"

Jen gulped. "Sure," she replied, as harrowing memories of her experiences inside Smolder's Castle came flooding back into her mind. An uneasy silence filled the hall, with Jen quickly realizing just how unconvincing her one-word answer had been. She hastily added, with a nervous smile, "But it was worth it all to see Blythe disguised as Targot."

"You should have seen him grovel!" shouted out Tamhorn as he began to chuckle. "He's a natural, our Blythe!" Much laughter and hilarity then erupted, thankfully erasing at once the unease. It was all at the expense of poor Blythe, of course, but he didn't appear to mind. He simply smiled a self-deprecating grin, as Deeron proudly patted his mane.

"Now," said Deeron, "let us celebrate this day, and embrace the return of our future!"

Very quickly, Deeron's Hall became a blaze of dance, laughter, celebration and golden light. The six magic stags, led by Tamhorn, decided to recreate the same circle dance that they had performed on the edge of the forest, overlooking Marsh Valley. Just as before, they stomped with their hooves - *stomp-stomp-stomp-stomp* - as wisps of golden light meandered above and around them all. It also wasn't long before Arog, just as before, began his chant.

"Dance-now-Emily, dance-now-Jen," were the words he repeated over and over as others joined in, and many eyes fell upon them both. The unexpected request rather caught the two girls off-guard, but a shrug and a smile from Jen soon coaxed Emily into action. They both entered the circle and first began to skip around, mixing in twists and jumps along the way. It wasn't long, however, before they were dancing their now-familiar deer dance, causing golden wisps of light to form translucent antlers above their heads! Once more, a kaleidoscopic scene of magic, dance, music and light had been created, at the greatest party ever to be held at Deeron's Hall.

What was more, for the very first time none of the magic conjured generated anything other than joy in response. The sight was a truly mesmerizing experience for those deer, and more particularly fawns, who had never before witnessed the magical power of the Wandiacates' dance. This was a moment they would never forget.

Soon after their performance, Emily and Jen stood with Tamhorn, Blythe and Leif. Although they were all incredibly tired, everyone still managed to savour the merriment and carnival atmosphere going on around them. Everyone, that is, except for Leif who seemed, to Emily at least, to be rather gloomy, prompting her to ask,

"What's wrong, Leif? You look a bit down about something."

"Well," he replied, a little reluctantly, "I was just thinking how much we're all going to miss you two when you return home today." He forced a soft, conceding smile. "It's been fun having you here, you know, and we can't thank you enough for what you've done for us."

Emily grasped Leif around his neck and hugged him hard. "We're going to miss you all too!"

"How couldn't we!" gasped Jen, as she grabbed a slightly taken aback Blythe. Each of the three magic stags received a hug at least twice as emotions ran high, and was only interrupted by a very noticeable quiet descending across Deeron's Hall. Blythe looked up to see Arog and Deeron exchange a few words, and then both proceed to walk outside in silence. Deeron's face at that moment revealed astonishment and shock.

"What's going on?" he asked, to no one in particular.

"I suspect that Arog may also be planning to leave us," replied Tamhorn, with a soft sigh. "Perhaps even today."

Arog's intended and eventual departure had been common knowledge throughout the herd for some time, but its sudden and impending arrival was no less shocking for anyone. Especially today, of all days, when the sweet taste of victory had barely even been sipped! An anxious hush continued unabated throughout Deeron's Hall, broken only by frantic whisperings and muttered conjecture. It was when Deeron and Arog finally walked back in, that total silence fell. They both stood side-by-side, just beyond the large double-doors, encircled by the entire herd.

"Arog has an announcement to make," said Deeron impassively, stepping sidewards to receive his address.

"Er, well," stumbled a hesitant Arog, rather nervously, "I've given this a lot of thought, and have finally reached a decision about what I must do, now that the antlers are returned to their rightful place." The silence surrounding him, now so intense, was almost deafening. "I've decided to remain here with you all, to help maintain the…"

"HOORAY!" A loud chorus erupted from the herd, cutting short his speech.

"Three cheers for Arog!" someone cried, causing everyone to join in with the "Hip-hip, hooray! Hip-hip, hooray! Hip-hip, hooray!" Poor Arog didn't know where to put himself, honour having always made him feel uncomfortable, even at the best of times. He managed a simple yet awkward smile as he turned to Deeron beside him and said,

"I really wasn't expecting this."

"You should," replied Deeron, smiling warmly. "You mean a great deal to us, Arog. We all know that without you, the battle could not have been won, and none of us would be here now. Our home is your home, for as long as you choose."

"I'm touched," he said modestly, "and I thank you."

The festivities continued long into the morning and proceeded to spill outside, where many more hugs, kind words and long goodbyes were expressed with the other stags. Eventually, both girls managed to sit themselves down propped up against the castle wall in the courtyard, blearily gazing at the goings on as Bill lay alongside Jen with his head flopped on her lap. All three were utterly exhausted, but were at last enjoying some relaxation underneath the basking rays of a warm summer sun. As Bill lay fast asleep, Emily struggled to keep her own eyes open as tiredness began to overwhelm her. Jen, through her sleepy eyes, caught sight of Deeron walking out of the Hall close by them.

"Deeron," she weakly called over, "shouldn't we be getting back soon?"

"It has all been arranged," he replied cheerily, crouching down beside them. "There's no need to worry."

"That's a relief," said Emily with her eyes closed, almost sighing each word as she shuffled about her position. "'Cause right now, I'm too tired to worry about anything."

"Then get some rest, both of you."

"How are we getting back?" asked Jen, now with her eyes closed as well. The simple fact was that neither she nor Emily had even considered how to return home.

"Don't concern yourselves," replied Deeron, calmly and quietly. "You'll be woken when it is time."

As Deeron spoke, Emily and Jen felt waves of fatigue rush into their bodies, forcing their tiredness to grow evermore acute. Jen tried to fight it, knowing that if she succumbed she would be asleep for many hours, and they would miss the Horn Dance later that day. She tried, but simply could not overcome the relentless and pulsating surges of exhaustion washing over her. They both fell farther and farther towards slumber.

"Don't forget us, will you?" said Deeron.

"As if!" replied Emily with a broad smile and a final fidget, before she and Jen both fell headlong into deep, intense and restful sleep.

Horn Dance on the Green

Jen found herself lying on a bed of dry leaves somewhere in the forest, not knowing where she was or what she was doing there. A dusky light dully illuminated her strange surroundings, enough to see that she was alone. Besides feeling incredibly tired and weak, Jen also felt distinctly uneasy about her situation and so tried to get up. A dark shadow suddenly loomed over her, causing Jen to crane her neck so as to try and see what was happening. Above her, a gigantic crow suddenly swooped down, hurtling towards her open-mouthed with outstretched, fully extracted claws!

"Give me the Wandiacates!" it screamed. "Give me the Wandiacates!"

Jen struggled to stand up, only to immediately fall back down again. Something had wrapped itself around her left ankle, preventing her from moving! She grabbed whatever it was, and pain instantly shot into her hand. Jen looked down to see barbed wire, everywhere! She couldn't stop and deal with this, or even think about it right now. She had to get away! The noise above her was deafening, and she could barely breathe or even see. She scrambled desperately onto her feet, managing to lurch forward and free herself of the wire. Then she ran. Jen ran for all she was worth.

But, what was happening now? Jen's legs weren't working! She stumbled clumsily from one to the other, but they refused all demands to go faster! Sounds of crockery clattering about could suddenly be heard above the cawing, squawking and flapping. Jen felt seriously claustrophobic. She couldn't see! How on earth was she going to get anywhere if she couldn't see? The clatter became louder. She tried to breathe slowly. She thought pleasant thoughts. *'I have to do this... I can do this... the pillar's not far...'* Jen let go. She paced forward... again... again... Her foot slipped. She fell.

"WHOOOA!"

Jen awoke with a start and a gasp of air, momentarily confused as well as petrified. She found herself manically gripping the arms of the armchair in which her twisted body lay slumped. Releasing her grip quickly, she exhaled a huge sigh of relief as her eyes registered the fact that she wasn't actually falling, but was instead back in the study of the farmhouse. Jen was home at last, although she had absolutely no idea how she had got there.

She gazed around slowly, trying to adjust to her surroundings. Emily was still asleep in the chair beside her, whilst Bill lay curled up on the rug. The study was just as it had always been, with no sign of a fire and every book back in its rightful place on the bookshelves. Even the exploding patio door Jen had seen shatter glass everywhere bore not a mark of damage. Everything was tidy, in place and intact. She continued to stare, completely bewildered, as both Emily and Bill began to rouse.

"Where...?" Emily blinked blearily, before turning to Jen aghast as she asked, "How on earth did we get back here?"

"Beats me," replied Jen with a shrug, as she stroked Bill who had padded over to say hello. "All I remember is feeling sleepy in the courtyard at Deeron's Hall. That's it! There's nothing else between then and now."

Emily thought hard, trying desperately to recollect anything of the return journey herself. After a few moments, she added ponderously, "No, me neither."

"Also," Jen leant forward and began to whisper in a disbelieving tone, "this room was a wreck when we left it! Look at it now! There's not even a book out of place! How come?"

Before Emily could even think of an answer, the sound of clattering crockery was suddenly heard coming from the kitchen. They both instantly sat up, as though alarmed by the presence of someone else in the house. There could be no mystery as to who the intruder was, however. Staring at each other, Emily & Jen together mouthed the very same name.

"MARTHA!"

"What ARE we going to say?" whispered Jen frantically, as she suddenly appeared very worried. "We've been gone for nearly FIVE days!" Emily attempted to pull herself together, both physically as well as mentally, so as to better deal with the situation.

"Remember the dream though, Jen," she prompted, eyeing the door to the kitchen suspiciously. "We couldn't have found those antlers without her help. There's no way. Martha knows where we've been, she has to!"

"So what do we say?"

Emily thought for a moment. "Nothing," she replied, firmly. "Let her make the first move. Just act as normal. Come on." She grabbed Jen's arm and pulled her up out of the chair, and towards the door. Bill by now was beginning to scratch at the door anyway as he was undoubtedly famished, as were they all.

Jen gently pushed the door open and instantly caught sight of the back of Martha, as she stood at the sink washing up. Bill bounded through to get to his bowl with such force that Jen lost her grip on the door handle and the door flew wide open, bashing hard against the back wall. Martha quickly glanced around, then wiped her hands with a tea towel and picked up a tray nearby.

"Here you are," she said cheerily, placing the tray on the kitchen table. "Brunch." The table had already been laid for them, while on the tray was spread a feast of hot scrambled eggs, baked beans, butter, toast and just about every kind of jam. "Tea's brewing, and there's more toast on the way. Come on, Bill, here's yours."

"Oh wow!" exclaimed Emily, almost overcome with joy to see cooked human food in front of her once more, after having spent almost a week living on nuts and fruit. "Thanks, Martha!" Whatever concerns Emily had harboured over Martha's response now completely vanished, as ravenous hunger overcame her. She sat down and quickly began helping herself to what was on offer.

Jen was also incredibly hungry and so did likewise, but as she ate, she pondered deeply Martha's apparent lack of interest concerning their absence. Even after everything that had happened since, Jen still hadn't forgotten Martha's previous bizarre antics, especially as much of it had occurred in this very same kitchen. That behaviour simply didn't tally with her being involved with or otherwise supporting Deeron's fight against Smolder. It just didn't add up, and Jen knew it was a question that would bug her for evermore unless she at least tried to find an answer.

"There you are." Martha placed the tea and toast gently down on the table, and then resumed the washing up.

"Martha," asked Jen rather timidly, "is there something you'd like to ask us?" Emily stopped chewing mid-mouthful, flashing Jen an anxious stare as Martha froze and appeared to ponder the question.

"Actually," she replied in a rather stern tone, turning round to face them both, "there is…" In that moment, Emily's wide eyes looked as though they were about to pop out of her head! Jen eyed Martha intently. "I'd like to ask you both whether you honestly think that those filthy clothes you're wearing are suitable for welcoming back your mother today!"

For Jen, this unexpected news felt like a punch in the stomach. "Mum's coming home?" she asked, almost whispering.

"Yes," replied Martha flatly, as she then began to hurriedly clear away the crockery. "In fact, she should be here any minute, so hurry up both of you. I'm up to my eyes already today, without all this extra washing to do. Bill, you're first in the tub. Come on." She led Bill out into the yard.

Emily and Jen suddenly felt the mortal world thrust back upon them with remorseless speed, as they both disappeared upstairs into their separate rooms to shower and change. With so little time before Jen's mum arrived home, there was no opportunity for discussion as to what had just happened, leaving Emily to consider alone whether Martha might have actually planned all this in order to divert their attention. If so, she had certainly succeeded. As for Jen, she anxiously deliberated over Martha's choice of words, specifically the 'welcoming back your mother' part. Did this mean that her father would not be coming back, or was it simply a slip of the tongue?

One thing Emily and Jen did know was that it was wonderful to at last be clean again. Jen's foot was still badly bruised and they both had many scratches as well as some nasty cuts, but considering what they had gone through, they had both been remarkably lucky really. As soon as she could hear Emily's hairdryer, Jen wandered into her bedroom and slumped down on the bed.

"I just know it's all gone wrong, Em," she said, solemnly. "Dad's left us."

"You don't know that," replied Emily, trying to sound optimistic. "Martha could've got it wrong. Besides, her hearing's not exactly the best, is it?"

"What?" Jen was struggling to make out Emily's words above the noise of the hairdryer.

"Martha!" replied Emily, almost shouting. "Her hearing!"

"Oh." Jen gave Emily an irritated frown, as she failed completely to make any connection between Martha's partial deafness and her father not coming home.

Emily switched off the hairdryer. "Wait and see," she said, with a reassuring smile. Moments later, Martha was heard announcing from the staircase that a car had just pulled into the drive.

"This is nothing compared to what we've just been through though, is it, Em?" asked Jen, staring earnestly.

"No," she replied. "It's nothing. Besides, Deeron said that some of the goodness would be passed onto us, so life can't all be bad can it?"

"I guess not," said Jen with a sigh, as she pulled herself up off the bed and went downstairs.

Emily thought it best to remain in her room for the time being, and so spent quite some time looking out across the forest, just as she had done on her very first day at Oak Dale Farm. She wondered how she was going to cope with leaving both this place and her best friend Jen, knowing as she did that her time there was rapidly coming to an end. Emily would soon have to return home to her family, the new baby, and to school and normal everyday life.

However she managed it though, Emily King resolved to herself that manage she would, as she was not the same girl who'd arrived at the beginning of summer. Every problem in her life, and all her fears and doubts, seemed to pale into insignificance compared to what she had had to overcome in the magical world. She sensed courage and strength from within herself now, and felt more able to deal with the obstacles that would inevitably come her way in the future. "Maybe it's because I'm a Wandiacate that I feel like this," she whispered, with her face up close to the windowpane.

"Emily!" Jen's voice calling from downstairs broke her thoughts. "Come and meet mum!" Emily wiped her breath from the glass with a sleeve, and then went downstairs to join them in the sitting room.

"Emily," greeted Jen's mother warmly, "how wonderful it is to meet you at last. I'm Megan."

"Hello," replied Emily cheerily, as she shook her beautifully manicured hand.

"I wrote to your mother last week," she began, as they both sat down, "and invited her to come and stay once the baby is born. We have so much to catch up on. We both spent a summer here together once when we were young girls, just like you two have."

"Oh we know that," said Jen, rather flippantly. "Martha told us."

Megan briefly searched Jen and Emily's faces, before breaking into a broad and generous smile. "Well, you will always be welcome here, Emily. Jen needs a good friend at the moment, and I have a feeling that's you."

"Dad's not coming home." Jen gave the news in a calm and very matter-of-fact way, although Emily could still detect a sigh in her voice. All she could offer by way of sympathy was a simple 'oh well, so now you know' half-smile, but Jen's gaze was actually focused on the forest outside. Emily wondered whether perhaps she might also be feeling stronger now.

"It will all be for the best in the end," said Megan, heartened by her daughter's courage and acceptance. She grabbed Jen's hand from across the sofa. "You just can't keep people in a place where they don't want to be. They end up feeling like prisoners."

"The greatest gift of all - freedom to live our lives." Jen recited Deeron's words with another gentle sigh, as she continued to stare out of the window. Eric's head suddenly appeared through a nearby open window, looking very summery in a bright yellow shirt.

"Come on, yow lot," he exclaimed, "or we'll miss it!"

"Miss what?" asked Jen, slightly resenting the intrusion.

"The Horn Dance, of course! What else?"

"I nearly forgot again!" exclaimed Emily, slapping her hand across her mouth as she stared horrified at Jen.

"Again?" enquired Megan, as they all stood up to leave. Emily froze as she suddenly realized the impossible situation she had managed to get herself into. Fortunately, Jen quickly came to the rescue.

"Oh, it's nothing," she said, attempting to sound dismissive and prevent any further questions. "Emily forgot the date of it when I took her to see the antlers last week, that's all."

"Oh, I see," said Megan, rather doubtfully.

"Wakes Monday," began Eric cheerily, as they filed outside to join him, Martha and Bill for the short walk into the village. "Yow see, Emily, Wakes Monday follows the first Sunday after the 4th September every year. Now technically, this means that it falls on the Monday between the 6th and the 12th inclusively. It's a very old tradition, y'know, and I've got a leaflet about it. Yow can borrow it if yow like."

Emily at this point was trying her hardest not to burst out laughing, as was Jen. Maybe it was the fact that Eric knew nothing of their adventure, or because he was so unaware of what the Horn Dance was really about. Perhaps it was just a release for them both. Whatever it was, they both burst out laughing regardless. Emily tried to soften any insult to Eric by giggling out the words, "Thanks, Eric, I'd love to." but it only made things worse. Even Jen's mother had to bite her lip. Martha just smiled, seemingly oblivious to it all.

"I don't see what's so funny," said Eric quietly and clearly offended, as they all walked to the village.

Once inside the village, they made their way along a narrow path which ran along the back of some houses and into the churchyard. Just beyond the lychgate at the front lay the village green, where quite a crowd had already gathered. Emily, Jen and Bill separated from the others, and managed to commandeer a spot in-between the throng of onlookers who had likewise come along to watch.

Before very long, a procession honed into view, coming towards them along the main road. A total of twelve people, all dressed in costume, made their way onto the green. Six men, each with a set of antlers, then arranged themselves into two lines of three, so as to face an opposite number. An accordionist began to play the Horn Dance theme, and the men with the antlers danced.

"Look Bill," whispered Emily, "they're pretending to be the six magic stags!" They weren't actually dancing like deer at all, as their routine consisted mainly of a repeated phrase where each line advanced towards the other and then separated. The dance that Jen and Emily had both seen and performed was very different from this. What they were witnessing now had been handed down through many generations of mortals, of whom none could have had any idea of the power being created in the magical world.

"The last time we saw those antlers, they were under the tractor!" whispered Jen, as the dancers swapped sides and began again the sequence, whilst a young boy kept time throughout by tapping on a triangle. It was at this point Emily noticed that the very tips of some of the antlers were starting to emit a deep golden glow, as though they were suddenly energized by the dance. The radiance then expanded along the line to the antlers of the other dancers, ultimately connecting with the other side as it spread and wove its way to illuminate every single branch. Before long, the Horn Dance had become a ring of light, shining so brightly now that even the surrounding onlookers shone a golden glow!

"Do you see what I see, Jen?" she asked, hesitantly.
"Oh yes," replied Jen, her eyes glued to the dance.

Both girls then noticed that as the dancers came together, a pulse of golden energy fell to the ground. The effect was faint at first, but every time the phrase was repeated, the stronger the pulsations became! Energy flowed outwards in all directions as the light trace penetrated far down like shockwaves. Emily scanned the crowd, trying to find a face amongst them that registered something of what she and Jen were witnessing. Clearly, no one else saw anything unusual, as they simply smiled and clapped along to the dance, just the same as before. One person whose face she didn't observe, however, was Martha who stood on the other side of the green, watching them both carefully.

Very soon, Emily and Jen could even feel the warmth of the golden light being created. The dancers were now moving around in a circle with their antlers raised high. As they walked into the centre and locked antlers together, Emily and Jen watched as the golden light now hovered. Then, like a long trail of transparent haze, the light rose high over the heads of everyone and floated off in the direction of Needwood Forest. Jen stared utterly transfixed, and wondered if this was similar to what Fauld had said he had seen from Marsh Valley the previous night. As for Emily, she imagined it to be Deity's long dress of sinuous golden light, gathered up by her to ensure that all the energy and goodness generated began its rightful journey to the magical world, and to Deeron's six magic stags.

As the music finally died, loud applause and cries of "More!" from the spectators brought Emily and Jen back down to earth. The dance was over, and the mortal world was back. For a few moments, there was a great deal of bustling with the crowd as everyone began to move in different directions.

"Let's follow the antlers back to the church," said Jen, making sure Emily and Bill were still with her.

"Right."

They fought their way towards the church by walking across the green. Jen's mum caught sight of them and waved. Jen suddenly gazed at her, slim and smart in her navy cotton dress. She looked relaxed and happy.

"We're going for a drink, girls," she called over. "Do you want to come?"

"We're going to the church," replied Jen. "We'll be home later."

"Don't be too long then, as it's barbecue tonight. And keep an eye on Bill. Don't let him near the road!"

"Okay."

Bill looked at Megan with a hint of disgust. Just because he had allowed Martha to shower him down did not mean he was satisfied to comply with family pet rules any more. Bill reckoned that he understood humans far better than they understood each other, or even themselves. Anyway, he had plans of his own to go back into the forest and visit his friends the stags one day. He wasn't going to be content with his ordinary, everyday humdrum routine again.

As they stepped inside the candlelit church, the hustle and bustle of the crowd drifted away.

"That's it for another year," said the vicar, helping the last dancer to hang the antlers back on the hook. "Thanks very much." He then slipped away into the vestry, presumably to do a last bit of tidying. The dancer turned slowly to Emily and Jen, causing them both to gasp in absolute astonishment.

"Nick!" they said together.

"All this time, and I never knew you were one of the dancers!" said Jen, completely flabbergasted.

Without saying a word, Nick simply stared deeply into the eyes of both girls. Emily quickly felt uneasy and so took one step back, concerned that he might be about to act all weird and aggressive again. As she did so, Nick's eyes changed colour - one into opal-cream, and the other emerald-green. Both girls' jaws dropped, as they realized they were now staring straight back into the eyes of Arog!

"You will prosper from this day on," he said with a kind smile, and in a voice that was clearly not his own. "You are Wandiacates. Never forget."

The voice coming from Nick's own lips was also unmistakably Arog's. Not only did Nick now have Arog's eyes, he also had his voice! For several seconds, both Emily and Jen fell completely dumbstruck.

"NICK?" Jen eventually exclaimed, very loudly and sounding thoroughly exasperated. "How…?"

Nick blinked. Instantly, Arog's eyes were no more. His own dark brown variety now stared back at them.

"I told you that forest were dangerous," he said softly in his own voice again, as he walked past them and back up the aisle.

Emily and Jen could do nothing but gaze after him, as Nick stepped out into the churchyard and a late afternoon summer sun. They stood for quite some time at the door of the church, watching him disappear into the crowd, wondering what on earth had just happened. It was like putting the very last piece of an incredibly hard jigsaw puzzle into place, and then not knowing what the picture was meant to be. All they knew was that Martha and Nick fitted into that image somehow.

They might find out one day. Then again, they might not. Besides, things are rarely what they seem to be, and sometimes you just have to accept that things are strange and unexplainable. Even though some people say there is always a logical explanation, the reality is there may not be. For Emily, Jen and Bill, the past week had supplied more than enough evidence to support that opinion.

With a simple shrug of the shoulders, Jen slid her arm through Emily's, and they set off for home together. The sinking sun hung golden-edged clouds high over the forest like paper lanterns, as cool air drifted down the quaint village streets and enveloped the houses. With evening approaching, the forest itself seemed to be settling down to sleep, like a big contented cat. As they approached the farm gates, Bill bounded off ahead as usual to be the first inside. Jen stopped and looked at Emily.

"Now, for the very last time, do we need an explanation for where we've been since that night of the storm?"

Emily shook her head. "No," she replied. "Tell you what, though. If anyone does ask, let's say that we went to share a honey drink with Deeron and got a bit delayed. Then, just watch their faces."

They both laughed, and closed the old white gate to *Oak Dale Farm* behind them.